When the trials begin,
in soul-torn solitude despairing,
the hunter waits alone.
The companions emerge
from fast-bound ties of fate
uniting against a common foe.

When the shadows descend,
in Hell-sworn covenant unswerving
the blighted brothers hunt,
and the godborn appears,
in rose-blessed abbey reared,
arising to loose the godly spark.

When the harvest time comes,
in hate-fueled mission grim unbending,
the shadowed reapers search.
The adversary vies
with fiend-wrought enemies,
opposing the twisting schemes of Hell.

When the tempest is born,
as storm-tossed waters rise uncaring,
the promised hope still shines.
And the reaver beholds
the dawn-born chosen's gaze,
transforming the darkness into light.

When the battle is lost,
through quake-tossed battlefields unwitting
the seasoned legions march,
but the sentinel flees
with once-proud royalty,
protecting devotion's fragile heart.

When the ending draws near,
with ice-locked stars unmoving,
the threefold threats await,
and the herald proclaims,
in war-wrecked misery,
announcing the dying of an age.

—As written by Elliandreth of Orishaar, c. −17,600 DR

FORGOTTEN REALMS®

THE SUNDERING

PAUL S. KEMP
THE GODBORN

FORGOTTEN REALMS®

THE SUNDERING

Book

II

THE GODBORN

©2013 Wizards of the Coast LLC.

Published by Wizards of the Coast LLC. Manufactured by: Hasbro SA, Rue Emile-Boéchat 31, 2800 Delémont, CH. Represented by Hasbro Europe, 2 Roundwood Ave, Stockley Park, Uxbridge, Middlesex, UB11 1AZ, UK.

Prophecy by: James Wyatt
Cartography by: Mike Schley
Cover art by: Tyler Jacobson
First Printing: October 2013

9 8 7 6 5 4 3 2 1

ISBN: 978-0-7869-6541-0
ISBN: 978-0-7869-6436-9 (ebook)
620A6851000001 EN

The Hardcover edition Cataloging-in-Publication data is on file
with the Library of Congress

Contact Us at Wizards.com/CustomerService
Wizards of the Coast LLC, PO Box 707, Renton, WA 98057-0707, USA
USA & Canada: (800) 324-6496 or (425) 204-8069
Europe: +32(0) 70 233 277

Visit our web site at **www.dungeonsanddragons.com**

For Jen, Riordan, Roarke, Delaney, and Sloane.

PROLOGUE

Marpenoth, the Year of Holy Thunder (1450 DR)

PAIN WRACKED VARRA, KNIFE STABS OF AGONY THAT KEPT time with her contractions. She lay on her back in a straw-filled birthing bed in the abbey—the Abbey of the Rose, Derreg had called it—her knees bent, the sheets damp and sticky with sweat and blood. *Her* blood.

Too much of it, she knew.

She saw her fate reflected in the worried eyes of the homely, middle-aged midwife who patted her hand and mouthed soft encouragement, saw it in the furrowed brow and filmy but intense gaze of the balding, elderly priest with blood-slicked hands who reached into Varra time and again to no avail.

Varra searched her memory but could not remember their names. The previous hours—had it been just hours?—had passed in a blur. She remembered traveling in a caravan across Sembia, fleeing before a storm of shadows, an ever-growing tenebrous thunderhead that threatened to blanket all of Sembia with its pall. Undead had attacked the caravan, unliving shadows, their keening voices announcing their hunger for souls, and, in a moment of thoughtless bravery, she had led them off into the forest to save the others.

There, terrified and stumbling through the underbrush, she'd happened upon a man, a dark man who had reminded her of

1

Erevis, her child's father. The howls of the undead had filled the woods behind her, all around her, their keens a promise of cold and death and oblivion.

"Who are you?" she'd asked the dark man, panting, her voice tense with growing panic.

"I'm just fiddling around the edges," the man had said, and his narrow, sharply angled face had creased in a mirthless smile. He had touched her pregnant belly—then not yet bulging—and sent a knife stab of pain through her abdomen.

The memory of his touch caused her to squirm on the birthing bed. She moaned with pain. Bloody straw poked into her back. The light from the lanterns put a dancing patchwork of shadows on the vaulted stone ceiling, and she swore she heard the dark man chuckle.

"Be still, woman," the priest said sharply. Sweat greased his pate. Blood spattered his yellow robe.

"He did something to the child!"

"Who?" the midwife asked, her double chins bouncing with the question. "What do you mean?"

"The dark man!" Varra said, screaming as another contraction twisted her guts. "The man in the forest!"

The midwife glanced at the priest knowingly and patted Varra's hand. "It'll be all right," she said, mouthing words they all knew were a lie. "It's fine. You're not in a forest and there's no dark man here."

The priest mopped his brow, smearing blood across his scalp, and reached into Varra again. Pain ripped through her, a wave of agony that ran from pelvis to chest. She gasped and the priest pulled his hands back, looked up, and shared a glance with the midwife. Varra read in their faces the words they didn't say aloud.

"What's wrong with my child?" she said, and tried to sit up. The bloody sheets clung to her back. The effort caused her more pain, agonizing pulses. The room spun. She feared she would vomit.

"Please be still," the priest said, and the midwife gently pressed her back down on the birthing bed.

Pain and exhaustion caused Varra's vision to blur. Her mind floated backward into memory, to the forest.

"Run," the dark man had said to her, and she had, tripping, stumbling, and cursing her way through the brush. The unliving shadows had pursued her, closing, their wails loud in her ears, coming at her from all directions. She had stumbled into a meadow and fallen. She recalled the sweet smell of the purple flowers, the dusting of silver pollen that fogged the night air and glittered in Selûne's light. She remembered curling up among the blooms as the shadows closed in, like a child herself, wrapped in the meadow's womb. She'd put her arms around her belly, around her unborn child, knowing they were both about to die, and wishing and praying that she were somewhere else, somewhere safe, anywhere.

And then, as if in answer to her wish, the motes of pollen had flared bright silver and she recalled a sudden, disconcerting lurch of motion.

"He saved me," she murmured to the midwife, knowing she wasn't making sense to anyone but herself. "The dark man. He saved me."

"Of course he did, dear," the midwife said, caressing her hand, obviously not listening.

And he'd also saved Varra's child, from the undead if not the perils of childbirth.

She came back fully to the current moment, to the pain.

"Derreg?" she said, blinking tears and sweat from her eyes.

"I'm here," he said from behind her, and she drifted again.

The magic of the meadow's flowers had . . . *moved* her, and Varra had found herself elsewhere, disconcerted, nauseated. A soft rain that smelled faintly of ash fell out of a black sky.

She'd felt drowsy, as if she'd been sleepwalking and had only just awakened.

Sitting low on the horizon, the setting sun tried to poke through a roof of dense dark clouds, but only a few stray rays penetrated the shroud. It was almost night.

The sheer, cracked face of towering mountains hemmed her in. She was in a pass.

Her mind tried to make sense of events. How had she arrived here? Some magic, some miracle of the meadow . . .

Her child moved within her. She gasped, her knees went weak, and she nearly fell when she saw the growth of her belly.

"How?" she whispered, and ran her hands over the now-swollen mound of her abdomen. The swell of her stomach seemed more miraculous than her inexplicable translocation. Moments ago, she had been little more than a month pregnant.

Then she remembered. The dark man had touched her belly. He'd done something to the baby; he must have.

Even as the thought registered, the contractions began, like a hand squeezing her womb. Her wonder turned in an instant to fear, and fear to terror.

She was alone in an unknown place, and somehow soon to give birth. Her heart beat so fast she grew lightheaded. She tried to calm herself with long, deep breaths. The rain and the breeze summoned shivers. She had to find shelter, help. Gods, she needed help.

She stumbled through the rocks, picking her way through the boulders, the stands of trees, calling out over the patter of the rain. The unliving shadows appeared to be gone. Perhaps the caravan was nearby? Or perhaps there was a village in the vicinity, a cottage, something, anything. She had to risk a shout.

"Help! Anyone! Help, please!"

She realized that she didn't even now where she was. She'd been in a forest. Now she was in a mountain pass.

"Gods," she said, tears falling down her face. "Gods."

She wandered the shadowed landscape, shouting until her voice was hoarse, watching with a sense of dread as the sun sank. At last her legs would bear her no farther and she sagged to the ground under a cluster of pines, exhausted, wrapped in the aroma of pine needles and rain.

She would give birth alone, outside, in the dark. The realization pressed against her chest, made it hard to breathe.

"Help!" she called, expiating with a scream the pain of another contraction. "Help! Someone please, help!"

Over the rain she heard voices.

She froze, afraid to let hope nest in her chest. She cocked her head, listened, tried to hear above the thump of her own heart.

Yes, voices!

"Here!" she cried. She tried to stand but another contraction ripped through her and forced her back to the bed of pine needles. "Over here! Help me, please!"

The ground vibrated under her and she soon saw what caused it. A patrol of armed and armored men mounted on warhorses moved through the pass at a rapid trot. A blazing sun and a rose—both incongruous in the bleak, shrouded land—were enameled on their breastplates. They looked about, as if seeking her, their mounts trotting and snorting.

"The call came from around here," one of them said, and pulled his horse around.

"I heard it, too," said a second.

"Where are you?" another shouted.

"Here!" she called, and held up a hand. Relief put more tears in her eyes but gave her voice strength. "I'm here."

Helmed heads turned to her. The men pulled up their horses.

"Here in the pines!"

"It's a woman!" one of them shouted.

Several of them swung out of their saddles, pushed through the pine limbs, and hurried to her side. They smelled of sweat and leather and horse and hope.

"She's with child!" said a young man whose helm seemed too large for his head. Even under the trees their bodies seemed to attract the last, meager rays of the setting sun, and the fading light limned their armor and shields. She could not take her eyes from the rose. Her memory blurred subsequent events, compressed what must have been close to an hour into moments. The oldest of the men, his long, gray-streaked hair leaking from beneath his helm, his face seamed with lines and scars that his trimmed beard could not hide, had kneeled beside her.

"Rest easy," he said. He closed his eyes and placed the fingertips of one hand on her arm.

She felt his mind touch hers, as if evaluating her soul. She did not welcome the violation, but she was too tired to resist. After a moment he opened his eyes and nodded, seemingly satisfied.

"What is your name, goodwoman?" he asked.

His deep voice reminded her of a rolling brook. It calmed her.

"Varra," she said, and winced as another contraction knotted her abdomen.

"You'll be cared for, Varra."

He took a small holy symbol, a stylized rose, in his hand and placed both of his palms—gnarled and scarred from years of battle—on her stomach. He intoned a prayer to Amaunator. A soft glow spread from his palms to her abdomen, warming her, easing her pain, and quelling her fear.

"You need a midwife," he said. "And a priest skilled in childbirth. I can get you to both. Can you stand?"

She nodded, and he helped her to her feet. He stood almost as tall as Erevis and smelled like the rain.

"Where am I?" she asked.

"You're with me. And safe."

The simple words took her by surprise, recalling, as they did, her wish from the meadow. Her eyes welled. The man removed his heavy cloak and draped it around her shoulders.

"How did you come here?" he asked her, guiding her toward his horse.

She felt the eyes of the other riders on her, their gazes heavy with questions. They'd already remounted.

"How did you find the pass? Are others with you?"

She swallowed, shook her head. "I was with a caravan, but . . . I think I'm alone now. And . . . I don't know how I came here. What . . . pass is this?"

"She could be in service to the Shadovar, Derreg," said a young, squat rider.

"Don't be a fool," the older man, Derreg, snapped. "Look at her. She is no servant of the shades."

"The shades of the desert of Anauroch?" Varra asked, wincing in anticipation of another contraction.

"Desert?" said the young rider, his face pinched in a question. He looked to Derreg. "She babbles."

"Erwil, ride toward the foothills," Derreg said. "See if anyone else from her caravan is about." To Varra, he said, "Do you think you can ride?"

She took stock of her condition, nodded, grunted as another contraction pained her.

"She rides Daybreak with me," Derreg said to his men. "Nav, Greer, ride for the abbey. Tell the Oracle we found her. And tell the abbot we return with a pilgrim in the midst of labor. Then rouse Erdan. He has experience in these matters."

Two of the riders wheeled their mounts and rode off.

"Abbey?" Varra asked, leaning heavily on Derreg. "Pilgrim? Oracle?"

"The Abbey of the Rose," Derreg said, as he assisted her toward the warhorse he had called Daybreak. "You're a pilgrim, yes? Come to see the Oracle?"

She had never heard of the Abbey of the Rose. "I . . . don't know."

He studied her face, the age lines in his brow deepening with his frown. "Where are you from?"

"Sembia. North and west of Ordulin."

Derreg's eyes narrowed. He studied her expression as he said, "Ordulin is a wasteland. It was destroyed in the Shadowstorm. And Sembia is a vassal state to Netheril and the shades."

She stared at him uncomprehending.

"Are you all right?" he asked.

She felt lightheaded. She shook her head. She must have misheard. "I don't understand. I just left . . ."

A contraction doubled her over. When it passed, strong hands took hold of her and lifted her gently atop Daybreak. She sat sidesaddle as best she could. Derreg mounted behind her, enclosed her in his arms as he whickered at the mount.

She hissed with pain as the horse started to move. She kept one hand on her belly, felt the movement of her child within.

"The abbey isn't far," Derreg said. "Tell me if it becomes too much to endure."

"It's tolerable," she said. "But please hurry."

The rest of the patrol fell in around them as they rode through the pass. The way narrowed as they followed a winding, circuitous path of switchbacks and side openings. A mist formed around them, thick and pale, obscuring vision. Whispers sounded in her ears, sibilant words suggesting a meaning that slipped away just prior to understanding. She thought she heard Erevis's name in their whispered tones, and another name, too: Erevis's real name—Vasen.

"Try to ignore the whispers and whatever else you see," Derreg said to her softly.

She nodded, alone with her pain. "Please hurry."

Faces formed in the mist, men and women with eyes like holes. They dissipated moments after forming, fading like lost memories. She squeezed her eyes shut, but still the fog tugged at her clothes, pawed at her belly. Still the voices hissed in her ears, speaking of her child.

It's the child, they said.

He'll dream of the father.

And the father of him.

"They know me!" she said, terrified.

"No," Derreg said. "They're the voices of spirits that serve the Oracle and guard the way, but they're harmless to us. They only confuse. Don't heed them."

Varra swallowed, nodded, and ignored the voices. She soon lost all sense of direction. The pass was a maze, and the voices of the spirits thickened her perception, dulled her mind. The moments passed with agonizing slowness. She tried through force of will to delay the birth of her child.

The birth of Erevis's child.

The child, the voices said. *The child.*

She squeezed her eyes shut, wondering where Erevis was, if he was safe. He had left her to save his friend and she had reconciled herself to it, but she missed him still, and always would. She hoped he was well, but Derreg's words resounded in her mind—Ordulin is a wasteland. Sembia is gone.

How could that have happened so fast?

"Oh, gods," she whispered, as realization broke over her. It seemed impossible, and yet . . .

"What's wrong?" Derreg asked.

"What year is it?" she said, her voice breaking on the rocks of the question. She braced herself for the answer. Her heart pounded in her ears.

"Year?" Derreg said. "By Dalereckoning, 1450."

The child squirmed within her and she cried out.

The child is come, said the voices.

"Are you all right?" Derreg asked.

She nodded as one pain passed, replaced by another.

1450.

How was that possible?

Seventy years had passed in what felt to her like moments. She wrestled with understanding but failed. She could not make sense of it. Her child was seventy years old before he was ever born.

She began to weep, not with pain but with grief for all that she'd lost, all she'd left behind.

"How can this be?" she whispered, and had no answer.

If Derreg heard her, he offered no answer, either.

They emerged from the mist, leaving the voices of the spirits behind. Through tear-filled eyes, she watched the last, glowing sliver of the sun sink behind the western mountains, watched the long shadows of the peaks stretch across the pass. The already meager light faded to black. They had reached a forested vale. Huge cascades fell from cliffs and a simple stone abbey was nestled in the trees.

The priest's head appeared between her knees. Sweat slicked his thin hair to his pale, age-spotted scalp. The dim lantern light put shadows in the hollows of his cheeks.

"If I'm to save the child, you must not push until I say."

"Breathe in and out slowly," the midwife said.

Varra swallowed, nodded. The rush of her heart boomed in her ears. A contraction girdled her pelvis in agony. She screamed, and the portly midwife, wincing, sopped up more blood from the bed, cast some of the sheets into the gory pile on the floor.

"I'm thirsty," Varra said.

"Almost," the priest said, not hearing her as he stared into her body and tried to save her child.

"Do something!" said Derreg from somewhere behind Varra. "She's in too much pain." He had refused to leave her since bringing her to the abbey.

"We're doing all we can, Derreg," the priest said, tension putting an edge on his voice.

"Do more!" Derreg said.

Varra focused on her breathing and stared up at the vaulted ceiling. Her entire frame of reference distilled down to an awareness of only her abdomen, the birth canal, the child she was soon to deliver. But there was no ease from the pain. Her vision blurred. She feared she would be too weak to push when the priest told her to do so. She feared she would never see her child.

She screamed again as the priest manipulated the child within her, a dagger in her belly.

"Get the child out!" Derreg said, stress causing his voice to break.

The priest looked up from between Varra's legs, looked first at her, then past her to Derreg.

"I can't. It's dying. The cord is . . ."

He trailed off, but his words left Varra hollow.

"No," she said, and tears wet her cheeks. "No."

The priest looked at her, his expression soft, sympathetic. "I'm so sorry."

"You are not trying hard enough, Erdan!" said Derreg, and she heard him move across the room toward the priest, although he remained behind Varra, out of sight.

The priest's soft voice never lost its calm. "I've done all I can, Derreg. We must . . . take steps if the woman is to have a chance."

Varra felt Derreg's hand on her head, on her hair, a protective gesture that soothed her, warmed her.

How strange, she thought. She realized in the clarity of the moment that in another time, another place, he was a man she might have loved, despite the difference in their ages.

"Her name is Varra," Derreg said. "And there must be something—"

"Cut the child out," Varra said, her voice as soft as rain, its quiet resolve slicing through the room.

Derreg's hand lifted from her head as if he were recoiling.

The priest looked as if she had spoken in a language he could not understand. "What did you say?"

The midwife squeezed Varra's hand. "You're not clearheaded—"

"Cut my child out," Varra said, louder, her mind made up. Her body tensed, a contraction gripped her, the child moved within her, and she screamed. "Cut it out! I'm already dead! I see it in your face!"

The priest and the midwife stared at her, eyes wide. Neither gainsaid her words.

"I'm already dead," Varra said, more quietly, the words spiced with her tears, her grief.

The priest swallowed, his tracheal lump bouncing up and down. "I haven't prepared the correct rituals, and I do have not the needed tools . . . "

"A knife will do," Varra said, and managed to keep her voice from faltering. The room began to spin. She closed her eyes until it subsided.

"A knife?"

"There's little time," Varra said.

"Right, of course," the priest said, looking past her to Derreg, as if for permission.

Derreg's hand returned to Varra's head, cradling it as he might an infant, as he might a daughter. His fingers twisted gently in her sweat-dampened hair. She reached up and covered his hand with hers as her tears fell. His skin felt as rough as bark. His bearded face appeared next to hers, his breath warm on her cheek.

"You don't have to do this," he said.

"It's my child," she said, three words that said everything there was to say about anything. Her eyes went to the sheets piled along the wall, a crimson pile. "I'm dead already. We both know that."

The priest produced a small knife and held it aloft in a shaking hand. The lantern light flickered on its blade. Stress squeezed sweat from his blood-smeared brow.

The midwife's clammy fingers clenched Varra's hand. Varra alone seemed to feel calm.

"Derreg, listen to me," Varra said. "Someone . . . did something to the child, changed it. I do not know how, but it's *my* child. Mine. Do you understand?"

His hand squeezed hers. He buried his forehead in her hair.

She breathed in the smell of him—he still smelled of the rain—and wondered how she could have come to care for him so much in mere hours, in mere moments. How cruel that they'd had only hours to share rather than a lifetime.

"I understand," he said.

She swallowed in a throat gone dry, nodded. To the priest, she said, "Do it."

The priest winced, steeled himself to his work.

"This will pain you," he said, but did not move.

"Do it," Varra said. "Do it now."

But he didn't. He couldn't. His hand shook uncontrollably.

The midwife took the knife from the priest's hand, stared for a moment into Varra's eyes, and began to cut.

Varra walled off a scream behind gritted teeth as the edge slid across her abdomen and opened her womb, spilling warm fluid down her sides.

The midwife's resolve spread to the priest and he moved forward to assist.

Spots formed before Varra's eyes. Sparks erupted in her brain. She might have been screaming, she could not be certain. She felt the priest and midwife manipulating the hole they'd made in her, felt them reaching inside her.

She *was* screaming, she realized, swimming in pain, in blood.

She focused on Derreg's hand, its solidity, the gentle way it cradled her own. Warmth radiated from his flesh, dulled the edge of her agony.

He would never leave her, she thought. Never.

Something warm and wet pattered on their joined hands. Her fading consciousness mistook it for blood at first, but then she realized it was tears. Derreg's tears. She felt his mouth near her ear and he whispered words of faith.

"From ends, beginnings, from darkness, light, from tragedy, triumph. Night gives way to dawn, and dawn to noon. Stand in the warmth and purifying light of Amaunator who was Lathander and fear nothing. Fear nothing, Varra."

She felt herself fading, slipping. The room darkened.

"Care for him," she whispered to Derreg.

"Him?" Derreg said.

Varra nodded. She knew the child would be a son, a son for the father, the spirits in the pass had told her. "His name is Vasen. After his father."

"I will, Varra," Derreg said. "I promise."

Varra heard a rush like roaring surf. The room darkened. She could no longer see. She felt herself drifting, floating in warm water, sinking . . .

She heard a tiny cough, then a newborn's cry, the defiant call of her son as he entered a world of light and darkness.

She smiled, drifted, thought of Erevis, of Derreg, and feared nothing.

Derreg had slain many men in combat, had seen battlefields littered with corpses, but he had to force himself to look on Varra's body, at the blood-soaked bed, at the opening in her abdomen out of which Erdan, the priest, had mined the child. Her face, finally free of pain, looked as pale as a new moon.

He could not release her still-warm hand. He held onto it as if with it he could pull her back to life.

"She is gone," the midwife said. "Gone to light."

Derreg nodded. He'd known Varra perhaps two hours, but he had felt a connection with her, a whispered hint of what might have been had they met under other circumstances. Through sixty winters he had never married, and now he knew why. He was to meet his love only in the twilight of his life, and he was to know her for less than a day.

He thanked Amaunator for that, at least.

"What's wrong with it?" the midwife said, her exclamation pulling Derreg's attention from Varra.

Hand to her mouth, the midwife backed away a step from the birthing bed, a step away from the child. Erdan, eyes as wide as coins, held the baby out at arm's length, as he might something foul.

The child, pinched, dark, and bloody, his legs kicking, cried in sharp gasps. The umbilical cord still connected him to Varra, and a thin vein of shadow twined around the cord's length and slowly snaked toward the child as if the baby—Vasen, Varra had named him—had received nourishment not only from blood but also from darkness. Vasen's eyes flashed yellow with each of his wails.

"It's born of the Shadovar!" said Erdan, and looked as if he might drop the child. "Look at it! The darkness moves toward it!"

Vasen's appearance and the coil of shadow around the umbilical made the claim hard to deny, but deny it Derreg did.

"He's born of this woman, Erdan. And his name is Vasen."

The child kicked, wailed.

"It must be killed, Derreg," Erdan said, although uncertainty colored his tone, and he paled as he spoke. "If the Shadovar learn of the abbey . . ."

"Killed?" the midwife said, and put her hand to her mouth. "A child? You cannot!"

"No," Derreg said, his hand still holding Varra's, feeling it cool. "We cannot. You heard me give this woman my word. I'll keep it." He let go of Varra's hand and held out his arms for the child. "Give him to me."

Erdan looked dumbfounded, his mouth half open. His two rotten front teeth looked as dark as Vasen's skin.

"Give him to me, Erdan. It's not a request."

The priest blinked, handed the blood-slicked boy to Derreg, then wiped his bloody hands on his yellow robes.

Vasen stilled in Derreg's hands. His small form felt awkward, fragile. Derreg's hands were accustomed to holding hard steel and worn leather, not a babe. Shadows coiled around the baby, around Derreg's forearms.

"You'd damn us all for the child of a stranger?" Erdan said, his tone as much puzzled as angry.

Derreg did not bother to explain that he did not regard Varra as a stranger. "I gave my word."

"I must take this to the abbot. I take no responsibility—"

"Yes," Derreg snapped, unable to keep the sharpness from his voice. "You take no responsibility. I understand that quite well."

Erdan tried to hold Derreg's gaze, failed.

"Give me the knife," Derreg said.

"What?"

"The knife, man. I can't use a sword on the cord."

Muttering, Erdan handed Derreg the small knife he'd used to cut open Varra's womb. With it, Derreg cut the shadow-veined umbilical, separating boy from mother, then wrapped him in one of the sheets stained with Varra's blood.

"You must find a—" the priest began.

"Shut up, Erdan," Derreg said. "I know he'll require a wet nurse. I'm childless, not a dolt."

"Of course," Erdan said. He stared quizzically at the boy. "The shadows, Derreg. What is he if not a shade?"

"What he is," Derreg said. "Is my son."

Holding the boy against his chest, Derreg stepped to Varra's side and leaned over her so the boy could see his mother's face. Her mouth was frozen in a half smile, her dark eyes open and staring.

"That is your mother, Vasen. Her name was Varra."

"You know the abbot will consult the Oracle," said Erdan. "You risk much."

"Perhaps," Derreg said. He stared down at the tiny, bloody child in his arms—the tiny nose, the strange yellow eyes, the dusky skin, the thin black hair slicked back on his small head. He resolved that he would not turn Vasen over to the abbot, no matter what the Oracle said. "If the Oracle sees danger in the child, I'll take him from here. But I won't abandon him."

Erdan studied him for a moment, then said, "I will see to the woman's—burial. And we'll see what the abbot and Oracle say. Perhaps I'm mistaken. I was . . . surprised by the boy's appearance and spoke hastily. Harshly, perhaps."

"It's forgotten, Erdan," Derreg said softly. He knew the priest to be a good man.

"I'll prepare her . . . body for the rituals," said the midwife. "I, too, was—"

The lantern light dimmed and the shadows deepened. The child uttered a single cry and burrowed his face into Derreg's chest.

Derreg felt pressure on his ears, felt the air grow heavy and found it difficult to draw breath. The shadows in the far corner of the room swirled like a thunderhead, their hypnotic motion giving Derreg an instant headache. He caught a pungent, spicy whiff of smoke, the smell somehow redolent of times old and gone.

"By the light," said the midwife, fear raising her voice an octave.

The shadows coalesced. A presence manifested in the darkness.

"Shadovar," Erdan hissed. "I told you, Derreg!" Then, to the midwife, "Get aid! Go!"

She ran from the room without looking back, stumbling over the bloody sheets in her haste.

The entire room fell deeper into darkness, the lantern's flame reduced to the light of a distant star.

Cradling Vasen against his chest, Derreg drew his blade and took a step backward, toward the door. "Go, Erdan. Now."

"You have the child," Erdan said, taking his holy symbol in his hand. "You go."

An orange light flared in the darkness—the glowing embers of a pipe bowl. They lit the face of the man who resided in the shadows, a man who *was* the shadows.

Long black hair hung loose around a swarthy, pockmarked visage. A goatee surrounded the sneer he formed around the pipe's stem. He was missing an eye and the scarred, empty socket looked like a hole that went on forever. The embers in the pipe went dark and the man once more disappeared into the shadows.

"Maybe you should both stay," the man said, and the lock bolt on the door slid into place.

17

Erdan looked at the door, at the man, back at the door, his rapid breathing audible.

"You won't need your blade, knight of Lathander," the man said to Derreg. "Or is it Amaunator these days? I haven't kept up."

Erdan intoned the words to a prayer and the pipe flared again, showing the man's face twisted in a frown.

"Close your mouth," the man said to Erdan, his voice as sharp-edged as a blade. "Your words are empty."

Erdan's mouth audibly shut. His eyes widened and he doubled over and pawed at his face, moaning behind his lips as if they were sealed shut.

"Priests," the man said contemptuously, shaking his head as the light from the pipe died and the darkness engulfed him.

"Release him," Derreg said, nodding at Erdan, and advancing a step toward the man. The baby went still in the cradle of Derreg's arm.

The man took a long drag on his pipe, and the light showed him smiling. "Well enough. He's released."

Erdan opened his mouth, gasped. "By the light!"

"Hardly by the light," the man said. "But you needn't fear. I'm not here for either of you." He nodded at Vasen. "I'm here for him."

Derreg cradled Vasen more tightly to his chest. The boy remained eerily still, his yellow eyes like embers. Derreg recalled Varra's words to him about a dark man who had changed the boy. He tightened his grip on his blade's hilt.

"You're the child's father?"

The man exhaled smoke and stepped closer to them, shedding some of the darkness that clung to him. He moved with the precision of a skilled combatant. Twin sabers hung from his belt and the hilt of a larger sword—sheathed on his back—peeked over his shoulder. His one good eye fixed not on Derreg but on Vasen, then on Varra. Derreg could read nothing in his expression.

"Are you the father?" Derreg repeated. "The dark man?"

"Oh, I *am* a dark man," the man said, smiling softly. "But I'm not the father. And I'm not the dark man you mean, at least not exactly."

He was suddenly standing directly before Derreg. Had he crossed the room?

The man extended a finger toward Vasen—the baby still did not move—but stopped before touching him. A stream of shadow stretched from the man's fingertip and touched Vasen, for a moment connecting man and child, an umbilical of another sort, perhaps.

"How peculiar," the man said, and withdrew his finger.

"How so?" Derreg asked, and turned his body to shield the child from the man's touch.

"His father was Erevis Cale," the man said, still staring at Vasen. "And I've been searching for this child for some . . . time."

Derreg heard the echo of some distant pain in the man's utterance of Cale's name. He knew the name, of course. His father, Regg, had spoken of Cale often, had watched Cale destroy a godling at the battle of Sakkors.

"Erevis Cale? Abelar's traveling companion?"

Shadows spun about the man. His lips curled with contempt. "*Traveling companion*? Is that how he's remembered?" He shook his head. "You've lost much more than half this world to the Spellplague. And you'll lose more of it yet if the cycle runs it course."

"The cycle?" Derreg asked.

"You're Drasek Riven," said Erdan, his voice rapid, excited. "By the light, you are!"

The man inclined his head. "Partly."

Derreg did not understand the cryptic comment. He'd heard Riven's name in tales, too. "You can't take the child, Drasek Riven. I gave my word."

"Do you think you could stop me?" Riven asked.

Derreg blinked and licked his lips, but held his ground. "No. But I'd try."

Riven leaned in close, studied Derreg's face. His breath smelled of smoke. "I believe you. That's good."

"You haven't aged," blurted Erdan, stepping closer to Riven, curiosity pinching his wrinkled face into a question. "You're not Shadovar?"

Riven turned to face Erdan and the priest blanched, retreated. "My kinship with darkness runs deeper than that of the Shadovar, priest. And I won't tell you again to keep your mouth closed. You're a witness to this, nothing more."

Erdan's eyes widened even as his mouth closed.

"You knew my father," Derreg said. "He spoke of you sometimes."

"Just sometimes, eh?" Riven drew on his pipe, a faint smile on his face, a distant memory in his eye. "I confess I'm not surprised."

"When he talked about those days he spoke mostly of Dawnlord Abelar."

"Dawnlord?" Riven looked up and past Derreg. His brow furrowed as he wrestled down some memory. "What is that? Some kind of holy title?"

"Of course it's holy," said Erdan, his tone as defiant as he dared. "His tomb is in this abbey. Pilgrims come from across Faerûn to lay eyes on it."

"You . . . question his holiness?" Derreg said.

Riven chuckled. "He was a man to me, and men are never holy."

"You blaspheme!" Erdan said.

Riven sneered. "Priest, I saw *Dawnlord* Abelar run his blade through an unarmed man trying to surrender. How does that square with your understanding of the man?"

"You lie!" Erdan exclaimed, then, realizing what he had said, backed up a step.

"Often," Riven acknowledged, "But not about that. Maybe you think killing Malkur Forrin made him less holy? You might be right. But it made him more of a man. And that murder is why you have an Oracle."

Derreg shook his head. "I don't understand. The Oracle is Abelar's son."

"You miss my meaning," Riven said and shook his head. "No matter. Myths sometimes outrun the man."

Riven took a draw on his pipe, blew out a cloud of fragrant smoke. He looked at Derreg, his eye focused on a memory. "I once promised your father that we would share a smoke but . . . other things got in the way. How did Regg die? Well, I hope?"

A fist formed in Derreg's throat, old grief blossoming into new pain. He pulled Vasen tighter against his chest. For a moment, he considered refusing to answer, but changed his mind. "He died an old man, in his sleep. The light was in him."

Riven's face did not change expression, although his eye seemed to see something Derreg could not. "It pleases me to hear it."

Voices and shouts carried into the room from the hall outside. Riven drew on his pipe, unconcerned.

"What do you want?" Derreg asked. "Why are you here?"

Riven jerked the large blade from the sheath on his back. Derreg lurched backward, his own blade held before him. Vasen began to cry. Erdan froze, rooted to the spot.

"To see the boy. And to give him his father's weapon." Riven flipped the weapon, took it by the blade, and offered Derreg the hilt. "This is Weaveshear."

The weapon was as black as a starless night. Shadows curled about its length, extended outward from the blade toward Vasen. The child extended a hand, cooed.

"That's a weapon of darkness," Erdan said, and made the sign of the rising sun, the three interior fingers raised like sunbeams.

"That it is," answered Riven.

Derreg stared at the blade. "The boy won't need it."

"No?"

"No. He has me."

Riven scowled, shadows swirling around him. He lowered the weapon and advanced. Although short of stature, Riven nevertheless seemed to reach to the ceiling.

Derreg knew he had overstepped and his mouth went dry, his heart pounded.

"You'll take this blade and you'll keep it safe and when that boy is of age, you'll tell him who his father was and you'll give him that weapon. I owe Cale that much. And so do you. All of you."

"I—"

"Nod your godsdamned stubborn head, son of Regg, or I swear I'll remove it from your neck."

Derreg did not care to test whether the threat was earnest. He fought down a prideful impulse and nodded. Riven offered him the blade once more, and Derreg took it. Shadows curled around his wrist. He felt as if the weapon was coated in oil. It seemed to squirm in his grip.

"Well enough," Riven said, and the shadows about him slowed. He took a step back. "We're done here now."

Riven turned and shadows started to gather around his form. Derreg could barely see him.

"Why don't you take him?" Erdan blurted.

"Shut up, Erdan," Derreg said.

Riven did not turn. Shadows curled around him, slow, languid. "Because I'm hunted, and my only safe haven is no place for a child. He'll be safe here for a time and he should have what peace this life can afford." He paused, staring at the child. "I fear it won't be much. I'll return if I can, but I'm doubtful that will be possible. Meanwhile you keep him. And you prepare him."

"Prepare him for what?"

"For what's coming."

"What do you mean? What's coming?"

Riven shook his head. "I don't know for certain. Others will be looking for him."

"Why?"

"Because of who his father was, because grudges die harder than gods. And because the Cycle of Night is trying to find its end. He's the key."

"I . . . don't understand."

"Nor I, not fully. Not yet. Someone's scribbling new words in the book of the world, and I was never much of a reader." He smiled, and it reached his good eye. "Two and two, it seems, still sum to four, even in this ruined world. He got that right, at least."

"What?" Derreg's head was spinning. "He?"

"Someone I once knew." Riven shook his head, as if to clear it of an old memory. "I can't stay any longer. My presence compromises the child's safety." He looked around. "Your Oracle has done good work here. This valley is . . . peaceful. I especially like the lakes. Tell the Oracle I was here. Tell him to do his part. And ask him if he still enjoys jugglers."

"What?"

"He'll know what I mean."

The darkness gathered, but before it obscured Riven entirely, he turned and looked at Derreg, at Vasen.

"What's his name? The boy."

"Vasen," Derreg said, and felt Vasen's yellow eyes fix on him when he spoke the word.

"Vasen," Riven said, testing out the word. "A good name. Well met, Vasen. Welcome to the world. When we meet again, I think you'll not be pleased to see me."

Derreg blinked and Riven was gone. The room lightened. Vasen began to cry.

Erdan let out a long breath. "What just happened?"

"I'm not certain."

"That wasn't a man."

"No," Derreg said. "That was not."

CHAPTER 1

Eleint, the Year of the Awakened Sleepers (1484 DR)

GLACIERS AS OLD AS CREATION COLLIDED, VIED, AND SPLINtered—the crack of ancient ice like the snap of dry bones. The smell of brimstone and burning souls wafted up from rivers of fire that veined the terrain. Cania's freezing gusts bore the innumerable screams of the damned, spicing the air with their pain. Towering, insectoid gelugons, their white carapaces hard to distinguish from the ice, patrolled the banks of the rivers. Their appetite for agony was insatiable, and with their hooked polearms they ripped and tore at the immolated damned who flailed and shrieked in the flames.

Mephistopheles perched atop an ice-capped crag a quarterleague high and stared down at his realm of ice and fire and pain. Plains of jagged ice stretched away in all directions. Black mountains hazed with smoke scraped a glowing red sky lit by a distant, pale sun.

And he ruled it all. Or almost all.

His gaze fixed on the mound of shadow-shrouded ice, far below, that had defied his will for a century, and his eyes narrowed. His anger stirred the embers of his power, and the air crackled around him, baleful emanations of the divinity he'd stolen from the god, Mask.

Staring at the shadowy cairn, he sensed that events were picking up speed, fates being decided, events determined, but he couldn't see them. Matters were fouled and he suspected the shadowy cairn had something to do with it.

"Permutations," he said, his voice as deep and dark as a chasm. "Endless permutations."

He had schemed for decades to obtain a fraction of the divine power he now held, intending to use the power he'd gained in a coup against Asmodeus, the Lord of Nessus, a coup that would have resulted in Mephistopheles ruling the Nine Hells. But events on one of the worlds of the Prime had made a joke of his plans.

The Spellplague had ripped through the world of Toril, recombining it with its sister world, Abeir, and causing chaos among gods and godlings. A half-murdered god had literally fallen through the Astral Sea and into the Ninth Hell. Asmodeus had finished the murder and absorbed the divinity.

Mephistopheles, who had plotted for decades to become divine, had managed to take only a fraction of a fraction of a lesser god's power, while the Lord of the Ninth had become a full god through luck. By chance. And Mephistopheles was, once more, second in Hell.

Worst of all, he feared that Asmodeus had recently learned of his plans. Mephistopheles's spies in Nessus's court spoke of mustering legions, of Asmodeus's growing ire. A summons had reached Mephistar, Mephistopheles's iron keep. Asmodeus's words had been carried on the vile, forked tongue of the Lord of Nessus's sometime-messenger, the she-bitch succubus, Malcanthet.

"His Majesty, the Supreme Overlord of the Hells, Asmodeus the Terrible, requires His Grace's presence before his throne in Nessus."

"Supreme, you said?"

"Shall I tell His Majesty that you take issue with his title?"

Mephistopheles bit back his retort. "He sends me Hell's harlot to convey a summons? To what end is my presence required?"

Malcanthet had ignored the question, offering only, "His Majesty wished me to inform you that time is of the essence."

"And my time is limited. I will attend when I'm able."

"You will attend within a fortnight or His Majesty will be forced to assume that you are in rebellion. Those are the words of His Majesty."

Mephistopheles had glared at her while his court had muttered and tittered. "Get out! Now!"

Malcanthet had bowed, smirking, and exited the court, leaving Mephistopheles to stew in uncertainties, his court to gossip in possibilities.

Mephistopheles had managed to put off a reckoning with Asmodeus for decades. He'd made excuse after excuse, but the Lord of the Ninth's patience had finally worn thin. Mephistopheles had little time and few options. He wasn't ready. Far below, the cairn of ice mocked him. Shadows leaked from it, dribbled out of its cracks in languid streams. Often he'd tried to burn his way to the bottom of the cairn, but the ice would not yield. He'd had hundreds of whip-driven devils tear into the mound with weapons and tools, all to no avail. He'd attempted to magically transport himself within the hill and failed. He could not even scry what lay at its bottom.

And yet he had his suspicions about what lay under the shadow-polluted ice.

"Erevis Cale." Saying the name kindled his anger to flame.

Mephistopheles had torn out Cale's throat on Cania's ice and taken the divine spark of Mask then possessed by Cale. Then, while Mephistopheles had been distracted by his triumph, Cale's ally, Drasek Riven, himself possessed of another divine spark, had materialized and nearly decapitated Mephistopheles.

The pain remained fresh in Mephistopheles's mind. His regeneration had taken hours, and by then, Cale's body had been covered by the cairn that vexed him so.

Unable to destroy the cairn, finally Mephistopheles had simply forbade anyone from approaching it. Intricate, powerful wards allowed no one to go near it but Mephistopheles himself.

Staring at the cairn, his anger overflowed his control. He leaped from his perch and spread his wings—power and rage shrouding him. Millions of damned souls and lesser devils looked up and then down, cowering, sinking into their pain rather than look upon the Lord of Cania enraged.

He tucked his wings and plummeted toward the cairn, Erevis Cale's tomb. He slammed into it with enough velocity and force to send a shock wave of power radiating outward in all directions. Snow and ice shards exploded into the air. The damned of Cania uttered a collective groan.

He looked down, his breathing like a bellows, his rage unabated. The hill remained unmarred—a mound of opaque ice veined with lines of shadow. He aimed his palms at the cairn's surface and blasted the ice with hellfire. Flame and smoke poured from his hands, engulfing the cairn, the back blast cloaking him in fire and heat. He stood in its midst, unaffected, pouring forth power at the object of his hate. Around him, ice hissed, fogging the air as it melted. Shadows poured from the hill in answer, a dark churn that coated him in night.

The ice renewed itself as fast as his fires could melt it. The shadows swirled amid the storm of power and snow and ice—mocked him, defied him. He channeled fire and power at the hill, relenting only long enough to let the shadows disperse, the spray of ice and snow to settle. And when it did, he saw what he always saw: the unmarred cairn.

It was protected somehow and he did not understand it. Something was happening, something he could not see. Mask was in the center of it, the cairn was in the center of it, and he could not so much as melt its ice.

And now—*and now*—Asmodeus was coming for him.

Ropes of shadow leaked from thin cracks in the cairn's ice and spiraled around Mephistopheles's body. He threw back his head, stretched his wings, flexed his claws, and roared his frustration at the cloud-shrouded red sky. The sound boomed across his realm, the thunder of his rage. Distant glaciers cracked in answer. Volcanoes spat ash into the sky.

When at last he was spent, he fell into a crouch atop the cairn, put his chin in his hand, and considered his options.

He saw only two courses: He could ask forgiveness of Asmodeus and abase himself before the Lord of Nessus, foreswearing rebellion, or he could obtain more power, enough to equal Asmodeus's, and so empowered, pursue his planned coup.

He much preferred the latter. And yet if he moved to obtain more divine power, he'd be moving blindly. Mask had put in place some kind of scheme—was the cairn not evidence of that?—and Mephistopheles did not want to stumble into it and inadvertently serve Mask's ends. Mephistopheles feared losing the divinity he'd already gained in an effort to gain more, for he had no doubt that Mask had plotted for his own eventual return.

But he had little choice. Time had grown short. Over the last hundred years he'd scoured the multiverse for information about Erevis Cale and Mask, trying to suss out Mask's play so that he could thwart it. He'd tortured mortal and immortal beings alike, eavesdropped on the whispered conversations of exarchs and godlings, listened to the secrets carried in the planar currents, wrung what information he could from the nether with his divinations.

And he'd learned only one thing, one tantalizing clue: Erevis Cale had a son.

He'd come to believe over the years that the son had something to do with the secret buried under the ice, *his* ice, that the son was at the center of Mask's scheme, and that if he could find the son, he could end Mask's plans, whatever they were, at a stroke. Then he'd have had the freedom to move against the two men who, like Mephistopheles, held fractions of Mask's power.

He'd pacted with many mortals over the decades, promising them rewards if they brought word of Erevis Cale's son. He'd bargained with so many that he'd lost track of them. But none had ever located Cale's son. It was as though the son had simply disappeared.

And now events had, at last, outrun Mephistopheles's ability to plan ahead of them. He could no longer wait to learn the full picture of Mask's scheme. He could no longer spare time searching for Cale's son. Asmodeus was coming for him, as he did for any who dared plot rebellion. Mephistopheles would need more power to face the Lord of Nessus. And he knew where he could get it.

Drasek Riven and Rivalen Tanthul each possessed a spark of Mask's stolen divinity. If Mephistopheles killed them, he could take their divinity and face Asmodeus as a peer.

He looked down at the cairn, imagined Erevis Cale's frozen body buried somewhere under its ice. He tapped the ice with a clawed finger.

"I haven't forgotten your son. And I won't. And your dead god won't be coming back, whatever his schemes."

For answer, only more shadows.

He shook them off, stood, cupped his hands before his mouth, and put a message in the wind for Duke Adonides, his majordomo, blowing it in the direction of Mephistar. The gust tore over Cania's icy plains.

"Prepare the legions to march on the Shadowfell. Drasek Riven is to die."

Riven stood in the uppermost room of the central tower of his citadel—a fortress of shadows and dark stone carved in relief into the sheer face of a jagged peak.

The plaintive, hopeful prayers of Mask's few remaining worshipers in Toril bounced around in his head, the background noise of his existence, a din that made him want to dig out his remaining eye with his thumbs.

Lord of shadows, hear my words . . .

From the darkness, I speak your name, Shadowlord . . .
Return to us, Lord of Stealth . . .

"I'm not your damned god," he said, and drew on his pipe.

As best he could, he pushed the voices to the back of his consciousness. There'd been many such voices a century earlier, but they'd gradually faded and there were only a few now. He wondered, not for the first time, if Rivalen or Mephistopheles— who also possessed some of Mask's power—also heard them, or if the fading hopes of Mask's faithful were his burden alone to bear. He suspected the latter, and he wondered what that meant.

Annoyed, he exhaled a cloud of pungent smoke and let his gaze follow it out the tall, narrow window and down to the shrouded land beyond his citadel.

The starless black vault of the plane's sky hung over a landscape of gray and black, where lived the dark simulacra of actual things. Shadows and wraiths and specters and ghosts and other undead hung in the air around the citadel, or prowled the foothills and plains near it, so numerous their glowing eyes looked like swarms of fireflies. He felt the darkness in everything he could see, felt it as an extension of himself, and the feeling made him too big by half.

The Shadowfell had been his home for the past one hundred years. More his home now than Faerûn, he supposed, and the realization annoyed him further. He'd never wanted to be a god, never wanted to spend his days in shadow, listening to the whines of the faithful, caught up in the machinations of beings he hadn't even known existed when he'd been only a man. Back then, he'd wanted only to drink and eat and gamble and enjoy women, but now . . .

Now he still wanted to drink and eat and gamble and womanize, but the divinity squirmed within him, a toothy thing that chewed at the corners of his humanity, eating away at the man to make room for the god. And unless he did something soon, it would consume his humanity altogether. He hated it, hated what it had done to him, and for what it insisted he hear and know.

For as the divinity opened holes in the man, knowledge not-his-own filled the abscesses. The fractional divinity within him revealed its secrets only gradually, a slow drip of revelation that had been unfolding over decades, a plodding education in godhood. He wondered if that, too, was his burden alone to bear. Because if Mephistopheles and Rivalen did not experience it the same way, well . . . what did that mean?

At the least it meant that new memories bubbled up from time to time, popped in his mindscape, and loosed their stinking contents into his consciousness. Riven consulted them not as a man looking back on his own experiences but as a scholar would a scroll written in a language in which he was barely fluent. Mask kept his secrets even from Riven, letting him in on the game only a little at a time.

And the game, it turned out, had been a long con. Mask had played them all, including his mother, Shar.

Mask had been Shar's herald on Toril, the prophet who started her Cycle of Night, a divine process that had repeated itself countless times across the multiverse, and had, in the process, destroyed countless worlds. And each time, on each world, the cycle ended the same way, *had* to end the same way—with Shar consuming the divinity of her herald. The divine cannibalism of her own offspring allowed the Lady of Loss to incarnate fully, and once she did, she reduced everything in the world to nothing.

Cycles of Night had left the multiverse pockmarked with holes. Voids of nothingness were the footprints Shar left as she stalked through reality. Riven knew the amount of life she'd destroyed in the process, and it nauseated even him. And apparently it had been too much for Mask, also, for when it came to Toril, he hadn't played his part.

"The cycle must be broken," Riven said, the words exiting his mouth, but not feeling at all like his own words.

On Toril, Shar had consumed only a portion of Mask's divinity, for he'd hidden the rest away, and what she'd consumed was not enough to finish the cycle, not enough to allow her to incarnate. Mask had trapped his mother halfway through her incarnation. She existed now within a hole in the center of the Ordulin Maelstrom, raging, gazing out through a window of nothingness at a world that had defied her, at least temporarily. Mask had frozen Toril's Cycle of Night.

But Shar was still hungry, and she wanted the rest of her meal.

Riven possessed some of Mask's divinity, Mephistopheles possessed some, and Rivalen Tanthul, Shar's nightseer on Faerûn, possessed the third portion. The divinity could only come out of them one way—with their deaths. And as much as Riven hated godhood, he hated being dead even more. He wouldn't be feeding himself to Shar anytime soon.

He'd learned more as Mask's memories showed him the game. He finally remembered what he'd done—what *Mask had done*—to Cale's son, Vasen. And he'd learned of Mask's plan to return.

"To end the cycle, resurrect the herald," he said, the words once more like foreign things on his lips.

Mask had changed Vasen in the womb, given him a very special ability, and pushed him forward in time to hide him. Vasen was the key. Vasen could release the divinity in Rivalen, Riven, and Mephistopheles, and do it without killing them. But he had to do it with all three of them present, and he had to do it while Shar looked on. That meant it had to be done in the Ordulin Maelstrom.

If it went right, Mask would reincarnate. If it went wrong, the Cycle of Night would re-start and run its course.

"This should've been Cale," Riven muttered.

Riven had never had Cale's mind for plans, and he struggled to keep everything straight in his head.

"I should've died, not him."

But then again, Cale wasn't dead.

Mask had seen fit to reveal that bit of information to Riven recently. Riven had wrestled with the implications for days. He didn't quite see how it fit into the rest.

All he knew at this point was that Cale was alive. Alive and trapped under Hell's ice for a century.

"Damn, damn, damn."

Mask had either kept Cale alive somehow when he should've died or brought him back to life immediately after his death. Riven didn't know which, and didn't understand why. He didn't even understand how. He presumed that Cale, too, must have still had some of Mask's divinity, a tiny sliver that Mephistopheles hadn't taken. That was the only explanation.

Riven's head spun as he tried to think through all the players and their plots. Everything was complicated, wheels within wheels, plans within plans within plans, and somehow Riven had to sort it out and end up on the right end of things.

Yet he suspected that Mask had kept still more secrets from him. Riven could spend a decade planning, then learn something new tomorrow that changed everything, put everything in a new light.

He put it out of his mind for the moment, looked out on his realm, and tried to enjoy his pipe.

Flashes of viridian lightning periodically knifed through the dense churn of low clouds, painting the landscape for a moment in sickly green. Gusts of wind summoned dust as fine as ash from the foothills, whipped through the plains and caused the twisted grass and oddly angled branches of the Shadowfell's trees to hiss and whisper. The miasmic, gloomy air, soupy with shadows, thronged with undead, pressed down on Riven's mood.

He'd long ago had enough of the Shadowfell, but he left the plane only when absolutely necessary. His close connection to it meant that he was strongest when here, weaker when away. He knew Mephistopheles and Rivalen both would kill him if they could, each for their own reasons, and he dared not give them a moment's weakness to exploit, not unless he must. They'd both tried to scry him from time to time. He felt their divinations pawing at him, making the air around him charged and itchy, but the spells never quite latched onto him. His divinity allowed him to slip almost all scrying.

But the Lord of Cania and the nightseer knew where he was. And he knew where they were.

"The three of us," he said. "Stalemated."

His voice drew one of his dogs, bitches he'd had for decades. She pushed through the door behind him, padded over, and plopped down at his feet with a tired exhalation.

His mood immediately improved. Her short tail beat against the smooth stone floor. When he looked down and smiled around his pipe, she flopped on her side to show her age-fattened belly.

Shadows slipped out of her flesh. She'd been a tan, white, and brown mutt once, but years in the shadows, years with Riven, had turned her dark. The Shadowfell had seeped into her, the same as it had into Riven, turning them both into shadows of themselves.

She whined for attention, tail still thumping, and Riven took the hint. He scratched her chest and stomach and she answered with happy sighs and more wags. He tried not to follow the implications of her graying muzzle and labored breathing. Unlike Riven, she was not divine, not immortal. Shadowstuff had extended her life, but it would not keep her alive forever.

"I shouldn't have brought you here," he said, and she just wagged happily. He should have let his girls die in peace in Faerûn, still themselves, still normal.

Her sister, also as black as ink, caught wind of the petting and ambled in. She plopped down and showed her stomach, too, and Riven surrendered fully. He set his pipe on the floor and vigorously scratched and petted each of them. They rolled over and put their heads on his legs, licked his hand. Shadows spun around all three of them. He smiled, thinking how they must look, the dark god and his fat, tail-wagging shadow hounds.

"You're good girls," he said, patting their heads, stroking their muzzles.

He would have been dead inside without them, he knew that. He sometimes felt that they were the sole thread connecting him back to his humanity. And he missed his humanity. He missed *need*, the satisfaction that came from striving for ordinary things and achieving them. Divinity had expanded his mind but dulled his body to pleasure. He could partake of food, drink, and women, but he experienced all of them at a distance, almost as an observer, not a participant. The curse of a divine mind, he supposed. For some reason the pleasure he felt smoking his pipe remained sharp, so he smoked often. Jak Fleet, an old companion of his, would have smiled to see it.

"All right, girls," he said, and patted them each one last time before grabbing his pipe and standing. They watched him stand, forlorn, as dogs do.

He drew on his pipe, thinking, planning. He'd put things in place as best he knew how. Now he had to wait for Vasen—he'd be over thirty by now—to come to him, for he dared not visit Cale's son again. After that, he had to rescue Cale. Then he had to resurrect a god or destroy the world, one or the other.

"Damn," he said.

He thought of his old life, thought of Cale, Jak, and Mags. Mags.

He made up his mind. He'd need Mags, someone he could count on, someone he could trust. He'd risk leaving the Shadowfell one more time before all the pieces started to move.

Magadon stood behind the bar of his tavern, wiping one tin tankard after another with a dirty rag. He'd closed an hour earlier and his now-empty place—a rickety taproom he'd named the Tenth Hell, to amuse himself—felt hollow. It still carried an echo of the day's stink, though: smoke and beer and sweat and bad stew.

Daerlun, and indeed all of Faerûn, had changed much over the eighty years he'd owned the place, but his tavern remained more or less as it was since the day he'd first bought it. He'd done nothing but minimal maintenance.

It was frozen in the past. Like him.

He, too, had changed little over the years. He'd let his horns and his hair grow long, and he'd grown more powerful in the Invisible Art, but little else. He was passing time, nothing more and nothing less. He served his ale and his stew, his weapons and gear stored under the bar, while he waited.

Damned if he knew for what. Something.

The tavern was a two-fireplace, decrepit wooden building that attracted a decrepit clientele who didn't mind a half-fiend barkeep. The building nestled against Daerlun's eastern wall, squalid and lonely. If the Shadovar and their Sembian allies ever marched on Daerlun—which had declared itself an independent city decades ago—they'd come from the east, and Magadon's tavern would be among the first buildings to burn. Maybe there was meaning in that.

The threat of war with the Shadovar had loomed over Daerlun for decades, as much a shadow on the city as was the miasmic air of neighboring Sembia. Over time the populace had gotten so used to the threat of an attack that it had gone from danger to jest: "As probable as Sakkors floating up to the walls," they'd say, in reference to something deemed unlikely.

But the jests had been fewer of late. Teamsters and peddlers and soldiers spoke in quiet tones of skirmishes in the perpetual dark of the Sembian plains, of Shadovar forces blockading the lands south of the Way of the Manticore, of battles being fought in the Dales. An open call for mercenaries had gone out from Sembia, and Magadon imagined shiploads of blades-for-hire sailing into the ports of Selgaunt and Saerloon. The war would eventually reach Daerlun and its towering, obsidian walls. If the Dales fell to Sembia's forces, Daerlun would fall next. Magadon didn't think it would be long. Sakkors had been sighted once or twice on the distant horizon, floating on its inverted mountain, hanging in the dark Sembian sky like a promise of doom.

Sakkors. Magadon had not actually seen it himself in many years, but then he didn't need to. He'd seen it long ago and dreamed of it often. The sentient crystalline mythallar that powered the city and kept it afloat—it called itself the Source—had permanent residence in Magadon's mind.

Long ago Magadon had nearly lost himself in the Source's vast consciousness. He'd augmented his mind magic with its power and become a godling, at least for a moment. In the process he'd also become a monster, but his friends had saved him, and he'd stood with Erevis Cale and Drasek Riven and defeated a god.

Thinking of those times made him smile. He considered those days the finest in his life, yet things felt incomplete to him. That was the reason he could not move on. That was the reason he tended bar and bided his time.

The Source still called to Magadon, of course, but because he'd grown stronger over the decades, its call no longer pulled at him with the insistence it once did. Instead the Source's mental touch felt more like a gentle solicitation, an invitation. He could've blocked them—a simple mind screen would have shielded him—but the Source's touch had become familiar over the years, a comforting reminder and a connection to a past he wasn't yet ready to let go.

Clay lamps burned on a few of the tavern's time-scarred tables, casting shaky shadows on the slatted wood walls. He stared into the dark corners of the room, a little game he played with himself, and let a doomed flash of hope spark in his mind. He gave the hope voice before it died.

"Cale? Riven?"

Nothing. Shadows danced, but none spoke. Cale was dead, Riven was a man-become-a-god, and Magadon hadn't seen him in almost a century.

He blew out a sigh and hung all but one of the tankards he'd cleaned on their pegs behind the bar. He filled the one he'd kept from the half-full hogshead and raised it in a salute. After draining it, he set to closing down the tavern for another night, all of it routine. His life had become rote.

He went to the tables, each of them wobbling on uneven legs, and blew out the lamps. The low fire in the hearth provided the room's only light. He checked the stew pot on its hook near the hearth, saw that almost nothing remained, and decided to leave cleaning it for the morning. He took the iron poker from the wall, intending to spread the coals and head to his garret next door, where he'd lay awake and think of the past, then fall asleep and dream of the Source.

All at once the air in the room grew heavy, pressed against his ears, and a cough sounded from behind him. He whirled around, brandishing the poker. Instinct caused him to draw on his mental energy and a soft, red glow haloed his head.

The darkness in the tavern had deepened so that he could not see into the corners of the room. He stood in a bubble of light cast by the faint glow of his power and the fire's embers. He slid to his left, holding the poker defensively, and put his back against the hearth. He'd left his damned weapons behind the bar.

"Show yourself," he said.

He charged the metal poker with mental energy, enough to penetrate a dragon's scales. Its end glowed bright red. The light cast shadows on the walls.

"I said: Show yourself."

"You carry that instead of a blade now?" said a voice from his right.

Magadon whirled toward the voice and shock almost caused him to drop the poker.

"Riven."

The darkness in the room relented. The weightiness in the air did not.

"Nice that someone remembers that name," Riven said. He stepped from the darkness, emerged from it as if stepping out from behind dark curtains, all compact movement and blurry edges. Sabers hung from his belt. A sneer hung from his lips. He hadn't aged, but then he wouldn't have. Magadon reminded himself that he was not talking to a man but a god.

Riven glided across the room, his footsteps soundless, and Magadon could not think of a single word to say. Riven smiled through his goatee and extended his hand. Magadon hesitated, then took it. Shadows crawled off Riven and onto Magadon's forearm.

"It's good to see you again, Mags. I don't have long. My being here puts you at risk."

"At risk? From what? I don't—"

Riven was already nodding. "I know you don't. I know. And that's as it must be. Mags, the Cycle of Night either succeeds or fails. And that's up to us. Maybe."

Magadon's head was spinning. His thoughts were inchoate. "The Cycle of Night?"

Riven nodded, started pacing, dragging his fingertips over the tabletops as he moved, the shadows clinging to his form. "This is a shithole, Mags."

"What?"

Riven chuckled. "I caught you by surprise here. Apologies. I need you to be ready when I call. I just . . . need someone I can rely on. Can you do that?"

Magadon could not quite gather his runaway thoughts. He resisted the impulse to cough out another stupid question. "I don't know what you're talking about."

Riven looked almost sympathetic. "I know you don't. But that's good for now. I don't even know what I'm talking about half the time because they're not my words and only half my thoughts."

Magadon blinked, confused.

Riven looked at him directly, his regard like a punch. "Can you be ready, Mags?"

"I . . . don't know."

Riven nodded, as if he'd expected ambivalence. "Where's your pack? Your bow and blade?"

Magadon started to find his conversational footing. "Behind the bar."

"A barkeep," Riven said, chuckling. "Not how I saw things going for you."

"Not how I saw things going for me, either," Magadon admitted with a shrug. "It's been a hundred years, Riven. You show up, you talk about things as if I should know what they are, but I don't and—"

"I found Cale's son. Thirty years ago. I found him."

The words stopped Magadon cold. "Found him where? He was alive thirty years ago? He'd have been over seventy years old."

Riven shook his head. A pipe was in his hand, although Magadon had not seen him take it out. "You have a match?"

Magadon shook his head.

"Gods, Mags. You used to be prepared for anything." He shook his head. "No matter."

He put the pipe in his mouth and lit. He inhaled, the glow of the bowl showing the pockmarks in his face, the vacancy where his left eye should have been. The smoke joined the shadows in curling around him.

"He's not seventy," Riven said. "He was newborn thirty years ago. It's a long story."

"How could he have been newborn thirty years ago? Cale would've been dead seventy years by then."

A smile curled the corners of Riven's mouth. "I told you it was a long story."

"I've nothing but time."

Riven nodded, blew out a cloud of smoke. "But I don't."

"You're telling me he's still alive? The son?"

"He's alive and he's the key, Mags."

Magadon shook his head, unable to make sense of things. "The key to what?"

"The key to fixing all this, undoing it, making it as it should have been, stopping Shar's Cycle of Night. But it'll have to happen in Ordulin."

Magadon was still not following, although the mention of Ordulin turned Magadon's mind to the Shadovar, to Rivalen Tanthul, Shar's nightseer. Magadon had been captured and tortured by Rivalen and his brother, Brennus, long ago. "Rivalen and the Shadovar are involved?"

Riven nodded. "More than involved. Rivalen's trying to complete the Cycle, and he's clever, Mags, very clever. But maybe too clever this time. Your father's involved in this, too, although he's a bit player. And so are you. Or at least you are now."

"My father?" The last time Magadon had seen his father, Mephistopheles, the archdevil had flayed his soul. He banished the memory.

"You all right?" Riven asked.

Magadon nodded. "Where's Cale's son?"

Riven's eye looked past Magadon, to the east. "He's out there in the dark. A light in darkness, is what they say. He's safe, though."

"You tell me where he is, I can go to him. Keep him safe."

Riven shook his head. "No, you can't. He's where he's supposed to be. Now he's gotta come to me. Besides, I need you here."

"For what?"

"I told you. To be ready when I call."

"What does that even mean? You're talking in circles."

Riven grinned around his pipe stem. "I don't know what it means yet. I'm figuring this out as we go. I just know I want you ready. I'll need your help. Just like always, just like it was back before . . . everything."

"Like it was back before," Magadon echoed. He pointed with his chin at the stew pot, still hanging over the embers. "Do you eat? Now that . . . you are what you are? There's a little stew there. Or an ale, maybe?"

"I eat," Riven said, losing his smile. "But it's not the same anymore. It's like I can't help but analyze instead of just enjoy it." He shook his head. "It's complicated."

Magadon put a hand on Riven's shoulder in sympathy, but Riven pushed it aside and cocked his head, as if he'd heard something, and a half-beat later a loud thud sounded from above, a powerful impact on the roof that cracked a crossbeam and shook the entire tavern. Dust and debris sprinkled down.

Magadon looked up. "What—?"

Another thud, the crossbeam cracked further, and the entire roof sagged.

"Shit," Riven said, exhaling smoke. The pipe was already gone and he had his sabers in hand. Magadon had not even seen him draw them.

A heavy tread on the roof, creaking wood, a scrabbling on the roof tiles, as of blade or claw.

"They must've followed me," Riven said, taking position beside Magadon, his body coiled, shadows swirling. "They must've been watching me in the Shadowfell somehow, waiting. Or maybe they've been here the whole time? See anything unusual recently?"

"What? No."

Another thump, more splintering and dust, more tension.

Magadon drew on his store of mental energy, shaped it, formed it into a cocoon of transparent force that surrounded his body and would protect him as well as plate armor. He tightened his grip on the poker, looked up at the bowed roof.

"*Who* followed you?" he whispered.

"Agents of your father," Riven said, his voice low and edged.

"Devils, then."

A crash and a sharp prolonged splintering as the roof gave way entirely. The main crossbeam hit the floor with a boom, in the process crushing a table and two chairs. Tiles and wood planks and two winged fiendish forms poured down through the hole. The devils hit the floor in a crouch, narrow eyes on

Riven and Magadon, tridents clutched in clawed hands, membranous wings tucked behind their back.

The fiends—Magadon recognized them as malebranche—stood taller than even a very tall man. Thick muscles clotted in bunches under their gray, leathery skin. Each wore ornate vambraces and a pauldron over one shoulder. Two curved horns jutted from their brows, overlooking vaguely reptilian features. Their oversized mouths had a pronounced underbite, and a pair of tusks stabbed upward from their lower jaw.

"Shadows aren't the same here as they are in the Shadowfell," one of them said, its voice gravelly. The other grabbed a chair and hurled it at Riven. Riven ducked under it casually. The chair smashed against the hearth and splintered, spilling the stew pot.

"They're about the same," Riven said with a sneer.

The devils opened their mouths in a deep growl. Licks of flame danced between the tines of their tridents.

"They can't get out alive," Riven said. "Neither escapes."

"Understood," Magadon said. He pulled from the deep pool of mental energy that filled his core, shaped it into a field of latent force, and transferred it once more to the tip of the poker he held. A halo of red energy formed around the point.

The devils leaped at them, the tree-trunks of their legs propelling them forward like shot quarrels. Magadon hurled the energized poker at one of them, while Riven bounded forward with preternatural speed, meeting the larger malebranche's charge with a charge of his own.

The fireplace poker flew true and slammed into the smaller fiend in mid-leap. The latent power with which Magadon had charged the tip allowed the makeshift weapon to strike with exaggerated force. The impact knocked the fiend out of the air and into a table. It bellowed with pain and rage, the poker sunk a hand span into its hide.

Meanwhile, Riven faced the other devil, his blades a whirlwind of steel, his movements trailing shadows. He sidestepped the devil's charge and a stab from its trident, leaped over another stab, slashed and spun and cut. The devil retreated under Riven's onslaught, bumping into tables, stumbling into chairs, its trident too slow to parry the speed of Riven's assault. Two clay lamps hit the ground and shattered, spilling their oil.

Riven, his speed and skill that of a god, carved flesh from the devil in gory ribbons. The creature roared, ichor spraying from its wounds, and stabbed at Riven with its trident again and again, hitting only empty air. Its trident scraped the floor, and the flames between the tines ignited the oil.

The devil Magadon had knocked prone jerked the poker from its flesh and intentionally toppled another table into the flames. The lamp atop it broke, spilling its oil. Tables caught fire, a chair, another chair, the floor. Smoke clotted the air.

Magadon cursed and sprinted across the common room. The fiend leaped to its feet and gave chase. Magadon jumped over the bar, sending two tankards and a plate clattering to the floor, and landed in a heap on the other side. He scrambled to his feet and looked back to see the fiend coiling for a leap.

Drawing from his reserve of mental energy, Magadon formed it into a spike of force that bound the devil's leg to the floor. The fiend leaped anyway, and the floor planks that now adhered to its clawed feet tore loose, the dislodged nails and wood screeching like the damned. Thrown off balance, the fiend fell forward into a table, splintering it under its weight.

Behind it, more smoke and flames. Riven and devil dueling in the flames. The room would soon be an inferno.

Magadon grabbed for his bow and quiver and had both in hand by the time the devil had regained its feet. Magadon nocked, charged his arrow with mental energy, drew, and fired into its face. The missile sunk into the devil's throat and it screamed, staggered back, clutching at its neck. As it did, it made a wild throw with its flaming trident, and the huge weapon struck Magadon squarely in the chest.

Although the tines did not penetrate the field of force that sheathed him, the sheer power of the blow drove him backward against the wall, cracked ribs, and drove the air from his lungs. Dislodged by the impact, tankards rained from their pegs. The hogshead fell to the floor, broke open, and covered the floor in beer.

Gasping for air, coughing on the growing cloud of smoke, Magadon staggered back to the bar and reached for another arrow from his quiver. The devil he'd shot spun frenetically around the burning common room, toppling tables and chairs, screaming, its breathing an audible squeal through the hole Magadon had put in its throat.

Behind the wounded devil, Riven continued his dissection of the larger devil. Riven's blades were a blur, slashing, stabbing, cutting. The devil roared and spun, lashed out with claws, trident, even a kick, but nothing landed. Riven was too fast, too precise. The fiend bled dark ichor from dozens of wounds. Its flesh hung in scraps from its body. A final crosscut from Riven's saber severed its head.

As Magadon nocked another arrow, the surviving devil finally pulled the arrow from its throat, screaming in agony. It fixed its eyes on Magadon, its huge chest rising and falling. It spit a mouthful of black ichor and rushed him.

Magadon sighted and powered his arrow with enough mental energy to fell a horse. The tip glowed an angry, hot red. He picked a spot between the devil's eyes and prepared to draw.

Before he could loose his shot, Riven stepped through the shadows, covering the length of the room in a single stride. He appeared in front of the devil, his sabers sheathed. He held a thin loop of reified shadow in his hands.

He dodged a surprised slash from the fiend's claws, spun, and looped the line of shadow around the fiend's neck. Before the devil could respond, Riven leaped atop the fiend's back, wrapped his legs around the devil's mid-section, and pulled the line taut around the fiend's throat.

The devil reared back, eyes wide, choking, gasping for breath, shooting a mist of blood from the hole Magadon had put in its throat. It spun, reached back to claw at Riven, staggered around the room, bumping into tables, chairs, walking through the flames. Throughout, Riven rode its back in calm, deadly silence, the shadow garrote choking out its life.

Magadon relaxed, set his bow on the bar, and his body lit up with pain, the suddenness of it like a lightning strike. The tip of a black sword exploded out from his abdomen and showered the bar in blood. He gasped, screamed, looked down uncomprehendingly at the dark wedge of steel protruding from his guts. His mouth was filling with blood. He gagged on it. His vision blurred.

"Shit!" He heard Riven shout. "Mags!"

"I'm all right," he tried to say, but he wasn't, and no words emerged, just a gurgle of blood. He put a hand on the gore-slicked bar to stay upright as his knees started to buckle. His clothing was already soaked in blood, his thoughts overwhelmed by pain.

A chuckle from behind.

He turned his head—it seemed to take forever—and saw a male devil standing behind him, holding the dark blade on which Magadon's dying body hung. It wasn't another mal-ebranche. It looked almost human, save for its violet skin and the two thin horns that jutted from its head. Shadows and leather armor wrapped its lithe body. Magadon recognized it as a breed of stealthy fiend used by other devils as quiet killers and assassins. It must have entered the tavern with the mal-ebranche, invisible or clad in darkness. Magadon had missed it. And it had killed him.

"Riven," Magadon tried to say, but it just came out an inarticulate gurgle of blood. He tried to focus but his eyes wouldn't hold onto anything but the devil's face, the red eyes, the fanged mouth.

The fiend gave a smile as it twisted the blade in Magadon's guts, then jerked it free, scraping ribs, widening the wound. A gush of warmth poured from the slit. Magadon screamed.

Desperately he grabbed at the pain, focused on it, lived in its center for a moment, a moment during which he ignored the blood and shit seeping from the hole in him. He grabbed at the devil with arms gone weak. He lurched, staggered, and would have fallen had he not gotten hold of the fiend by the forearm.

The devil tried to shake him loose but Magadon held on. The devil pulled back his blade for another stab but before he could Magadon made a spike of his will and drove it into the fiend's mind.

The devil sensed danger immediately. It resisted the mental intrusion, tried to shake Magadon's grip loose, but its desperation fed Magadon's physical and mental grip. His fingernails sank into the fiend's skin and his mind put a psychic hook in the devil's consciousness.

The devil stabbed him again, but Magadon was beyond pain, and heard, more than felt, the blade slice his flesh and organs, grate on bone. Lights flashed before his eyes, sparks, then darkness. He was fading, falling, but he held onto the fiend's mind and used their connection to set up an empathetic connection. When he felt the connection take firm hold, felt the psychic bridge between them, he grinned, tasting blood, and transferred the wounds and every damned bit of pain in his ruined body through the connection and into the devil.

The fiend's eyes went as wide as coins. It dropped its blade as its fanged mouth opened in a wail of pain. Shadows swirled around it, a storm of darkness. A jagged hole opened in the devil's abdomen, spilling gore, as the hole in Magadon pinched closed and painfully healed.

"This is for you, bastard," Magadon grunted, pushing his agony into the dying devil. He shoved the creature backward and the fiend stumbled back against the wall, tripping on tankards, trying and failing to push its innards back into its abdomen.

Magadon reached back to the bar and grabbed an arrow in his fist, sidestepped a feeble stab by the devil with its sword, and plunged the arrow into the fiend's eye, deep into its horned head.

The devil fell to the floor and Magadon rode him down, the two of them slick in shared gore. He pulled the arrow out and drove it into the fiend's other eye.

Magadon stood, breathing hard, his legs still weak, and found Riven right behind him, crouched atop the bar, backlit by the glow of the spreading flames. Shadows made a slow swirl around him. Somehow he reminded Magadon of a crow.

"Like old times," Riven said.

Magadon stood upright, wobbled, nodded.

"You all right?" Riven asked. He wasn't even breathing hard. In passing Magadon wondered if he breathed at all.

Magadon looked at the gory arrow in his hand, his blood-soaked clothes, the corpse of the devil behind him, his burning tavern.

"I'm good," he said. He picked up the hogshead from the floor and found that the spill hadn't drained it entirely. He filled two tankards and gave one to Riven.

"It's a shit brew," he said, draining his.

Riven drained his, too. "Best I've had in a long while, Mags."

Riven's pipe appeared in his hand, already lit, and he took a long draw.

"Fire brigade will be coming," Magadon said, as he watched his tavern burn, a thick column of smoke pouring through the hole in the ceiling. His fiendish blood protected him from heat and fire. Riven, too, would feel no threat from flames.

"Too late for this place," Riven said. "Sorry, Mags."

Magadon shrugged. "I'd had enough of it anyway."

Riven nodded. "Let these bodies burn. If these three had been working for your father, we'd have had ten score fiends here by now, and maybe the archfiend himself."

The mere hint of Mephistopheles's name, spoken by a godling, caused a cool wind to waft through the bar. Flames hissed and popped, the sound suggestive of dark words.

"These three were working for themselves, probably trying to get in your father's favor. Their mistake."

"Aye."

Riven took another draw on his pipe, exhaled the smoke. "Well?"

Magadon eyed his old friend, more god than man, while the life he'd built burned down around him.

"I'll be ready," he said.

"Well enough," Riven said, and Magadon thought he looked relieved. "Link us, then."

"A mind link?"

"So I can call you when I need you. Just leave it laying there so I can pick it up if I need it. And don't look around in there, Mags. You won't like it any."

The thought of linking minds with a god disconcerted Magadon, but it needed to be done. He opened his mind, drew on his mental energy, reached out for Riven's mind.

The shock of contact caused him to gasp. Mindful of Riven's admonition, he kept the link superficial and narrow. Still, he sensed at a distance the scope of Riven's mind, his expanded perception of time and place, the voices of the faithful that echoed through his mindscape.

"Gods," Magadon said softly.

"Gods, indeed," Riven said. "Makes a man a monster, Mags. No way to avoid it."

"I'm . . . sorry."

Riven shrugged. "We've all got our burdens. And don't feel sorry for me just yet. Things will get ugly for you before all's said and done. Count on it."

Magadon smiled ruefully. "When has it not?"

Riven grinned. "Stay sharp, Mags. See you soon. And Mags? He's alive."

"Who?"

"Cale. And we're going to get him."

"What? Wait!"

The darkness gathered, folded Riven into it, and he was gone.

He's alive. He's alive. The words and their implication pushed all other thoughts out of Magadon's mind.

Cale was alive. And his son was alive.

Grinning like a lunatic, Magadon gathered his weapons and gear. He donned his wide-brimmed hat, fitted it over his horns, and walked unharmed through the flames and into the night-shrouded streets of Daerlun. Already some passersby had gathered. The fire wouldn't spread, though. It'd burn up his garret and the tavern, but nothing else.

One of them, a tall, gaunt bald man who held an open book in his hands, struck Magadon oddly. He wasn't looking at the burning building like the rest of them. Instead he wrote something in his book with a quill.

The man must have felt Magadon's gaze. He looked up from his book.

His eyes had no pupils. They looked like opals set in his skull. He grinned.

Goose pimples rose on Magadon's skin. He had no idea why. Something about the man . . .

"Hey, are you all right?" shouted another of the gathered passersby, a sailor with drink-slurred speech. "You all right, friend? Look at your clothes! Gods man!"

The bald man had gone back to his book, writing, his mouth bent in a secretive smile.

"I said, are you all right?" the sailor shouted again.

Magadon looked at the sailor, raised a hand, and smiled. "I'm fine."

He was better than fine. He was good as he'd been in a hundred years.

CHAPTER TWO

Magadon walked for a time, thinking. The streets bustled even at the late hour: Mule-drawn wagons of supplies moved toward the barracks, and groups of grim-faced soldiers stood on corners, monitoring the traffic and the passersby. The city was preparing for war. Every day hundreds of soldiers marched out of the city to the parade grounds outside the towering basalt walls that ringed Daerlun, and there drilled for hours. Scouts mounted on veserabs—giant-winged lamprey-like creatures—swooped over the city, carrying messages from Cormyrean nobles to High Bergun Gascarn Highbanner. Rumors had an alliance brewing between Daerlun and Cormyr. Magadon wasn't sure that would be enough to thwart a Sembian assault, when it came.

He didn't realize it until he arrived, but his boots had carried him to the east gate. Beyond the dark, basalt wall, the shroud of Sembia's shadowed night hung across the sky. Lines of green lightning flashed, the veins of Sembia's sky. He felt the gentle touch of the Source's consciousness brushing against his own.

Sakkors was out there, floating in the dark. As was Cale's son.

And with that, he knew what he would do.

The gate was closed and the guards stiffened at his approach. But their minds were ordinary and easily manipulated by his mind magic.

"I'm on official city business by order of the high bergun," he said, and pushed acceptance of his statement into their minds. "I need to get out of the city right now. Apologies for the late hour."

"Of course, of course," said the gate sergeant, a heavyset bearded fellow whose breath smelled of onion and pipe smoke.

In moments, Magadon stood outside the gates, with the basalt walls of the city behind him. He stared across the plains at the distant wall of shadowed air that blanketed Sembia. He'd walked Sembia in the dark before, with Erevis Cale at his side. They'd braved the Shadowstorm and trekked to Ordulin. The memory made Magadon smile.

"Walking in our footsteps, old friend," he said, and started off.

Using the Source's mental emanations, he kenned the direction and distance of Sakkors. It floated in Sembia's perpetual night south of the Thunder Peaks, about halfway between Daerlun and Ordulin. And Riven had said that whatever was to happen must happen in Ordulin.

Riven said he wanted Magadon's help. But how could Magadon be of assistance to a god? The same way he had assisted in the murder of a god a century before. He would draw on the power of the Source to augment his own. He felt the Source's mental emanations, answered them with his own.

See you soon, he projected.

He avoided the roads—fearing he'd encounter Sembian troops—and instead moved rapidly across the plains. His bow and woodcraft kept him fed and his mind magic and stealth kept him unobserved. Even traveling cross-country he spotted Shadovar patrols from time to time, once including what appeared to be a prisoner-transport caravan. He stayed well south of the Thunder Peaks and the Way of the Manticore, but he still saw signs of the gathered Sembian troops there. Even the perpetual gloom could not hide the light, like faintly burning stars, from thousands of campfires in the distance. The Sembians had blocked the road between Daerlun and Cormyr on the one hand and the Dalelands on the other. Whatever army the Dalelands had to face, they'd face alone.

Magadon did not take time to investigate any of it more thoroughly. Riven had asked him to be ready, so he kept moving east, moving directly for Sakkors, for the Source.

The twisted, malformed trees and whipgrass of the Sembian countryside saddened him. He'd walked the plains when they'd been lush with old trees and fields of barley. Now the leafless skeletons of old elms and oaks rattled in the gusty wind. He put a hand on the trunk of any old elms he encountered, a moment of bonding between two living things that had once seen a Sembia under the sun.

He stayed off the roads and skirted wide around villages, although many appeared abandoned, their fields fallow and weedy. Possibly the villagers had fled as Sembian forces marched east, or possibly something worse had happened to them.

Monsters prowled the plains. From time to time Magadon heard growls and roars in the distance, occasionally caught motion out of the corner of his eye. Often he nocked an energized arrow into his bow, but he never had to fire. The creatures that stalked the darkness left him unmolested.

The pull of the Source grew stronger as he covered the leagues. And as he grew closer, he sensed an undercurrent to its pull, a sadness. The Source's mind seemed dulled and melancholy. He didn't understand it. As he neared it, as he sensed the full scope of its power, he grew nervous. He feared he could lose himself in it again. But by the time he actually spotted Sakkors in the distance, a dark star hanging in the lightning lit sky of Sembia's night, he knew for certain he could resist its pull. He could use the Source and still keep himself. He'd been broken once before by using it, shattered, really, but his reassembled self was stronger than the original.

Small, dark figures flitted around the floating mountain on which Sakkors stood. They looked tiny from afar, but Magadon knew them to be Shadovar cavalry mounted on scaly-winged veserabs. The Source seemed finally to sense him fully, and its pull grew plaintive. It wanted him to come closer, to deepen their connection.

He eyed a stand of pine directly under the floating mountain and drew on his reserve of power. A dim orange glow haloed his head, and a mirror of the glow shone in the spot he'd mentally chosen under Sakkors. He activated the mind magic and it moved him instantly to the wooded spot under Sakkors.

The mountain floated over him, huge and ominous. And somewhere within its center was the Source.

Magadon opened his mind and let the Source's touch wash through him, let part of its power, its ancient consciousness, become part of his own. He sensed right away that it had lost no power, but it *had* lost acuity, and in an instant Magadon understood.

The Source *had* been calling to him, for a hundred years it had been sending mental energy out into the world in a desperate effort to reach out to him.

It missed him. It wanted him near.

Why? He projected, but knew the answer before the Source offered it.

The Source was dying, its sentience slowly fading away. Worse, it was aware of its impending demise, the slow erosion of its self-awareness. It was afraid.

And it was alone, surrounded by beings that didn't understand it and could not connect with it.

I'm so sorry, he projected.

The Source's fear and sadness tightened his chest, caught him up in its swirl, and swept through him. He sank to the bed of pine needles, weeping, and wrapped his arms around his knees.

It had wanted him to come to it, for a century, and he had not answered. He'd failed it.

Forgive me, he projected.

It did. In fact, it had nothing for him but affection, and his connection with it, and his sympathy, mitigated its sadness and alleviated its fear. It welcomed his companionship the way a thirsty man welcomed a drink, another mind to keep it company as it faded. It had simply not wanted to die alone.

I'll stay with you throughout, he promised. *When the city moves, I'll move with it. I won't leave you.*

He felt its gratitude. He made a place for himself under the city, hidden by his mind magic and the pine trees, and kept company with the oldest consciousness he'd ever encountered. Shadovar patrols came and went, sometimes cavalry on veserabs, sometimes soldiers afoot, but none ever noticed him.

Over the days and nights, the Source showed him many things, events from its past, possible futures, jumbles of nonsequential nonsensical things that he could not follow. Time passed oddly for him as he walked in the Source's dying thoughts. Its consciousness took odd turns, made strange connections, moved from things extraordinary to things mundane. He came to understand that he'd lost himself in the Source the first time not because of the Source's malice but because of its loneliness. It was a consciousness with no body, and it had wanted mental and emotional companionship so much that its over exuberant consciousness had simply overwhelmed his. He'd been unready then. But one hundred years had passed since, and he was ready now.

Magadon experienced months and years in moments, lived lives in hours, laughed and cried and raged. But always he kept a firm hold on himself, on his purpose.

There may come a time when I need your help, he said. *Will you help me?*

The Source answered, in its way, that it would if it still could.

Magadon broke his connection with the Source only once, to send a message to Riven through their mind link. He didn't know if Riven would receive it, but he wanted to try.

I'm ready, he projected, and nothing more.

Then he waited, keeping deathwatch on the Source, his thoughts often turning back to Riven's words.

Erevis is alive. And he has a son. And his son is the key to everything.

Vasen had never known the father whose blood ran in his veins, but Erevis Cale lived on in him somehow, haunting his dreams. Vasen always saw him as a dark man with a dark sword, a dark soul. In the dreams he never saw his father's face, and rarely heard his voice. They somehow communed without truly seeing one another, in blindness, in quietude, and over the years through the sense-starved dream connection Vasen believed he'd come to understand what Erevis would've wished for him to know—the depths of loss, the pain of regret. Everything he'd learned of his father seemed to circle around regret.

Vasen was dreaming now, he knew. He saw only darkness before him, deep and impenetrable. Frigid air stirred his hair, felt like knives on his skin. Erevis spoke to him, each word a treasure, his deep voice pushing aside the silence of the dreamscape.

"I am cold, Vasen. It's dark. I'm alone."

Vasen knew solitude all too well. He'd spent his life among others, but always apart from them. Vasen tried to move but could not. Something was holding him in place. The cold was growing worse. He was shivering, going numb, paralyzed.

"Where are you?" he called.

"Vasen, you must not fail."

The words hung there for a time, heavy, portentous, filling the darkness.

"Must not fail at *what*?"

"Find me. Write the story."

"How? How can I find you? You're dead!"

Vasen felt colder. He wanted to ask more questions, wanted to see his father's face at long last, but the darkness receded.

"Wait! Wait!"

Vasen caught a flash of glowing red sky, rivers of fire. He heard the screams of millions in torment.

He awoke on his pallet, shivering, heart racing. He stared up at the cracked, vaulted ceiling of his quarters in the abbey. The gauzy, dim gray of a newly birthed morning filtered through the single window of his quarters. He could count on one hand the number of days he had seen more than an hour or two of sunlight in the past year. He'd gotten used to Sembia's perpetual shroud long ago, the same way he'd gotten used to many things.

Letting the dream slip from the forefront of his mind, he sat up, his flesh still goose pimpled, and recited the Dawn Greeting, the words softly defiant in the ever-dim light.

"Dawn is Amaunator's gift. His light dispels darkness and renews the world."

He sat on the edge of his sleeping pallet for a time, bent over his knees, his head in his hands, thinking of Erevis, the legacy he could not escape even when asleep. He'd been dreaming of his father more and more in recent months. He examined his calloused hands, his skin the color of tarnished silver, his veins a deep purple. Shadows webbed the spaces between his fingers and spiraled up his forearms, gauntlets of night. He stared at them a long while, the curves and whorls and spirals, the script of his blood. When he shook his hands, the darkness dissipated like mist.

The light of your faith is stronger than the darkness of your blood, Derreg had often told him, and most of the time Vasen credited the words. But sometimes, after awakening from a dream of Erevis and sitting alone with only his shadow for company, sharing time with the darkness he felt lurking around the edges of his life, he wasn't so sure. Erevis's life haunted Vasen's; Vasen's heritage occluded his hopes. He sometimes had the feeling that he was doomed to live a history written by someone else, unable to turn the page to get to his own life. The shadows that cloaked him, that he could not escape, were the story of his life.

Write the story.

What did that even mean?

Derreg had told him often that Vasen had to prepare himself, had drilled it into him with such fervor that Vasen's childhood had been no childhood at all. It had been training of mind, body, and spirit since he'd been a boy.

"Prepare for what?" Vasen had asked through the years.

"For whatever comes," Derreg would answer softly, and the concern in his eyes spoke louder than his words. "And you must not fail."

And now Erevis echoed Derreg in Vasen's dream. The voices of his two fathers, the one of his blood, the other of his heart, had merged into a single demand.

You must not fail.

He stared at the symbol inlaid into the wall over the hearth, a blazing sun over a blossoming red rose.

"I won't," he said. Whatever came, he would bear it. And he would not fail.

Hard raps on his door startled him. As always when his emotions spiked, shadows leaked from his skin.

"Hold a moment," he said.

He stood and the morning chill resurrected his goose pimples. The fire in his hearth had burned down to ash and embers. He pulled on his tunic, his holy symbol on its sturdy chain, splashed water from the washbasin on his face, and padded the few steps to the door of his small chamber. He opened the door and blinked in surprise.

The Oracle stood in the doorway, his red, orange, and yellow robes glowing softly. His eyes were the solid, otherworldly orange of a seeing trance. A shining platinum sun, with a rose raised in relief on the circle of its center, hung from a chain around his thin neck. He stared not at Vasen but at a point just to Vasen's left.

The Oracle's guide, a large, tawny-coated fey dog with intelligent eyes, stood beside the elderly seer, tongue lolling, tail upright and entirely still. Vasen realized that he had never once heard the dog bark.

"O-Oracle," Vasen said, shock summoning a stutter from his mouth and shadows from his flesh. He had never heard of the Oracle entering a seeing trance outside the sanctum.

The Oracle smiled, showing toothless gums and deepening the web of grooves that lined his hawkish face. Age spots dotted the skin of his scalp, visible through the thin fluff of his gray hair. His skin looked parchment thin and lit with a soft, inner glow.

"His light and warmth keep you, Vasen," said the Oracle. Despite his age, his voice was the steady, even tone of the valley's cascades, so different from the voice he used when not in a trance.

"And you, Oracle."

"You may go, Browny," the Oracle said to the dog. The creature licked the Oracle's hand, eyed Vasen, and disappeared in a flash of pale light. Vasen always marveled at the dog's ability to magically transport itself.

Standing face to face with the Oracle, Vasen keenly felt the differences between them. The Oracle's pale skin, deprived of direct sunlight for a century, but illuminated by the inner glow of his trance, contrasted markedly with Vasen's dark skin, dimmed as it was by the legacy of his bloodline. The Oracle was lit with Amaunator's light. Vasen was dimmed by Erevis Cale's shadow.

"Do you . . . wish to come in, Oracle?" Vasen said. He realized the words sounded foolish, but was not sure what else to say.

Again that toothless grin. "Vasen, did you know that Abelar Corrinthal was my father?"

The abrupt conversational turn took Vasen aback, but he managed a nod. "My father told me."

"Which father?"

Recalling the dream that had awakened him, Vasen had trouble forming a reply. "Derreg. My adoptive father. I've never known another. You know this, Oracle."

"But you see Erevis. Sometimes. In your dreams."

Vasen could not deny it. "Yes. But they're just dreams, and he's long dead."

"So it's said."

Shadows leaked from Vasen's skin. Once more the goose pimples. "What do you mean?"

"I see him, too, Vasen son of Varra."

Vasen swallowed the bulge in his throat. "And what do you see when you see him?"

"I see you," the Oracle said.

"I . . . I don't understand."

"I don't either. I met Erevis Cale. Did you know that?"

"I didn't, but I wondered sometimes."

"Why did you never ask?"

Vasen answered truthfully. "It seemed a betrayal of Derreg. And I was afraid. I didn't want to . . . know him."

"He was hard to know, I think. I saw him twice when I was a boy. The first time he was a man haunted. The second time, he was no longer a man at all, but he was still haunted."

"Haunted? By what?"

"Doubt, I think," the Oracle said, then changed the subject. "Your father, your adoptive father, was the son of Regg, who rode with my father. Did you know that?"

"Yes. Of course."

Vasen could not shake the impression that he and the Oracle were simply reciting words written out for them by someone else. He still did not understand the purpose of the Oracle's visit.

"You, like your father, and like his father before him, swore to remain here and protect this abbey, to protect me. And you have done so."

Vasen did not answer. He felt humbled by the Oracle's acknowledgment.

"You have been here the longest with me and have done credit to the memory of Derreg and Regg. You have even become the first blade. But change comes to everything."

"It does," Vasen said haltingly. "But what's to change?"

"The world. I see a swirl of events, Vasen, but I cannot make sense of it. Gods, their Chosen, gods beyond gods, the rules of creation, the Tablets of Fate. Wars, Vasen. We see it already in the Dales. War is sweeping Toril. Something is changing. And in the midst of it all I see shadows and I see a growing darkness that threatens it all."

Vasen's head swam. He could make no sense of the Oracle's words.

"I am one hundred and six years old, Vasen," the Oracle continued. "Where will you go when I die?"

The question startled Vasen. "What?"

"Already pilgrims come only rarely. Traveling the realm of the Shadovar is too dangerous. Monsters walk the plains and, where they do not, Sembian soldiers march. When I die, still fewer will come."

"They will come to see your father's tomb."

"Perhaps some."

"They will come to see your tomb, as well, to honor your memory, the work you've done here. A light in the darkness, Oracle."

The Oracle smiled and Vasen saw that it was forced. His lined face wrinkled with remembered pain.

"That, I fear, will not be."

"Are you . . . dying?"

"We're all dying," the Oracle said. "So I ask again: Where will you go when I go to the Dawnfather?"

Vasen shook his head. He had dedicated his life to service and had never conceived a life for himself outside the valley. He had no family anymore, no real friends. The pilgrims and his comrades-in-arms respected him, but none were friends. His blood and appearance made him different. He lived his life in solitude.

"I don't know. Perhaps I'll remain here. This is my home."

The Oracle smiled, as if he knew better. "Indeed it is. Here, there is something you must have."

From the pocket of his robe, he withdrew a thick silver chain from which hung an exquisitely made charm of a rose. Age had left the silver black with tarnish.

"This was my father's . . ."

Vasen held up his hands. "Oracle, I cannot—"

"Abelar Corrinthal, Dawnlord of the Abbey, my father, would be pleased for you to have it. This I know."

Vasen felt himself flush. He could not refuse the Oracle. He bowed his head to allow the charm around his neck. The touch of the symbol, once worn by Dawnlord Abelar, made the hair on the back of his neck stand on end.

"It is tarnished," the Oracle said. "But scratch away the tarnish and there is silver and light beneath. Many things are that way."

Vasen took the Oracle's point. "I understand."

"The darkness in you is not born of Erevis Cale."

Vasen stiffened. "Who, then?"

"You separate yourself from everyone, from everything except your duty because you think yourself bound by the past to a future you cannot change. And you intend to face that future alone."

Vasen's anger kindled in the heat of the truth. Shadows swirled from his skin.

"Is that not true? Isn't that what you see for me?"

The Oracle shook his head. "No, I see hard choices before you, but I don't see what you will choose. They're to be *your* choices. Remember that. Nothing is foreordained. Nothing is written."

Write me a story.

"And listen to me carefully," the Oracle said, continuing. "You do not need to face them alone. You should *not* face them alone."

Vasen's anger dissolved in the face of the Oracle's concerned tone. He bowed his head again. "I apologize for my outburst. Thank you for your words, Oracle."

The Oracle smiled softly. "It's nothing. And you may regret your gratitude someday."

"Never."

"Listen to me, Vasen. The light is in you, and burns brighter than the rest of us because it fights the darkness of your blood. Will you remember that?"

"I will."

Smiling, the Oracle said, "Very good. Then be well, Vasen son of Derreg and Erevis and Varra."

"Wait! Is that . . . all?"

But it was too late. The Oracle's face slackened and the glow left his skin. The orange light of Amaunator fled his eyes and they returned to the filmy, bleary eyes of an old man. He sagged, his aged body unable to so suddenly bear his weight. Vasen caught him to prevent a fall. He felt like a bundle of sticks under his robes.

"It's Vasen, Oracle."

"Vazn," said the Oracle in his slow, awkward way. "Where Bownie?"

"You sent Browny away," Vasen said. "I'm sure he's nearby, though."

"Bownie!" the Oracle called, alarm in his expression. "Bownie!"

Vasen found it difficult to reconcile the sure, powerful voice of the Oracle when he was in a trance with the childlike voice of the mentally infirm Oracle when he was not.

A soft pop and flash of light announced Browny's return to the Oracle's side. The dog nuzzled the Oracle's hand.

"Bownie came!" the Oracle said, grinning.

"I'll escort you back to your sanctum, Oracle," Vasen said.

The Oracle shook his head. "No, Vazn. When the bell calls, have pilgrims sent to me for a seeing. I speak to them, then all leave this day. All. You take them."

The latest group of pilgrims—the first in months—had arrived less than a tenday earlier, dodging Sembian troops along the way. They would be disappointed to leave so soon.

"They only just arrived, Oracle. And the Dales are wracked by war. We'll have to take them north through the foothills toward Highmoon. Even that way may be closing. Sembian troops are massed all along the borders of the Dales."

"I know. But they go, Vazn."

Vasen knew better than to dispute with the Oracle. "Very well."

The Oracle smiled at him. "Farewell, Vazn."

"The light keep and warm you, Oracle."

He watched the Oracle, one hand on Browny, totter off down the corridor.

Vasen closed the door, mind racing. First the dream, then a personal visit and seeing from the Oracle. What did it all mean?

He took the rose holy symbol from his neck. Thin threads of shadow spiraled from his fingertips, around the rose. He imagined Dawnlord Abelar using the symbol to channel the power of Amaunator while facing the nightwalker at the Battle of Sakkors.

He studied its petals, the stem, the two thorns. It was so finely crafted it could have been an actual rose magically transformed into metal, not unlike the rose gardens around the abbey that the Spellplague had petrified. With his thumbnail, he scratched at the tarnish of one petal to reveal a line of shining silver, light under the darkness.

Smiling, he returned it to his neck. He would try to be worthy of it.

His eyes fell on the dusty, locked chest he kept in one corner of his chamber and he lost his smile. The chest held the dark, magical blade once borne by Erevis Cale: Weaveshear. Vasen had held its cool, slippery hilt only once, when, as a boy, Derreg had first given it to him. Shadows from the blade had mingled with the shadows of his flesh. The weapon had felt an extension of him, but the familiarity had frightened him and he had never touched it again. And he would not touch it today. Today was a day for light and hope, not shadow and somber remembrances.

Mindful of the Oracle's words, he donned his padded shirt and mail, his breastplate, slung his shield over his back, strapped his weapon belt with its ordinary sword around his hips, and headed out.

As was his habit, he would commune with Amaunator at highsun, walk the vale, and see his mother's grave before he took the pilgrims back out into the dark.

Rain fell in straight lines from the dark Sembian sky, beating the whipgrass into a flat, twisted mat. The sky cleared its throat with thunder. The stink of decay suffused the air, as if the entire world were slowly decomposing.

"Quickly!" Zeeahd said, his voice as coarse as a blade drawn over a whetstone. "Quickly! It will come soon, Sayeed."

Sayeed swallowed, nodded, and kept pace with his brother's hurried, shambling steps. He would have offered Zeeahd a reassuring touch, an arm to steady him, but Sayeed disliked the way his brother's flesh squirmed under his hand.

They walked—walked because horses would bear neither of them—under a bleak sky and over sodden, spongy earth. They moved cross country because Sembian soldiers and wagon trains had become too common on the roads.

Sayeed's rain-soaked cloak hung from his shoulders like a hundredweight, like the burden of the fourteen decades he'd lived.

Beside him Zeeahd sagged under the weight of his own burdens. He wheezed above the hiss of the rain, and the hump of his back was more pronounced than usual. Zeeahd's wet robes hugged his form, and their grip hinted at the shape of the warped body beneath, the flesh polluted by the wild magic of the Spellplague.

Around them thronged the pack of mongrel cats his brother had summoned when they crossed into Sembia's shadow-shrouded borders.

"Feral cats?" Sayeed had asked.

"Feral, yes," his brother had answered, staring at the creatures with his glassy eyes. "But not cats."

Sayeed counted thirteen of the felines, although the numbers seemed to change slightly from time to time. They held their tails low and the rain pressed their mangy fur to their bodies, showing with each stride the workings of bones and muscles. Their heads looked overlarge on their thin necks, their legs disproportionately long. They seemed composed entirely of black eyes, thick sinew, and sharp teeth.

Dark clouds stretched across the sky, blotting out the sun. It was midday but was as dark as dusk in winter. Sayeed and Zeeahd had been walking through perpetual night for many tendays, avoiding airborne Shadovar patrols and Sembian foot soldiers as they traced a winding path across the ruined Sembian countryside. Rumors spoke of pitched battles in the Dalelands, as Sembia moved against its northern neighbors.

Sayeed and Zeeahd wanted nothing of war. They had come in search of the Abbey of the Rose and its oracle.

"What if this abbey and its oracle are just myth? Then what do we do? Both could be stories the Sembians tell themselves to preserve hope."

"No," Zeeahd said, shaking his head emphatically. "They exist."

"How do you know?"

Zeeahd stopped and turned on him. "Because they must! Because *he* told me! Because this," he gestured helplessly at his body. "This must end! It must!"

Sayeed knew who Zeeahd meant by "he"—Mephistopheles, the archdevil who ruled Cania, the eighth layer of Hell. Merely thinking the archfiend's name caused Sayeed to hear sinister whispers in the falling rain. He took a moment to drink from his waterskin: a habit, nothing more, the ghost of a human need. Sayeed did not need to drink, or eat, or sleep, not anymore, not since he had been changed. If the Spellplague had fouled his brother's body, it had perfected

Sayeed's, although the price of perfection had been to make him as much automaton as man.

"Why are you slowing to drink?" Zeeahd called. "I said we must hurry!"

Zeeahd's agitation conjured coughs from his ruined lungs, thick and wet with phlegm. The cats mewled and crowded close to him, their feral, knowing eyes watching with terrible intensity. Between hacks, Zeeahd tried to shoo the animals away with his boot, and Sayeed tried to ignore the unnatural way his brother's leg flopped at the hip as he kicked at the cats. The coughing fit ended without a purge and the disappointed cats wandered back into their orbits, tails sagging with disappointment.

"The cats disgust me," Sayeed said.

"Not cats, and they're a gift," Zeeahd mumbled, as he wiped his mouth with a hand partially covered in scales. His dark eyes stared out at Sayeed from the deep, shadowed pits of their sockets. His hatchet-shaped faced was dotted with pockmarks, the result of a childhood illness.

Sayeed looked past his brother, across the plains, and his mind moved to old memories. "I can't picture our mother's face. Can you? She had long brown hair, I think."

Zeeahd drank of his own waterskin, swished and spit. The cats pounced on it, saw it was naught but water, and left off.

"It was black," Zeeahd said.

"I used to dream of her, back when I slept."

"You'll sleep again, Sayeed. And dream. When we find the Oracle, we'll make him tell us—"

His voice cracked and broke into a cough. Sayeed moved to help but Zeeahd waved him off with a hand, and one cough followed another into a wracking, wet fit.

Once more the cats crowded close, mewling, circling, jostling for position as Zeeahd fought the poison the Spellplague had put in him. He hunched over in the rain, coughing, warring with the foulness of his innards.

Sayeed could only watch, disgusted. He looked away and tried to remember his mother, the exercise helping distract him from the shifting swells and lumps that bulged under his brother's robes, the mucous-filled gasps, the wet heaves.

Sayeed could not recall his mother's eyes, or even her name. His memory was fading. It was as if he were someone new every day, someone he hated more and more. He remembered with clarity only one day from the distant past, one moment that connected who he was now to who he had been before the Spellplague—the moment Abelar Corrinthal's men had chopped off his right thumb with a hatchet.

He remembered screaming, remembered the knight who'd cut off the digit apologizing for the mutilation.

Zeeahd's coughing intensified, turned into a prolonged heave, and the sound pulled Sayeed back into the present. The cats meowed with excitement, circling, tails raised, eyes gleaming as Zeeahd gagged. And finally the felines received what they wished.

Zeeahd's abdomen visibly roiled under his robes and he vomited forth a long, thick rope of stinking black sputum. The grass it struck smoked, curled, and browned. The cats pounced on the mucous, hissing and clawing at one another, a fierce caterwaul, each lapping at the phlegm.

Zeeahd cursed and wiped his mouth.

"Thrice-damned cats," Sayeed said, stomping a boot on the ground near the felines, splashing them with mud. The cats arched, hissed, and bared their fangs but did not back away from their meal. Sayeed had never seen them eat anything other than the black result of his brother's expulsions.

"They're not cats . . . but damned, indeed," Zeeahd said. He cleared his throat again and the creatures, having devoured the first string of mucous, turned to him, hoping for another meal. When none was forthcoming, they sat on their haunches and licked their paws and chops.

Zeeahd lowered his hood, threw his head back to put his face to the rain. He ran a hand over his thin, black hair. With skin pulled taut to reveal sunken eyes and cavernous cheeks, he looked skeletal, the living dead.

"The purgings only slow the advance of the curse," Zeeahd said. "I need someone soon, Sayeed. A vessel. Otherwise the curse will run its course."

Sayeed nodded. Their use of vessels had left a trail of aberrations in their wake.

"Come," Zeeahd said, and threw up his hood. "We must get to the next village. The urge is strong." He inhaled as well as his ruined lungs would allow and stared down at the cats. They looked up at him, far too much intelligence in their eyes.

"I can't let it happen to me," Zeeahd said softly.

"Let what happen?"

His brother seemed not to hear him and Sayeed was, as always, left to wonder.

The Spellplague had transformed both of them, but differently. Sayeed had been made unable to sleep and increasingly dull to life's pleasures and pains, his emotions and appreciation of physical sensations had been ground down to nubs.

Zeeahd, on the other hand, had been killed. But the blue fire had not left him dead. Instead, it had somehow filled him with pollution and returned him to life. Sayeed well remembered how Zeeahd looked upon his return; the panicked eyes, the animal scream of terror and pain. He had shivered with cold but, inexplicably, smelled of brimstone, of rot. Zeeahd had pawed frantically at his own body, his breath coming in strained gasps.

"What is it?" Sayeed had asked.

"I'm . . . unchanged?" Zeeahd had said, his tone amazed and relieved. "I was torn, Sayeed, burned, flayed. For centuries. I saw the master of that place and he spoke to me, made me promise to seek . . ."

Sayeed had thought him mad. "Master? Centuries? You were gone only moments."

Zeeahd had not heard him. "I'm unchanged! Unchanged!"

But he was not unchanged. His laughter had turned to wheezing, then coughing, then his first purging, and both of them had stared in horror at the squirming black mass expelled from his guts.

"Oh, gods," Zeeahd had said. He'd wept as if he understood some truth that Sayeed did not. "It's in me still, Sayeed. That place. It's a curse, and it wants to come out."

Only later had Sayeed learned that Zeeahd's soul had gone to Cania, where his brother had forged a pact with Mephistopheles to seek out someone the archdevil could not find alone. And only later had Sayeed learned what the purging actually meant, what it would require, again and again until Mephistopheles set them free of their afflictions.

"Come on," he said, hating himself for saying it. "We'll find you someone."

They walked on, two men who weren't men and thirteen cats who weren't cats, bent under the weight of the rain. In time they came upon a packed-earth wagon road.

"Must be a village near," Sayeed said, scanning the shapeless black expanse of the plains. Wisps of shadow clung to the trees and scrubs, a black mist.

Zeeahd nodded, his head bobbing strangely on his neck. His voice, too, sounded odd when he spoke.

"Let's hope so."

Gerak awoke before sunrise, or so he judged. Dawn's light rarely penetrated Sembia's shadow-shrouded air, so he relied for timekeeping on the instincts he'd sharpened as a soldier.

He stared up at the ceiling beams of the cottage, listening to the soft roll of distant thunder through the shuttered windows, the patter of rain on the wood-shingled roof. He hoped it was ordinary precipitation. Ten days earlier a stinking black rain had fallen, and whatever it had borne in its drops had fouled the soil. Soon after, the barley crop had begun to wither and the autumn vegetables—especially the pumpkins—had browned on the vine. They'd done what they could to minimize the loss, but the whole village keenly felt the absence of a greenpriest of Chauntea. The villagers' own prayers to the Earth Mother, whispered in small, secret gatherings, as if in fear the Shadovar in their distant cities and floating citadel would somehow overhear, went unanswered. Winter would bring hardship for them all. Another black rain would ruin the harvest altogether.

He and Elle would have to put up as much food as they could before first snow.

And that meant he would have to risk a hunt.

The thought of it sped his heart, although he wasn't sure if that was out of fear of what he might encounter on the plains or out of fear of Elle's reaction.

She lay beside him, her form covered in the tattered quilts, her breathing the deep, regular intake of sleep.

Moving slowly, so as not to awaken her, he swung his legs off of the straw-stuffed mattress and sat on the side of the bed. He tried to squelch a cough but only half managed. Elle did not stir.

He sat there for a time, his bare feet flat on the cold wood floor, and waited for wakefulness. The damp air summoned the aches that lurked in his joints and muscles, and he massaged first one shoulder, then another. Age was turning him brittle.

He tried to swallow away the foul taste of morning but could not summon the spit. He grabbed the tin cup on the bedside table, swished the leftover tea, and drank it down. Cold and bitter, like the morning.

He rubbed the back of his neck and considered the one-room cottage, lit faintly in the glow of the hearth's embers: furniture he'd made from the straight, dark limbs of broadleaf trees, bowls and cups and pans that had served three generations. He tried to imagine their baby crawling on the floor, but could not quite do it. He tried to imagine how they would provide for the baby and could not quite do that, either.

Elle's pregnancy had been a surprise to them both.

Gerak had resigned himself to childlessness long before. Ten seasons of marriage had produced not a single pregnancy, so they had assumed one or both of them was sterile. At the time, Gerak had thought it just as well. The world seemed too dark for children.

And then Elle had told him, her voice quaking.

"I think I'm with child, Gerak."

The joy he'd felt had surprised him, as if the child were a key to a locked room inside him that held happiness, that held possibility. In a moment, the stakes of his life had been raised—a child would rely on him.

The realization terrified him.

He wondered if they should leave Fairelm. Many of their friends and neighbors had already abandoned the village—the Milsons and Rabbs the most recent. They had braved the darkness, the Shadovar, and the Shadovar's creatures, and made for the sun. He didn't know if they'd gone west for Daerlun or north for the Dales. He wasn't sure it mattered. War or the threat of war seemed everywhere in Sembia. The big cities were the sites of musters, the borders were the sites of battles, and the villages and towns in between were left to fend for themselves. He didn't know what to do.

Elle was still able to travel, and they owned a wagon, a pack horse. They could sell their remaining chickens, gather up their goods, and head northeast. Gerak knew how to handle a blade and was matchless with his bow. Maybe they could avoid the soldiers, and Gerak could protect them from the creatures that prowled the plains.

He tried to coax another drop of tea from the cup. Nothing. He tried to coax from himself the will to leave. Nothing.

Leaving seemed too dangerous, and felt too much like surrender, like a betrayal, and neither was in him. He had been raised in the cottage, as had his father and grandfather before him. And despite the perpetual shadow that covered Sembia, despite the dire creatures that prowled the countryside, despite the sometimes harsh rule of the Shadovar, his father and grand-father had managed to eke out a living from the land. They had taken pride in it.

And so did he.

He hadn't always. He'd thought a farmer's life contemptible in his youth, and had run off to serve in one of the Shadovar's many wars. He'd killed more than a dozen men with his bow, but only one, the last, with his blade. Killing felt different up close. Gerak had seen his reflection in the dying man's eyes and that had been all he wanted of war ever again.

He ran a hand through his hair—it was getting long—and scratched at the three-day beard that covered his cheeks. He exhaled, ready at last to start another sunless day. As he started to rise, Elle's voice broke the quiet and stopped him.

"I'm awake," she said.

He sat back down. He knew her tone well enough to under-stand that her thoughts had probably veered close to his own. She, too, was worried about the future. He put his hand on the rise of her hip.

"You've been awake this whole time?"

She rolled over and looked up at him. Her skin looked less pale in the light of the embers. Her long, dark hair formed a cloud on the bolster. Under the quilt, she had one hand on her belly, which was just beginning to swell with their child.

"The rain awakened me hours ago. I started worrying for the crop and then my mind whirled and I couldn't fall back asleep."

"Try not to worry. We'll manage. Are you cold?"

Without waiting for an answer, he rose, walked across the cool floor, and threw two logs onto the embers. The logs caught flame almost immediately and he returned to the bed and sat. She had not moved.

"Are *you* worried?" she asked.

He knew better than to offer her a falsehood. "Of course I am. I worry about how we'll feed ourselves and the baby, mostly. But then I remind myself that my parents endured difficult years, too, especially after I left to fight, and yet here this cottage stands. The crops will recover and we'll endure."

"Yes, but . . . do you worry about . . . the world?"

He took her meaning and offered her a falsehood after all. "The world is too big for my worry. I'm trying to focus on our bellies."

"And if the Shadovar come for a quota of the crop to supply the troops? They say there's war in the Dales."

The fire caused shadows to dance on the walls, and Gerak flashed on memories of his military service, when he'd served the Shadovar in battle against Cormyreans.

"They say lots of things, and the Shadovar haven't come for a quota in years. The farms near the cities must produce enough. Or perhaps they eat magic in the cities these days."

She did not smile at his poor joke but at least it smoothed the worried furrows from her brow. She inhaled deeply, as if to purge the concerns that plagued her, and when she exhaled a playful look came into her eye, the same look he'd first seen on her ten years ago, the look that had caused him to want her as a wife.

"You snore loudly."

"I know. You should nudge me."

"No," she said, and snuggled more deeply into the quilts. "I like the sound sometimes."

"You like strange things, Sweets."

"Taking you for a husband seals that ward, I'd say."

"I'd say," he agreed with a smile. He bent and kissed her on the crooked nose she'd broken years before when she'd stepped on a rake. He placed his hand over hers, on her belly, so that both of them had their unborn child in their palms.

"We'll be all right," he said and wanted her to believe it.

"I know," she said, and he knew she wanted to believe it.

He stood and stretched, groaned when his muscles protested.

"Why're you up so early?" she asked.

He hesitated for a moment, braced himself, then dived in.

"I'm going on a hunt, Elle."

"What?" Instantly she sounded fully awake. The grooves had returned to her brow, deeper than before.

"We need to put up some meat," he said.

She shook her head. "No, it's not safe. We saw Sakkors in the night sky only last month. The Shadovar keep their creatures away from the villages but let them wander the plains. Only soldiers and those with official charters walk the roads safely."

"Neither the Shadovar nor their flying city will take an interest in a lone hunter. They just want no one in or out of Sembia without their permission, especially during a time of war."

"No one has come to the village in months, Gerak. Why do you think that is? It's not safe."

He could not deny it. Peddlers and priests and caravans had once roamed the Sembian countryside, tending to the villages. But Fairelm had seen nothing in a long while, nothing but old Minser the peddler, who seemed to enjoy spinning tales more than selling wares. But Minser had not returned in more than a month. The village seemed to have been forgotten out in the dark of the plains, all alone and surrounded by monsters.

"There are worse things than Shadovar," she said. "Don't go. We can manage—"

"I have to. I'll be gone not more than two days—"

"Two days!" she said, half sitting up.

"Two days," he said, nodding, his resolve firming up as he spoke. "And when I return, we'll have a stag or three to dress and smoke. And that'll keep us in meat through the winter and then some. You and the baby need more than roots and tubers and we need the chickens for eggs."

"I need my husband and the baby its father."

He bent and put his hand on her brow. She covered it tightly and lay back, as if she had no intention of letting go.

"Nothing will happen to me."

"How can you know?"

"I'm a soldier, Elle."

"You were a soldier. Now you're a farmer."

"Nothing will happen to me."

She squeezed his hand. "Swear it."

"I swear."

"If you see something bigger than a deer, you run away. Promise."

"I promise."

She gave his hand another squeeze and let it go.

He cleared his throat and went to the chest near the hearth, feeling Elle's eyes on him. He opened the lid and removed the weapon belt and the broadsword, still oiled and sharp, that he'd earned as partial payment for his military service. He had not worn more than an eating knife and dagger in what felt like a lifetime, and when he strapped on the heavier blade, the weight felt awkward on his waist.

"I used to feel awkward *without* this on," he said, and Elle said nothing.

His bow sat in its deerskin case near the chest, his two quivers, both stuffed with arrows, beside it. He undid the tie on the case and removed the yew shaft. He strung it with practiced ease and placed his hand in the grip. It felt as smooth and familiar as Elle's skin. He imagined himself sighting along an arrow, a stag in his sight.

His talent with the longbow had been a matter of comment among his fellow soldiers, and he had not let his skills atrophy over the years, even after taking up the plow for the sword.

"Wait for the rain to end, at least," she said.

He strapped the quivers on, did a quick count on his various arrows. "The sooner I leave, the sooner I'll return."

"You'll get sick from the wet."

"I won't."

"Then at least eat something before you go."

"I can eat when I—"

"Eat, Gerak. The rain and cold is bad enough. I won't have you out there with an empty stomach."

He smiled, nodded, went to the small table he'd made, and broke off a large chunk of two day old bread from a loaf. With it, he swabbed yesterday's stew slop from the bottom of the cauldron hanging near the fire. Elle watched as he ate. There was no meat in the turnip and kale stew and the absence only strengthened his resolve to hunt. He would fill his waterskin in the pond and could forage for additional food in the field, should he need it.

"You eat, too, Elle."

"I will. The baby's always hungry. Takes after its father, I suppose."

He went to the bed once more and gave her a lingering kiss.

"There's ample stew and bread. A few eggs in the coop. I'll be back before you know it."

She stayed strong, as he knew she would. "You're leaving me here with none but the fools and cowards."

"You manage fools and cowards quite well, Sweets."

"Again, I think our marriage seals that ward." She smiled as she spoke and he thanked the gods for it.

"I think I like you better asleep."

She turned serious. "Be careful, Gerak."

"I will," he said, and pulled on his boots and cloak. "Go see Ana while I am gone."

"A good idea," she said. "I'll take her a couple eggs. They're suffering."

"I know. See you soon."

He opened the door and the wind rushed in.

"Wait," she called. "Take my locket. For good fortune." She leaned over and took the locket, a bronze sun on a leather lanyard, from the side table.

"Elle, that's—"

"Take it," she insisted. "Minser sold it to my mother. Told her it'd been blessed by one of Tymora's priests."

He came back to the bed, took the locket, secreted it in a pocket of his cloak, and gave her another kiss.

"I'll take all the luck I can get."

She smiled. "You need your haircut."

"You'll cut it when I return," he said. "Everything will be fine."

With that, he headed out into the storm. He opened his mouth to the sky and tasted the rain, found it normal, and thanked Chauntea. The crops would live another day. He stood for a moment, alone in the dark, alone with his thoughts, and eyed the village, nestled amid the elms.

The other cottages sat quiet and dark, each a little nest of worry and want. The dozen or so elms rose like colossuses from the plains, whispering in the wind. The rain beat a drumbeat on his cloak. Gerak had always liked to think that the elms protected the village, wood guardians that would never let harm befall those who sheltered under their boughs. He decided to keep thinking it.

Holding his bow, he pulled up his hood and cut across the commons to the pond, where he filled his waterskin. Then he headed up the rise and toward the open plains.

CHAPTER THREE

THE LIMBS OF THE MALFORMED TREES RATTLED IN THE WIND and rain. Sayeed recalled the Sembia of a century before, before the Spellplague, even before the Shadowstorm; fields of barley, forests filled with game, rivers that ran fast and clear, merchants everywhere. But all of that was dead.

Like him, Sembia was alive while dead.

The last time Sayeed had walked the Sembian plains, the nation had been in the midst of a civil war, and he and Zeeahd had worn the uniforms of the overmistress's armies. They and many others had been captured and maimed at the order of a Lathandarian, Abelar Corrinthal. Sayeed had taught himself to fight left-handed over the intervening years. And now Sembia was in the midst of a war again. Damp air and bad memories caused the nub of Sayeed's thumb to ache distantly.

"Why do you slow?" Zeeahd barked over his shoulder.

Sayeed had not realized he had slowed. He hurried forward, the cats eyeing him as he moved through them to his brother's side. Zeeahd's hood obscured his face.

"I was . . . thinking."

"About?"

"The plains dredge up old memories."

Zeeahd grunted.

"I was thinking about the Spellplague. About why we were . . . changed as we were. I wonder if there's purpose in it."

Zeeahd spat, the cats pouncing on the spittle. "There's no purpose in it. We were on that ship when the blue fire struck, just the wrong place at an ill time. And we were there because of this."

Zeeahd held up his own right hand, the stump of his thumb a mirror of Sayeed's, although marred with scales and a malformed joint.

"And we owe *that* to Abelar Corrinthal. Look for no more meaning than that. Men do awful things to other men. That's the world."

"That's the world," Sayeed echoed.

"We'll be free of all this soon," Zeeahd said. "The Lord of the Eighth promised. We need only find him the son."

The son. They'd been seeking their prey for decades, scouring Faerûn. By now, the son of Erevis Cale would be an old man. Or dead.

"You think this Oracle will tell us how to find him?" Sayeed asked.

"We'll *make* him tell us," Zeeahd said. "And if the son is already dead of age, we'll find out where his corpse is and give that to Meph—to the Lord of Cania. And he will free us. Come on. We must find a village."

Zeeahd picked up his pace, his gait lumbering, awkward, bestial. Sayeed fell in after him.

Over the next several hours the rain picked up until it fell in brown, stinking sheets. The whipgrass under their feet squirmed at the foul water's touch.

"Do you require shelter?" Sayeed asked Zeeahd. "Sleep?"

"No," his brother said, in a voice deeper than usual. The hood of Zeeahd's cloak hid his face. "You know what I require, and I require it soon."

They hustled through the rain, the wet ground sucking at their boots, the anticipatory cries of the hungry cats driving Sayeed to distraction. His brother wheezed, coughed frequently, and spat a black globule every few steps—to the delight of the cats, who feasted on it.

After a time, moans began to slip through Zeeahd's lips and his form roiled under the robes. Sayeed could not help but stare. He'd never seen his brother so bad.

"Stop looking at me!" Zeeahd said to Sayeed, half turning his cowled head, his speech slurred and wet from malformed lips.

Sayeed licked his lips and looked away, queasy. The plains looked the same in all directions. The road they traveled appeared to lead nowhere. He feared that they would not be able to stop whatever was soon to happen to his brother.

A small, secret part of him wished that whatever was to happen would happen. His brother disgusted him. Their lives disgusted him. He tried to exorcise the traitorous thoughts with a half-hearted offer of aid.

"How can I help, Zeeahd?"

Zeeahd whirled on him. "You can find me a vessel! Or become one yourself!"

Sayeed's eyes narrowed. His hand went to the hilt of his blade.

As one, the cats turned to face him, all eyes and teeth and claws.

He tightened his grip on the hilt, prepared to draw.

But a sound carried out of the rain, the distant scream of a woman from somewhere ahead. The cats arched their backs, cocked their heads.

"You heard it?" Zeeahd asked, still eyeing Sayeed out of the depths of his cowl. "It's not a phantasm of my mind?"

"I heard it," Sayeed said slowly, and relaxed his grip on his blade. More screams carried through the rain, terrified wails, dogs barking feverishly. "Someone requires aid."

"Come on," Zeeahd said, turning and staggering over the wet earth toward the screams. Despair raised his voice. "Hurry. I can't continue like this."

They ran over the slick earth, Sayeed leading, the cats trailing. Twice Zeeahd slipped and fell. Twice Sayeed turned back, lifted his brother to his feet, and felt the flesh and bone of his brother's body swell and roil under his touch, as if something were nested in his flesh, squirming underneath it in an attempt to burst forth. Bile touched the back of his throat and shock pulled a question from him before he could block it with his teeth.

"What in the Hells is in you, Zeeahd?"

Zeeahd kept his cowled head turned away from his brother. His voice was guttural. "I told you before! I don't know. He put something in me. To make sure I did his work. It'll . . . change me." He shoved Sayeed ahead. "Please, hurry."

Closer now, Sayeed distinguished the screams of several women and men, the frantic barking and growls of not one but two dogs. He topped a rise and crouched low amid a stand of broadleaf trees. Zeeahd crawled into position beside him, wheezing and moaning. The cats formed up around them, silent and staring.

Below them, the ribbon of the packed-earth wagon road stretched east to west. Two wagons lay overturned on it. A flotsam of household goods lay scattered in the grass: rain-sodden blankets, a small table, broken stoneware. Two bodies lay among the debris, both torn open at the abdomen, the ropes of their entrails smeared on the grass, glistening in the rain. A third corpse lay a few paces from the first two, arms and legs at grotesque angles, the skin drawn tightly against the bones, mummified, as if sucked dry.

A misshapen bipedal creature twice as tall as a man stood in the road. It appeared almost skeletal, but sickly black flesh and bands of muscle wrapped the bones here and there. Overlong arms ended in finger-length black talons, and large, pointed ears walled a hairless, misshapen head. Green light burned in the depths of its sunken eye sockets. The fanged mouth was opened wide and a pink tongue as thick as Sayeed's wrist and as long as his forearm dangled grotesquely from the opening. Currents of dark energy swirled around it, gathered on its claws.

It shrieked in hunger and hate, a high-pitched, ear-splitting sound that would have stood Sayeed's hair on end a hundred years earlier.

Zeeahd coughed, spat a globule of dark phlegm. The cats pounced and consumed the black mass in a moment. "It's a devourer. An undead that draws power from the Shadowfell."

Two men—simple villagers, to judge from the homespun they wore and the wooden axes they wielded as weapons— circled the devourer at a distance of two paces, the weapons trembling in their grasps. A mastiff, barking frenetically, harried the devourer opposite the two men.

A boy's body lay on the ground near the devourer's feet, his head nearly ripped from his neck. A girl lay not far from the boy, her dress torn and covered in mud, face down, unmoving. The bodies of three other children lay around the road, their clothes and bodies torn, pieces of them scattered about like the wagon's debris.

Two women hovered on the outskirts of the combat, shouting, cursing, crying, hurling rocks and stones and whatever they could find at the devourer, all to no effect. A second mastiff stood near the women, barking and growling.

"Run!" the tall, bearded man shouted to the women. "Run!"

"I won't leave you," the thick-set woman answered, crying. "Leave us be, creature!"

The bearded man lunged forward, axe held high. Before he could bring his weapon to bear, dark energy flared around the devourer, a cloud of darkness veined with green streaks that knocked the man from his feet. The second man, much younger, perhaps the first man's son, shouted in anger, bounded forward, and sank his axe into the devourer's leg. The weapon barely bit and the devourer showed no sign of pain. The creature lashed out with its overlong arm and claw and caught the young man across the face. The impact spun the youth completely around. Blood sprayed and he fell to the mud without a sound.

As he fell, the younger of the two women screamed in despair, her hands clasped before her as if in prayer. The dogs' barking grew manic. The heavier woman tried to pull the younger girl away, but she seemed frozen to the spot.

The devourer lumbered forward, grasped the older, bearded man and lifted him triumphantly into the air. The man's arms were pinned against his body, his axe hanging futilely from his fist.

"Run!" the man screamed at the women, his face twisted with pain and fear. "Please run!"

The devourer pulled the man close and ran its tongue over his face, leaving a road of blood and blisters and a ruined eye in its wake. The man wailed, legs kicking against the devourer's chest, all to no effect. The devourer opened its fanged mouth as if in glee, tongue dangling. The dark energy that animated the creature spun and whirled in a black cloud around the man and the undead.

Green lines flared within the cloud, baleful veins connecting the man to the devourer. The man's screams rose to a high pitch, and then turned to a distorted wail as his body began to shrink in on itself, the hole of his mouth appearing to get larger as the skin drew tight against his bones. The green lines pulsed, netted the dying man. A green glow formed within the devourer's abdomen, a vile egg.

The energy flared, causing Sayeed to see spots, and the man's wails stopped. When his vision cleared, Sayeed saw the devourer drop the shriveled, lifeless form of the man to the mud and turn to face the women.

Within the devourer's abdomen, caged by the bars of its ribs, squirmed a tiny, naked effigy of the man, the devourer pregnant with horror. The effigy's eyes and mouth were wide with pain and terror.

Sayeed knew what had occurred: The devourer had caged the man's soul and would use it to power its own unholy force.

Seeing that, the women finally broke entirely. They shrieked and turned to run. The older slipped and fell in the mud, and the younger turned to help her. The devourer keened. Green energy flared from the effigy in its abdomen, traveled to its claws, and shot out toward the women and their dog. It struck all of them at once, and the barking and screaming ended, cut off as if by a blade. All three fell to the sodden earth, limp.

The tiny body within the devourer watched it all and opened its mouth in a wail of despair. The devourer ran its tongue over its lips and fangs, shuddered as if in ecstasy.

The surviving dog whined, turned circles in its agitation.

Sayeed stared at the small form of the trapped soul, wondering if he could die were his soul so trapped. It had been so long since he'd rested. He wondered if he could find peace in the belly of a horror. What would it would be like, to have his soul slowly—

"What are you doing?" Zeeahd said. "I need someone alive!"

Zeeahd stood and pushed past Sayeed while drawing his sword. He spoke words of power, his voice ragged and deep, and extended his blade in the direction of the devourer. A twisting spiral of smoking, deep red flames exploded from the steel and slammed into the devourer's chest.

The creature staggered backward, bent, flesh charred and smoking, steadying itself by placing one clawed hand on the wet ground. Its green eyes scanned the rise, fixed on Zeeahd and Sayeed, and flashed with unholy light. It crouched, flexed its claws, and shrieked.

The cats hissed in answer.

The surviving dog took to barking and growling but did not get within the devourer's reach. The soul of the trapped man writhed, veins of green energy pulsing from it to feed the devourer.

Black energy swirled from the devourer's form. Green light flared in its abdomen, and the tiny effigy of the man imprisoned there squirmed, shrinking ever smaller as the devourer consumed him for power. As the effigy shrank, the burns Zeeahd had inflicted on the flesh of the devourer healed, the flesh knitting closed.

A coughing fit seized Zeeahd and he bent double, slipped in the wet, and fell to the grass on all fours. His form twisted under his clothing, getting taller, thinner. Sayeed started to help him up—feeling his brother's bones twisting—but Zeeahd pushed him away.

"Go!" he said, and coughed. "That's all I can do for now."

Sayeed stood, drew his blade, and readied his shield.

Zeeahd's hand reached up and closed on his wrist. His brother's hand was feverishly hot, although he still kept his visage hidden within the cowl.

"That creature cannot give you peace, Sayeed. Your soul and mind would live on in its form, regenerating constantly, forever sating its appetite. You would suffer eternally." Another cough, then, "The Lord of the Eighth has promised me a cure. Promised *us* a cure. Only through him will we find an end to this. He has already gifted me with hellfire. You saw, Sayeed. You saw."

The devourer shrieked again and padded across the grass toward them, stepping heedlessly on the corpses of those it had slain, driving the bodies deeper into the mud.

"I saw," Sayeed said to his brother. He didn't trust Zeeahd—he hated Zeeahd—but what choice did he have?

The devourer broke into a loping run.

Sayeed didn't wait for it. He roared and ran down the rise, his armor clanging, meeting the creature's charge head on. The thrill of battle filled him, the only thing he felt with clarity anymore.

They closed in five strides. The devourer slashed with one of its huge claws, but Sayeed deflected it with his shield and did not slow, instead slamming his body into the devourer's larger form while he drove his blade into the creature's abdomen, through the effigy, and up through the neck. The enchanted blade vibrated gleefully in his hands as it found purchase in flesh, and the movement made the already deep wound jagged, more painful.

The devourer and the effigy both keened with pain. Dark energy swirled around them, a black fog that pulled at whatever withered bits of Sayeed's soul remained. The stink of the creature, like a charnel house, filled Sayeed's nostrils. The devourer shoved him away, nearly causing him to slip on the wet earth, and bounded after him, claws slashing. Sayeed parried with his shield and ducked under another blow, but the creature pressed, heedless of Sayeed's blade.

Sayeed slashed the creature's arms, leg, but the devourer grabbed his face with an enormous clawed hand and squeezed, the nails piercing Sayeed's cheeks, penetrating gums, and scraping teeth. Blood poured into Sayeed's mouth. He felt no pain but nearly vomited at the taste of the creature's foul digits in his mouth.

With preternatural strength, the devourer lifted Sayeed by his head and cast him five paces away. Sayeed hit the ground in a clatter of metal, rolled with the momentum, and bounced to his feet. Already the flesh of his face was knitting closed. He spat out the taste of the devourer's fingers and a mouthful of blood.

The devourer cocked its head and licked its fangs with the rope of its tongue, perhaps puzzled that Sayeed had not remained prone.

Sayeed's weapon shook in his hands, hungry for more violence. Sayeed, eager to feed it and high on the rush of battle, roared and charged anew. He blocked an overhead claw strike with his shield and cleaved the creature at the knee. His blade bit through flesh and sheared bone, severing the leg.

As the devourer fell, it lashed out with its other claw, catching Sayeed on the shoulder, ripping through mail and flesh, and spinning him around with the impact. A blast of dark energy from the devourer engulfed him, cooled his body, and once more pulled at his soul.

His rage proved the hotter and he resisted the dark magic. He spun and drove his blade downward into the prone creature's chest. He left it there, pinioning the creature to the ground, while the devourer tore at his legs and abdomen. Black energy from the devourer churned around him, a seething cloud of unholy power. Sayeed felt the blood running warm from his body, but ignored it. Straddling the creature, he took his shield by the sides, lifted it high, and slammed the sharpened edge of its bottom into the devourer's neck. The slab of enchanted metal severed the devourer's head, ending its shrieking, extinguishing the green light in its eyes. The dark energy around Sayeed subsided as the head fell away from the body, tongue still dangling from its mouth like some grotesque pennon.

Sayeed stood over the corpse while the rain fell, while his body healed its wounds. With battle over, the rush left him, and he once more returned to his usual emptiness.

The devourer's corpse began to leak shadows, the stink of them like rotting meat. Its flesh fell away from bones that began to crumble. The trapped soul in its abdomen, like a malformed fetus, was the last to go, screaming as it dissolved into putrescence.

As Sayeed watched the rain wash the stain of the creature from the plains, he recognized that he was no more human than it had been. He should have felt fatigue, soreness, pain, but he did not. He occupied flesh, he moved, but he felt nothing, not unless he was killing something.

Standing there, he realized there was nothing left in him but hate, for himself, for his brother, for the world. The Spellplague had done more than transform his body. It had transformed his soul, robbed him of hope. He'd once tried to kill himself, slitting his own throat with a dagger. For a brief, glorious moment, his vision had blurred and sleep and death had seemed within reach. But his flesh had healed far more quickly than he could bleed out.

He wanted to die but the world would not let him.

Hearing his brother shambling near, he recovered himself, his blade, his shield. He used the grass to wipe the ichor from both. His brother was grunting like a beast. Sayeed tried to block out the sound, tried to quell the impulse to drive his blade into Zeeahd's guts, expose whatever foulness polluted his brother's flesh.

The surviving dog hovered at a distance, whimpering, unwilling to approach. Sayeed sheathed his blade and turned to the dog.

"Here, boy! Come!"

The mastiff bared its fangs, turned a circle, whined, and did not come any closer.

Animals always saw them for what they were, he and his brother.

Zeeahd lumbered among the carnage, gasping, awkward with the bulges and swells forming under his robes. The cats followed, their eyes glowing red in the dim light.

"Are none alive? Sayeed, are none alive?"

Zeeahd sounded as if he might weep.

Sayeed felt nothing for him.

"Sayeed!"

Sayeed sighed, sheathed his weapon, and slung his shield. He went to the women, the younger and the older, and kneeled beside them, found them both dead. The men and all the children were dead, too, all except one.

"The girl is alive," he said, and gently rolled her over onto her back. She looked pale, her dark hair pulled back and tied with a leather tie. Her breast rose and fell with her shallow breaths. She might have been fifteen winters old.

The dog whined. The cats hissed at it, eyed it hungrily.

"Excellent! Excellent!" Zeeahd said, and waddled over. His voice was wet, as if he had a mouthful of liquid. "Leave her to me. Leave her, Sayeed."

Sayeed stood, backed away a few steps. He made another attempt to win over the dog—he didn't know why—but the mastiff would have none of it.

Zeeahd kneeled at the girl's side, cradled her in his arms, and spoke words of healing. They came awkwardly to his brother's lips, accustomed as they were to uttering arcane words that harmed.

The girl moaned and her eyes fluttered opened. Sayeed saw the panic form in them.

"Let me go! Let me go!"

"Be at ease, girl," Zeeahd said, his words sloppy, wet with drool. "You're safe now."

Sayeed realized that his mouth was dry and that he still had the taste of the devourer in his mouth. Odd that he could barely taste even the finest food, but the foulness of a devourer lingered. He drank from his waterskin, swished, spit.

Thunder boomed.

The cats ringed Zeeahd and the girl, although they stared out at the growling dog with unmistakable hunger in their eyes.

"What happened?" the girl asked. "Who're you? Where're mama and papa?"

Zeeahd used his roiling girth to shield the girl from the sight of the corpses. "You were attacked. You were with your family?"

She craned her neck and looked around Zeeahd at the carnage.

Sayeed saw her expression fall, saw the light fade from her eyes. She had just died, although her body still lived. In that moment, she had become him.

"Not my mum and dad. Oh, no. Oh, no." Tears leaked from her eyes, snot from her nose.

Zeeahd daubed at both, as gentle as a wet nurse, and wrapped the distraught girl in his overlong arms, enveloping her in his cloak. His body pulsed and seethed under the sodden cloth.

"There, there, my girl," he said, his voice the gentle roll of thunder before the lightning. "It's all over now."

Sobs shook the girl's small frame. The cats milled in a circle around them, their meows like a question. Zeeahd tried to shoo them while tending the girl. His hand poked from his cloak and Sayeed saw its malformation, the claws, the leathery skin, the fingers almost twice the length they should have been.

"That creature!" the girl said through her sobs. "It was awful. Oh, father!"

"There now," Zeeahd said. "The creature is no more and that's all that matters. What's your name?"

"Lahni," the girl said, her voice muffled by Zeeahd's cloak. "Lahni Rabb."

"That's a beautiful name," Zeeahd said, and stroked her hair.

Sayeed took another drink from his waterskin. He wished it was wine; he wished he could drink himself into unawareness. But even drunkenness was denied him. He toyed with the idea of decapitating Zeeahd, an idle thought that made him smile.

The mastiff whined, barked uncertainly, sniffed the air, hackles raised.

"The dog won't come," Sayeed said, because he had nothing else to say and the silence was awful.

The dog turned a circle, agitated. Spit frothed on its muzzle. It began to shiver, as if in fear, but did not abandon the girl.

"That's our dog," said Lahni. "Papa's dog."

"What's its name?" Zeeahd asked.

"King," she said.

"King," Zeeahd said. "That's a fine name. We'll see to the dog."

He waved an arm in the direction of the dog and the cats tore off past Sayeed toward King. The guttural sounds that emerged from their mouths were nothing Sayeed had ever heard from cats. The dog barked once in alarm, wheeled around, and fled, the cats in pursuit.

"What is this?" Zeeahd asked, his malformed fingers closing on a charm the girl wore on a leather thong around her neck. "Is it amber?"

"Mum gave it to me for my fifteenth lifeday."

"It's beautiful," Zeeahd said. His clumsy fingers nearly dropped the amber charm.

"Oh, mum!" the girl said, and melted into Zeeahd's grasp, sobbing.

Zeeahd stroked the girl's hair, harder, harder.

"That hurts," she said.

"I know," Zeeahd said. "I know."

"Stop," she said, fear creeping into her voice. "You're hurting me."

"I can't stop," Zeeahd said, his voice guttural.

"Please . . ."

"I'm sorry," Zeeahd said, his voice little more than grunts.

The girl pulled back, looked up into his cowl, and her eyes widened. "What's wrong with your face? Oh, gods! Help! Help!"

Sayeed had braced himself, but the girl's screams still hit him like a knife stab. He wanted to turn away but his feet seemed rooted in place, stuck in the mud, stuck in the horror of his life with his brother.

Zeeahd held the struggling, screaming girl in his hands, his form roiling, and half turned to Sayeed, his face thankfully lost in the shadow of his cowl. "Stop looking at me, Sayeed!"

The words freed Sayeed to move. He turned away, bile in the back of his throat, acrid, harsh.

Lahni screamed, a pitiful, terrified shriek.

"One kiss for your savior," Zeeahd grunted in the voice of a beast. He began to cough, to heave. "Just one."

"Help! Help!"

The girl's pleading stopped, replaced by muffled sounds of terror, a wet gurgling.

Sayeed tried not to hear his brother's retches, the girl's abortive wails, the final, violent wet heave followed by blissful silence.

Sayeed stared off at the plains, at the darkness, at the rain, and tried to make his mind as blank as his emotions.

"It's done," Zeeahd said at last.

Sayeed steeled himself and turned.

His brother, his form more normal than it had been in a tenday, stood over the limp, prone form of the girl. She looked tiny on the ground, her arms thrown out, her head thrown back, like a broken flower. Open eyes stared up into the rain. A rivulet of black phlegm hung from the corner of her mouth. The tendril of black mucous wriggled like a living thing and disappeared into her mouth.

"She was a girl," Sayeed said. "Just a girl."

"I know that!" Zeeahd said, wincing. "Do you think I don't know that? This is the price I must pay to keep the curse at bay. He holds me between worlds to ensure I do his work and find the son."

"Mephistopheles?"

Thunder rumbled and the darkness seemed to deepen.

"Do not say his name!" Zeeahd said in a hiss. He looked about, eyes wide with fear.

Somewhere, out in the plains, the dog, King, yelped with pain.

"We can't continue like this," Sayeed said dully. "I can't."

"We'll have release," Zeeahd said. "We need only find the son. Bear with it a while longer."

In the years they'd sought Cale's son, Zeeahd's divinations had revealed nothing; consultations with seers and prophets had not availed them. It was as if the son had fallen out of the multiverse. But recently, Zeeahd's divinations had pointed them to the legendary Oracle of the Abbey of the Rose.

"The Oracle will know how to find him," Zeeahd said.

Sayeed looked past his brother to the girl, Lahni, lying still in the grass among the corpses of her family. He hoped the Oracle would know. Sayeed just wanted to sleep. He'd never wanted anything more in his life. His brother had turned into a monster serving the Lord of Cania. Sayeed had turned into a monster serving his brother.

The cats padded out of the shadows, their paws and muzzles covered in the dog's blood. They stopped, sat, and licked their paws clean while they eyed Sayeed and Zeeahd.

Sayeed didn't want to see the remains of the dog, if there were any. He turned back to his brother to find him staring at the cats.

"Why do we keep doing this, Zeeahd? I'm so tired."

Zeeahd peeled his eyes from the bloody felines. "Because we must. Because my pact with him is the only hope we have. And because I'm getting worse."

Vasen's adoptive father, Derreg, had buried Varra in the common cemetery atop a rise in the eastern side of the valley. When Derreg died, Vasen laid him to rest beside Varra. They'd known each other only a short time, but Derreg had insisted that he be buried beside Varra in the cemetery for layfolk rather than in the catacombs under the abbey.

The stones that marked their graves were the same as those that marked all the other graves on the rise. A simple piece of limestone etched along the bottom with the spraying lines of the rising sun.

Vasen sat on his haunches before the graves. He'd plucked two of the pale orchids that grew at the base of the mountains and placed one on each of their graves.

"Rest well," he said. "I'll return when I can."

He stood, turned, and looked out and down on the vale. The Abbey of the Rose sat in a deep, wooded valley, a gash hidden in the heart of the Thunder Peaks. A hundred years earlier, the Oracle, then only a child, had led the first pilgrims to the valley, telling them that it was a protected place into which the Shadovar could not see.

"We will be a light to their darkness," he'd said, or so the story went.

And, as with all of the Oracle's pronouncements, the words had proven true. The vale had remained unmolested by enemies, its location a secret to all but a select number of the faithful.

Ringed on three sides by cracked limestone cliffs that merged with the sloped sides of pine-covered mountains, the vale felt like a world unto itself, a pocket of light in the heart of shadow, a singular thing, like the rarely seen sun. Vasen loved it.

Foaming cascades from melting glaciers poured out of notches in the eastern and northern cliff faces, falling with a roar to the valley floor. The rushing waters joined to form a fast-moving river that bisected the vale before carving its way farther down the mountains. Smaller brooks and streams branched from the river to feed the vale's lush vegetation. Dozens of tarns dotted the terrain, their still waters like dark mirrors.

Vasen took one last look back at his mother's grave, at Derreg's, then headed down the rise. When he reached the valley floor, he picked his way along the many walking paths that lined the pine forests. Pilgrims had trod the same paths for decades. Nesting cowbirds fluttered unseen in the branches; they'd head for warmer air to the south soon.

From time to time the canopy thinned enough overhead that he could glimpse the sky, the whole of it the gray of old metal, as if the Shadovar had encased the world in armor.

Despite the impenetrable sky, Vasen's faith allowed him to perceive the sun's location. He always knew where he could find the light. Yet he felt comfortable, even welcome in the shadows. He credited his blood for that, and it only rarely bothered him.

He had mostly reconciled himself to his dual existence. He told himself that his connection to both light and shadow gave him a better appreciation of each. He existed in the nexus of light and shadow, a creature of both, but a servant of only one.

His hand went to the rose symbol the Oracle had given him. Silver under the tarnish, light under the darkness.

"Where will you go when I die?" the Oracle had asked him.

He kicked a piece of deadwood and frowned. He could scarcely conceive of the Oracle's death. The Oracle was the fixed star of Vasen's existence. Vasen's sworn purpose was to protect him. Without the Oracle, without the oath, what would Vasen have? Who would he be?

He didn't know. He lacked family and friends. Without a purpose . . .

He inhaled deeply to clear his somber mood. The air was thick with the smell of pine and wildflowers, the scent of his home.

"Wisdom and light, Dawnfather," he said softly. "Wisdom and light."

Ahead, a beam of sunlight escaped the cloak of the shadowed sky and cut a line down through the pines, a golden path that extended from the hidden sun to the hidden vale.

Vasen whispered his thanks and hurried forward to the boon. He placed his hand in the beam's light and warmth. Shadows leaked from his dark flesh, the blade of Amaunator's sun and the darkness of his blood coexisting in the light.

The beam lasted only a few moments before the sky swallowed it again, but it was enough. The Dawnfather had heard, and answered.

His spirits lightened, Vasen turned the direction of his thoughts from his own concerns to those of the pilgrims he would soon lead out into the dark.

He asked Amaunator for wisdom and strength, prayed that his light and that of the Dawnswords would be enough to see them all to safety.

A voice broke the spell of solitude. "Well met, Dawnsword."

Surprise pulled a rush of shadows from Vasen's flesh. He turned to see one of the pilgrims standing on the path a few paces behind him. The man had come with the most recent group from the war-torn Dalelands.

"The light keep you," Vasen said, recovering himself enough to offer the standard greeting between believers. "Are you . . . lost? I can escort you to the abbey if—"

The man smiled and approached. He wore a gray cloak, dark breeches, and a loose tunic. The compact stride of his lithe frame wasted little motion.

"Oh, I've been lost for years. But maybe I'm finding my way now."

The man's eyes struck Vasen immediately—pupilless orbs the color of milk. Vasen might have thought him blind had he not moved with such confidence. Tattoos decorated his bald head, his clean-shaven face, and his exposed neck—lines and spirals and whorls that made a map of his skin. He held an oak staff in his hand and carved lines and spirals grooved its length, too.

"I didn't hear you approach. Orsin, isn't it?"

"So I tell myself these days. And you're Vasen."

"Aye. Well met," Vasen said, and extended a hand.

Orsin's grip felt as if it could have crushed stone.

"Do you mind if I join you?" Orsin asked. "I was just . . . walking the vale."

Ordinarily Vasen preferred to prepare his mind and spirit in solitude. But he remembered the Oracle's admonition— "Things change, Vasen."

"Please do. I was just walking, too. And the company of a brother in the faith would be welcome."

Orsin hesitated, an awkward smile hanging from his lips.

"Something wrong?" Vasen asked.

"Not wrong, but . . . I should tell you that I'm not a worshiper of Amaunator."

Given the context, the words struck Vasen as so unlikely that he thought he might have misheard.

"What? You're not?"

Orsin shook his bald head. "I'm not."

Now that he thought about it, Vasen did not recall seeing Orsin at dawn worship, or at any of the Oracle's sermons, or at anything else associated with the faith. Concern pulled shadows from Vasen's skin. He tensed.

"Then what . . ."

Orsin held his hands loose at his side. Perhaps he read the concern in Vasen's face. "I'm not an enemy."

"All right," Vasen said, still coiled, eyes narrowed. "But are you a friend?"

Orsin smiled. The expression seemed to come easy to him. "I was, once. I'd like to be again."

"What does that mean?" Vasen asked.

"I ask myself the same thing often," Orsin said.

Vasen's faith allowed him to see into a man's soul, and he saw no ill intent in Orsin. Besides, the man would have been magically interrogated in the Dalelands before being brought to the vale. And had he been hostile, the spirits of the pass would have barred his passage. Still, Vasen could not imagine anyone other than a follower of Amaunator risking the Sembian countryside to come to the abbey.

"I'm . . . at a loss," Vasen said. "I'll need to tell the Oracle."

"Oh, he knows."

"He knows?"

Orsin smiled, shrugged. "He does."

"I'm confused. Why are you here, then?"

Orsin's milky eyes were unreadable. "That, too, is something I often ask myself. The answer, usually, is happenstance. I just follow the wind."

Vasen could not quite make sense of either the reply or the man. He could tell Orsin was not giving him the entire truth, yet he sensed no lie in Orsin's words.

"You're a strange man, Orsin."

"Would it surprise you to know that I've heard that before?" Orsin chuckled. "Does this change your answer? May I still walk with you?"

"Oh, I insist you walk with me now."

"Very good, then," Orsin said, and used his staff to scribe a line in the dirt before their feet.

"I hesitate to ask," Vasen said. "What's that you just did?"

He wondered if perhaps the man were mentally unsound.

"Lines mark borders, a beginning. This is before," Orsin said, and used his staff to point to one side of the line. Then he pointed to the other side. "This is after. I hope there's a friendship on this side."

The words, so guileless, touched Vasen.

"Then I do, too," Vasen said, and together they stepped over the line. Orsin's steps were so light on the undergrowth that they made almost no sound.

"Where are you from?" Vasen asked him. He made a note to ask Byrne and Eldris about Orsin. In particular, he wanted to know how Orsin had slipped through the interrogation they performed on all would-be pilgrims. A non-worshiper getting through suggested a problem. The battles being fought in the Dales could not be an excuse for carelessness.

"I'm from the east, Telflammar," Orsin said. "Do you know it?"

Vasen shook his head. It was just an exotic name he'd heard from time to time, although perhaps coming from Telflammar explained Orsin's exotic appearance.

"It's very far from here," Orsin said, looking off in the distance. "It was . . . changed in the Spellplague."

"What wasn't?"

"True, true," Orsin said. "And you? Where are you from?"

Vasen made a gesture that took in the vale. "I'm from here."

"Sembia?"

"Not Sembia, no. Sembia belongs to the Shadovar. I was born in this vale, and it belongs to us."

"Us," Orsin said. "You're . . . not Shadovar?"

Vasen had heard the question often from pilgrims and it no longer offended him. "No. I'm . . . something else."

"Something else, but . . . akin to shadows, yes?"

Vasen held up a hand. "Listen. Do you hear that?"

Orsin looked puzzled. He cocked his head. "The water?"

Vasen nodded. "The cascades. They're the first thing I hear when I lead pilgrims to the vale or return from taking them home. Hearing them, I know I'm home."

"You walk much but never far."

Vasen liked that. "Yes. Never far. Are you interrogating me, Orsin of Telflammar?"

"So it seems," the man said with a grin. "You've spent your entire life here?"

"Since the day I was born. Only the Oracle has been here longer. All the others, even the abbot, rotate in and out. The gloom is not for everyone."

"No, but it calls those it calls," Orsin said. "And nothing lasts forever."

Orsin's words reminded Vasen of the Oracle's words earlier. His expression must have turned somber. Orsin picked up on it.

"I'm sorry. Did I speak out of turn? I meant that the darkness couldn't last forever."

Vasen waved off the apology. "No need for sorry. Your words just put me in mind of words someone else said to me recently."

"I see."

"And if anything can last forever, I fear it's this darkness."

"I think not," Orsin said.

Vasen smiled. "You're sure you're not a worshiper of the Dawnfather?"

"Very good," Orsin said with a chuckle. "Very good." The end of Orsin's staff put little divots in the earth as they walked. "Where are we walking?"

"I'm just following the wind, same as you."

They came to the river's edge. The burbling water, shallow and fast moving, cut a groove in the valley's floor. Trees jutted at odd angles from the steeply sloped bank. Round rocks like cairn stones lined the bank. Vasen felt a chill, and it reminded him of the dream of his father.

Directly across the river stood another pair of pilgrims—a middle-aged man with a scarred face who held the hand of a plump, long-haired woman, probably his wife.

Vasen held a hand aloft in greeting and called, "The light warm and keep you."

The pilgrims stared at him for a moment, finally raised their hands in a tentative wave, and mumbled an echo of his blessing. They hurried on without another word.

"My appearance makes some uncomfortable," he said, pointing a finger at his eyes, which he knew glowed yellow in dim light.

"My appearance does the same," Orsin said. He looked in the direction the pilgrims had gone. "Seems unfair, since they owe their safety to you."

"Fairness does not enter into it," Vasen said. "It's my honor to serve."

"And true service often demands solitude."

Vasen heard something forlorn in Orsin's tone, an echo of his own feelings. "You speak as one who knows that firsthand."

Orsin nodded. "I do."

"Well, neither of us walks alone today, yeah?"

"Very good. Not alone. Not today."

Abruptly, Vasen made a decision that surprised him. "Come on. I'll show you a place."

Orsin's eyebrows rose in a question but his tongue did not utter it.

Vasen followed the bank of the river for a time. Ahead, through the thinning pines, he saw the cracked, pale face of the eastern wall of the vale, and above it, crags like teeth. The shadows of the mountains fell across the forest, darkening the already dim air further. Vasen felt the deepening darkness draw around him like a blanket, thick and comfortable.

He turned right, leaving the river behind. The ground sloped upward, and the pines, older and taller than elsewhere in the vale, towered over them. The scrub overgrew the walking path.

"Few come this way," Orsin observed.

"I usually come here alone," Vasen said. He'd always felt drawn to it.

"Thank you for letting me accompany you, then."

Eventually they came to Vasen's destination: a large tarn of still, dark water. Tall pines, the oldest in the vale, ringed the water, standing silent, dignified sentinels. One of the tall pines bordering the tarn had fallen over years earlier, blown down in a storm, perhaps. Half of its roots lay exposed, and a portion of it extended out into the tarn. Weather had stripped it of much of its bark, but still it lived.

When they stepped within the circle of the trees, sound seemed to fall away. The distant rush of the cascade, the stirring of birds, the hum of the wind, all diminished. Near the tarn there was only stillness, silence, shadows.

Orsin spoke softly. "This place is waiting."

Vasen nodded. "That's always been my feeling, also. I come here to meditate and commune with the Dawnfather. Although . . ."

He did not say that the tarn pulled at the part of him he owed to Erevis Cale, the dark part, the shadow.

"Although?" Orsin prodded.

"For other reasons, too."

Orsin looked at the earth, the trees, the tarn. "I don't think this is the Dawnfather's place. None come here but you?"

"None but me for a very long time," Vasen acknowledged. "What do you mean, this isn't the Dawnfather's place?"

Orsin did not answer. He glided forward, his pale eyes fixed on the dark water. Vasen followed, his skin inexplicably goose pimpled.

"Who are you, Orsin?" Vasen asked. He felt as if much hung on the answer. He wondered why he had brought the man with him to his place of solitude. They'd only just met. He'd been walking with the man for half an hour and Vasen knew essentially nothing of him. "I think I should take you back to the abbey, explain matters to the Oracle—"

"I'm a walker," Orsin said over his shoulder. He reached under his tunic to remove something, a disc of some kind, a symbol. "A hopeful wanderer. And a congregation of one."

"Is that—?"

Orsin was nodding. "This is the symbol of my faith. This place doesn't belong to the Dawnfather, but it's holy still. And now I know why my path brought me here, why you brought me here."

Kneeling at the water's edge, Orsin held the symbol—a black disc bordered with a thin red line—over the water.

Vasen did not recognize the symbol but felt as if he *knew* it. He froze when shadows flowed up from the surface of the water to enwrap the symbol, twisted around Orsin's hands. Orsin murmured words, a prayer, that Vasen could not hear.

Vasen looked at his own hands, also leaking shadows. His entire body was swimming in them, wrapped in them. Once more, he felt as if he were living life in a story written for him by another.

Write the story.

Orsin stood and turned to face Vasen. His white eyes widened slightly when he saw the mass of shadows swirling around Vasen.

"This place was left here. For me, maybe, but I think more likely for you. You're connected to it. So I'll ask you the same question you asked me. Who are you?"

Vasen looked at his hands, leaking shadows.

"You're a shade but not a Shadovar. How? Tell me."

Vasen cleared his throat. He tried to pull the shadows back into his form but they would not diminish. "My . . . father."

Orsin took a step toward him, his fingers white around the disc of his holy symbol.

"Who was your father?"

Vasen looked past Orsin to the tarn, its deep, black water. "His name was Erevis Cale."

Orsin's hands fell slack to his side. "That . . . can't be."

"You've heard his name? I thought you came from the east."

Orsin took his symbol in both hands, held it to his chest. "Erevis Cale died more than a hundred years ago. You're too young to be his son. It's not possible, is it? How can it be?"

"Magic sent my mother here while I was still in the womb." Vasen took a step toward Orsin, toward the tarn. "How do you know my father's name?"

Vasen's hand went to the hilt of his blade. Suspicion lodged in him, grew. Orsin seemed not to notice, or not to care if he did.

"Erevis Cale was the First of the Shadowlord." Orsin brandished the symbol, held it out for Vasen to see. "The First of Mask." Orsin was shaking his head, pacing now along the edge of the tarn. "I was led here to see this, to meet you, but why? I don't see it. I don't see it."

Vasen said nothing, could say nothing, just stood in the midst of the shadows gathering around them. He let his hand fall from the hilt.

Orsin stopped suddenly, looked over at Vasen.

"This is their place, Vasen. Mask. Your father. This is *their* place."

For a moment Vasen could not speak. His dreams of Erevis Cale reared up in his mind, dark visions of a cold place. "No. Mask is dead. Erevis Cale is dead. This can't be their place."

"I keep the faith alive, Vasen," Orsin said. He gestured at the fallen tree. "It's like that tree. Uprooted by a storm, broken on the rocks, but still it hangs onto life. So, too, does the Shadowlord's faith. In me and maybe a few others."

"You . . . worship a dead god?"

"Not quite dead," Orsin said. He pointed at the tarn as if it signified something. "This tarn is different from all of the others in the vale, yes?"

Vasen stepped to Orsin's side, his eyes on the water. "It is. Deeper. No one has touched its bottom."

The faint light of the dying, shrouded day cast their darkened reflection on the water, faceless and black, only half formed.

"You've tried?"

"Once. The water gets too cold and the depth is too great. It's like . . . a hole."

Orsin inhaled deeply, put a hand on his hip, and looked up at the mountains. "I think I've stood on this ground before."

Vasen shook his head. "You've never been to the abbey before. I'd remember if you had."

Orsin smiled, no teeth, just a faint rise at the corners of his mouth. "There was no abbey here, then."

Vasen could not control the swirl of shadows around him. "The abbey has been here since before you were born."

"The spirit is eternal, Vasen," Orsin said, nodding at some truth only he understood. "The body is not. Before going to its final rest, a spirit is often reborn into a new body. Sometimes this happens many times." His white eyes looked distant as he fixed them on the dark water of the tarn. "But the essence of the spirit, its core, is the line that tethers its lives to one another through time. A thread that connects them all."

Vasen thought he better understood the tattoos on Orsin, the grooves in his staff. "And you . . .?"

"Have been reborn many times." He smiled. "It seems I have a disquieted spirit."

"Are you—? I don't—"

"I'm not human, Vasen, at least not fully. The essence of the planes runs in my veins. In the Dalelands they called me a deva. But I've been called other things in other places, in other lives. Aasimar. Celestial. But deva suits me well enough. And Orsin suits me best."

Vasen tried to process everything he was learning, to make sense of it. "And you came here—?"

Orsin shrugged. "Following the thread of previous lives. I told you the truth. I follow my feet where they lead." His gesture took in the tarn, the vale. "I'm here now to see this. To see you, I think."

Vasen felt the threads of his life being drawn into a knot, his dreams of Erevis, the Oracle's words, Derreg's admonition to be prepared, the appearance of Orsin.

"Why? To what purpose?"

Orsin disappointed him with a shrug. "I don't know. Maybe I'm just walking a path that allows me to meet those I've known before. That'd be pleasant, I think."

The hairs on Vasen's neck stood on end. "Us? Then you think we've known each other before?"

Orsin smiled. "I believe so."

Vasen had no words. He didn't know if he believed Orsin, but he could not deny the connection he felt with the deva. He'd felt it the moment he'd seen him, like reuniting with an old friend. *That* was why he had brought him to the tarn. *That* was why he had tolerated the questioning.

"Thank you for bringing me here," Orsin said. "You've renewed my faith. It had been . . . flagging."

"You're welcome?" Vasen managed.

"Very good," Orsin said, chuckling. The deva tucked his holy symbol back under his tunic and took another look around. "Odd, not so, that a place holy to the Shadowlord is in a place holy to the Dawnfather?"

"Perhaps not so odd," Vasen said, thinking of his own soul, his own life, the tarnished holy symbol he bore.

Orsin watched him and seemed to take his meaning. "No, perhaps not. Shadows require light, after all."

The distant peal of the abbey's bell sounded three times, breaking the spell of the moment.

"That's the call to gather," Vasen said.

Neither man moved. Vasen eyed the tarn, the trees, seeing all of them as if anew. He took the rose holy symbol in shadow-shrouded hands.

"Wisdom and light," he whispered.

The bells sounded again, three peals.

"We must go," he said. "The pilgrims are to leave the vale."

Orsin's pale eyebrows rose. "All of them? So soon?"

Vasen nodded. "Including you, I'm afraid."

"Why now?"

"Because the Oracle commands it. He sees things we cannot. That's his burden."

Orsin's expression fell, but he recovered with a smile. "Strange to say farewell so soon after we met. Strange, that I would have come so far only to cross paths with you for so short a time."

"You won't have to say it quite yet," Vasen said. "I'll be leading the pilgrims' escort back to the Dales. The war there makes things especially dangerous. I should have gone last time. Although, then, perhaps," he said with a smile, "I wouldn't have let you come."

Orsin chuckled. "So the shade-but-not-Shadovar will take us back to the sun, then. Very good. Very good. The lines of our lives will stay crossed, for a while longer at least." He scraped another line into the soft earth and eyed Vasen. "Revelation means a new beginning. We walk together yet, Vasen Cale."

No one had ever called him Vasen Cale before. He allowed that it sounded right.

Together, they stepped over the line and walked back toward the abbey.

CHAPTER FOUR

GERAK FOLLOWED THE SELDOM-USED ROAD OUT OF FAIRELM for a few hours before cutting across the plains. The rising sun's light did not penetrate the dark clouds and rain; it might as well have been midnight. But Gerak knew the terrain well enough to navigate it in the dark. The wet caused his cloak to hang heavy from his shoulders. He did his best to keep his bow dry. As always, he kept his eyes and ears sharp.

A lifetime ago his father used to take him to a wood that was two day's trek out of Fairelm. Game had been plentiful then, but it had been more than two years since Gerak had ventured there. If Tymora smiled on him, he would make it there in safety, take a deer or two, rig a sled, and drag the carcasses back to the village. After drying and smoking the meat, he and Elle would use it to get them through most of the winter.

Fording flooded creeks and picking his way through intermittent stands of broadleaf trees and whispering whipgrass, he made his way toward the wood. He had trod the plains alone before, many times, but it felt different this time. He felt exposed, a man walking a darkness not meant for men. The black pressed against him, made it hard to breathe. The sounds of his breathing and footfalls broke a silence that felt lurking.

He crested a rise and looked back the way he had come, hoping to catch a final glimpse of Fairelm. But the village was gone, swallowed by the darkness. He stood there a moment, reconsidering his decision to leave on a hunt, but finally pushed away the uneasy feeling that plagued him and continued. Elle and the baby needed real food.

As the day wore on to afternoon, the hidden sun lightened the nearly impenetrable ink, turning it merely to oppressive darkness. Around midday, a high-pitched shriek sounded from somewhere out in the black, a terrified, distant wail that put Gerak in a crouch and sent his heart to pounding. He did not think it was human, and it was always difficult judging distance on the plains. It could have originated a bowshot away, or it could have originated half a league distant.

Moving in a low crouch, he stationed himself behind a rotting broadleaf stump, sweaty hands around the shaft of his bow, and waited. The sound did not recur and he saw and heard nothing more to give him alarm. After calming himself, he renewed his trek.

He walked all day, the wet ground pulling at his boots, as if the earth would suck him down under the sod. Several times he felt certain that eyes were upon him, hungry leers out in the dark, just beyond eyeshot. Always he would nock an arrow and put his back to a tree or rock, his senses alert to any sound or motion, but he never saw anything. Twice he doubled back, and once he hid in a ditch, his sword in hand, and lay in ambush, but nothing seemed to be following him.

Or at least nothing he could see.

He told himself that stress was pulling phantasms from his mind. He passed the first day out in the lonely dark without seeing another living creature, except once, a flight of pheasants far too distant to bother with an arrow. The absence of even small game did not bode well for what he might find in the wood.

The rain relented by nightfall, and before the air turned once more from merely dark to total pitch he gathered kindling and wood and found a suitable campsite under a stand of pines that swayed in the rising wind. There was risk in a fire, but he needed the warmth and the light. Besides, he'd scratch out a fire pit so the flames wouldn't be visible from too far away—one benefit of the shadowed air.

With his sword he scraped a fire pit out of the wet sod. The kindling resisted his flint and steel but he eventually won it over, and a fitful, smoky fire provided a dim counterpoint to the night. He had never been so happy before in his life to see flames.

He stripped off his pack, staked up the tarp that would serve as his tent, and sat before the flames for a time, thinking, trying to keep from shivering. He needed to dry out his cloak, so he shed it and laid it out near the fire.

Some kind of animal brayed in the distance. Overhead, he heard the flap of wings, large wings. Furtive movement at the edge of the firelight drew his eye, a small night creature that vanished before he could nock an arrow or note its shape.

Sitting out there alone, he turned maudlin. He thought of his father, Fairelm, the cottage, Elle, the baby. He realized that he was attached to the farm because it had been his parent's. And that was not enough of a reason to stay. Sembia was no place to raise a child. The land did not belong to men anymore, not really. It belonged to the darkness, and was no place for his family. Staring into the fire, he decided then and there that he would take Elle and the baby out of Sembia.

Having made the decision, he felt a weight come off him. He considered heading back to the cottage first thing in the morning, but decided against it. He was only a half day away from the woods where he hoped to take a stag. It would take some time for him and Elle to gather up their things and sell what they couldn't carry. In the interim, they'd have need for some meat.

Thunder rumbled in the distance, and his stomach echoed the sound. He thought of just enduring it—he'd gone without food often enough in recent years—but he did not relish the thought of going to sleep hungry. Besides, he'd need energy tomorrow. He remembered whatever small creature had crept up on his campfire, the pheasants he'd seen in the air. There was food out there. He just had to find it.

His mind made up, he threw enough wood on the fire to keep it burning for an hour or two and stalked off into the plains. He didn't wander far, wanting to keep the fire visible at all times.

Selûne was not visible through the swirl of clouds. Instead, her light created only a dim shapeless yellow smear in the sky, but once his eyes adjusted it was enough for him to see by. He realized that he had not had a clear view of the moon in many years. He would do better by his child.

In time he reached a low-lying area of tall whipgrass that looked promising. Knifewing pheasants were migrating south across the Inner Sea, and the birds roosted in whipgrass, feeding on the seeds, grasshoppers, and crickets. He'd seen a flock earlier in the day. They would be grounded for the night.

The birds were notoriously keen eared, so he knew he would not be able to sneak up on one and take it while it nested. He'd just have to be ready when they went airborne. Taking a shot in the dark would be difficult, but the moonlight, feeble as it was, would help. And Tymora smiled on the brash.

He started forward into the grass, holding his bow in one hand, two fowl-tipped arrows in the other. The ground softened as he advanced and he sometimes skirted puddles. Moving slowly, he imitated the pheasants' ground coo—his father had taught it to him as a boy—and listened for a response. Eventually soft coos and a rustle of wings answered him.

Three, maybe four knifewings were near.

He moved closer to the sound, gliding through the terrain like a ghost, and nocked both fowling arrows. He eyed the sky. The moon lightened the clouds enough to provide some contrast with the rest of the darkness. Estimating the location of the pheasants, he circled around to give himself a shooting angle against the light part of the sky.

Ready, he gave a sudden, sharp whoop that sounded perilously loud in the dark.

Wings flapped and five startled knifewings launched into the air. He took aim, the two arrows each held between a pair of fingers, tracking their motion. He waited for the birds to rise high enough against the sky to give him a clear shot. When they did, he targeted two near each other, adjusted his finger pressure to alter trajectories, and let fly. The arrows hissed through the rain and struck. Feathers flew and both birds spiraled to the ground while the other three vanished into the night.

Grinning, and pleased to have lost none of his accuracy, Gerak kept his eyes on the exact spot they fell and hurried through the grass. Despite the darkness, he found them after a short search. He'd hit both in the body and both had died instantly. No need to wring necks.

He carefully withdrew his arrows from the carcasses, wiped the small amount of blood clean on the grass, and replaced the arrows in his quiver. He carried only four fowling arrows and could not afford to lose them. Grabbing both birds by the neck, he stood and tried to get his bearings from the fire.

He didn't see it. Fear tightened his chest. Thunder rumbled, closer now, and a light rain started to fall. He imagined the precipitation putting out his fire, leaving him stranded on the plains until morning, and the fear he felt threatened to turn to panic.

He cursed, turned a circle, the birds dangling futilely from his fist. He wasn't sure which direction his camp was. He'd gotten turned around when he'd angled himself to take the shot and now he wasn't sure.

He needed to get to some higher ground and to do so fast. The rain was picking up. He eyed the terrain, spotted a rise capped with the twisted, malformed trunks of mature broadleaf trees, and tore off for it. As he ran, he nearly lost a boot to the muck.

He climbed the rise, heart racing, and looked around.

There! He saw the glow of his fire, maybe two bowshots distant.

He did not realize he had come so far.

He sagged with relief, hands on his knees. His heart started to slow, his breathing to grow more regular. His legs felt watery under him.

And that was when he noticed it.

The rain had sputtered out and the plains were quiet as a grave. Even the night insects had fallen silent.

His breathing sounded loud in his ears, too loud. He remembered the whoop he'd used to startle the pheasants. The sound must have been audible for half a league.

He cursed in a whisper.

He edged toward the broadleaf, wanting to put something at his back, feeling terribly exposed atop the rise. He inhaled deeply, held his breath, remained still, and focused his hearing.

Nothing.

A breeze from the east kicked up, carrying the faint scent of putrid meat—a dead animal, maybe, or so he hoped.

How had he missed it before?

Because the wind changed.

"Damn it," he said. A rotting animal would attract predators.

Thunder rumbled again, a promise of renewed rain. He looked at the glow of his fire and considered making a run for it. A natural predator would avoid a fire.

But not all predators on the plains were natural.

The wind gusted, causing the whipgrass to whisper, the leaves of the broadleaf to hiss, the limbs to creak.

A deep-throated bellow sounded from out in the darkness to his right, a wet snarl that reminded him of a rooting pig. His heart leaped against his ribs and the sound of flapping wings sounded from all around as two-score startled knifewings rose into the air. He found it hard to breathe. His muscles failed him, left him standing still in the dark, exposed, alone atop the rise. Sweat ran in cold rivulets down his back.

Whatever had made that sound might be able to see him, to smell him.

Move! His mind screamed. *Move!*

He felt heavy footsteps thudding into the sod, out there in the dark. He had no idea what it could be, but his mind summoned nightmares. He knew that aberrant creatures stalked Sembia's plains, horrors that no man should see. A second grunt carried through the darkness, closer this time, and punctuated with wet inhalations, the sound of a creature with a scent.

His scent.

It had him.

Terror freed him at last. Fueled by adrenaline, he turned and leaped, grabbed hold of the lowest branch on the broadleaf, and scrambled up. The sound of his boots on the trunk, his soft grunts of exertion, sounded like shouts in his ears.

The creature heard him, for it bellowed loudly, and the heavy tread of its footsteps bounded toward him. He climbed a few limbs higher, frantic, awkward, catching scrapes and cuts in his haste, then froze, afraid to make more noise. He was not safe in a tree, not for long. He knew that.

He got his feet as steady as he could on a thick limb, clutched his bow in a sweaty palm, and fumbled for one of his arrows. His breath would not slow down. It was loud, too loud. His heart thudded in his chest so hard he swore he could hear it through his ribs.

A large form lumbered out of darkness on two legs, a misshapen bulk half again as tall as a man, and thudded into the broadleaf. The impact caused the tree to shiver, sent a shower of leaves and seed pods earthward, and nearly dislodged Gerak. He caught himself only by firing his nocked arrow wildly as he grabbed for a limb. The creature seemed not to notice the pointed shaft that stuck in the earth near its feet.

In shape, it looked vaguely human, and Gerak wondered if it weren't some kind of troll. Folds of flabby skin drooped from its obese arms, legs, and mid-section. Torn, muddy rags covered skin the sallow yellow of an old bruise. Long, lank hair hung from the creature's head, a head far too small for the rest of the bloated body, like capping a bucket with a sewing thimble.

It circled the base of the tree, sniffing the ground, raising its face to the sky to sniff the air. Small, dark eyes looked out from a pinched face. Its mouth looked malformed, the lips stretched and hugely swollen.

Gerak hoped that the foliage and the darkness hid him from the creature. He dared not reach for another arrow, not with the creature right below him. It would see the movement.

Another low growl. The creature's stink, like spoiled milk, made Gerak wince. It fell to all fours and sniffed the bole of the tree where Gerak had gone up.

Gerak's breath came fast.

Still sniffing, the creature got to its hind legs and put distended hands on the tree, as if it would climb. Its tiny eyes, nearly invisible in the flabby folds of its face, started to work their way up the tree trunk.

Gerak tried to shrink into himself, tried to find calm, and failed at both. He moved his hand slowly, so slowly, for his quiver.

As his fingers closed on the fletching, the creature froze, cocked its head, and gave a curious grunt. It dropped back to all fours. An eager snort escaped it, and its sniffing took on a note of urgency. It scrabbled around the bole of the tree, moved away a couple paces, its face to the wet earth. When it reached the pheasants—the pheasants Gerak had dropped in his panic—it let out a roar of pleasure and seized both in its sausage-like fingers, then began shoving them into its mouth, feathers, bones, and all.

The wet slobbering and satisfied grunts of the creature, together with the wet cracking of the bird carcasses, made Gerak nauseous. Still, he took the opportunity to pull an arrow, nock it, and draw. He sighted at the back of the creature's thick neck, figuring he could sever the spine if not kill it outright. Something on its neck caught his eye: a leather lanyard, like a necklace. He hesitated, struck by the oddness of its presence. The creature bounded a few steps away, perhaps searching for more pheasant, and its movement took it clear of Gerak's firing line. The boughs of the broadleaf blocked the shot.

Moving slowly, his eyes fixed on the wrinkles of the creature's neck; he shifted his position. The limb creaked under his feet. The creature's head jerked up, wide nostrils flaring as it sniffed the air. Gerak froze awkwardly, the muscles of his calf already starting to scream. Sweat oozed from his pores. He still did not have a good shot. He might have to just risk shifting position again.

The creature growled, a deep wet sound. The tone of it, calculating, suspicious, put Gerak's hair on end.

He'd get only one shot, if that. He sighted along the arrow's shaft, waited for the creature to move into position.

It held its head cocked, lank hair spilling to the side. It was listening. It shifted on its weight, its feet sinking into the soft earth.

A single loud pop from the right—the wet wood from Gerak's distant fire, caused the creature to snort and Gerak to start. The creature roared and tore off in the direction of Gerak's camp, the stumps of its feet puckering the sod as it went.

Gerak did not hesitate. The moment the creature disappeared into the night, he dropped from the tree, bow in hand, and ran in the opposite direction of the camp until he reached a natural ditch. He slid into it, soaking his clothes in mud and organic stink—it would help mask his smell—and remained still.

The creature's roars carried across the plains. A shower of sparks went up from the area of the campsite, the creature's form a frenzied silhouette in the dim light of the floating embers. It was destroying the camp.

He cursed, thinking of his lost gear, thinking of Elle's locket still sitting in the pocket of his cloak.

The creature rampaged through his camp for a time and then the plains once more fell silent. To be safe, Gerak waited another half hour, cold and shivering. All remained quiet. He crept out of the ditch and ran in a crouch for the campsite.

He didn't care about anything there except Elle's locket.

Brennus stood in the doorway of his scrying chamber. A tarnished, solid silver scrying cube, two paces wide on each side, rested on the floor in the center of the round vaulted room. Shadows curled around the cube in thin wisps. The dim light of the Tears of Selûne, their glow diffused by the shadowed air of Sakkors enclave, gleamed feebly through the vaulted, glassteel roof.

His homunculi, tiny twin constructs made from dead flesh and Brennus's own blood, climbed down his robes from their usual perch on his shoulders and pelted across the chamber ahead of him. They took turns tripping each other, clambering over one another in their haste, a chaotic ball of leathery gray skin, thin limbs, high-pitched expletives, and squeals of outrage.

Smiling, Brennus followed them until he stood before the cube. In his hand he held his dead mother's platinum necklace. He'd found it a hundred years earlier, and plumbing its mystery had been his obsession ever since. Her ghost haunted his thoughts, her voice whispering two words in his mind over and over.

Avenge me.

Again and again over the decades he returned to his scrying cube, his divinations, seeking a way, any way, to make his brother, Rivalen, pay for the murder of their mother. But always the exercise ended in frustration. Rivalen was too powerful for Brennus to confront.

Brennus had caught hints of a plan by Mask to foil Shar—and anything that hurt Shar would also hurt Rivalen—but they remained only hints. He couldn't see how things fit together. He'd thought for a long time that Erevis Cale's son by Varra would play some role, but the son had seemingly vanished from the multiverse. Brennus had watched Varra, pregnant with the boy, disappear from the forest meadow and he'd never been able to locate her. One hundred years had passed since then. Varra and the child would be dead by now. He thought all of it might have some connection to the mysterious Abbey of the Rose, a temple to Amaunator supposedly hidden somewhere in the Thunder Peaks. After all, Erevis Cale had been allied with worshipers of Amaunator at the Battle of Sakkors. But Brennus had never been able to divine the location of any temple in the Thunder Peaks, and now he wondered if the Abbey of the Rose wasn't a myth.

So, with nothing else to go on, Brennus was reduced to compulsively spying on his brother, waiting and hoping for an opportunity, a moment of vulnerability, that he suspected would never come.

"Look now?" asked his homunculi, their two voices synchronous.

"Yes."

The homunculi squeaked with delight and clambered up his cloak, their tiny claws snagging but not harming the magical fabric. They took their usual station, one on each of his shoulders, bookends to his head.

"Show, show," they said.

Brennus put a hand on the smooth, cool face of the scrying cube and uttered the words to a divination. Goaded by the magic, the smears of tarnish began a slow swirl. Abruptly the face of the cube took on dimension, depth. The swirls and whorls of black constituted themselves into recognizable shapes.

"The dark city," the homunculi said, their tones hushed.

"Ordulin," Brennus said. "But it hasn't been a city for a long time."

Maps called it the Maelstrom, and not even the Lords of Shade set foot within it. None save one.

The scrying cube showed Ordulin from high above. The dark, miasmic air around the ruined city made everything look dull, diffuse, cloudy pigments on a surreal painting. Once-grand buildings lay in shattered heaps, the broken bones of a broken city. Streaks of green lightning split the sky from time to time, ghastly veins of light that cast the ruins in viridian light. Shadows formed and dissipated in the air, wisps of reified darkness.

Undead flitted among the bleak ruins: specters, living shadows, ghosts, wraiths, hundreds of them, thousands, the glow of their eyes like a sky of baleful stars. The hole in the center of the maelstrom—the hole his brother and his brother's goddess, Shar, had created when they'd loosed the Shadowstorm on Sembia—drew undead the way a corpse drew flies. Ordulin was a graveyard, haunted by its past and ruled by Brennus's brother, who had murdered their mother.

He held up a hand and intoned a refinement to the scrying ritual. The homunculi mimed his gesture, murmuring nonsense syllables.

The perspective in the face of the cube changed and the arcane eye of the divination streaked toward the blasted ground, wheeled through the shattered stone and wood, and stopped in the center of the ruins, at the edge of what once was a large, open plaza. Chunks of weathered statuary and jagged blocks of a fallen citadel lay scattered across the cracked flagstones, monuments to destruction.

A shield-sized hole hung in the air in the center of the plaza, a colorless distortion in reality that opened onto . . . nothing, an emptiness so profound that looking at it for more than a moment made Brennus nauseated. The homunculi squealed and pulled the loose folds of his robes before their eyes. It seemed slowly to swirl, but Brennus was never certain. What he was certain about was that the hole represented the end to everything. He'd noticed that it grew over time, a miniscule amount each year, the mouth of Shar that would eventually devour the world. He hated it, hated Shar, hated his brother, who was her nightseer, her Chosen, and a godling in his own right.

Rivalen sat at the edge of the hole on the cracked face of a once-enormous statue. He stared into the maelstrom, his hands in his lap, unmoving. As always, Brennus wondered what Rivalen thought of when he looked into the work he'd wrought, the apocalypse he'd sown. Did he welcome it? Regret it? Did he even think like a man anymore?

The wind stirred Rivalen's cloak and his long, dark hair. Shadows leaked from him in long tendrils. He stared at the hole as if he could see something within it, as if he wanted something from it.

"The nightseer," the homunculi said, and covered their faces with their clawed hands.

Brennus said nothing, merely watched his brother a long while. He had no purpose in it anymore, other than to fuel his hate and remind himself of his mother. He relaxed his grip on the necklace he held.

"I'm going to kill you," he promised his brother. Shadows oozed from his skin, swirled around him, marked his anger with their churn. "For her. I'm going to kill you for her. I'll find a way."

The homunculi, sensing his frustration and sadness, patted his head with their tiny hands and made cooing noises.

A cascade of green lightning veined the sky above Ordulin. Brennus blinked in the sudden glare, and when the spots cleared from his eyes he saw that his brother was gone. He saw only the hole, the ruins.

"Nightseer gone," the homunculi said.

Before Brennus could acknowledge them, a voice spoke from behind him.

"Gone from there," said Rivalen's deep voice, as the power of his presence filled the room and put pressure on Brennus's ears. "Because I've come here."

The homunculi squealed in terror and curled up in the cowl of Brennus's cloak, trembling. Brennus swallowed and turned to face his brother.

Rivalen's golden eyes glowed in the dusky crags of his angled face. The darkness in the room coalesced around him, as if drawn to his form. The weight of his regard threatened to buckle Brennus's knees, but he thought of his mother and held his ground.

"Every day I feel your eyes on me, Brennus."

Brennus felt his back bump up against the still-warm metal of the scrying cube. He relied on his hate to give him courage.

"Then perhaps you've felt my hate, too."

His words caused the homunculi to squeal with alarm and try to burrow more deeply into his cowl, but Rivalen's neutral expression did not change.

"Yes, I've felt it," Rivalen said. He glided over the floor toward Brennus, his form lost at the edges, merged with the darkness. He seemed to displace space as he moved, causing the room to shrink, sucking up the air.

Brennus tried to steady his breathing, his heart, tried to slow his rapidly blinking eyes. He knew he looked a fool and it only made him angrier.

"What do you want?" Brennus asked, and was pleased to hear the steadiness in his voice. The shadows leaking from his body merged with those swirling around Rivalen and were overwhelmed by them.

"That's my question to you," Rivalen answered. His golden eyes drifted to Brennus's hand, to the jacinth necklace he held there. "Ah. Still that."

Brennus dared take a step closer to his taller brother. He knew Rivalen could kill him easily, but he did not care. "*Always* that."

The darkness around Rivalen intensified. His eyes stayed on the necklace. "That damned trinket."

Brennus clenched his fist around the necklace. "Our mother wore it the day you murdered her."

Rivalen's eyes came up, met Brennus's, flared in the black hole of his face. "You never told me how you found it."

"You're not all-knowing? Ask the whore you worship or the hole you stare into everyday."

Rivalen held out his hand. Shadows rose from his palm, wound around his fingers. "Give it to me."

Shadows stormed around Brennus and words leaped out of his throat before he could stop it. "No! Never!"

"I can take it if I wish."

Rage boiled in Brennus, the steam of his anger leaking around the lid of his control. He uttered a guttural cry of hate, extended a hand, shouted a word of power, and unleashed a blast of life-draining energy that would have shriveled a mortal to a husk.

But Rivalen was not mortal, not anymore, and the beam of energy slammed into his chest, split, and ricocheted off in several directions, all to no effect.

Rivalen's eyes narrowed. Power coalesced in him as the darkness about him deepened. He stepped toward Brennus and his form seemed to grow, to fill the room. His hands closed on Brennus's robes and lifted him into the air. The homunculi squealed with terror.

Imminent death steeled Brennus's courage. He glared into his brother's impassive golden eyes, squeezed his mother's necklace so hard the metal pierced his skin. Blood ran warm and soaked his fist before his regenerative flesh closed the wound.

Rivalen pulled Brennus close until they were nose to nose. "Give it to me."

Brennus spat in his brother's face, the face of a god, the globule running down Rivalen's cheek.

"You'll have to kill me first."

Rivalen's eyes flared. He studied Brennus's face, perhaps measuring his resolve, then threw him across the length of the scrying chamber.

Brennus hit the far stone wall hard enough to drive the breath from his lungs and crack ribs. His body began immediately to regenerate itself and he winced as shadowstuff reknit his broken ribs. He grimaced as he stood, shouting at his brother.

"A hole, Rivalen! You've had a hole in you since you murdered our mother for your bitch goddess! Now the hole is all you have! How does it feel? How does it feel?"

"Mother died thousands of years ago, Brennus."

The impassivity in Rivalen's voice drove Brennus to distraction. Shadows swirled and he pointed his finger at his brother.

"You don't get to call her 'mother.' You call her Alashar or don't speak of her at all. And she did not just die. You murdered her."

Rivalen did not deny it, did not apologize for it, said nothing at all. He stepped forward to the scrying cube, his expression thoughtful, and put his palm to its face. The entire cube turned black as onyx. In a moment the darkness lightened and an image began to resolve in the cube's face.

Brennus's breath left him in a rush. "Is this? This cannot be."

"It is."

"Don't do this."

"It's done."

His mother's face formed on the cube. She was lying on her back amid a meadow festooned with purple flowers. Her long dark hair haloed her head. The wind stirred her clothes, caused the flowers to sway.

Brennus recognized the meadow. It was the same meadow where he had found her necklace, the same meadow from which Erevis Cale's love, Varra, pregnant with Cale's child, had disappeared.

His mother's pale face looked pained, but Brennus did not think the pain physical. Her breathing was rapid, too rapid.

Brennus found himself walking slowly toward the cube.

His mother reached out a hand, her arm visibly shaking.

Brennus felt as if he could almost reach out and touch her. His hand went up to take hers into his.

"Mother," he said softly, but her eyes were not on him. He was seeing an image of events that had occurred thousands of years before.

"Hold my hand, Rivalen," she said, her voice a whispered gasp. Brennus saw that her other hand held the necklace Brennus now held.

Rivalen's voice answered her, his voice from the time when he had been a young man, before he'd become a shade, before he'd become a god.

"We all die alone, mother."

She closed her eyes and wept. Tears fell down Brennus's cheeks in answer. He stood next to Rivalen, his hate a wall between them.

"Your father will learn of this," Mother said.

"No. This will be known only to us. And to Shar."

"And to me," Brennus said through clenched teeth, as he watched the scene.

She stared at where Rivalen must have been standing, then closed her eyes and inhaled deeply.

"What did you wish for, mother?" Rivalen asked.

When she opened her eyes, Brennus was pleased to see that the hurt in her eyes was gone, replaced by anger.

"To be the instrument of your downfall."

"Goodnight, mother. I answer to another mistress, now."

Rivalen removed his hand from the scrying cube and the image faded.

"No," Brennus said. "No." He put his hands on the cube, tried to reactivate it with his own power but it remained dark, a void, a hole. Tears streamed down his face but he did not care. "Show me the rest."

"You know the rest."

Brennus stared at the cube, his mother's face floating at the forefront of his memory.

"Bastard. You thrice-damned bastard. Why did you show me that?"

Rivalen, taller than Brennus by a head, stared down at him. "I thought it was time you saw what I was capable of."

"I always knew what you were capable of."

"I also thought it was time to remind you that my patience is not infinite."

"I'm going to kill you," Brennus said, wiping stupidly at his tears. "I'll find a way."

Rivalen put a hand on Brennus's shoulder. "Your bitterness is sweet to the Lady, Brennus."

Brennus slapped his brother's hand away. "Get out of here."

Rivalen turned away. "You see nothing, Brennus. You understand so little. I'm unmatched in power here on the Prime, but what use is my power?"

Brennus did not understand. The Lords of Shade had traveled the planes freely, always had. "You're bound here?"

Rivalen shook his head. His left fist clenched, a small gesture of frustration. "Not bound, no. Hunted. My power protects me here. But elsewhere . . . there are those who want what I possess."

Brennus's mind latched onto the import of the sentence. His brother feared someone, or something. Brennus could use that, perhaps. "The divinity you stole?"

Rivalen whirled on him, shadows swirling. "The divinity I *took*."

"You, and Erevis Cale, and Drasek Riven."

"Cale is gone. Mephistopheles holds his power now."

Comprehension dawned. "Mephistopheles wants your power. He's hunting you. He needs it for his war with Asmodeus."

Rivalen shrugged. "No matter. I can't safely leave this world, even as it marches to its inevitable end. I'll be the last living thing on this planet, Brennus, screaming into the void as everything dies."

"You'll be dead before that," Brennus said.

Rivalen smiled. "I could kill you easily." He snapped his fingers. "Like that. But I won't. At least, not yet. Do you know why?"

Brennus refused to respond, but Rivalen spoke as if he did.

"Because we're all already dead. And my bitterness, too, is sweet to the Lady."

"Wallow in it, then," Brennus spat. "Suffer with it."

The shadows gathered around Rivalen. "I will. And because I do, so will everyone else."

The darkness took him and Brennus stood alone in the scrying chamber. Sweat and shadows poured from his flesh. His heart thumped against his ribs. The homunculi emerged tentatively from the blanket of his cowl, exhaling audibly when they saw that Rivalen was gone.

"Lady was pretty," one of them said.

"Yes," Brennus said, turning back to the dark scrying cube where he had seen the image of his mother. He put his hand on the silver face of the cube, replaying the images in his mind, her words. They made him smile.

"You would have made her laugh," he said to the homunculi.

His mother had encouraged Brennus's skill with constructs and shaping magic. She'd always loved the little creatures and moving objects he'd create for her. His father, the Most High, had forced him to turn from the "frivolity" of shaping to the serious study of divination.

Something about the image Rivalen had shown him stuck in his mind, something odd.

"What did you wish for, mother?" Rivalen had asked her.

Realization struck. The meadow had been a magical place, perhaps powerful enough to grant wishes. Such places had existed in ancient Faerûn. Varra had vanished from the same meadow as undead shadows had closed in on her. Brennus had seen her curl up in the flowers, had seen a flash, had visited the meadow and found the flowers gone, as if consumed.

"Gods," he breathed, and shadows swirled around him in an angry storm.

Varra had wished herself away from there.

And the meadow had granted her wish.

"Where would she go?" he mused aloud. And then it struck him. "*When* would she go?"

Hope swelled in him, the antipode of Shar's despair. He hurried to his library to renew his search.

Rivalen rode the darkness back to Ordulin, back to his haunt among the cracked stones of the plaza. Upon arrival, his expanded consciousness took in every shadow in the maelstrom. The darkness was an extension of his mind and will. In the emptiness of the ruins he heard the voice of his goddess, who whispered dooms in his ears.

Wind gusted, tore at his cloak and hair. Forks of green lightning flashed again and again across the inky vault of the sky, dividing it into a shifting matrix of jagged angles, the bursts of light painting deeper shadows on the ruined landscape.

The hole of Shar's eye hung in the air before him, slowly rotating, imperceptibly expanding year by year, a void that would in time consume the world. Even Rivalen could not stare at it for long without feeling dizzy, nauseated. The hole took up space, but seemed apart from space, not a thing that existed but a thing that was the absence of existence.

Its depth seemed to go on forever, a hole that tunneled through the multiverse, a hole that would pull him and everything and everyone into its emptiness and stretch them across its length until all of existence was so thin that it simply ceased to be.

He felt her in there, Shar, or at least felt her essence. Her regard radiated out of the hole, like a poisonous annihilating cloud. The Shadowstorm had begun the Cycle of Night and heralded her arrival on Faerûn, and *The Leaves of One Night*, a singular tome sacred to Shar, held her here. Rivalen had recovered the tome from the ruins of the Shadowstorm. But she was trapped now, stuck in the middle of her incarnation.

Small pieces of *The Leaves of One Night*, tiny bits of parchment, whipped in the wind around the hole like wounded birds, orbiting it the way the Tears orbited Selûne, darting in and out of the void, as if Shar were reading them page by page.

But she wasn't reading them. She was writing them, writing them for Rivalen, so that he could read them and finish the Cycle of Night.

"Write the story," he whispered to himself.

Once, long ago, he'd possessed *The Leaves of One Night*. He had tried to read it and found the pages empty. He'd heard voices upon touching the book, true, but he'd been unable to understand them. The words, like the pages, had been meaningless, empty. He'd thought the emptiness of the pages and the raving of the voices profound, meaningful somehow. How wrong he'd been. They'd merely been incomplete. They'd merely been waiting.

He watched them flutter around Shar's eye, moths to the flame of her spite. He could see the black ink on the pages, characters, words, but the language was nothing he'd ever seen before. He needed a mortal filter to translate it, a despairing soul to serve as the lens. And that mortal filter would suffer in the process.

He intended to use Brennus. He'd lied when he said he hadn't killed his brother because they were already dead. He hadn't killed Brennus because he needed him, and because Brennus was not yet ripe for picking. The bitterness in his brother grew with each passing year, a tumor in Brennus's soul. Rivalen had heightened it by showing Brennus the murder of their mother.

Rivalen would read the book's words through the lens of his brother's bitterness and despair.

The thought made Rivalen smile. Shadows whirled around him.

The Leaves of One Night were said to articulate Shar's moment of greatest triumph—a ritual that would destroy a world—but also to suggest her moment of greatest weakness.

Of that Rivalen was doubtful.

He longed to read the book. He desired an end. He was tired; he existed only to complete the Cycle of Night, only to end Toril. And when that was done, either his goddess would reward him after death or he would pass into nothingness. Both appealed to him more than the state in which he currently existed.

Both Shar and Rivalen were aware that the powerful were moving in Toril. They knew that the gods and their Chosen were plotting, that something was happening with the overlapping worlds of Abeir and Toril. Wars were being fought all across Faerûn, the Silver Marches, the Dalelands. Rivalen understood those events no better than anyone, but he didn't need to, because he knew that all of it was for nothing. When he succeeded, the gods, their Chosen, and everyone else would precede him into the void, and then he would follow them to his own end.

Distantly, numbly, he admired Shar's ability to turn what had been his zeal to preserve himself into a zeal to end himself. When he'd first turned to her worship, when he'd murdered his mother to seal his oath to Shar, he'd done so, strangely, with a sense of hope. He'd recognized even then that everything must one day end, that Shar would have her eventual victory, but he'd thought that worshiping her would allow him to extend that day far into the future and that in the meanwhile he'd have power to make the world as he wished it.

How she must have laughed at his naiveté. How she must have laughed hundreds of times, thousands of times on other worlds, with other nightseers, whose worship started in hope and ended in nihilism and annihilation

"My bitterness is sweet to the Lady," he whispered.

Lightning split the sky. Darkness reigned. Shar's eye looked out on the world in hunger.

CHAPTER FIVE

Vasen stood toward the rear of the abbey's northern courtyard, near a columned gate, arms crossed over his chest. A mail shirt and breastplate sheathed him under his traveling cloak. Sword and dagger hung from his weapon belt. His pack, stuffed full with the supplies he'd need for the journey, as well as some extra for needy pilgrims, lay on the ground near his feet. His most important possession, the rose holy symbol given him by the Oracle, the symbol that had belonged to Dawnlord Abelar, hung from a lanyard around his throat.

The air smelled damp, rife with the promise of autumn's coming decay. Distant thunder rumbled in the black, starless sky, vibrating the earth under his feet, threatening to drop rain on the open-air courtyard. The gathered pilgrims did not seem to mind. At the moment, they did not see the darkness. They were, instead, awaiting the light. They had their backs to Vasen—young and old, thin and fat, tall and short—facing the high balcony that jutted from the side of the abbey's sanctum, where the Oracle would soon appear.

Cracked, age-pitted flagstones paved the courtyard, trod underfoot for decades by groups of pilgrims just like those who stood upon them now. The stones in the center of the courtyard had been inlaid with colored quartz to form a sunburst pattern, a symbol of Amaunator's light, defiant in the face of the perpetual darkness. None of the pilgrims stood upon the sunburst. Instead they surrounded it, orbiting it in faith.

Roses of gray stone, petrified by the passage of the Spellplague's blue fire a hundred years earlier, bordered the courtyard on three sides. They had been red and yellow once—or so Vasen had heard—but now they, like the sky, were forever gray, their forms eternally fixed, unchanging, bound forever to the valley.

Like Vasen.

Vasen felt eyes on him and turned. Orsin stood beside him, a larger pack than even Vasen's slung over his shoulders. Vasen had not heard him approach. The man's quiet was disconcerting, as was his gaze, with his eyes like opals, as if he were not man or even deva but some kind of construct.

"You move with less sound than a field mouse," Vasen whispered to him.

The corners of Orsin's mouth rose slightly in a smile. "Old habits." He cleared his throat. "Is it acceptable if I remain?"

"What do you mean?"

"Since I'm not of the faith," Orsin explained. "I'd understand if you wanted me to wait outside the courtyard and—"

Vasen shook his head. "No, no, stay. The Oracle's light won't diminish in the presence of your Mask-shadowed soul."

Orsin grinned and lowered his pack to the ground. "Nor your shadowed flesh."

"Indeed," Vasen said, and smiled. "Is this also ground you stood upon in another life?"

He meant the words as jest, but Orsin seemed to take them seriously, and glanced around.

"Not this particular ground, no. But I've stood on the ground to your right hand before."

Shadows leaked from Vasen's hands. "A joke, yes?"

Orsin smiled and nodded. "A joke, yes."

"You're more than a little strange."

Orsin clasped his hands behind his back. "Well, then, quite a pair are we."

Vasen chuckled. "Quite a pair."

For a time they stood beside one another in silence. Vasen admitted that Orsin at his side felt *right*, and the feeling struck him oddly. He had no one in his life he'd call friend, never had. Comrade, yes. Trusted ally, brother in faith, these he had in abundance. But a friend? He had none. His blood, the shadows that clung to him, set him apart from everyone else.

Except Orsin. And while they weren't exactly friends, he certainly felt . . . comfortable with the deva.

A distant chime rang from somewhere within the abbey and its sound cut through the murmur of the pilgrims. They fell silent as the chime sounded ten times, a ring for each hour of daylight at that time of year.

"Dawn follows night and chases the darkness," Vasen whispered.

The chiming ended and the pilgrims shifted as one, their collective movement an expectant assurance over the cobblestones. They inhaled audibly as the Oracle emerged from an archway, his hand on his dog, Browny, and stood on the second-floor balcony overlooking the courtyard.

"The Oracle," one of the pilgrims whispered.

"Look at his eyes," said another.

Kindled by Amaunator's touch, the Oracle's eyes glowed orange in the dim light. His colorful robes seemed illuminated from within, a stark contrast with the dull gray of the day. He seemed more real than the world, too bright for Sembia's drab air, a portion of the sun come to earth. Age lines seamed his clean-shaven face, crevasses in his flesh. His platinum holy symbol hung from a thong around his neck—a rose in a sunburst.

Vasen's hand went to the symbol he wore, a rose, the symbol of Amaunator in his morning guise of Lathander. It felt warm to the touch, sun-kissed.

The Oracle patted Browny, and the magical dog lay on the balcony beside his master. Putting his hands on the balustrade, the Oracle stared down at the assembled pilgrims. Vasen imagined him seeing not the world but the possibilities of the world. A smile pulled the Oracle's lips from his rotted teeth and he raised his hands. Heads bowed, including Vasen's, including Orsin's, and a reverent hush fell.

"His light keep you," the Oracle said, his voice forceful, portentous.

As one the pilgrims and Vasen looked up and recited the ritual answer. "And warm you, Oracle."

The presence of so many faithful warmed Vasen's heart, as it always did. It pleased him that, for the moment, at least, no shadows leaked from his skin.

"You braved the journey to this abbey to see the light that lives in the darkness."

"Yes, Oracle," the pilgrims answered.

"You need not have come. The light lives not here but in each of you. We are all but humble servants to the Dawnfather."

Smiles around, murmured thanks, nodded heads.

"I hope that the time you spent here, although brief, has kindled a blaze in your heart."

More nods and murmured assent.

"Carry that with you always as the world changes around you. The path ahead is fraught for all of Toril. Be a light to others, a torch in the deep that shows the way. Will you do this?"

A resounding shout. "We will!"

The Oracle nodded. "I have met with each of you, seen for each of you."

Orsin shifted his feet at that and Vasen didn't miss it. The Oracle continued:

"I know you all would have preferred to remain longer. But it is important now that you return to the lands of the sun, before the war in the Dales, a war that has already cost many of you a great deal, makes it impossible to get you safely through. Go forth with his light and warmth upon you. Be a light to a world in which war and darkness threaten."

"Bless you, Oracle," said many.

"Thank you, Oracle," said others.

"The light is in him," said another.

And with that, the Oracle backed away from the balustrade. Browny stood and came to his side. The Oracle placed his hand on the large canine's shoulder and the two of them moved off into the abbey.

The moment he removed himself from view, the pilgrims turned to one another smiling, laughing, embracing, alight with the Oracle's blessing. Vasen turned to Orsin.

"You seemed affected by his words when he mentioned a seeing. Did he see for you?"

"He did," Orsin said. "The first day I was here."

Vasen was mildly incredulous. "The first day? But you're not . . ."

"Among the faithful? Very good. He knew that."

Vasen had never heard of the Oracle performing a seeing for someone not of the faith. "Then what did he—" He stopped himself mid-question. "Forgive me. His words are for you alone. I was just . . . surprised to hear this."

Orsin wore a peculiar expression, a half smile, perhaps. "As was I. And I'll tell you what he told me, if you wish."

Vasen stared at Orsin but said nothing.

"He told me to walk in the woods of the valley this day, and to do so exactly where we met."

Shadows curled out of Vasen's skin. His eyes went to the balcony, now empty. "That's what he told you?"

Orsin nodded. "He wanted us to meet, I presume."

Vasen nodded absently, puzzled.

"When do we leave?" Orsin asked.

"Right now," Vasen said. He stepped forward and called for the pilgrims' attention.

Faces turned toward him and he watched their expressions fall. They'd gone from looking upon the face of the Oracle, lit with Amaunator's light, to looking upon Vasen, with his dusky skin and yellow eyes.

"The Oracle has spoken. Today is the most auspicious time for us to leave."

Resigned faces, nods.

"I'll lead the squad of Dawnswords that will take you back to your homes."

Shadows leaked from his skin, wisps of night that diffused into the dusky air.

More nods.

"I didn't lead you here, but I'll lead you back. I've made this passage many times. The rules are the same going out as they were coming in. Stay close together. You experienced the pass coming in and know how easy it would be to get lost there. Don't heed the voices of the spirits. They won't harm you. Once we've cleared the mountains, make little noise. The aberrations of the plains are attracted to sound. As we near the Dalelands, we'll have to watch carefully for Sembian troops. We know ways to get through. Fear not."

The import of his words caused the pilgrims' expressions to cloud. He saw fear settling on them, watched it fill the lonely places in their spirit that their courage had left vacant. They'd always known in theory what it would mean to once more dare the dark of the Sembian plains and run the gauntlet of an ongoing war, but the reality of it, its immediacy after only ten days in the valley, was hitting them now.

Vasen continued, his tone even. "Be aware of your surroundings. You're all eyes and ears until we see the sun. Signal to me or another Dawnsword if you notice anything that causes you alarm. Anything. And if I or another member of my squad gives you an instruction, follow it without question or delay. Your life and ours may depend on it. Do you understand?"

Nods all around, murmured assent.

The youngest of the pilgrims, a boy of ten or eleven, took hold of his mother's hand, fear in his wide eyes. She absently mussed his hair, her own gaze distant, haunted. An elderly gray-haired woman, so thin she looked like a bag of dry sticks, smiled crookedly at Vasen.

He winked at her, smiled. "I'll die to keep you safe. My oath on that. Now, gear up. Your packs are already prepared and await you in your quarters. We leave within the hour."

"Only an hour?" someone asked.

"The Oracle has spoken," Vasen said, and that was that.

The pilgrims filed past him as they returned to their quarters to gather their packs. Several touched his shoulder or offered him a thankful gaze. He smiled in return, nodded.

After they'd all gone, Orsin grinned and said, "Your words didn't brighten them quite so much as the Oracle's."

"My work isn't to brighten their spirits, but to keep them, and you, alive."

Orsin shouldered on his pack. "Very good. I guess we'll soon know how well you do your job."

Gerak approached the campsite in a half hunch, an arrow nocked, senses primed. The ground all around showed pits from the creature's heavy tread. The creature had flattened his tent, tore the tarp, scattered the logs from the fire. Fitful streams of smoke leaked from the spread embers. With almost no light to work by, Gerak fumbled through the mess of the campsite and sought his cloak. He found a shred of it stomped into the muck, another shred elsewhere, and his heart fell. The creature had torn it to bits and trod it underfoot. He found a few more bits of it but not the part with the pocket, not the part with the locket.

He sank to the ground near the remains of the fire, put his hands on his knees, and tried to figure out how he'd tell Elle about losing it.

"So much for good luck," he muttered.

He'd spend the night hungry and cold. He never should have ventured out of Fairelm. Instead, he should have packed up with Elle, left the damned village, and headed for the Dales.

He felt the vibrations in the ground at the same time the creature's roar split the night. Adrenaline had him on his feet in a heartbeat, an arrow nocked and drawn. The creature barreled out of the darkness, all flabby bulk and sour stink and ear-splitting roars. He fired, and the whistle of his arrow was answered with a satisfying *thunk* and pained shriek as it sank to the fletching in the creature's flesh.

But the bulk kept coming. Gerak backstepped, dropping his bow and trying to draw his sword, stumbling on the broken, muddy earth. His boot stuck in the muck, tripped him up. He fell onto his back as he pulled his blade free.

The creature rushed him, snarling, slobbering, arms outstretched, clawed fingers reaching for him. Shouting with fear, he stabbed his blade at its midsection as one of its hands slammed into the side of his head.

Pain. Sparks exploding before his eyes. He flashed on the creature devouring the pheasants, bones and feathers and all, and imagined himself consumed entirely, clothes and bones and flesh.

Instinct and adrenaline kept his hand around the hilt of his blade even as his body went numb and the creature's bulk fell atop him and drove him a hand span into the soft earth, a grave of his own making. His breath went out of him in a *whoosh*. The creature spasmed atop him, a mountain of stinking flesh, its bulk crushing him. A huge hand closed over his face and shoved his head into the sodden ground. Water from the saturated earth got into his eyes, nose, his mouth. Panic seized him as he inhaled water. Desperate, terrified, he stabbed and stabbed with his blade. Distantly he was aware of warmth, the pained snarls of the creature, its shifting bulk atop his body. He couldn't breathe. More sparks, his field of vision fading to black. He was failing, dying. He blacked out for a moment; he didn't know how long, but when sense returned he realized that the creature was no longer moving.

He'd killed it?

He was too exhausted and pained to feel much relief. Its stink filled his nostrils; its weight made it hard to breathe. He was face to face with its bloated countenance. Its eyes were open, thick black tongue lolling from its mouth. The brown eyes gave Gerak a start.

They looked entirely human, almost childlike.

Squirming to the side, he maneuvered himself from under the creature and stood, covered in mud, blood, and stink. He stared down at the creature's bulbous form, the folds of flesh, the network of burst veins on the surface of the skin. The tip of his sword stuck out of its back.

With a grunt, he rolled the creature over so he could retrieve the blade. The rags it wore were the muddy, torn remains of a homespun and trousers. He pulled his blade free, wincing at the stink it freed. He remembered the lanyard he'd seen, and used his blade to lift a fold of flesh at the creature's neck.

Hung from the lanyard was a charm, a dirty cube of amber.

At first his mind refused to draw the conclusion. He stood perfectly still, eyeing the charm, the clothes, insisting that it wasn't what he thought it was.

But it was. He knew the charm. It had belonged to a little girl from Fairelm, Lahni Rabb.

But her family had left Fairelm days earlier. Had it killed her and taken the charm? Or . . . ?

He stared at the creature. Its hair. The brown, childlike eyes. The torn homespun.

The reality hit him and he vomited into the grass until his stomach had nothing left to give. He sagged to the ground.

"Lahni," he said. It seemed obscene to connect her name to the bloated, twisted form before him, but it was her. He was sure of it. And he'd killed her. Some magic or curse had changed her into something awful and then he'd killed her.

"Gods, gods, gods," he said.

He tried not to think about what might have happened to the rest of her family.

Sickened, he cast his blade away and kneeled beside her— the tiny, waifish young girl he could still picture running and laughing in the village commons. He reached out a hand but did not touch her.

"I'm so sorry, Lahni."

What could have done this to her?

Thunder sounded. A trickle of rain started to fall.

He sat there for a long while, engulfed in night, wrapped in a sense of grief not just for Lahni and her family but for himself and Elle and the baby, for all of Sembia. The land itself was corrupted by darkness. He had to get out, get Elle out, but he could not just leave Lahni there. He had to do something with her body, burn it. It was the least he could do.

He found his wood axe amid the scattered debris of the camp, split some dead broadleaf limbs he found nearby, and started to build a pyre around Lahni's body. He took her by the wrists to move her a bit and get some of the logs under her. As he did he realized that she was holding something in her closed hand.

He uncoiled Lahni's swollen, misshapen fingers, already stiffening in death, to reveal Elle's locket—a bronze sun. Of all the things in the campsite, she'd taken Elle's locket. He remembered once, long ago, Lahni telling Elle how beautiful the locket was. Elle had mussed her hair, thanked her, and Lahni had run off.

Emotion bubbled up in Gerak, raw, bitter, and he couldn't swallow it back down. He wept as he worked, and in time had built a serviceable pyre. A pyre for an adolescent girl that Sembia had turned into a monster. He gently placed Elle's locket back in her hand.

"I'm sorry," he said to her again, and worked on the kindling. When it took, he tended the logs until the fire was going strong. He thought he should say something, a prayer, but he could not manage one.

"The gods damn this place," he said softly, as the flames darkened Lahni's bloated body. "The gods damn it all."

He watched for a while, until he was sure it was going, then gathered what he could find of his gear and headed back out. He had to get back to Fairelm and get Elle away.

He walked with his bow in one hand, his sword in the other. He had no intention of stopping, and he put leagues behind him before exhaustion made his vision blurry and caused him to stumble. Still he pressed on. His purpose compelled him, a fishhook of fear set deep in his guts, pulling him back to Fairelm and Elle.

After two hours, he was blinking so much with fatigue that he could hardly see. His legs felt as if they were made of lead, slabs of meat attached to him at the hip. He stumbled, fell, crawled, and finally collapsed. He attempted to stand but couldn't. His face hit the wet ground. His strength went out of him, drained away into the ground. Shivering with cold and exertion, he decided he'd rest for just a moment. Just a moment . . .

Rain fell as the pilgrims gathered on the high rise that over-looked the valley. They stood in a huddled, sodden, miserable mass, hoods pulled over their heads. All but Orsin. He stood apart from the others, dressed only in his tunic, trousers, tattoos, and boots. The rain seemed not to bother him. The pilgrims gave him a wide berth. He was not one of them, and they must have sensed it.

The deva caught Vasen's gaze, nodded.

The pilgrims stared down at the valley, its towering pines backed by the teeth of the mountains, the vein of the river, the pitted stone walls of the abbey nestled among the greenery. Not for the first time, Vasen wondered what the valley would look like bathed in sunlight. He imagined the river flecked with silver, the bits of mica in the walls of the abbey glittering like jewels, the snow caps of the mountains shining like lanterns. It saddened him that the valley would never see unadulterated sunlight. He vowed to himself that when he saw the pilgrims to the Dales, out from under the Shadovar's shroud, he would allow himself a few hours of sunlight before returning to the darkness.

"Your thoughts wander, First Blade," said Byrne, standing beside him.

Vasen turned to look into Byrne's heavy lidded eyes, over-hung by thick brows. A jagged scar marked Byrne's temple. Vasen sighed.

"My thoughts seem to do that a lot of late."

"It's the time of year," Byrne said, gesturing at the sky with a gloved hand. "Winter approaches. The mind wanders in hopes of finding spring. But soon we'll see the sun."

"We will," Vasen said with a firm nod. "The pilgrims are ready? You've done a head count?"

Byrne nodded, his conical helm falling over his eyes. He seated it more snugly on his head and said, "Twenty-three, plus the four of us."

The four of them. Four servants of Amaunator would lead the faithful through the Shadovar's perpetual night. Eldris, Nald, Byrne, and Vasen, the first blade. Veterans all, good men. Each of them knew the markers to follow across the plains to the Dales, to safety, to the sun.

"Take position, then," Vasen said to Byrne. "A prayer, and then we move."

"Aye."

Vasen pulled his long hair back into a horse's tail and secured it while Byrne, Eldris, and Nald took position around the pilgrims, shepherds ringing their flock. When they were ready, Vasen ran his hand over his beard and addressed the pilgrims. He saw the fear in their eyes and did what he could to dispel it.

He drew his blade and held it high. Byrne, Nald, and Eldris did the same. Shadows snaked from Vasen's flesh, spiraled around his forearm and hand, but he channeled the power of the Dawnfather, and his blade glowed with a bright, rosy hue. It fell on the pilgrims, on the Dawnswords, its power steeling their spirits, amplifying their hopes, even while painting their shadows on the ground. Vasen felt both the warmth of the light and presence of the shadows. The glow elevated the pilgrims' expressions. Many made the sign of the rising sun and bowed their heads.

"We walk now into darkness on a journey toward the sun," Vasen said. "A common faith binds us, a common purpose. We are each warmed by the light that's in our fellows. In faith we'll hold the darkness at bay. His light keep us."

"And warm us," the pilgrims answered.

Vasen and the Dawnswords lowered their blades, the glow faded, and Sembia's darkness once more crept close. Everyone awaited Vasen's order to begin. Before giving it, he turned and called Orsin to his side.

The other Dawnswords eyed him strangely, but Vasen did not care.

"Vasen?"

Vasen raised his eyebrows, nodded at the ground, at Orsin's staff.

"Lines signify new beginnings, you said. Maybe draw one?"

Orsin smiled. "Very good. Very good, indeed." He dragged a line in the mud.

"We go," Vasen called, and the column moved, crossing the border Orsin had drawn.

The sky relieved itself in a drizzle as they walked the labyrinthine pass, navigating its switchbacks, its hidden paths, its deadfalls. Orsin hovered near the front of the column, near Vasen. The other Dawnswords assisted those who stumbled or bore the packs of those who sagged under the weight.

The air thickened with moisture as they moved. Mist gathered around their feet, rose to their knees. Ahead, a wall of swirling gray, within which lived the spirits of the pass. Vasen did not understand what the spirits were. He only knew they had been harvested from elsewhere by the blue fire of the Spellplague and deposited in the pass. Perhaps they couldn't leave. Perhaps they didn't wish to. They seemed to answer to the Oracle in some way that Vasen did not comprehend. They let Dawnswords and pilgrims pass unmolested. Others, they led astray. From time to time through the years, the Dawnswords had found errant wanderers in this or that switchback, dead for lack of food or water, their eyes wide with fear.

The mist swirled around him as they neared the fog, climbed up his thighs. His flesh answered with shadows. Muttering filled his ears, whispers, a meaningless chatter that threatened to cloud his thinking.

He touched the holy symbol at his throat, uttered a prayer, drew upon Amaunator's power, and channeled it into his shield. Energy charged the metal and wood. It began to glow with light, grew warm in his grasp. The voices in his head fell back to distant whispers.

Behind him, Nald, Eldris, and Byrne did the same, and soon Amaunator's light hedged the pilgrims.

"Stay within the glow," Vasen said. "It will be as it was when you came through the first time. You'll hear the spirits, perhaps even see them, but heed nothing. They won't harm you directly, but if you wander in the pass, it will be hard to find you again. We won't stop until we're through. Hold hands with the person nearest you. If one of you stumbles or cannot keep up, shout for aid immediately."

Grunts and murmurs of assent answered his words. A child whimpered. A cough, cleared throat.

Vasen led them into the wall of the fog and it enveloped him immediately, deadened sound, attenuated his connection to the world, to himself. He felt cocooned in it. Even with the light from his shield he could see only a few paces. But he'd known what to expect, so he kept his wits.

"Stay together," he called over his shoulder.

Behind him he heard the footsteps of the pilgrims, the soft crunch of sandal and boot on rock, but the sound seemed distant, and he seemed separated from them by more than mist. The reflected light of his shield glowed white on the whorls and eddies of the mist. He sought the markers as he moved, boulders with glowing sigils etched into the base. He found the first, the glowing rose of Amaunator's dawn incarnation scribed into the stone.

"We're at the first marker," he said. "Nald? Byrne? Eldris?"

"With you," they all answered.

Two more markers and they'd be clear, the way etched into Vasen's memory as clearly as the markers were etched into rock.

In the churn of the mist he saw ghostly faces outlined, mouths open and full of secrets, eyes that were holes into which one could fall forever. Whispering from all around him, the sound like the hiss of falling rain, the words hard to distinguish, an eerie sibilance.

A bearded face before him, mouth open in a scream.

A woman's visage to his left, eyes wide with terror.

A child's gaze, forlorn, lost.

He kept his mind focused, his feet on the path, same as always.

Snippets of phrases rose out of the inchoate storm of whispers.

"The City of Silver," said a man's voice.

"Elgrin Fau," hissed a woman.

Vasen ignored them, as he had countless times before.

"You must free him," said a boy's voice.

"You're the heir. Write the story."

The words halted Vasen in his steps. They recalled to his mind the dreams he'd had of his father, the words of the Oracle.

"Byrne?" he called. "Nald?"

No response. Had he gotten separated? Had he lost his charges?

"Eldris?"

He turned a circle, realizing immediately that he'd made a mistake. The mist had scrambled his senses. Dizziness seized him. The world spun and he stumbled on a boulder, nearly fell. The light from his shield dimmed. Shadows poured from his flesh, mixed with the mist. He put his hand on the holy symbol at his throat, held onto it as if his life depended upon never letting go.

The whispers intensified. The mist closed in on him, a funereal shroud. He muttered a prayer, tried to drown them out, but they grew closer, louder, a rush in his ears, the cascades of the valley falling all around him in a foam of voices.

"Save him," said a deep voice.

"You must."

"Save him. Then write the story."

"Save who?" he shouted, but he already knew the answer.

The air around him grew cold, freezing, knives on his flesh. His teeth chattered. He tried to speak, to call for his comrades, but frost rimed his lips and prevented speech. The wind picked up, pawed at his cloak with frozen fingers. The whispers of the spirits gave way to screams, prolonged wails of agony. He smelled brimstone, the stink of burning flesh.

"What is happening?" he tried to shout, but no words emerged, just a croak and a cloud of frozen breath.

The mist parted before him to reveal distant mountains larger than any he'd ever seen, jagged ice-covered towers that reached to a glowing red sky. Smoke poured into the sky in thick columns. He stood on a precipice overlooking a plain of ice. Below, he saw a mound of ice, like a cairn, alone in a flat frozen plain. Shadows curled out of cracks in the mound. A river of fire cut through the plain, veins of red in which, in which . . .

"By the light," he whispered, and sweated darkness.

Souls burned in the river, their screams rising into the air with the smoke. Towering insectoid devils stabbed at them with long polearms, lifted them from the fire like speared fish.

"Cania," a deep, powerful voice said to his right.

He turned but saw no one.

"Is that where he is?" Vasen called. "In Hell? Tell me!"

No answer. He turned back to look upon the horror once more, but the vision of Cania, of Hell, had faded. Warmth returned, as did the mist, as did the dizziness, the whispers.

"Save him," said another voice. "He is cold."

Vasen stumbled on legs gone weak, but before he fell a hand closed on his shoulder and pulled him roughly around. He brought his shield to bear, readied his blade.

But it was Orsin. Orsin had pulled him around.

"You wander," the deva said. "Are you unwell?"

"No. Yes. They showed me things, Orsin. Horrible things."

Orsin's pupilless eyes fixed on Vasen, the pale orbs strangely analogous to the mist. Worry lines in his brow creased the lines of ink on his flesh.

"I've seen nothing," he said. "But I hear them. They whisper of Elgrin Fau, the City of Silver. They speak of your father. It was not so when I journeyed through the mist on my way to the temple. Then I heard only jabberings."

"It's never been so," Vasen said, his thoughts clearing. "And what's the City of Silver? And how could they know of my father?"

Orsin looked around as if he could decode an answer from the swirl of the mist, from the malformed faces staring out of the gray at them. "I don't know. Maybe something has changed?"

Vasen held onto the deva like a lifeline. "Changed. Aye."

Orsin patted Vasen on the shoulder. "We'll speak more of this when we clear the mist."

Orsin's words moored Vasen, reminded him of his duty. He shook his head to clear it, called out. "Eldris? Byrne? Nald? Speak!"

One after another they called out, their voices not far from him.

"And the pilgrims?" Vasen called, his voice hollow in the mist.

"Accounted for," answered Byrne.

"All is well," Orsin said. "It was you we worried after. You spoke strangely and walked off."

"And you followed? You could have been lost."

Orsin pulled back, showed Vasen his quarterstaff, scribed with lines, his flesh, made into a map from the tattoos that covered him. He smiled. "I seldom lose my path, Vasen."

Despite himself, Vasen smiled. "No, I suppose not. You have my thanks. Come on. Let's get everyone clear of here."

Rather than walking a few paces behind, Orsin walked beside Vasen, to his right, and Vasen welcomed his presence. The spirits receded to silence, as if they'd had their say, and the column had only to manage the fog and switchbacks as they journeyed through the pass.

"This is a maze," Orsin said.

"A challenge to even those who seldom lose their path, not so?"

Orsin chuckled. "Very good."

"The pass has kept the abbey safe for a century. When he was only a boy born dumb, the Oracle entered his first seeing trance and led the survivors of the Battle of Sakkors through the pass."

"Sakkors," Orsin said. "Where Kesson Rel fell."

"Yes," Vasen said, and shadows leaked from his skin.

A whisper went through the spirits of the mist.

"He fell to your father and Drasek Riven and a Shadovar, Rivalen Tanthul," Orsin said.

"He fell, too, to the light of the servants of Amaunator. Among them my adoptive father's sire, Regg, and Abelar Corrinthal, the Oracle's father."

"Shadow and light working as one," Orsin said.

"Yes," Vasen said, and eyed Orsin sidelong. The deva's hand was over the holy symbol he wore under his tunic. Vasen continued, "And when the survivors reached the valley, the Oracle pronounced it the place where light would thrive in darkness. The abbey was built over the next decade and there it has stood since."

"I hear your pride in the accomplishment."

"The Order does Amaunator's work here. Good work. I'm privileged to serve."

"I don't doubt it," Orsin said. He walked in silence for a time, then said, "I'm pleased our paths crossed, Vasen."

"I share the sentiment. Although our meeting appears to have been no accident."

"No," Orsin agreed. "No accident."

They said nothing more as they led the pilgrims out of the pass. As the mist thinned and finally parted, the dark sky spit a heavier rain.

CHAPTER SIX

VASEN LED THE PILGRIMS DOWN TOWARD THE ROCKY FOOT-hills of the Thunder Peaks. He stopped them there. Beyond the hills stretched the Sembian plains, a vast expanse of whipgrass dotted with large and small stands of broadleaf trees and pines. Occasional elms and maples, the giants of the plains, loomed like protective parents over the smaller trees. The bleak Sembian sky merged into the dark of the plains at the horizon line, the one blurring into the other. All was darkness and rain.

Vasen scanned the sky for any sign of a Shadovar patrol. The floating city of Sakkors had not been seen so far north in a long while, but Vasen would take no chances with pilgrims in his charge. Now and again the Dawnswords had seen airborne Shadovar patrols, two or three soldiers mounted on the flying, scaled worms they called veserabs, but even those had grown uncommon. Vasen suspected the Shadovar had diverted the bulk of their forces toward Cormyr and the Dales. The Dawnswords scouted the area around the Thunder Peaks and knew a Sembian force was encamped on the plains south and west, blocking the passage between the southern Thunder Peaks and the sea. Probably to hold any forces from Cormyr that might otherwise try to aid the Dales, which had already endured months of attacks by Sembian forces.

"Hurry now," he called to his men, the pilgrims. "We're exposed in the foothills. We have to reach the plains as rapidly as possible."

With the hale assisting the elderly or weak, the group moved quickly through the boulder-strewn hills. Vasen knew his mother had been found in the foothills, among a stand of pine, not far from the pass. Pines still dotted the hills, and each time he walked there, he felt connected to her. He wondered if the trees under which she'd been found still stood.

Soon the rocks and gravel surrendered to scrub and whip-grass. Vasen led the group to a stand of broadleaf trees he knew and they stood under it, fatigue in the eyes of the pilgrims.

"Rest a moment," he said. "Eat. We move quickly from here. The less time we spend on the open plains, the less likely we are to be spotted. We're three days from the Dales. Three days from the sun." He forced a smile. "That's not long, is it?"

"No," some said.

"Not long," said others.

The pilgrims pulled bread, cured mutton, and goat cheese from their packs. Orsin sat apart, cross-legged on his pack, eyes closed, hands on his knees. He seemed to be meditating or praying. Vasen, Nald, Eldris, and Byrne moved among the pilgrims as they ate, keeping spirits high.

"He's a strange one, yes?" Byrne said softly to Vasen, nodding at Orsin.

"He is. Of course, many say that of me."

To that, Byrne said nothing. Both of them knew it to be true.

"He's an honorable man, I think," Vasen said.

"He's not of the faith, though," Byrne said, and gave a harrumph.

"He's of *a* faith," Vasen said, and left Byrne to visit with the pilgrims, offering encouraging words and blessings to ease pain and warm spirits. Amaunator had gifted all of the Dawnswords with the ability to channel their faith into various miracles.

"How do you fare?" Vasen asked a heavyset woman of maybe forty winters. He thought her name was Elora. Her son sat beside her, a boy of perhaps ten. Vasen searched his memory for the boy's name—Noll.

"As well as I might in this rain."

"Do you need anything I can provide? You or Noll?"

"We're fine."

"Fine, goodsir," said the boy, around a mouthful of cheese.

"You hale from the Dales?" Vasen asked, to make small talk.

A shadow passed over Elora's face. "Archendale. Before the Sembian attack. Then Daggerdale."

Vasen could see loss in her face. Judging from the fact that she and Noll traveled alone, he could guess what.

"If there's anything I can do for you, sister," Vasen said, and touched her lightly. "You need only ask."

She recoiled slightly at his touch and he saw that his hand leaked shadows. He pretended not to notice her response, stood, and moved to walk away.

"Are you a . . . Shadovar?" Noll blurted at his back.

The question silenced the other pilgrims.

Vasen felt their eyes on him. A child had asked the question, but they were all thinking it. He turned, shadows leaking from his flesh.

Elora colored. "Noll!"

Her son spoke around a mouthful of cheese. "I didn't mean to be rude, momma."

Vasen produced a smile to reassure Noll. He'd heard the query often enough, and not always from children. With his dusky skin, long dark hair, and shining yellow eyes, he looked not unlike a Shadovar.

"I'm not," he said, and left it at that. "Be at ease."

"Then what are you?" asked Noll.

"Boy!" said the middle-aged man. "You go too far."

"Forgive the boy," another man said. "His mouth outruns his sense."

"There's nothing to forgive," Vasen said, loudly enough for everyone to hear. "I'm a man, a servant of Amaunator and a follower of the light, the same as you." He smiled at Noll and winked. "I've found that to be quite enough to keep me busy."

Noll grinned in return, bits of food sticking to his teeth.

"Now gather your things, all of you," Vasen said. "Time to move."

Groans answered his proclamation, but the pilgrims did as he bade. As they gathered their things, Eldris walked to Vasen's side and put a hand on his shoulder.

"They meant nothing by it, First Blade."

"I know," Vasen said.

Soon they set off. Sticking to the route he'd traveled many times in the past, they made rapid progress. Always Vasen kept his eyes to the sky, watching for any sign of the Shadovar. His lineage allowed him to see in the darkness as if it were noon, so everyone relied on him to spot danger before they could.

The rain picked up after a few hours, the water of the downpour as brown as a turd and carrying the faint whiff of decay. He considered calling a halt but the pilgrims seemed to be holding up, even the old. Vasen saw that Noll had his face to the sky, his mouth open to drink.

Before Vasen could speak, Orsin tapped the boy on the shoulder. "Don't drink that or your pee will come out green."

The boy grinned.

"He's right," Vasen said, seriousness in his tone. He admonished himself for not telling the pilgrims not to drink the rain.

The boy colored, lowered his head, and grinned sheepishly.

Orsin offered Noll his own waterskin and the boy drank deeply.

Vasen nodded gratitude at Orsin, and said to the pilgrims, "Drink only from your waterskins. Rain like this can make you sick."

They murmured acquiescence. Elora cuffed Noll in the back of his head.

Orsin fell in beside Vasen.

"I should've told them before," Vasen said, shaking his head at his oversight. "Sometimes I assume they know what I know."

"No way to anticipate the boy would drink rain that smells like death."

"He must have drank all his water at the first break," Vasen said.

"Maybe," Orsin said. "Or he's just a boy drinking the rain because he's bored and that's as boys do."

"He didn't drink much," Vasen said, hoping Noll wouldn't get ill.

"He didn't," Orsin agreed. "And he's young."

The wet pasted the pilgrims' cloak hoods and hair to their scalps, their robes and cloaks to their bodies. They trudged through muck that pulled at their feet, stumbling often. But despite the rain and the bleak sky, they smiled often at each other. Each carried a symbol of their faith blessed by the Oracle—a wooden sunburst and rose—and most held it in hand as they trekked, heads down, prayers on their lips. Despite the rain and the black churn of the Sembian sky, the pilgrims held Amauntator's brightness in their spirit. Vasen found joy in their happiness, although he kept an eye on Noll. The boy seemed fine, if a little pale.

Byrne sat beside Vasen under a broadleaf tree while the pilgrims took another rest. As usual, Orsin sat apart from the rest of the pilgrims, with them, but not of them. The deva stared off into the rain with his peculiar eyes, maybe seeing things Vasen did not. Old lives, perhaps.

Byrne drank from his waterskin, offered it to Vasen.

"Word of the abbey and the Oracle is spreading," Byrne said, as Vasen drank. "The pilgrims speak of loose tongues in the Dales and beyond."

"That's always been a risk," Vasen said. "But no one knows even the general location of the abbey except those of the faith. And none of them could find their way back without us to guide them."

Byrne shook his head. "Still, too many know of us. The Oracle's on every tongue. He's sought by many. The war in the Dales is only making it worse."

Vasen pushed his wet hair out of his eyes. "Aye. The times are dark, Byrne. People crave light."

"Aye, that. But if loose tongues bring the Shadovar down on us while we have pilgrims," Byrne said. "Then what light shall we cast?"

Vasen stood, offered Byrne a hand, and pulled him to his feet. "That'll depend on how well we fight."

"There are only four of us here, First Blade."

"Five," called Orsin.

Byrne raised his eyebrows in surprise. "The man's ears are keen." He raised the waterskin in a show of respect. "Five it is, then. I'm called Byrne."

The deva stood, approached, and took Byrne's hand. "Orsin. And even with five we will need to fight very well, indeed, should we encounter Shadovar."

"Truth," Byrne said.

Vasen shouldered on his pack. "Let's hope we don't have to fight at all. Time to—"

A deep growl from somewhere out in the darkness of the plain pulled their eyes around. Vasen drew his blade. The pilgrims stared at one another, wide-eyed. They huddled close. A few of them drew eating knives, little use in a combat. Eldris and Nald stationed themselves before the pilgrims. Vasen, Byrne, and Orsin drifted a few steps toward the sound, ears primed, weapons drawn, all of them knowing the horrors the plains of Sembia could vomit forth.

The sound did not recur. Vasen called his men to him.

"Appear calm and unafraid," he said to them. "Eyes and ears sharp. And watch the boy, Noll. He drank more of the rain than I'd like. Let's move."

The group left the shelter of the pines and re-entered the stinking rain. All of the Dawnswords carried bared blades, and Vasen didn't breathe easy until they had put a league under their feet.

During the trek, Noll began to cough. At first Vasen told himself it was merely the ague, but hope faded as the coughing grew worse. Soon the boy hacked like an old man with wetlung. Vasen had never seen disease root so fast.

Noll stumbled as he walked. His mother, Elora, tried to help him.

"Assist them," Vasen ordered Eldris, and Eldris did, letting Noll lean on him as they walked.

"The rain has infected the boy," Orsin said.

Vasen nodded. "I'm worried. Illness from the rain is usually days in the making."

"Can he be helped?"

"Byrne," Vasen called, and nodded at Noll.

Byrne hurried to the boy's side and the group halted for a moment while the Dawnrider placed his holy symbol—a bronze sun—on Noll's forehead and invoked the power of the Dawnfather. Byrne's hands glowed with light, the holy symbol glowed, too, and Noll smiled and breathed easier. Byrne mussed his hair.

The reprieve lasted only a short while. Soon Noll was coughing again, worse than before.

"What's wrong with him?" Elora called. While Eldris sought to calm her, Byrne came to Vasen's side.

"The healing prayer did not rid him of the disease."

"No," Vasen said. Healing prayers could close wounds, even fix broken bones, but against disease they were useless. "If we can get out of this storm, I can see him healed."

Thunder growled in answer, the spite of the Shadovar's sky.

"I'll find shelter, then," Orsin said, and darted off into the darkness.

"Wait!" Vasen called, but the deva was already gone, one with the darkness and rain.

"What now?" Byrne asked.

Vasen eyed Noll. "We keep moving until we find shelter. Orsin will find us. He doesn't seem to get lost."

Another round of lightning veined the sky, celestial pyrotechnics that elicited a gasp from the pilgrims. A prolonged roll of thunder shook the earth. Soon the rain fell in blistering sheets, blocking even Vasen's vision. Vasen could not believe that the Oracle had deemed their departure time an auspicious moment. They'd walked into the worst storm Vasen could remember.

They pressed on because they had no choice, the Dawnswords shouting encouragement, scanning the terrain for shelter but seeing none. Noll lagged, stumbled, his coughing loud between the intervals of thunder. The boy would fail if they did not do something soon, and they were moving too slowly.

Vasen strode to the back of the column, where Eldris tried to keep Noll upright. Elora, her dark, curly hair pressed by the rain to her pale face, fretted over the boy. The rain failed to hide her tearful eyes.

"Can you not help him?" she said to Vasen, and took him by the hands. "Please, Dawnsword."

Vasen held her hands and spoke softly. "I hope so, but I need shelter to perform a more powerful ritual. I need a fire among other things, and no flame will hold in this downpour." He kneeled and looked the boy in the face. The wind whipped both of their cloaks hither and yon. Noll's eyes were bleary, his face wan.

"I'd like to carry you, Noll, but I can't do it all alone. Can you hold onto me?"

The boy's gaze focused on Vasen and he nodded.

Vasen shed his pack, shield, and sword as another round of lightning lit the plains.

"Come on!" shouted one of the pilgrims. "We'll be struck by a bolt standing here."

Eldris carried Vasen's gear and Vasen lifted Noll onto his back. The boy wrapped his arms around Vasen's neck, hooked his legs around Vasen's waist. Even through his armor Vasen could feel the heat of the boy's fever. He got a feel for the weight.

"Just hang on, Noll," Vasen said.

"You won't be able to carry him far," said Eldris.

"Far enough," said Vasen, and started off. To the pilgrims, he shouted, "Move! Faster now!"

The sky darkened further as night threatened and the storm strengthened, and still they'd found no suitable shelter and no Orsin. Lightning split the sky and bisected a twisted, long dead elm that stood a spear cast from the group. Wood splintered with a sharp crack and the two halves of the dead tree crashed to earth. The ruin spat flames for only a moment before the rain extinguished them.

"Where's a damned stand of living trees?" Vasen shouted, as another coughing fit wracked Noll. The boy's mother hovered near Vasen, fretting.

Vasen focused on putting one leg in front of the other. Shadows poured from his flesh. Noll was either past noticing them or didn't care. So, too, his grief-stricken mother. Fatigue threatened to give way to exhaustion in Vasen and still the rain did not relent.

Byrne drifted back to the rear of the column. "How do you fare?"

"Well enough. How fares the boy?"

Byrne checked the boy, returned his gaze to Vasen. "Not well."

Noll's mother wailed. "Not my boy. Not my sweet boy. I've already lost his father to the Sembian army. I can't lose him, too."

"Find someplace," Vasen said to Byrne. "Any place. We must try the ritual."

"There is nowhere, First Blade," Byrne answered.

A shout from the pilgrims drew their attention. Two of them were pointing off to the left, but the rain and darkness prevented Vasen from seeing anything. Lightning ripped the sky anew.

"There! There!"

Vasen saw. One hundred paces away, Orsin stood atop a rise, waving his staff over his head. Hope for Noll rose in Vasen.

"Light us up so he knows we saw him," Vasen said to Byrne.

Byrne nodded and uttered a prayer lost to the howl of the wind. His shield began to glow, the warm, rosy glow of

Amaunator's blessing. So lit, Byrne headed toward where they'd last seen Orsin.

"Hurry now, everyone," called Vasen. "Quickly. Quickly."

Sloshing through the sopping plains, the group followed Byrne toward Orsin, who came down from the rise to meet them. Thunder rolled.

"I've found a cave. It'll bear us all."

Vasen grabbed him by the cloak, leaned on him for strength. "How far?"

Orsin's eyes looked like moons in his face. "Less far the faster we move."

Vasen let him go, and all of them staggered through the storm. Fatigue and the weather made Vasen's vision blurry, but Orsin appeared to know exactly where he was going. They topped a rise, descended, found below a sizeable stream turned river by the storm, and followed it a ways. It cut a groove in the landscape, the banks falling steeply to its edge.

"Not far," Orsin said.

"Almost there!" Vasen shouted to the pilgrims. None responded. They just kept plodding forward.

Orsin pointed and Vasen saw it—a cave mouth in the riverbank on the opposite side of the stream. Orsin pulled Vasen close so he could hear.

"There's a ford ahead. Follow me."

Orsin led them to a narrower stretch of the rapidly flowing stream. He did not hesitate, stepping directly into the water.

"Make sure none are swept away," Vasen called to Byrne, Eldris, and Nald.

All nodded, and they, with Orsin, assisted the pilgrims across, carrying the frail and young on their backs. The water rose waist high at its deepest point. Flotsam spun past in little eddies, mostly fallen limbs and leaves. The current pulled at Vasen as he crossed. He moved slowly, methodically, taking care not to dislodge Noll. In time, all made it across, and they staggered into the cave. The relative quiet struck Vasen first. The rain had been a drumbeat on his hood.

Byrne placed his shield in the center of the cavern, prayed over it, and its rosy light painted their shadows on the walls— dark, distorted images of the real them.

The cave was ten paces wide and tunneled into the riverbank perhaps another twenty. Brown lichen clung to the cracked walls, oddly reminiscent of Orsin's tattoos. Smoke from old fires had stained the ceiling dark. At first the cave smelled faintly of mildew and rot, but the smell of the exhausted, sodden humans and their gear soon replaced one stink with another. Most of the pilgrims sagged to the floor around Byrne's shield, stripping off packs and wet clothes. Some wept. Others smiled and praised Amaunator for the shelter. Vasen had time for neither pity nor praises.

"I need wood for a fire," he said as he laid Noll down on the cave floor. "And bring me anything dry to cover him with."

The boy's face was as pale as a full moon. His eyes rolled back in his head. Heat poured off of him. Elora sat beside Noll, cradled her son's head in her lap, stroked his head. Coughs shook the boy's small frame. Black foam flecked his lips.

Several of the pilgrims brought dry blankets from the packs, and Vasen covered the boy with them. Byrne soon returned with several small tree limbs. Using his dagger, he rapidly stripped the sodden exterior from the logs to reveal dry wood. Nald set his shield on the floor, concave side up, and Byrne stacked the wood in it. Orsin tore a section of his tunic, shielded from the rain by his cloak, and shredded it for tinder. Flint dragged over a dagger sparked the tinder, and soon a small blaze burned in the bowl of Eldris's shield.

"What could have been in the rainwater to cause this?" Elora asked, her voice faint as Noll groaned. "What?"

Vasen shook his head as he stripped off his cloak. "Who can say? The Shadovar poison land and sky with their magic."

"It is cursed," Elora said, tears leaking from her eyes. "Sembia is cursed."

Vasen did not dispute it. He filled a tin cup from his pack with water from his waterskin and set it in the edge of the fire. Orsin nodded to him, backed away to stand among the flickering shadows on the wall.

While Vasen waited for the water to heat, he cleared his mind, stared into the fire, and began to pray softly. The pilgrims fell silent, watching. The sound of the rain outside fell away. Byrne, Eldris, and Nald soon joined him and formed a circle around the fire. Their voices fell in with his. Soon the pilgrims, too, joined. In a dark cave, in the midst of a black storm, the faithful of Amaunator raised collective voice in worship.

As the water warmed and then boiled, and without a break in his intonation, Vasen removed from his belt pouch a pebble taken from the river in the abbey's valley. He dropped it into the warm water while he, his fellow Dawnswords, and the pilgrims all continued their imprecation. The stone began to glow, a pale rosy light that diffused through the water. Vasen lifted the lanyard with his holy symbol from around his neck and lowered the rose into the glowing water while his prayers finalized the ritual. The glow intensified, the water shining brighter than the fire. For a moment, the rose looked not tarnished silver but red with life.

"It's ready," he said, and all fell silent except the thrum of the rain and the roll of distant thunder. He replaced his holy symbol over his neck and picked up the cup. Despite sitting in the heat of the fire, it was cool to the touch. He carried the glowing liquid to Noll, lifted the boy into a sitting position, and held the cup to his lips.

"You must drink," Vasen said.

Noll's bleary eyes sought focus and his hands fumbled for the cup. Vasen held it, too, wincing at the heat of the boy's flesh when their hands touched. Noll drank.

"All of it," Vasen said.

"Do it, sweet boy," said Elora.

Noll's head moved in what might have been a nod. A prolonged coughing spell prevented him from drinking for a time, but when it ended, he gulped what remained in the cup. Vasen lowered him to the ground, covered him with his blankets. The boy shivered, coughed more, the black foam still flecking his lips.

Vasen looked at Elora, her eyes stricken. "Now we must wait," he said.

She looked at her son, at Vasen. "I believe Amaunator will save him. I do."

Vasen touched her shoulder. "Your faith will help. Rest now. There's nothing more to be done."

She reached for his hand, did not blanch when shadows snaked from his skin to caress her flesh. "Thank you, Dawnsword. I'm sorry for . . . before."

Many pilgrims echoed her words or patted him on the back. Fatigue from carrying Noll, from carrying the pilgrims' hopes, settled on him. His legs felt like foreign things, detached from his body. He staggered and Orsin and Byrne were both there to steady him.

"You should eat," Orsin said.

"And rest," added Byrne.

"Rest first," Vasen said. "Watch the boy."

"Aye," said Byrne.

The rain had gotten through the flap of Vasen's pack, making his bedroll damp. He did not care. He did not bother to unroll it, just tucked it under his head along the wall and lay flat on his back on the cave floor, staring up at the smoke and shadow-stained ceiling, listening to the rain, the soft murmur of conversation. The pilgrims were talking about him, he knew.

Exhaustion overtook him in moments. The last thing he heard before falling asleep was the sound of Noll's coughing. For the first time in a long time, he did not dream of Erevis Cale.

Elden sat on his favorite chair in the sanctum of the abbey. He felt like a king on a throne, like the ones in stories. The others had made it his chair because he could see what they could not. He did not fully understand how he saw, but he did. And because he did, everyone treated him as if he were special. And maybe he was, although he didn't feel special.

He reached down to the floor beside his chair and felt for Browny's soft fur. The dog exhaled happily as Elden scratched his ears. The feel of fur under his fingers calmed Elden. He smiled when Browny licked his hand.

Pretty orange and pink and purple ribbons hung from the walls. Elden knew they were colors favored by Amaunator, the god of the abbey, but Elden liked them because they were pretty, because they reminded him of sunbeams.

He had not seen the sun in a long time. He missed it, but he'd long ago accepted that his life was a service to the light, even though he lived it in darkness. He did not understand exactly why, but he knew people came from all over to see him, because he could *see*. They looked so hopeful when they met him, lit with a light of their own. He liked that. He made them feel hope. And hope made *them* glow like the sun.

A tall bronze statue of Amaunator stood on the tiled floor in the center of the circular sanctum. The god had that same look of hope on his bearded face. He held a large, orange crystal globe in his open palm. It would have caught the light entering through the glass dome built into the ceiling, had there been any light to catch. But the sky remained as it ever was—dark, swirling with shadows. The dome in the ceiling, too, was a symbol of hope. Elden had hoped to see the unfiltered sun pour through it during his lifetime, but he doubted it now. Sometimes, if Elden asked, one of the priests would use magic to light the god's globe. He loved the globe when it was lit, shimmering, shiny. So shiny. It called to mind the spheres that jugglers used when entertaining children. Elden loved jugglers. He still carried a set of spheres that he'd been given as a boy, although it had been so long ago he could not remember who'd given them to him. A dark man, he thought. With only one eye.

That had been a good day.

But it had also been about the time that Papa had died. He had not seen it. Uncle Regg had told him about it afterward.

He stared at the statue, floating through memories a hundred years old and wondering why Amaunator had chosen him to see things. He had never asked to be gifted, had not even known such gifts to be possible. Soon after Papa had died, Elden had dreamed of a blazing sun, a sun no longer visible in the Sembian sky. He'd heard his father's voice in his head.

"Stare at the sun, Elden. And don't look away."

"It will blind me, Papa.

"I promise that it won't. It's all right."

So Elden had stared and had not looked away.

His eyes stung, though he hadn't been blinded. "It hurts, Papa."

"I know. I'm sorry, son. That's enough. Look away now. You were very brave."

"Where are you, Papa? Unka Regg said you died."

A long pause, then, "I did die, Elden. But it's all right. I'm all right."

Elden had not understood how Papa could be both dead and all right. Tears formed in his stinging eyes.

"Please come home, Papa. Me miss you."

"I am home, son. And you will be, too, one day. Listen to me now. When you awaken you will see things. Don't be afraid. Tell Regg and Jiriis and the others what you see. They'll listen to you and they'll know what to do. Be a light to them."

Elden did not understand the words, not completely, but that sometimes happened when people spoke to him. "All right, Papa. Papa?"

"Yes, Elden?"

"Please don't go."

"I must, son. I'm sorry. I know it makes you sad. I'm sad, too. Be strong."

"All right, Papa." But it wasn't all right.

"Elden, I love you very much. I'll be waiting for you."

Sobs finally broke through, shook Elden. "Me love you, too, Papa."

He'd never heard his father's voice again, and when he had awakened, his face tear-streaked, he had been able to see things others could not. Strange things. Frightening things. At first, he remembered the things he'd seen. He did not like that. Over time, he no longer remembered but he still saw. Others told him that he did, that he spoke to them even although he didn't remember. They said he was touched by the light, gifted with prophecy. Regg, Jiriis, and the others had listened to him, just as Papa had said. He had led them to the valley, where they had built the abbey and become a light in darkness.

He leaned back in his chair, his eyes on the statue. The face of Amaunator looked serious under his beard, the deep-set eyes staring out at some distant point from under the domed helm. Elden wondered what the god was looking at. He wondered if Papa was with Amaunator.

Thinking of Papa made him happy and sad at the same time. He reached for Browny again, stroked the dog. Elden had lived more than one hundred years, but he felt that things were changing. Not so many people came to see him anymore. Maybe the darkness kept them away. Or maybe he'd cast what light he was to cast.

He replayed his father's voice in his head.

I love you very much.

He smiled and tears filled his eyes.

Everyone in the abbey called Papa Dawnlord. Elden did not know for sure what "dawnlord" meant, but that was all right. He knew it meant they liked Papa. Everyone liked Papa. Their voice dropped when they spoke of him. But to Elden, Papa was just Papa—a tall man of kind smiles and soft words.

The pain of losing Papa still hurt, even after a hundred years. Elden missed him more than ever.

I'll be waiting for you.

Sensing Elden's sadness, Browny stood, whined, and nuzzled his hand. Elden rubbed the dog's big head, his muzzle. The dog sighed contentedly.

Elden sensed changes but did not know what to do with the feeling.

"Me need to see Papa, Bownie," he said.

The dog stood, stretched. Elden closed his eyes for a moment, willed his inner eyes to see, and entered a seeing trance.

Images swept through the Oracle's head—the growing menace of the Shadovar, two shade brothers in the center of events, both pained with loss but each alone. A second pair of brothers appeared to him, not shades but Plaguechanged, and behind them lurked the shadow of an archdevil. He saw the hole in the center of Sembia where Ordulin once had stood. He saw Vasen, his image bisected down the middle, half of him in shadow, half of him in light, such bright light. He saw a tattooed deva surrounded by shadow, standing at Vasen's side. And he saw the one-eyed man, now a god, who had given him the juggler's toys so many years ago—Drasek Riven. All of the images he saw whirled past his inner eye, a swirl of shadows and light and violence. He did not try to interpret what he saw. He had not entered a trance to see. He had entered the trance to speak.

"The shrine, Browny," he said, and put his hand on the back of the large blink dog. The dog triggered its power, and in an instant the Oracle and Browny stood in the dawnlord's shrine. Two elaborately carved, magically preserved wooden biers sat in the center of the large, round room, ringed by a candelabra-lined processional the pilgrims used to view the shrine. Dried roses and other small offerings covered the biers, the floor around them. A soft glow from a ceiling-mounted glowglobe suffused the chamber. The light was never allowed to die in the shrine.

The lids of the biers featured carved images of the Oracle's father, Abelar Corrinthal, and Jiriis Naeve, sculpted in lifelike relief. After Abelar's death, Jiriis had sworn to serve and protect the Oracle for as long as she lived, just as Vasen did now. She'd loved Abelar and had insisted that she be laid to rest beside him. Jiriis had been the first to hold the title of First Blade. Vasen Cale, the Oracle knew, would be the last.

With Browny at his hip, he walked to his father's resting place. Spells and subtle use of wood chisels had carved a perfect image of his father from the wood. His shield, inscribed with a rose, rested on his feet. He held his blade at his waist. The image showed not armor but burial robes, and his father's strong-jawed, bearded face looked at peace.

Inscribed under his father's feet, the words:

ABELAR CORRINTHAL, SERVANT OF THE LIGHT, WHO RODE A DRAGON OF SHADOW INTO BATTLE AGAINST THE DARKNESS AND FELL IN GLORY.

Beside him lay Jiriis, her fine features and high cheekbones as delicate as the Oracle remembered them in life. The sculpted image, however, did not capture the loveliness of her red hair.

Browny curled up on the floor near Abelar's bier.

"I did what you asked, Papa. We were a light for a long time. But now darkness encroaches. Erevis Cale's son stands in the center of it, and I cannot foresee the direction of his life. I gave him your holy symbol, the rose you loved. I think you would have wanted that. I will give him something more when the time comes."

He ran his fingertips over his father's face, over Jiriis's. Tears pooled in his eyes, ran down his cheeks.

"I miss you both. I wish we could have spoken this way when you were still alive." He thought about his words for a moment, then chuckled. "Then again, maybe we spoke to one another in the ways that matter. Love doesn't require perfect words, does it?"

He took a look around the chamber, at the ribbons of warm color that decorated the walls, at the high windows in the round, a symbol of hope that light would one day return. Perhaps it would.

Browny stood, sensing that it was time to depart.

"I love you, Papa, and I will be home soon."

He placed his hand on Browny's back. The dog had been his companion, guide, and bodyguard for more than a decade, and there had been another before him, and another before that.

"The pass, Browny," the Oracle said, and the dog looked up, a question in his dark eyes. "The debt is nearly paid. I must release them."

The Oracle pulled his cloak tight about him as the dog again activated his power and in an instant moved the two of them from the abbey to the spirit-guarded mountain pass that shielded the vale from unwanted incursion.

The wind pawed at the Oracle's robe but he did not feel the chill. Browny stood close, hackles raised, sniffing the air. The fog swirled, thick and gray. The Oracle felt the spirits' awareness focus on him. Their sentience coalesced the fog into forms discernibly human. The outlines of men, women, and children stood all around him, dozens, their eyes like empty wells, their outlines shifting in the wind. He saw the anticipation in their expressions, the hope. He would leave neither unanswered.

With the aid of Abelar, Regg, and the servants of Lathander, the spirits had helped slay Kesson Rel the Godthief during the Battle of Sakkors. The Oracle spoke above the whisper of the wind, above the whisper of the spirits.

"Kesson Rel cursed Elgrin Fau, the City of Silver, your city, to perpetual darkness in the Shadowfell. But shadow and light came together on the field of battle, in the shadow of Sakkors, and there combined to kill the Godthief."

One of the spirits glided forward, a thin, aged man in robes.

"Avnon Des," the Oracle said.

The spirit inclined his head in acknowledgment. "You come to free us, Oracle, yet we don't wish release. We vowed to serve the Order in gratitude for the Order's role in destroying Kesson Rel. We will hold true to that vow until the darkness is lifted."

The other spirits nodded agreement, even the children.

The Oracle held up a hand. "Your oath is fulfilled and your service to me has ended. The world is changing, Avnon Des. The Spellplague was but a symptom of it. The war of light and shadow against the darkness of this world is no longer mine or yours to fight. It falls to others now. Shar's cycle will run its course, or it will not. I cannot foresee its end."

The spirits rustled in agitation.

"You've kept the vale and abbey safe for a century," the Oracle continued. "But the time is past. I have only one more favor to ask. Return to the Shadowfell, but not Elgrin Fau. Go to the master of the Citadel of Shadows. You serve him now. Tell him I still enjoy juggling. Tell him I said . . . I know the burden he carries."

They looked at one another, back at the Oracle, and nodded.

"The light is in you, Avnon Des," the Oracle said.

Avnon Des, the First Demarch of the Conclave of Shadows, smiled in return. "And there is shadow in you, Oracle. Farewell."

Avnon turned to face the others, and their collective whispering sounded like wind through leaves. As one, they faded from view, returning to the Shadowfell. The Oracle stood his ground until they were gone. With them went the mist. The pass was exposed, unguarded for the first time in more than a century. The Oracle put his hand on Browny.

"Light and shadow, Browny, will combine to fight the darkness. And I don't know if they will prevail. Return me to the abbey."

A lurching sense of abrupt motion and he once more stood in the abbey's sanctum. He enjoyed the quiet for a moment, the solidity of the walls. He could scarcely conceive of no longer calling it his home. But so it would be.

"I need you to get Abbot Eeth," he said to Browny.

He would order everyone away. He would concoct some excuse, tell them that his vision demanded they go on a pilgrimage to Arabel while he resanctify the abbey alone. They would worry for him but they would obey. And after they were gone, he would remove all of the scrying wards that shielded the abbey from divination spells. Anyone would be able to find it, were they looking. And there were those who were looking.

He kneeled, faced Browny, and rubbed the dog's face and muzzle. The dog must have sensed something amiss. His stubby tail did its best to wag.

"I'm going to send them all away, Browny. And after they've gone, you must go, too."

The tail wag stopped entirely. The dog sat on his haunches and a question formed in his eyes.

"I know. But you must go. I am to be here alone."

Browny licked his hand, refused to move, started to whine.

"Why?" The Oracle put his forehead against the dog's head, rubbed his sides, and stood. "Because the chick has grown into a bird. And now we must kick him from the nest. Go fetch the abbot."

Yellow lines of power spiraled out from Brennus's outstretched fingers, flowed around and into one face of his scrying cube. Shadows spun around his body; sweat slicked his brow.

He was hunting a ghost.

"Come back," he murmured, and once again slightly tweaked the nature of his spell.

An echo of the images Rivalen had shown to him had to remain in the cube. They had to.

He pictured his mother's face, pictured the flower-filled meadow, her outstretched hand as she died.

On his shoulders, his homunculi hunched and mirrored his expression of concentration.

A charge ran through the line of his spell and a flash of light appeared in the cube. An image flickered, just for a moment, his mother lying amid a field of purple flowers. The image was blurry, not as clear as when Rivalen had shown it to him, but it was there. It was there.

"What did you wish for, Mother?" Rivalen asked, the replay of the images slurring his voice.

His mother, poisoned by her own son, said, "To be the instrument of your downfall."

The image fragmented on the face of the cube: eyes, nose, hands, all falling to pieces before fading altogether. Brennus cursed and his homunculi echoed him. He blinked, wiped the sweat from his face, adjusted his spell, and tried to pull the echo back, but the face of the cube remained black.

"Damn it," he said.

A soft knock sounded on the scrying chamber door.

"Not now," he snapped.

"Apologies, Prince Brennus," said Lhaaril, his seneschal. "But—"

Brennus irritably waved a hand and the ward on the door dispelled with a soft *pop*. The wood and metal slab swung open on silent hinges to reveal Lhaaril, standing alone in the dark hallway.

"You know I'm not to be disturbed in this chamber," Brennus said.

Lhaaril, his hands clasped across his stomach, bowed his balding head. Shadows poured from his flesh, a sign of his agitation. "Yes, Prince. Humblest apologies. But the Most High wishes to see you."

The words brought Brennus up short. His homunculi squeaked with alarm. Shadows slipped from Brennus's skin. "When? He sent a summons?"

"No," Lhaaril said, looking up, his glowing green eyes narrowed with warning. "He's here, Prince. Now."

The words did not quite register. "Here? On Sakkors? Now?"

From the dark hallway behind Lhaaril, the voice of Most High said, "Yes, Brennus. Now."

Lhaaril stiffened, glanced over his shoulder in irritation, back at Brennus, and spoke in a formal tone. "Prince Brennus, your father, Telamont Tanthul, the Most High."

"I think he knows who I am, Lhaaril," said the Most High, and glided around the steward.

The Most High towered over the seneschal, and his platinum eyes glowed feverishly out of the black hole of his sharply angled, clean-shaven face. An embroidered cloak hung from broad shoulders that age had not bowed. He held a polished wooden staff in one ring-bedecked hand. His body merged with the darkness, the outline of his form shifting, difficult to separate from the shadowed air of Sakkors.

"That will be all, Lhaaril," said Telamont.

The steward held his station, jaw stiff, upper lip drawn tight, and looked at Brennus.

Brennus nodded at him while he tried to gather his thoughts. "That's all, Lhaaril."

Lhaaril's exhalation was audible. "Yes, Prince Brennus. Shall I have a meal prepared for two?"

Brennus looked his father, asking a question wioth his eyes.

"I can't stay long."

"Very well," Lhaaril said. He bowed first to the Most High, then to Brennus, and exited the scrying chamber.

"This is a surprise," Brennus said.

His homunculi cowered, covered their faces with their hands.

"I imagine it is," the Most High said. "So . . . "

Brennus cleared his throat. "So."

Father and son regarded one another across the gulf of things unsaid. The silence grew awkward, but Brennus refused to break it. At last the Most High did.

"You and your constructs," he said, smiling, and nodded at Brennus's homunculi. "Like Rivalen with his coins."

"I'm *nothing* like Rivalen," Brennus answered, and could not keep a bitter edge from his voice. "And you've always hated my interest in shaping-magic, father. Mother encouraged it, but never you."

"No," the Most High said, irritation coloring his voice. "I didn't. Because I wanted you to focus on your gift with divination magic and—"

Brennus had heard it all before. "What do you want, Father?"

The Most High looked everywhere but Brennus's face. Brennus had never seen his father so discombobulated. "Do you think that Rivalen still collects coins?"

"Of course he doesn't," Brennus said. "What use would a god have for such things?"

Shadows swirled around the Most High. "Godling," he corrected. "Not a god."

"Neither," Brennus corrected in turn. "Murderer."

Telamont sighed. "Still that?"

"That."

Telamont glided toward Brennus's scrying cube. "I explained this to you before, Brennus. We needed him."

"*You* needed him. Do you still need him? He does nothing more than sit in his darkness and ponder his goddess. He can't be of use to you, now."

To that, the Most High said nothing.

"Or perhaps he's just too powerful for even the Most High to challenge now? Is that it?"

The sudden tension in the air caused Brennus's homunculi to squeal in alarm and secret themselves in the hood of his cloak.

The Most High turned to him, his platinum eyes mere glowing slits, the darkness about him deepening.

It took everything Brennus had not to back up a step or lower his gaze, but he thought of his mother and held his ground. Shadows swirled around him.

"You push and push, Brennus," the Most High said softly. "And then push again. My patience is not limitless."

Brennus's homunculi trembled. Brennus bit his lip and held his tongue.

The fire in the Most High's eyes diminished to coals. He cleared his throat.

"I didn't come here to fight with you. And Alashar . . . died long ago. I've come to terms with how it happened, with the . . . compromises I've made." He turned from Brennus and put his hand on the face of the scrying cube. "This was just used. What were you scrying?"

Brennus lied. "I was . . . searching for the Chosen. As you asked me to do."

The Most High turned once more to face him, and Brennus's lie crumbled under the weight of his eyes.

"And I was also searching for . . . something else. Something I hope to show you someday."

The Most High seemed not to hear him. He spoke absently, almost to himself. "Matters are afoot in Faerûn, in Toril. I don't mean the wars. The Dalelands will soon fall to our forces, but I mean something more than squabbles over territory. Something is changing. There's power in the air, stirrings." He seemed to remember himself and looked over at Brennus. "Have you felt it?"

"I have sensed something," Brennus said carefully, although he'd been so fixated on Rivalen and Mask and Erevis Cale's child that he'd had time to notice little else.

The Most High nodded. "I need you to refocus on the work I've asked of you, Brennus. Find the Chosen for me, as many as you can, as fast as you can. I believe they're important."

"Important, how? This change you feel, it's connected to the Chosen?"

Telamont nodded, turned, paced before the cube. "The Chosen and the Gods. Pieces are moving. I'll admit that it's still opaque to me. But yes, the Chosen are involved somehow. I need them found."

"And then? You hold them? Kill them?"

Using his divinations, Brennus had already identified a score of Chosen for the Most High, but it was painstaking, time-consuming work. Surprising work, too. He had not expected there to be so many Chosen. It was as if the gods had birthed a brood of them in preparation for something neither he nor the Most High had yet been able to discern.

Brennus had provided names, descriptions, and locations of those he'd found, and after that, he had no idea what happened. In truth, the only Chosen he was interested in was already dead—Erevis Cale.

The Most High stared into Brennus's face. "Just find them, Brennus."

Brennus nodded. "I hear your words, Most High. Will that be all?"

The Most High approached him, and his expression softened. "Must it be like this forevermore, Brennus? I barely see you. We were never . . . close like you were with your mother, but there wasn't always this distance. You no longer attend the Conclaves. Your brothers ask after you. Yder is overseeing war with the Dales, yet I suspect you know nothing of it. Our Sembian forces recently took Archendale. Did you know that?"

Brennus knew nothing of any of it. His obsession with Rivalen had driven him into isolation. "I've no interest in the movement of our armies. That's work for Yder. I have my own work."

The Most High's expression regained its imperious cast. "Your work is an obsession with your brother, with your mother, with revenge."

It was too much, and the shouted answer slipped Brennus's control before he could rein it in. "And it should be your obsession, too! He murdered your wife! You should want revenge! You! You fear him, though, don't you?"

The Most High's mouth formed a tight line. "You overestimate his power and underestimate mine. And now you've come dangerously close to overestimating my capacity for indulgence."

Brennus swallowed and said nothing, knowing an apology would sound foolish. Inside his cloak, the homunculi trembled uncontrollably.

"You do as I've told you," the Most High said. "Am I understood?"

Brennus stared into his father's face, bowed his head, and said, "Most High."

"Am I understood, Brennus?"

"Your words are clear."

The Most High studied his face, seemingly satisfied. His expression softened once again. "If it helps, I believe Rivalen is being punished, Brennus. He's gone mad. He thinks he's going to end the world."

Brennus blinked. "And you think he can't?"

"Of course he can't," the Most High snapped, and shadows swirled around him. "He stares at a hole in reality for days on end. His thoughts bounce around in the cage prepared for him by his goddess. He dreams only of darkness and endings and suffers for it."

"He should suffer."

"My point isn't so much about him as you. Live your life, Brennus. We have work to do in Faerûn."

"I will, Father."

The Most High stared into Brennus's face for a long moment before nodding. He pulled the shadows about him, was lost in them, and was gone.

Brennus swallowed down a dry throat, exhaled. The homunculi poked their gray heads out of his clothing, looked around, their pointed ears twitching.

"Father gone now?"

"Yes," Brennus said.

"Do as he ask?" they inquired as one.

"Eventually," Brennus said. He moved to his scrying cube and once more tried to resurrect the image of his mother's murder.

CHAPTER SEVEN

STANDING IN THE DOORWAY OF ANA AND CORL'S SMALL, WARM cottage, Elle drew her hood tight. The austere darkness of the late afternoon contrasted markedly with the warm glow of the cottage.

"Our thanks once more for the eggs, Elle," called Ana from behind her.

"You're welcome," Elle said, tying the string under her chin. "You'd do the same if your hens were producing."

"Even so."

"It's Idleday," Elle said, half turning. "So stay in and keep dry."

Ana tended a cauldron near the hearth. Her husband, Corl, sat in a rough-made chair before the fire, sharpening the blade of a hoe.

"Aye," called Corl. "There's naught to be done in this weather, anyway. And thank you, Elle. You're a saint."

Corl's sincerity touched her.

"Go feed that baby something," Ana said, smiling at her and nodding at Elle's belly.

"Aye," Elle said. She pulled the door closed behind her and stepped out into the muddy cart road. The namesake elms that ringed the village whispered and creaked in the wind. The rain smelled of decay. A shit rain, Gerak would have called it, and she would have frowned at his use of profanity. She worried for the village's crops. A fouled rain would harm an already fragile harvest. More of her neighbors than Ana and Corl would suffer.

The dark sky rumbled. The underside of the clouds looked burned, as if the world had caught fire and charred them black. But she knew how to read the sky, the subtle variations among the blacks and grays, and she thought the low, swirling clouds promised an end to the rain, and soon.

Odd, she thought, the things to which a person became accustomed. She'd grown up in Sembia's darkness and knew it as well as she knew the soil. But she'd never seen the unveiled sun and wasn't sure she'd know what to do if she ever did. But she hoped to find out one day.

The thought summoned a smile. She felt oddly hopeful. Gerak would return on the morrow or the day after, perhaps with fresh meat, and she carried his child in her womb, a life unexpected. She ran her hands over the bulge of her stomach and her eyes welled. The changes to her body wrought by the pregnancy seemed to make her weep over everything. She felt silly but smiled nevertheless.

She wiped her eyes as she walked the sloppy cart road, her mind on the baby, barely cognizant of the mud fouling her shoes and soaking the bottom of her cloak. She thought of a time years earlier, when Chauntea's greenpriests still traveled Sembia, using their magic to assist villagers with their crops. She remembered an elderly greenpriest, as thin as a reed, who had preached that where life grew there was always hope. Back then, Elle had rolled her eyes at the words. But now, with a child in her womb, she understood exactly what the priest had meant.

The child in her belly was hope.

Again her eyes welled. Again she smiled in embarrassment at her own sentimentality.

"Hope," she said, testing out the word. It sounded good, sounded right. She ran a hand over her belly. "If you're a girl, we'll call you Hope."

The sky rumbled with thunder. Elle refused to surrender her smile or her mood. She made a dismissive gesture at the sky.

"Bring your worst," she challenged.

She crossed the village commons, heading for her cottage. The Rins' milk cow was there, head down, chewing the grass. A scrawny barn cat slinked through the underbrush, probably stalking a field mouse. The Idleday weather had kept everyone else inside, even the children. Two fishing boats tethered to posts at the edge of the pond bobbed in the chop.

Before she reached the cottage the rain lost its stink and reduced to a drizzle. With the weather cooperating and leftover stew already in the soup kettle, she decided she'd walk a bit more, maybe stroll the edge of the village and enjoy the elms.

Shutters opened as she walked and she exchanged greetings with her neighbors.

"The rain is soon to stop," she called to Mora.

Mora looked up, nodded. "How's the loaf?"

Elle put her hand on her belly. "Rising."

"The gods keep it and you."

"And you, Mora."

Her feet carried her eventually to the two oldest elms in the village—the Gate Elms, everyone called them. The road from the plains went right between them and extended out into the darkness, a string that connected the village to the dangers of the plains. The road faded after only a short distance, devoured by Sembia's perpetual gloom. She stared at it a long while, rubbing her stomach. Gerak was out there somewhere, alone in the dark. She stood there under the leaves, sheltered from the drizzle, and wondered where he was, how he fared.

"Your daddy's out there," she said to Hope. "He'll be back soon."

She turned to go, but a sound from out in the plains caught her attention. A man's voice, she was sure, although she had not made out any words. Gerak returning? A lost traveler? She considered calling out but thought better of it. Gerak was not due to return and Fairelm had not seen a traveler in many months. She looked back at the village, the homes and barns and sheds within earshot were mere shadowy blobs in the gloom.

Her fine mood evaporated as distant thunder rumbled anew, the sky having its vengeance for her taunt.

"Probably nothing," she whispered.

Still, she sheltered near the bole of one of the elms, her hand on the bark, and listened. She put her other hand on the handle of the small eating knife she carried. It would make a poor weapon.

Long moments passed and she heard nothing more, so she allowed herself to exhale. Probably she'd imagined the sound, or transformed a distant animal's howl into a man's voice. The gloom sometimes fooled the senses. Turning, she started back toward the village.

The sound of rattling metal froze her, tightened her chest. A man's voice sounded from out in the darkness.

"Don't move," he said, and she didn't. Surprise shackled her feet to the ground, put a lump in her throat, sent her heart racing so hard she felt dizzy. Horrors lurked on the plains and some of them could speak like a man. She knew she should call out for aid, but her voice seemed to have died in the sudden dryness of her mouth.

She heard the slosh of something large in the mud of the road, drawing nearer, the jangle of chains. She imagined huge feet thumping in the earth, something snatching her from the darkness and stealing her away. Gerak and the neighbors would wonder what had happened to her, but no one would ever know. She'd become a warning tale for children.

Thunder boomed. She blanched at the sudden sound.

"There now," said the voice again, in a more soothing tone. "Good."

Good?

She realized that the voice was not speaking to her, and the realization slowed her heart and freed her from her paralysis. Movement in the gloom drew her eyes. She could not make out details but it did not appear the shadowy giant of her imagination.

"Who is out there?" she called.

The sound stopped. "Who asks? I seek Fairelm. This . . . is the road, isn't it? By the gods, Gray, if you've walked astray they'll be no barley for you for a tenday."

Gray? Didn't she know that name?

And all at once the voice and the sounds fell into place for Elle. Gray was a mule. The sound of jingling metal was the old mule's bridle. And the voice . . .

"Minser? Is that you?"

"Aye," said the peddler, and Elle heard the smile in his tone. "Is this Fairelm?"

Elle laughed with relief, her legs weak with it. "It is! It is! Come on so I can see you."

The slosh of Gray's hooves in the road grew louder, the sound no longer ominous but jaunty. The dimness relented as they closed and the shapes took on details. Minser's large covered cart containing pots, pans, cutlery, tools, jars, all manner of metal and clay goods, even a few items of glass. Minser sat hunched on the driver's bench like a dragon on his hoard. Gray, the largest mule Elle had ever seen, sullenly pulled the wagon through the muck, his ears flat on his head. Elle stepped away from the elm and waved.

"Minser! It's been so long! We thought something had befallen you."

Minser leaned forward on his bench to see her better. When he did, his jolly, round face split into a smile under his thick, graying moustache. "No, fair lady. Gray and me know these roads better'n the shades themselves. We steer clear of trouble. And we know how to shoot it when it shows." He held up the crossbow he kept beside him on the bench. "Besides, a creature'd hafta be senile to want to chew on these old bones."

He clicked at Gray to halt him before Elle, then heaved himself down off the wagon's bench. His belly bounced with every move he made. Elle rubbed Gray's muzzle, and the gentle giant of a mule whinnied with pleasure.

"He remembers you, lady," Minser said. "As do I." The peddler removed his wide-brimmed hat and made a show of bowing. "I'm pleased to see you well, Lady Elle."

"And I'm pleased to see you," Elle said, with a mock curtsey. "As will everyone else. Come, you should announce yourself."

"Of course," Minser said. "Will you ride?"

"I think I will," she said. Minser made a stirrup of his hands and assisted her up onto the driver's bench.

"Ayep," he said, and shook Gray's reins. The mule pulled the wagon forward. "You know, in the Dales and Cormyr, a traveler don't announce himself as they do here."

"In the Dales and Cormyr everyone can *see* a traveler when he arrives in a village. Here, the gloom makes sight uncertain. Hearing is best, unless you want to risk a startled crossbowman putting a quarrel in your hind end."

"You speak with truth," Minser said, chuckling.

"You've been to Cormyr and the Dales recently, then?" Elle asked. "The sun shines there still?"

"Only Sembia is darkened by the Shadovar, lady. I was in Cormyr at the end of summer, and the sun shines brightly there. Things are dire in the Dales, I hear. Sembian soldiers occupy Archendale and the other Dales brace for further attack. I myself saw Sembian soldiers, hundreds of them, on the march north. Stories of war in the far Silver Marches have even carried to these ears." He shook his head sadly. "All of Faerûn seems at war, milady. There's no place safe. I don't know what will come of it all."

"Well," Elle said. "You're safe here. And welcome."

"Ah, even in the gloom you shine brightly, milady."

Elle laughed. "You should have had a life at court, Minser. You've a flatterer's tongue."

Minser put a hand to his chest and feigned a wounded heart. "You hear that, Gray? A flatterer's tongue, she said."

Elle turned serious. "May I ask you a question? Why come back to Sembia? Gerak and I were considering leaving. The

Rabbs left several days ago. I wonder if you saw them on the road?"

"I did not, alas. Although they might have been avoiding the roads for fear of the soldiers."

"Well, if we left and saw the sun, I can't imagine ever returning."

Minser nodded as if he understood. "The road is in my bones, I'm afraid. Besides, even the darkest places need the light of Minser's pans and urns and stories. But maybe you *should* leave, lady? A life in the sun would suit you."

Elle smiled.

Minser fiddled with a bronze medallion he wore on his chest. Elle could not see it clearly but caught a glimpse of an engraved flower.

"Is that a religious symbol, Minser? Did you turn holy man while you were away?"

She was jesting, but Minser responded with seriousness. "This?" He withdrew the symbol from under the tent of his shirt. It featured a rose and sun—Amaunator's symbol. "A bit, milady, I'll admit. I picked this up . . . in a place of hope. A few months ago."

Elle touched his hand, his fingers like overstuffed sausages. "I've been thinking a lot about hope recently. I'm glad you're here, Minser."

"As am I," he said, and put the symbol back under his shirt.

Minser pulled up on the reins when Gray pulled the wagon to the village commons. A railed, wood-planked deck sat under the canopy of an elm. Seats made from old stumps sat here and there. The sounding bell hung from a post near the deck.

As they debarked from the wagon, Elle said, "You can share my dinner, if you'd like. And our shed is still waterproof, if you'd like to sleep in it rather than the wagon. There's a spot for Gray beside it. Keep him out of the rain."

Minser doffed his weathered, wide-brimmed hat and affected as much of a bow as his girth allowed.

"You remain, as always, gracious as a queen. It *is* a bit cramped in the wagon. It'll do in a pinch, but I admit your shed sounds appealing."

She smiled, nodded.

"And for your hospitality, you shall have your choice of cookware from my offerings. I have some fine kettles I acquired in Daerlun."

"Thank you, Minser."

Minser made a show of looking about. "So where, pray tell, is your king? And what sort of monarch allows his queen to walk about unescorted in such weather?"

Elle's voice dropped and she looked off to the plains. "Gerak is off on a hunt."

Minser recoiled. "In this? Is he mad?"

"I think possibly, yes."

Minser chuckled. "Well, I'm sure he's fine. I hope he returns before I move on."

"He'll return tomorrow or the next day."

Elle heard doors opening, the voices over the rain. At least some of her neighbors must have seen Minser arrive. They'd want to hear his stories and see what wonders his cart held.

"I'll set the table in two hours," she said. "Meanwhile, announce yourself so all know you're here. Not even the rain will keep them away."

Minser's mouth formed a smile in the thicket of his moustache. Elle noticed the wrinkles around his eyes. He stepped onto the deck—the planks creaked ominously under his weight—and rang the bell three times, the peals loud in the quiet.

"Ho, Fairelm! Ho! Minser the Seller has returned, with wares from as far west as Arabel and tales from the other side of the world!"

More shutters and doors were thrown open. Elle heard the exclamations of children and the happy chatter of her neighbors as they emerged from their cottages and went out to greet

Minser. It had been so long since Fairelm had seen a traveler, Minser's appearance might as well have been a festival.

Elle smiled as she walked back to her cottage. Minser's arrival in the village always heralded a good day or three, full of stories, interesting wares, and excellent beer. She was glad Gerak would return soon. He, too, would be pleased to see Minser.

After checking on her stew, she gathered all the extra blankets they had from the chest near their bed. Tattered and faded from many washes, the blankets had belonged to Gerak's parents. Minser would not mind their condition. She took a small clay lamp and the blankets to Gerak's tool shed and made a place on the floor for Minser to sleep. No doubt he had his own bedroll, but he would welcome extra blankets.

She returned to the cottage and lay down for a nap. The baby growing in her drained her of energy. She planned to be idle on Idleday. She fell asleep to the sound of laughter, Minser's voice spinning a tale, and the general hubbub of the gathering. It was as if Minser had brought the village back to life, back to hope.

A hand on his shoulder awakened Vasen.

Darkness.

The fire was mere embers and Byrne had extinguished the light from his shield.

Quiet.

The rain had stopped. He had no way to tell the time, to know how long he'd been asleep. Where were the pilgrims? How was Noll doing? He was still groggy from sleep, and had trouble orienting himself. He was vaguely aware of shadows crawling over his flesh.

Orsin's tattooed face loomed over him, lit only by the faint glow of the fire's embers. Concern showed in the deva's opalescent eyes.

"What?"

The deva held an inked finger to his mouth for silence. Vasen came fully awake as Orsin nodded at something beyond the cave mouth.

Noll coughed, the sound loud in the quiet of the cave. Orsin's grip on Vasen's shoulder tightened at the sound.

"Quiet that boy!" someone hissed from Vasen's right.

The pilgrims were crowded into the rear of the cave, some hugging one another, others holding eating knives in their hands. One of them had produced a truncheon from somewhere. All of them wore expressions of fear. Noll lay covered in blankets near the wall, still lost in fever, muttering incoherently, but his color had returned. Elora stroked her son's head, whispered softly to comfort him. She alone seemed unconcerned with what lay outside the cave's mouth.

Vasen lifted himself on an elbow, trying to move quietly in his armor, and saw that Byrne, Eldris, and Nald crouched near the cave opening, hugging the wall and looking out.

Noll coughed again, summoning sharp intakes of breath from the pilgrims. Vasen saw Eldris's jaw clench as he chewed on his own tension. Nald's hand opened and closed over the hilt of his bare sword. Vasen stood, pulled Orsin close, and whispered in his ear.

"What is it?"

"Shadovar," Orsin said.

The word flooded Vasen with adrenaline, pulled thick gouts of darkness from his skin. He crept toward the cave mouth with Orsin. Behind them, more coughs from Noll. Ordinarily the coughs would have been a good thing, indicative of the boy clearing his lungs. But at the moment the sound put them all at risk.

Elora tried to cover his mouth, but the boy, still incoherent, jerked his head to the side and cried out.

"That boy will get us all killed!" said one of the pilgrims, a man whose name Vasen could not recall.

Vasen turned and glared at him, pointed a finger leaking darkness at the man's face.

The man's mouth clamped shut and shame anchored his eyes to the floor.

Eldris held out Vasen's sword. Vasen took it, hugged the walls of the cave near his men, and peered out across the river. Orsin stood beside him. The cave's shadows engulfed them both, as thick as ink.

A veserab stood on the far side of the river, its head lowered to the stream to drink. Its cylindrical, serpentine body was twice as long as a man was tall, much of it coiled on the riverbank. From its sides sprouted membranous wings as large as sails. The dark gray hide, fixed with an elaborate saddle and harness, faded to a pale blue on its chest and underside. Its face resembled an open sore, a pink mass of flesh in the center of which was a rictus of fangs. To Vasen, the creature seemed an impossible a mix of lamprey, bat, and serpent. Its eyes looked like flecks of obsidian. A tongue as long as Vasen's forearm extended from the gash of its mouth to slurp at the water. A single Shadovar kneeled at the water's edge beside the veserab, filling his waterskin. Thick, viscous strands of shadow spiraled lazily around his form. Vasen's eyes fell to his own skin, where similar shadows swirled.

A gray tabard marked with the heraldry of Netheril covered the Shadovar's ornate armor. The thick plates featured vicious spikes at shoulders, gauntlets, knees, and elbows. Bald, gaunt, and with skin the color of old vellum, the Shadovar looked more like a corpse than a man. His eyes glowed red in the darkness.

A sudden, animal grunt from somewhere off on the plains behind the Shadovar caused Vasen's heart to jump and startled the veserab. Its wings flapped and it lifted its face into the air, long tongue wagging back and forth like an antenna. The Shadovar stood, patted the creature's side, and said something in his baroque, incomprehensible language.

A call sounded in the same language from farther down the riverbank. The first Shadovar shouted back, then said something to his mount. Vasen could not see down the river from where he stood in the cave's mouth, and didn't dare risk exposing himself by venturing out of the cave.

"Another one," Orsin whispered.

"Maybe more than one," Vasen said.

"Let's find out," the deva said. He crouched low and moved out into the brush, a few paces outside the cave. He looked down the riverbank, then looked back at Vasen and held up one finger.

Only one more Shadovar.

Vasen would wait them out. It appeared the shades had stopped only to water their mounts. They would be on their way back to Sakkors or Shade Enclave soon enough. He would not risk the pilgrims' safety or the abbey's discovery by attacking.

He made eye contact with Eldris, Nald, and Byrne. He did not speak but formed the words *we wait and do nothing* with his lips.

They nodded. Like him, they understood the stakes.

Noll coughed again, summoning a wince from the Dawnswords. The intake of breath from the pilgrims at the rear of the cave was sharp enough to cut wood.

The veserab, already skittish, grunted at the sound and again reared up, drool dripping from the circle of its fanged mouth, wings half spread. The muscles under its hide rippled. It extended its neck and the sore of its face opened like a blooming flower, revealing more pink flesh, more flaps of teeth. It chuffed at the air, sniffing for spoor. The Shadovar came to its side, the shadows around him swirling, a frown on his lips. He spoke softly to the creature while scanning the bank. The Shadovar would be able to see as well in darkness as Vasen, perhaps better

Orsin made himself small in the scrub. Vasen flattened himself against the wall, his fist clenching and unclenching on his sword hilt. By his side, Byrne softly breathed out, and Vasen caught the tail end of a whispered prayer in the exhalation.

The Shadovar's red eyes poured over the terrain, the scrub, the trees. His eyes went over and past the cave mouth, and Vasen allowed himself to hope.

The far Shadovar called to the near one, a question in the tone. The other answered a bit too casually, nodding across the river bank.

"They're coming," Vasen said to Byrne, and Byrne nodded. Another coughing spasm from Noll.

The veserab shrieked in agitation. The Shadovar gripped the reins and slung himself into the saddle, calling out to his comrade as he did so.

"Ready yourself," Vasen whispered to Byrne. "We can't allow either to escape."

Moving rapidly but methodically, Nald, Eldris, and Byrne sheathed swords, unslung their crossbows, cocked, and seated quarrels. Vasen kept blade to hand and prayer at the top of his thoughts.

The veserab coiled its body, tensed, and with an awkward shove vaulted into the air. For a moment, Vasen lost of sight of it, but only for a moment. It landed amid the scrub just to the right of the cave mouth, crushing shrubs and snapping saplings. Orsin crouched in the foliage ten paces from it.

The Shadovar called over his shoulder to his comrade. He cocked his head, his red eyes fixed on the cave mouth.

Noll broke into another coughing fit. The Shadovar slid out of his saddle, drew his sword, the blade like black glass, and advanced on the cave. Darkness clung to him, concealed his legs and lower body in a fog of darkness. The veserab lingered behind him, sucking in the air, its long tongue dangling between the rows of its teeth. Orsin crept closer to the creature, as silent as a ghost.

Noll's hacking ceased. The tension in the cave was as thick as the shadows. Many of the pilgrims whispered prayers.

The Shadovar halted.

Vasen held up a hand to order Eldris, Nald, and Byrne to hold. They nodded, but took aim nevertheless.

The darkness deepened around the Shadovar, he took a single step within it, and moved in an instant from the darkness in which he stood to the darkness in the mouth of the cave. His sudden appearance three paces before them elicited a surprised curse from Byrne and hurried shots from the crossbows. Two bolts went wide, but Byrne's struck the Shadovar in the chest. The darkness around the Shadovar killed the bolt's inertia, and the missile thumped weakly into his breastplate.

The pilgrims shouted in fear. Vasen voiced the prayer he'd kept behind his teeth, and his sword ignited with Amaunator's light. The Shadovar blanched before the sudden glare, his darkness overcome by Vasen's light, and Vasen bounded forward with a shout. He slashed at the joint in the Shadovar's armor between shoulder and neck, but the Shadovar recovered enough to duck under the blow and stab his sword at Vasen's abdomen. The black blade ground against Vasen's armor, and he lurched to his left before it could penetrate to his flesh. He slammed his shield into the Shadovar's face, felt the satisfying crunch of bone, and sent the shade careening backward three strides.

"Kill the mount!" Vasen shouted.

The veserab shrieked, spitting drool, and lurched like a serpent toward the combat, crushing scrub and saplings under its writhings. Byrne, Eldris, and Nald rushed past Vasen toward the creature, blades high and lit. The creature reared up, hissing. Vasen did not see Orsin anywhere.

He lunged at the Shadovar, noting with horror and fascination that the shade's broken nose already had ceased bleeding— the bones reshaping themselves as the flesh regenerated. The Shadovar spit a mouthful of blood, parried Vasen's overhead slash with his own blade, and loosed a kick that struck Vasen in the abdomen and doubled him over. Vasen's breath rushed out of him, but he got his shield up in time to block a slash that otherwise would have decapitated him. He swung his blade at the Shadovar's leg to drive him back a step.

They regarded each other for a moment, Vasen's light dueling with the Shadovar's darkness while Vasen's fellow Dawnswords surrounded the veserab and hacked at its flesh.

Vasen moved first, bounding forward and stabbing low. The shade sidestepped the blow and loosed a cross slash for Vasen's side, but Vasen swept the blade out wide with his shield and lashed out with a backhand. The pommel of his sword caught the Shadovar flush in the cheek, sent him reeling. From nowhere Orsin reared up behind the shade and leaped on his back, his quarterstaff drawn across the Shadovar's throat, his legs wrapped around the shade's waist.

The shade's red eyes flared with surprise and fear. The darkness around him swirled, churned. He spun a circle, gagging, trying to shed Orsin, but the deva covered him like a cloak, his arms hooked around his quarterstaff, squeezing. The shade tried awkwardly to bring his large sword to bear on Orsin, but the deva's position made it difficult.

Vasen did not hesitate. He lunged forward and stabbed the Shadovar through the midsection. The shade screamed when Vasen's glowing blade cut through the black armor, the gray flesh. Blood gushed from the wound. The shade staggered under Orsin's weight, then fell to the muck. The moment he hit the ground Orsin rolled off of him and Vasen stepped forward and with a downward slash decapitated the Shadovar.

"Their flesh regenerates only while they live," Orsin said. The deva was not even breathing hard. "This one is done."

But not the other.

To Vasen's right, the veserab wailed its dying shrieks as Eldris, Nald, and Byrne's swords rose and fell on its quivering flesh. Black blood stained their weapons, coated the creature's blue hide. Its wings flapped feebly as it made one last effort to get airborne, but it was too wounded to fly and only managed a clumsy lurch. The Dawnswords' blades ran it through. Its body spasmed as it died.

Vasen scanned the riverbank for the other Shadovar, spotted him twenty paces down the river, on the opposite side, strapping himself into his saddle.

"Shoot him!" Vasen said, pointing.

The second Shadovar's veserab shrieked in answer, showing its fangs. It beat its wings and tensed to take flight while Eldris, the best crossbowman among the Dawnswords, dropped his blade, took crossbow in hand, and cocked it rapidly.

Vasen ran in the Shadovar's direction, although he had no idea what he intended. Byrne, Nald, and Orsin trailed him.

The sails of the veserab's wings collected air and the creature rose into the sky, and with it went Vasen's hope. The pilgrims were more than a day away from the abbey, more than a day away from the Dales. The Shadovar would escape, report their presence, and a full patrol would come and find the pilgrims on the plains. Vasen would not be able to protect them.

Eldris's crossbow sang and a bolt sizzled through the shadows and tore a gash in the membrane of the veserab's wing. The creatures emitted a high-pitched shriek, lurched, beat its wings frantically, and spiraled back to the ground. A cloud of shadows swirled around the Shadovar and his mount. The huge creature lurched about on the ground, shrieking, flapping its wounded wing. The Shadovar spun in the saddle, his red eyes glowing in the black hole of his face. His gaze fixed on Eldris and he held forth his free hand. A column of dark energy streaked across the river at Eldris, blasted him in the chest, lifted him from his feet, and drove him to the earth.

"Eldris!" shouted Nald, but already Eldris had rolled to his stomach and climbed to all fours.

Meanwhile the Shadovar shouted at his mount, thumped it in the side with the flat of his blade.

"We can't let him escape!" Vasen said.

Byrne and Nald already had crossbows to hand and let fly, one bolt plowing into the soft earth beside the veserab, the other striking the Shadovar but dying in his darkness before ever reaching flesh or armor.

Vasen eyed the river, desperate. It was too wide. He'd never get across in time.

"Keep firing," he said, although he knew it would be futile.

Responding to the furious prompts of its master, the veserab again coiled its body and launched itself into the air. Its wounded wing made flight awkward, and for a moment it struggled to get height under it. The Shadovar shouted at it, slapped its side, all the while staring back at Vasen with hate in his face.

"Take this," Orsin said, and shoved his quarterstaff into Vasen's hand. Before Vasen could ask any questions, the deva was gone, sprinting over the uneven ground, zagging through the thick scrub and bounding over fallen logs, toward the river.

"What's he doing?" Byrne asked, reloading his crossbow.

"I don't know. Come on."

Vasen and Nald and Byrne ran after Orsin but could not approach the deva's speed. Orsin reached the river at a dead sprint and launched himself into the air. A column of shadow formed under Orsin's feet as he went airborne and Vasen, Byrne, and Nald stopped cold, gasping as Orsin sailed high into the air, completely over the river and into the airborne veserab and its rider.

"By the light," Nald said.

Vasen thought light had little to do with Orsin's feat.

The deva hit mount and rider in a tangle of limbs and wings and swirling shadows. Unready for the impact or the weight, the veserab lurched sidewise and lost altitude. It shrieked, its wings beating furiously to keep it airborne. Orsin hung on, swinging free in the air, one hand closed on the veserab's saddle strap, one hand around the Shadovar's ankle.

"Shoot it!" Vasen said. "Shoot it!"

Nald and Byrne fired again, one after another, the bolts slamming into the veserab's flank.

It keened with pain and lurched sideways. Blood sprayed from its wounded side, spattered the scrub below. Orsin swung like a pendulum but did not let go.

The Shadovar, nearly unseated by the lurches of the wounded veserab, managed to steady himself enough to hack downward at Orsin with his black sword. Orsin released his grip on the Shadovar's ankle to avoid losing a hand, but before the Shadovar could pull his arm and blade back, Orsin seized his wrist. The moment he had it, he twisted his grip somehow and the Shadovar shouted with pain. The sword fell from the shade's fist and spun to the ground. Still holding the Shadovar by the wrist, Orsin let go his hold on the veserab's strap and took the shade's arm with both hands. Using the arm as a lever, he flipped his legs up and got them under the armpit and around the Shadovar's neck. The veserab careened wildly through the sky as the men atop it struggled. A fog of shadows swirled around Orsin and the Shadovar. Vasen could see only glimpses of the tangle of limbs, the Shadovar's gauntleted fist rising and falling as he punched at Orsin.

"Come on!" Vasen said, and crashed through the scrub toward the river. He lunged into the cold water without stopping, Byrne and Nald on his heels. He hoped that his height would keep his head above water.

The veserab shrieked again, and so, too, did the Shadovar. Orsin dislodged the Shadovar from his mount and shade and man plummeted earthward in a cloud of shadows.

Vasen cursed, the current pulling hard at him, turning his straight course into a diagonal, but the water never rose above his chest and he cleared the river. Eldris and Nald called out behind him. Neither was as tall as he, and both were getting pulled downstream by the current.

"Help them, Eldris!" he shouted over his shoulder, not knowing if Eldris could even hear him.

He clambered up the muddy bank, his boots slipping in the mud, using the scrub to heave himself up. By the time he crested the top, shadows oozed from his flesh. Faith filled him and he channeled it into his blade. The weapon ignited, lit with a rosy light.

He spotted Orsin and the Shadovar twenty paces to his right. Darkness churned around the Shadovar and he appeared unwounded from the fall. Orsin circled him at a few paces, favoring a wounded leg.

Vasen charged straight at them. He shouted Orsin's name as he ran and hurled the deva's quarterstaff toward him. The weapon spun wildly as it flew, but Orsin bounded back from the Shadovar on one leg, caught it, and spun it over his head and before him so fast it hummed.

The Shadovar's red eyes glared as he looked first at Orsin, then at Vasen. He extended a hand at each and black energy streaked from his palms. Orsin tried to dive aside but his leg slowed him and the bolt caught him in the hip, spun him halfway around, and slammed him to the earth. Vasen interposed his shield and the bolt slammed into the steel so hard it drove him from his feet. The metal cooled at the magic's touch, and dark energy crept in tendrils around the shield's edge and dissolved the strap, but it dissipated before doing any more harm.

The Shadovar drew a secondary weapon, a black mace, from his weapon belt and stalked toward Orsin. The deva rolled to his side, tried to stand on his wounded leg—Vasen could see it was broken—and fell back to the earth, grunting with pain. The Shadovar would kill him easily.

Vasen leaped to his feet and renewed his charge, shouting a prayer to Amaunator and channeling the power of his faith into his shield. The entire disk blazed with light. He gripped its edge in his hands, spun a circle, and hurled it at the shade, who saw it coming a moment too late. The blazing shield cut through the darkness around the shade, slammed into his side, and staggered him, continuing to blaze with Amaunator's light. Wincing in the blazing light, the Shadovar recoiled and shaded his eyes with his own shield.

Vasen rushed toward him, his blade held in a two-handed grip. Orsin planted his quarterstaff in the soil and used it to pull himself to his feet, hopping on his one good leg.

Vasen hadn't taken four strides before the Shadovar's darkness extinguished the light from his shield. Vasen didn't care. His blade glowed with light enough.

He roared as he slashed downward, a blow to cleave the shade's helm and split his skull. The Shadovar parried with his shield, bounded a step back, and countered with a swing of his mace that clipped Vasen on the shoulder. A flash of pain, then numbness. His arm hung limp from his shoulder, but he held his blade in one hand and stabbed and slashed, driving the Shadovar back a step.

And then Orsin was there, barely mobile, but with his quarterstaff still a whirling, spinning line of oak. The Shadovar parried with shield and mace, backing up under the onslaught of metal and wood, the darkness around him whirling like a thunderhead.

Vasen ducked under a too-casual mace swing, stepped past the Shadovar's shield, and stabbed up under the shade's breastplate. He felt his glowing weapon grate against metal plates, pierce the mail beneath, slide into flesh, and grind against bone. The Shadovar grunted with pain, red eyes wide. He dropped his mace and grabbed at Vasen with his free hand, as if he would push him away. Orsin's quarterstaff slammed into the shade's temple, sending his helm from his bald head.

Vasen jerked his blade free and the Shadovar hit the ground like a felled cow, the darkness about him still swirling. Vasen straddled him, reversed his grip, and drove his blade downward . . . into the earth.

The Shadovar was gone.

"Damn it," said Vasen, looking around frantically.

Orsin sagged to the ground, wincing from pain. "He is not far. Their power allows them to step from shadow to shadow, but not over long distances."

Vasen spun around, eyeing the thigh-high whipgrass, the scrub bushes, the solitary broadleaf tree here and there. He saw nothing.

"He escaped us!" Vasen shouted, as Byrne, Eldris, and Nald climbed over the river bank. "He's near and sorely wounded!"

"He'll heal rapidly," said Orsin, feeling the break in his leg.

Vasen knew. He snatched his shield from the ground, picked a direction, and started walking.

"Light," Vasen called, and all four servants of Amaunator used the power of their god to light their swords. Holding them high, they scoured the nearby plains.

"Here!" Eldris called, and Vasen and the others sprinted to his side. Eldris crouched near a broadleaf tree.

"It's soaked with blood," he said, touching the bole of the tree and holding up his fingers, red with Shadovar blood.

Vasen sheathed his sword, darkness whirling around him. "Then he's gone. We'll be pursued soon enough."

"His mount abandoned him, at least," Byrne said, nodding at the dark sky. The wounded veserab was nowhere to be seen.

"That earns us some time, but only some," Vasen said. "He can move rapidly from shadow to shadow. A patrol will pick him up eventually."

"So they'll be coming," Nald said.

Vasen looked up at the sky, thick with darkness and nodded. "They'll be coming. Get the pilgrims ready. We need to move rapidly. Not the normal way. We take a direct path to the Dales."

Byrne's eyes widened. "You're certain that's wise, First Blade?"

"No, I'm not. But see to it."

"Aye."

As Byrne, Eldris, and Nald headed back to the cave where the pilgrims sheltered, Vasen hurried over to Orsin. The deva sat on the grass, his loose trousers rolled up over his thigh. Tattooed lines traced paths like veins the length of his leg. The man's flesh really was a map of sorts, the places he'd been drawn on his flesh in cryptic swirls and angles.

"Broken?" Vasen asked.

"And the ankle." Orsin nodded at his ankle. It was already purpling and the bones were angled all wrong. Only a furrow between his eyes suggested the pain he must have felt.

Vasen crouched beside him. "I can help you."

"Your chain."

"What?"

Orsin nodded at Vasen's chest.

It took Vasen a moment to realize what Orsin meant. The chain on which he wore Dawnlord Abelar's holy symbol was broken, its unlooped length hung up on a ridge of his armor.

His heart fell and he cursed. "I have to find it!"

He started to rise, remembered Orsin's leg, remembered his duty.

"After, of course. This may hurt, Orsin."

"May?"

"Will," Vasen acknowledged. "Ready yourself."

Using the symbol of Amaunator enameled on his shield as the focus for his power, Vasen gently laid the shield over Orsin's leg and intoned a prayer of healing. The shield glowed softly and warmth flooded Vasen's body. He focused the warmth in his hands, his palms, and placed them on the shield. The power passed through to Orsin's flesh and the deva hissed through gritted teeth as bones reknit and bruises faded. Vasen slung his shield and pulled the deva to his feet. Orsin tested his weight on the leg.

"Good?" Vasen asked.

"Good. Your symbol?"

"It must have fallen off in the fight," Vasen said, looking hopelessly at the ground around him. "It's . . . important to me."

"A silver rose," Orsin said.

Vasen was surprised the deva had noticed. "Yes. It belonged to the Oracle, and Dawnlord Abelar before that."

"I'll help you find it."

They slowly walked the area where they had fought the shade. Neither of them found the symbol. Eventually both of them got down on all fours, feeling through the grass, Vasen berating himself for his carelessness. He should have had it tucked under his mail shirt, not hanging free. He should have been more careful. Nine Hells, he could have lost it in the battle or he could have lost it while crossing the river.

"Vasen," Byrne called from across the river.

"I know," Vasen shouted over his shoulder, running his hands over the grass, hoping to feel the metal rose under his hands. Orsin stood, put a hand on Vasen's shoulder.

"I think it's gone," the deva said.

"I know."

"We should go."

Vasen hung his head. How would he explain to the Oracle?

"The pilgrims, First Blade," Byrne called.

And that was the word that dispelled Vasen's self-pity. The pilgrim's safety was more important than any holy symbol. He sighed, angry, sad, and stood.

"Thank you for helping," he said to Orsin.

"Of course."

"The lines on your skin? What exactly are they?"

Orsin looked down at his hands, covered in lines and swirls. "The story of my life."

"The story of your life can be read on your skin?"

Orsin nodded. "Much of it. Where I've been, at least. But the point of the story isn't to read it. It's to write it. A man writes his story in the book of the world, Vasen. Or so I tell myself."

Vasen heard an echo of his dream in Orsin's words. He tried to dismiss it as coincidence.

"Well, that's a good story," Vasen said, and Orsin chuckled.

"Very good. A good story, indeed."

Byrne, Eldris, and Nald already had the pilgrims geared up and ready to set out. Vasen and Orsin sidestepped down the river bank and waded into the water.

"You'll not jump it this time?" Vasen said to him, smiling.

Orsin smiled in return.

"How did you . . . manage such a feat?"

Orsin's eyes narrowed with puzzlement. "How do you cause your blade to shine?"

"You know the answer to that. With faith."

"And so it is with me. Your faith manifests as light. Mine . . . does not."

"But your god is . . . gone."

"Yes, but my faith is not."

"Well enough." They waded into the water. "You are a strange man, Orsin."

"I think you said as much once already."

Vasen chuckled. "I thought maybe you needed a reminder. Maybe you should write it on your skin?"

Orsin laughed. "Very good. Very good."

As they emerged on the other side of the river, Orsin adopted a more serious tone. "When there is time later, let's discuss some things."

Zeeahd's satiety unnerved Sayeed almost as much as his appetite. Having spat his pollution into the young girl, Zeeahd seemed almost giddy. He whistled as they plodded over the plains, saturated by the rain. The cats seemed gleeful, too. Their bloodlust temporarily sated, they fairly pranced around Zeeahd, tails held high.

For his part, Sayeed could not rid himself of the foul taste of the devourer's flesh, the memory of the girl's screams of terror, his brother's wet grunts as he expelled the evil in him.

"Her name was Lahni," he said to himself, not understanding why he felt the need to say her name aloud.

"What'd you say?" his brother asked, looking back, his voice high-pitched, irritating.

"Nothing," Sayeed said, knowing Zeeahd would not understand. "Protesting the rain."

The cats eyed him suspiciously, their fang-filled mouths more devilish than feline.

Zeeahd held his hands out, palms up to the sky. "I like the rain. Renews the spirit."

Sayeed said nothing. He feared he had no spirit to renew. He feared the Spellplague had stripped him of his soul and left a moral vacancy filled now by only his brother's ambition and his own resignation. He lived, but he did not *live*. And so it would go, forever. He swallowed down the despair evoked by the thought.

Zeeahd stopped. "I smell wood smoke."

The excitement in his voice made Sayeed nauseous.

Sayeed smelled it, too, the faint hint of a chimney's exhalation. Breakfast fires, maybe. Once, the aroma would have made his stomach growl with hunger. Now, he barely tasted the food that passed his lips. To the extent his senses let him perceive anything with acuity, it was invariably something foul. Like devourer flesh.

"Come, come!" Zeeahd said, and picked up his pace. "A village is near." He chuckled. "Perhaps Lahni's village."

Hearing his brother speak the girl's name sharpened Sayeed's irritation. He stared at his brother's cloaked form, Zeeahd's soul as distorted as his flesh, and wondered how it was possible to love and hate the same person so much. He flashed on an image of his sword driven through his brother's back, the blade exploding out of Zeeahd's chest in a spray of blood or whatever foul ichor now flowed in his brother's veins.

"Come on!" his brother called.

Sayeed came back to himself to find three of the cats sitting on their haunches before him, slit eyes staring at him knowingly. They lifted paws to fanged mouths and licked at the mud on their pads. Their eyes never left Sayeed's face.

"Out of my way," he said, but they did not move and he walked around rather than through them.

The smell of breakfast fires grew stronger with each step they took. And by the time they reached the village, the rain had sputtered to a stop. A dozen or more ancient elms sprouted from the plains, noble looking trees with vast canopies lost to the shadowed air, giants compared to the meager broadleafs that predominated elsewhere on the plains. They must have been saplings when the Spellplague struck.

Within the circle of the elms was a large pond and the village whose breakfast fires they'd smelled. A few dozen single-story wooden homes huddled around a common pasturage. Bark shingles covered the roofs. Smoke rose from several chimneys. Post fences made from stripped broadleaf limbs delineated small fields and gardens. A few rickety wagons sat here and there, small chicken coops, livestock pens. The village was so small Sayeed could have run from one end of it to the other in less than a fifty count.

The overgrown cart path they walked carried them between two of the elms, which formed a kind of natural gate. Sayeed heard voices coming from the village center, the chatter of earnest conversation punctuated with laughter and the occasional jovial shout.

"A collection of hovels," Zeeahd said, eyeing the village contemptuously. His good mood was already fading. Probably his hunger was already returning. "It smells of peasants and shit."

A herd dog stood in the open door of a rain-sodden woodshed, eyeing them, its hackles raised. Zeeahd's cats stared back at it as they walked past and the dog tucked tail and retreated into the shed.

No one seemed to be around. As Sayeed was about to announce their arrival, as was the custom, a boy of maybe ten winters with a too-large cloak thrown over his homespun hurried around the corner of one of the fences ahead. Head down, he clicked at a thin sheep that trailed him. When he caught sight of Sayeed and Zeeahd he froze, ten steps away but a world distant. The sheep, its head down against the rain, walked into him and bleated.

"Ho there, boy," Sayeed said, raising a hand in greeting.

The boy's sleepy eyes went wide. Sayeed and Zeeahd must have looked to him like ghosts stepping from the shadows.

Sayeed tried to look harmless, despite his armor, sword, and wild hair and beard. "There's no need to be afra—"

The boy turned and ran off toward the center of the village, slipping in the mud as he went. "Mother! Mother!"

The sheep trotted after him, oblivious.

"Fly back to the nest, little bird," Zeeahd said softly, and Sayeed knew his tone promised blood. "Predators are afoot."

They followed the boy's shouts toward the center of the village. The few local dogs and cats they saw slinked away as Sayeed, Zeeahd, and their cats drew near. Scrawny livestock lowed or bleated in their pens as they passed.

Ahead, they saw the village center. A raised, planked deck and a bell on a tall post had been built under the canopy of a large elm. It looked like the entire village had gathered there. Women, children, and men sat on stump stools or stood about, their eyes on the deck, where stood a large, fat man with a thick moustache, holding forth about something. A rickety peddler's cart stood to one side, still yoked to a large, graying mule. Some of the villagers were examining the cart's wares, smiling.

The boy Sayeed had frightened stood at the edge of the gathered villagers, a woman kneeling before him, probably his mother. The boy pointed back at Sayeed and Zeeahd while his sheep nibbled the grass.

"See! I told you more travelers had come! See!"

Dozens of eyes fixed on Sayeed and Zeeahd, questions written in their expressions. Eyes widened at the brothers' blades, their unkempt appearance.

The brothers walked toward the gathered villagers. The crowd formed up to await them, shifting on their feet, children hiding behind parents.

The peddler standing on the deck bowed and doffed his cap. "Minser the Seller at your service, goodsirs. This gem of a village is called Fairelm. And if I may be so bold as to speak for these good people, we bid you welcome."

The villagers did not echo the welcome.

Sayeed did not bow in return. His gaze swept the villagers, looking for anyone who might have been other than they appeared. He saw no one of note.

"My name is Sayeed," he said. "This is my brother, Zeeahd."

Their foreign sounding names caused a murmur of discontent to move through the crowd.

"Well met," Minser said. He waited a moment for a return greeting that didn't come, and the brothers' silence seemed to take him aback. He looked around at the villagers, perhaps hoping one of them would speak, but none did. He cleared his throat.

"Oh, yes, well. What has you two walking Sembia's plains under this bleak sky? There are dangers on the plains, although you look like a man familiar with a sword."

"We are merely travelers," Zeeahd said.

"We're just passing through," Sayeed added. "It is custom, is it not, to offer shelter and a meal to travelers?"

No one offered either. Eyes found the ground. The silence thickened. Finally the boy they'd frightened piped up.

"Those are strange looking cats."

Nervous laughter greeted the boy's words.

"Strange looking *men*," said a man's voice in the back.

Zeeahd stiffened at that, craned his neck. "Who said that?"

Sayeed took his brother by the arm, but Zeeahd shook it off. No one responded to the question.

"Who spoke so?" Zeeahd said. "It seems the custom in this stinking mass of hovels is to speak rudely to strangers."

Lots of angry looks, but no words, until a woman's voice from off to the side said, "And now who speaks rudely?"

Sayeed and Zeeahd turned to see a tall, strongly built woman with long red hair walking toward the crowd. Sayeed would have thought her attractive had he still felt such things.

The cats at Zeeahd's feet hissed at the woman as she approached, and her step faltered, her eyes on the creatures.

"You mind your tongue, woman," Zeeahd said. "Lest . . . "

Sayeed's hand on his brother's arm halted whatever threat he might have uttered, but the woman took his point and would have none of it. She put her hands on her hips and stuck out her chin.

"Lest what, goodsir?"

"Elle," said another woman in the crowd, a small, mousy looking woman with a mane of black tresses.

"No, Ana," Elle said, and glared at Zeeahd. "Say what you would, sir."

"Yes, lest what?" said another man in the back.

Most of the villagers' expressions grew vaguely hostile, although a few looked frightened. The children in the crowd, perhaps sensing the rising tension, looked upon events with wide, fearful eyes.

"Now, now," Minser the peddler said, as he lowered himself from the deck, huffing with the exertion of moving his fat. The crowd parted to let him through. He wore a fake, vacuous smile that annoyed Sayeed. "Things have gotten off poorly for no reason that I can see. I can assure you, goodsirs, that Fairelm is a village of unparalleled hospitality."

"Our homes are not hovels," spat a large, bearded man near the front of the crowd. Nodded heads greeted his assertion.

"Nor our women to be threatened," added another.

Minser gestured grandly, a king granting dispensation. Sweat beaded his brow. "Of course not! And I'm sure these men meant no offense! They misspoke, is all."

The cats lined up before Zeeahd, eyeing Minser coldly. The peddler's eyes went to them, to Zeeahd, back to the cats. He licked his lips nervously.

"Yes, well, um, perhaps you two could explain what brings you to Fairelm? If the good people here can be of assistance, I'm sure you'll have it. Within reason. And if not, well, then you can be on your way. Much of the day remains, and this is the best time to be traveling."

A round of "ayes" arose from the villagers.

Zeeahd stiffened, leaned forward, looking at Minser closely. "What's that?"

"What's what?" asked Minser.

"On your neck, what is that?"

Zeeahd advanced on the peddler, who nearly stumbled over himself backtracking. The crowd surged forward a step, but that was all. Sayeed put his hand to the hilt of his blade.

Zeeahd snatched at a lanyard hanging from Minser's neck and yanked it hard, snapping it.

"Sir!" Minser said, his face blotching red.

Zeeahd held the lanyard before him. A medallion hung from it, a medallion that featured a rose and a sun. The cats crept forward, gathering at Zeeahd's feet. Zeeahd's tone was sharp enough to cut flesh. "How did you come by this?"

The peddler stuck out his chest. "That is none of your—"

Zeeahd grabbed him by the shirt and pulled him close. His brother was much stronger than his slight frame would suggest. "How did you get this, peddler?"

"Let him go," Elle said, and angry murmurs formed in the crowd. They moved closer.

"Aye! Let him go."

The cats at Zeeahd's feet arched their backs, hissed, showed fangs. Sayeed moved to his brother's side, eyes cold.

"Keep your distance," Sayeed ordered them.

"Speak, Minser," Zeeahd said. "Your life depends on truth."

The peddler sputtered, terrified. "My life? You threaten me? What is this?"

"Speak!" Sayeed said, his eyes still on the crowd.

"I got . . . I got it at an abbey."

Zeeahd's hand gathered more of the peddler's shirt into his fist. His voice was as tight as bowstring, his eyes on Minser's face. "The Abbey of the Rose?"

Minser hesitated, nodded, his eyes moving from Zeeahd to Sayeed.

Sayeed glanced at the peddler, hope rising in him, making him as giddy as his brother.

"And while you were at the Abbey of the Rose, you saw . . . the Oracle?"

Several in the crowd made a sign with their hands: three fingers raised to the sky.

Minser gulped, nodded. "And . . . the sacred tomb of Dawnlord Abelar."

Sayeed whirled on him. "Who?"

"Did you say *sacred*?" Zeeahd asked, his voice low.

"He did," Sayeed said.

Sweat poured off of Minser's brow. He swabbed at it with a dirty hand, streaking his face with filth.

Hearing the name of Abelar Corrinthal, hearing him given a hallowed titled, his resting place called "sacred," all of it made Sayeed want to puke.

Zeeahd released Minser, and the fat peddler adjusted his shirt and his dignity.

"Thank you, Minser," Zeeahd said, faking a smile. "You must know where the abbey is, then."

Minser huffed. "No one knows where it is exactly. The Oracle sees who will come and sends Dawnswords to fetch them. But I doubt that you two—"

"And they fetched you?" Zeeahd asked.

Minser's mind seemed to be catching up with his mouth, so he held his tongue.

"Speak, man!" Sayeed said, his shout startling the peddler.

"Yes, they fetched me. I . . . wanted to see the dawnlord's tomb."

"The *sacred* tomb," Zeeahd said, closing his fist over the medallion. "Of *Dawnlord* Abelar."

Minser chewed the corner of his moustache. He seemed unable to make sense of things. "You . . . think him other than a good man?"

Zeeahd smacked Minser across the face, eliciting gasps from the crowd. "I *know* him to be other than a good man!"

Minser's mouth moved but no word emerged. A trickle of blood leaked from the corner of his lips.

"Something to say?" Zeeahd asked. "Say it, fat man."

The peddler's face reddened but still he made no sound.

Sayeed, caught up in Zeeahd's growing anger, held up his maimed hand, showing the stump of his thumb. "Your dawnlord took my thumb and that of scores of other unarmed men. He was a coward."

Gasps and uncomfortable expressions answered his proclamation.

"You're mad," someone said. "Leave here!"

"Dawnlord Abelar died a hundred years ago," said a burly man in a thick homespun, probably the village's smith

"He's jesting," said the fat peddler, rubbing his cheek, then blanched before Sayeed's hard gaze. "Aren't you?"

Another man's voice from deeper in the crowd said, "You look hale for a man of a hundred winters."

Uncertain laughter.

Sayeed sought the source of the voice in the crowd. His gaze killed the laughter.

"Jest?" Sayeed snarled. "You think I jest? About this?"

The smith's wife, Ana, tried to pull the man away from the front of the crowd. "Come on, Corl. Let's go now. Breakfast is ready."

"No one is going anywhere," Sayeed snapped, and whisked his blade free. He knew now how events would unfold. The cats did, too, for they meowed in excitement.

The crowd went wide-eyed at the sight of Sayeed's blade. A child wailed.

The red-haired woman, Elle, stepped forward, her arms held out to her sides as if she would protect the entire village with them.

"Why don't you put your blade back and be on your way, now? Please, just leave."

The villagers nodded heads, murmured agreement.

Zeeahd shoved Minser away, causing the fat man to stumble, and glared at Elle until she took a step back.

"I take no orders from you, woman."

"I meant no offense."

Zeeahd paced before all of the villagers, staring at them, fists clenched.

"Ah, but now I am offended! By this place! By all of you!" He glared at the crowd. "My brother spoke truth. One hundred years ago Abelar maimed unarmed men, us among them." He held up the stump of his severed thumb. "*Dawnlord* Abelar stole our livelihood, stole our *lives*." His voice rose as he spoke, spit flying. He made wild gestures with his hands. The cats trailed him like angry shadows, hackles raised, hissing. "*Dawnlord* Abelar condemned us to a cursed existence, a living hell, with only a devil's promise to give us hope. And you venerate him. You simplistic idiots. You wish to see? *Do you?*"

No one spoke. Everyone stared at Zeeahd, wide eyed.

"Then see."

He threw off his cloak, untied his tunic, and tore it from his body, revealing his torso.

The villagers gasped, turned away. Children screamed, started to cry. Sayeed simply stared, dumbfounded. He'd not seen his brother's exposed flesh in years.

Fissures and scars deformed skin that was the color of an old bruise. In places the flesh looked melted, like candle wax. Tumors bulged, the largest in the small of his back, and here and there were malformed lumps of vestigial tissue. A few red scales covered the flesh in places. His distended stomach looked like that of a starving man, like it would pop if it were pierced. Blue veins, visible through his skin, made a grotesque net on his flesh.

"You see now what your dawnlord wrought? Do you?"

As they watched, his skin bubbled and rippled, as if something moved below the surface of his tissue. He laughed, the sound manic, filled with rage.

"That is what Abelar did to me!" Zeeahd was respiring heavily, the sound wet and bubbling. He whirled on Minser, who quailed before his wrath, and pointed a finger in his face.

"You will take me to the abbey, peddler. And I will see the Oracle. And while I am there, I will also visit the *sacred* tomb of Abelar Corrinthal."

Minser sputtered. "I . . . I told you, I don't know how to find it. And even if I did—"

Zeeahd stalked forward and slammed the medallion into the peddler's brow, knocking the fat man to his knees and causing him to exclaim with pain.

"I think it's in that head, Minser. And I'll have it out one way or another."

He cast the medallion at the feet of the bleeding peddler. Elle stepped forward and tried to help Minser to his feet, but the peddler seemed in no mood to stand. Instead, he sat there, stunned and bleeding.

"I'm all right, lady," Minser muttered, but he was weeping. "I'm all right."

Elle whirled on them, face red with anger, a vein bulging in her forehead. "Get out of here!" she shouted, and pointed at the road. "Get out of here now!"

Zeeahd ignored her as he gathered his tunic and cloak. The cats paced around him, meowing, licking their chops, eager, hungry. Sayeed could not deny that he felt some of the same hunger, looking on the faces of the stupid peasants and their foolish reverence for Abelar Corrinthal. He had not come into the village intending to kill, but the desire to do so rose in him now, ugly and bloody.

"The peddler comes with us," Zeeahd said.

Sayeed stepped forward, pushed Elle away roughly, grabbed Minser by the arm, and jerked him to his feet.

"Leave him alone!" Elle said.

"It's all right, lady," Minser said, his speech slurred, daubing at his bleeding forehead. "I'll be fine."

The cats continued their insistent meowing. Zeeahd rubbed their heads.

"Hungry, are you?"

He looked up at the crowd, a sly smile on his face.

"Please," Elle said. "Just go."

"We are going," Zeeahd said. "But first, something for those who revere Abelar Corrinthal."

A nervous rustle from the crowd, one uncertain laugh, a cough.

"Come out," Zeeahd said to the cats. "Show them."

The villagers watched in wide-eyed horror as the cats' mouths opened so wide it looked as if their jaws were unhinged. Their faces seemed nothing but an open hole. Something wriggled within the cats' bodies, under the skin, causing their forms to bulge grotesquely. Their eyes rolled back in their heads and their bodies convulsed.

A woman screamed. Another fainted. Everyone took a step back. Terror moved in a wave through the crowd.

"What's wrong with them?" someone shouted.

"Gods!" said another.

Scaled hands reached out from within the cat's throats, took hold of either side of the gaping mouth, and began to pull back. The cats' skins stretched as blood-slicked diabolical forms wriggled out of the maws.

More screams, shouts of horror.

Diabolical forms wriggled forth in a slick, bloody mess of scales and horns and claws and teeth, the bodies much larger than the skin of the cats that contained them. They snarled as they emerged, drooling, shedding the feline skins like cloaks.

"The light preserve and keep us," Minser whispered beside Sayeed.

Sayeed backhanded him in the face with a gauntleted fist. The peddler did not even groan, just fell to the ground unmoving.

As the devils stretched, panic seized the villagers. They gathered children, screaming, and fled. All except Elle. She stood her ground, her hand to her mouth, terror in her eyes.

The gore-slicked devils crouched on all fours, their sinewy muscles coated in a blanket of long spines. Their slit-eyed gazes darted about as they fixed on one and then another of the fleeing villagers. Long black tongues ran over mouths fanged like a shark's. The one nearest Sayeed lifted its head to the sky and uttered an eager, clicking ululation.

"Feed," Zeeahd said to them, and gestured at the fleeing villagers. "All but this woman and the peddler. They're mine."

The devils snarled and pelted after their prey like a pack of wolves, howling for blood and flesh, their clawed feet throwing up clods of sod with every stride. One of them thumped into Elle as it passed, nearly knocking her down.

"The woman, Sayeed," Zeeahd ordered.

Two of the devils pounced on the villager who had fainted. They seized her by head and feet and tore her apart in a spray of gore.

Sayeed grabbed Elle by the wrist. She whirled, terror in her eyes, and kicked him hard in the groin.

"No! No! No!"

The blow might have doubled over another man, but Sayeed barely felt it. He pulled the woman close while she slapped and clawed at his face, her nails digging bloody furrows in his cheeks.

"Leave me . . . alone!"

Sayeed grabbed her by the hair and thumped her in the temple with the pommel of his sword. She sagged to the ground, as limp as a grain sack.

He stood over her and watched Zeeahd's creatures work.

The devils prowled heedlessly through the village, gleeful in the bloodletting. They overturned wagons, knocked down doors, shattered fences. From time to time they launched groups of spines from their backs, the missiles catching fire as they flew, thudding into flesh and wood and setting it all aflame. Screams sounded from all over the village, terrified shrieks from inside cottages and barns, wet ripping sounds from the street, gurgling groans of pain. The devils slaughtered everything within reach, not even sparing the livestock. Pigs squealed, impaled on devil's claws. Dogs, cows, goats, and cats were chased down and torn to pieces. The devils careened wildly through the streets, soaked in blood, bits of flesh and fur hanging from their claws, arms or legs dangling in their fangs, an orgy of gore.

Zeeahd came to Sayeed's side.

"It's beautiful, isn't it?"

When Sayeed said nothing, Zeeahd kneeled beside Minser and pulled him to a sitting position. Slaps to his face opened Minser's eyes. Seeing the slaughter, the peddler clamped his eyes shut, shaking his head.

"No, no."

Zeeahd slapped him, once, twice, a third time.

"Open your eyes, peddler! Open them or I will cut off your eyelids!"

Wincing, jaw clenched, his entire body trembling with the effort, Minster opened his eyes. He wept at the screaming, the blood.

"What have you done? What have you done? The light preserve us."

Zeeahd grabbed him by the hair.

"That will be your fate and worse, if you don't take us to the abbey. The light won't preserve you. Nothing will."

"You're a monster," the peddler said, sobbing. "A monster."

Zeeahd roughly released his hold on Minser's hair. "You have Abelar Corrinthal to thank for that, peddler."

Sayeed watched the devils work with a peculiar sense of detachment. He knew he should feel something—horror, sympathy, elation, something. But he felt nothing except tired. He might as well have been watching the slaughter of dinner chickens. He just wanted to get on with finding the abbey, the Oracle, and end his perpetual self-loathing and bitterness.

He ran his fingertips over his cheek and felt only smooth skin. The grooves that Elle's nails had carved in his face had already healed. Everything healed. Except his spirit. That wound where it should have been had never healed and never would.

"The Lord of Cania will cure us, Sayeed," Zeeahd said, as if reading his thoughts. "We need only get to the Oracle and from him, learn the location of Cale's son." He kicked Minser. "And now we have a way."

Fewer screams carried from the village. The devils had killed most everything. Sayeed heard mostly the sound of feeding, tearing meat.

Sayeed put a boot in Minser's belly. The peddler groaned, curled up into a fetal position on the ground. "And if this oaf cannot lead us to the abbey? He said—"

"He can and he will," Zeeahd answered. "Won't you, Minser?"

The peddler made no answer other than sobs.

When the devils had devoured their fill of the corpses, they stalked back to Zeeahd and Sayeed. Minser covered his eyes at their approach.

Their yellow, reptilian eyes glared at Sayeed as they passed. "Back now," Zeeahd said.

"We serve," one of the devils croaked, and each went to the bag of cat skin it had vacated, picked up the fur, extended the mouth over their horned heads, and began to squirm back inside. They seemed to diminish as they wriggled and writhed their way back into cat form. Soon the devils were gone and thirteen cats stared at Zeeahd and Sayeed.

"The woman?" Sayeed asked, although he suspected he knew the answer.

"I have something special for her rude mouth," Zeeahd said. His bare, scarred, distended stomach began to lurch and roll as he dredged up the poison he carried within him. "Put her on the deck."

Sayeed picked Elle up under her armpits and dragged her atop the deck. Her eyelids fluttered open when Sayeed dropped her there. She sat up, still woozy, recoiling as Zeeahd advanced on her, his body heaving with the effort to expel the darkness within him.

"Please, don't," Elle said, backing away crabwise. "I'm with child."

"Not anymore," Zeeahd said, the words distorted by the black phlegm filling his mouth and dribbling down his chin. As quick as an adder, he lunged forward, grabbed her by the wrists, and pinned her arms to her sides. He leaned in toward her face, his mouth open, drooling. She clamped her mouth shut, turned her head from side to side, making little grunts of fear.

Sayeed sheathed his sword and walked away. He'd rather survey the slaughter of Fairelm than watch his brother purge. He felt eyes on him and realized that several of the cats were following him, or perhaps they wished to revisit their slaughter.

Looking on the cats, Sayeed imagined something lurking within Zeeahd, too, some secret form waiting to burst forth from his brother the way the devils had heaved themselves out of the cats.

Blood, bodies, and gore littered the village's streets and buildings. The eyes of the villagers—where eyes still remained—stared accusations at him. Seeing the blood and death, he thought it was good that he no longer had a soul. If he had, by now it would be a withered, shriveled remnant of feeling, a thing that brought only pain, far worse than nothing.

CHAPTER EIGHT

GERAK AWOKE SHIVERING, FACE DOWN IN THE SODDEN WHIP-grass, the taste of Sembia's wretched soil in his mouth. He lifted himself to all fours, his body rebelling at even that slight exertion, and forced himself to his feet.

The rain had stopped. He eyed the dark slate of the sky, the shadow-polluted air. How long had he been asleep? Was it evening? He'd completely lost his sense of time.

He blinked away his exhaustion, slapped his face a few times, and started moving again. Thinking of Elle, of the baby, brought him strength. Exertion warmed his body, loosened his muscles, and soon he was making good progress. He alternately ran, jogged, or walked, stopping only to drink.

He saw the village's elms ahead, their massive height materializing out of the shadowy fog like columns supporting the sky. He did not smell any chimney fires, and their absence caused him a pang of concern.

He found the road that led through the gateway elms and picked up his pace. He was running by the time he entered the village.

Twenty paces in, he found a body. Or the pieces of a body. A headless torso lay in the street, the entrails spilling into the mud. Torn clothing, partially eaten flesh. The rest of the remains lay scattered elsewhere in the road, a head, an arm.

He stared at it for a long moment, unable to process what he was seeing. When the reality finally registered, bile rose and he vomited.

Another body lay nearby, the throat torn open, the abdomen split and emptied, the ribs visible.

A dead cow lay in a nearby pen, flayed, the exposed muscles glistening wetly, the poor creature's mouth frozen open in a scream of agony.

Gerak couldn't breathe. His heart was a drum in his chest. His vision blurred. He feared he would vomit again.

Something had come in from the plains, it must have, and attacked the village—some horror created by the Shadovar.

He started running for his cottage, heading around the edge of the village, spitting puke as he ran. He slowed enough to draw his sword, his fist white around the hilt. A buzz filled his ears, the muffled, internal roar of growing panic. He stumbled, slipped, and fell in the mud, but rose and ran on. Tears poured down his cheeks. Someone was speaking, despondent murmurings that sounded like a foreign language. It was him, he realized, the words drawn from his throat by the hook of his despair.

"Not Elle. Not Elle. Not Elle."

He passed more and more bodies, more body parts both human and animal, people he knew, friends and neighbors. Blood spattered everything. Viscera festooned fences and doorways as if placed there as part of some celebration of horror. He did not stop to look at the remains with care. He feared what he would see. Nothing was more important than getting to his cottage, to Elle. Nothing.

"Please, Elle. Please. Please. Please."

The cottage stood ahead, the door still closed. He saw no blood or bodies near it and prayed that Elle had hidden herself somehow, maybe in the shed. He slammed into the door, nearly knocked it from its hinges.

"Elle! Elle!"

She wasn't inside.

His heart fell to his feet.

The smell of her stew, still warm in the cauldron over the hearth's embers, filled the cottage, and its familiarity brought him to his knees. He dropped bow and sword, covered his face, and wailed like a child. Everything drained out of him. He did not even feel anger. He just felt . . . empty, hollow, a ghost, a shadow.

He cursed himself again and again. He should have taken her away from Fairelm years ago, left the village and the thrice-damned realm of the Shadovar. He would blame himself forever, hate himself forever. He never should have left her to hunt. He should have been here to defend her.

As if of its own accord, his hand went to the skinning knife he kept on his belt. He drew it from its sheath, held its blade before him, eyed the edge he kept so meticulously sharp. It could cut flesh and veins with the lightest touch, a simple pass over his wrist, a momentary flash of pain. He extended his arm, held the blade over his arm, saw the veins pulsing under his skin. Tears blurred his vision. He could join Elle with the smallest of gestures, the slightest movement.

A muffled scream from the direction of the village center stayed his hand. He was on his feet in an instant and sprinting out the door, sword and bow in hand. Another scream drew him on. He recognized it as Elle's voice, his Elle, and she was frightened, in pain.

"Elle! Elle! Where are you?"

Another scream pulled him onward. He made straight for the gathering elm in the center of the village.

He would kill whoever or whatever had slaughtered Fairelm, he would gut it, slit its throat, pull out its innards with his hands.

"Elle!"

He sprinted around the corner of the Ferrods' livestock pen, hardly noticing the heap of blood and gore that had been the Ferrods' cow, and into the commons. A thin, bald man, his shirtless torso covered in boils, scars, and tumors, had just finished . . . kissing her?

The man heard Gerak's approach and turned. His eyes narrowed in anger and he slid behind Elle, his forearm wrapped around her throat. Inexplicably, a dozen or more mangy cats, their faces all fangs and eyes, sat on their haunches around the man. She didn't look at Gerak; her eyes were open but vacant, staring out at something Gerak couldn't see.

Gerak's emotional state distilled down to a singular need to kill, to murder, to put arrows into this diseased bastard's eyes. He dropped his sword, drew an arrow and nocked, all of it instinctive, as rapid as thought.

"Get away from her, now!"

Elle gave no response to the sound of Gerak's voice, and the thin man's wide, fevered eyes squinted as he focused on Gerak. He smiled, showing the mess of his mouth, the crooked teeth of various sizes and shapes.

"Where have *you* been hiding?" the man said, his voice much deeper than the frame of his body would suggest.

Gerak trained his sight on the center of the face, a hard shot, but he'd made harder. He advanced and the shot got easier with each step he took.

"I said let her go."

A man lay on the ground near Elle, his face bloodied, his filthy shirt pulled halfway up, exposing a fat, hairy stomach. The man lurched up and shouted, "Gerak! Kill them! They want me to take them to the Oracle! I won't do it, Gerak!"

At first Gerak did not recognize him, but then the moustache and girth brought recognition: Minser. The peddler's unexpected presence made no more sense than his words.

Gerak put Minser out of his mind, walked slowly toward the man holding Elle, sighting along his arrow. A few more steps closer and he'd take the shot. The man maneuvered to keep Elle between them, but he seemed more amused than fearful.

"You know this woman?" the man said. He shook Elle and her arms and legs bounced sickeningly, as if unconnected from her body, as if she were a doll, as if she were already dead.

Gerak picked the spot he'd fire, right between the bastard's crazed eyes. He visualized the arrow's flight, prepared to loose.

"Gerak, look out!" Minser shouted, then screamed and curled into a ball as the cats pounced on him, clawing and biting.

Before Gerak could make sense of things before him, the splash and thud of heavy boots from behind whirled him around. A massive man in a battle-scarred breastplate, his hair long and disheveled, his eyes as dead as those of a fish, pelted toward him, a massive sword held high. Instinct and adrenaline seized Gerak—he sighted and released and his arrow sizzled through the air and slammed into the man's chest, knifing through the plate armor, sinking half the length of the shaft, and spinning the man to the ground, dead or dying.

Gerak spun back around while drawing another arrow—nock, pull, sight. The rat-faced man still sheltered behind Elle. The cats crawled all over Minser, nipping casually at his ears, fingertips, cheeks. The peddler lay curled up on the ground, screaming, crying.

"Get them off! Get them off!"

"Now you die," Gerak whispered to the man, and prepared to loose his shot.

An unexpected blow to the side of his head caused him to see sparks and drove him face down into the wet earth. He was distantly aware that he had fired his shot into the ground. Adrenaline allowed him to hold onto consciousness, but barely. He rolled over, bow held defensively before him, his vision shaky.

The large, armored man he had shot loomed over him, the arrow still sticking from his chest. The man leered behind his beard, raised a booted foot.

"You should be dead," Gerak muttered.

"I am," the man said, and slammed his heel into Gerak's face.

A crunch as his nose shattered, a flash of pain, more sparks, then darkness.

Sayeed grabbed Gerak by his cloak and dragged him through the mud toward his brother.

"What do we do with this one?" Sayeed asked.

The cats looked up from their torture of Minser, hope in their eyes.

Zeeahd looked at the woman prone at his feet, her eyes rolled back into their sockets and showing only whites, her mouth thrown open in a scream she'd never utter.

"He seemed fond of the woman," Zeeahd said. "Let them have each other."

The cats looked disappointed and left off tormenting Minser. The peddler lay huddled on the ground, weeping, bleeding from dozens of bites.

Zeeahd hopped off the deck and nudged the peddler with a toe. "Now you will take us to the Oracle."

Minser's face was still buried in his tunic. "I told you I don't know where the abbey is."

Zeeahd nodded at Gerak. "Then why did you tell him that you *won't* take us, rather than *can't?*"

Minser went still. He turned and looked up, his face bloody, tear-stained, one of his ears bleeding freely from a cat's bite.

"Don't bother to lie to me, peddler," Zeeahd said. "I know what I want is in your head. I'll have it."

Minser, bloody, muddied, somehow found the strength to summon a last bit of defiance. His double chin quivered when he spoke. "I'll die first."

"No," Zeeahd said, and kneeled to look him in the eye. "I won't let you die. Instead, I'll inflict pain. The cats will inflict it. My brother will."

Minser's lower lip joined his chin in quivering.

Zeeahd continued, "Pain today. Pain tomorrow. And the day after that, until finally you do exactly as I've asked. Is that what you wish?"

The cats gathered around the peddler, eyeing him, meowing. Minser began to shake. Sayeed saw terror root in Minser's eyes. It would live there the rest of his life. And yet still the peddler did not acquiesce. He closed his eyes and shook his head.

Zeeahd sighed like a parent exasperated with a child. "Start cutting off his fingers, Sayeed. Then feed them to the cats."

Sayeed drew his dagger and seized Minser's sweaty hand. The peddler shouted, tried to resist by balling his hand into a fist, but he could not hope to match Sayeed's strength. Sayeed locked the peddler's arm in place, pried his fist open, and put the edge of his blade to the base of Minser's index finger. The peddler shrieked. His body and breath had a stink born of terror. The cats gathered near, meowing excitedly.

"You are not men! You are not men!"

"Cut it off," Zeeahd ordered.

Sayeed let the blade bite just a little, and whatever little bits of resistance Minser still possessed crumbled.

"All right! All right! The gods forgive me, but I'll show you! Don't cut off my fingers! Just don't! I'll take you as far as I remember but that's not all the way. The Oracle sees when the worthy seek the abbey. He sends an escort and they lead followers through the pass. None know the whole way but them."

"A pass?" Sayeed asked. "It's in the Thunder Peaks?"

Minser hesitated, swallowed visibly, nodded.

"How far from here?" Sayeed said, shaking the fat man. "How far?"

"I think . . . two days' march," Minser said. "Maybe three."

"I told you, brother," Zeeahd said, triumph in his eyes. "We find the Oracle and he'll tell us where to find Erevis Cale's child. And then the Lord of Cania will free us of these curses."

"You *are* cursed," Minser said, weeping, head bowed. "Cursed in spirit. More devilish than those cats."

"Shut your mouth," Sayeed said, but only half heartedly. He could not work up any anger. He felt something he had not felt in decades, something alien, something he'd thought lost forever long ago: hope.

"What about my mule?" Minser asked diffidently. "What about Gray?"

"Your mule is coming with us," Zeeahd said. "My cats are carrying him around in their bellies."

Minser wept.

Growing fatigue slowed the pilgrims. Vasen, Byrne, Eldris, and Nald did what they could to keep spirits and strength high, but the encounter with the Shadovar riders had put a seed of fear in the pilgrims that flowered in the dark Sembian air. Eldris carried Noll, although it was plain the boy was healing.

Byrne, Vasen, and Orsin walked in the front of the column.

"This pace is too much," Byrne said. "They are failing."

"We can't let them," Vasen answered, eyeing the terrain ahead. "See to them. Word will get to Sakkors or Shade Enclave quickly. More Shadovar will come. We must get them to the Dales."

"And then?" Byrne asked. "War awaits them there."

"I know," Vasen said. "But what else is there, Byrne? This is the world. We just have to get them through safely."

"Aye," Byrne said. "This is the world."

Vasen put a hand on his shoulder. "Walk among them. Tell them stories. Give what solace Amaunator's blessings offer. And take comfort from what comfort you give."

"Yes, First Blade." Byrne faded back into the column, leaving Vasen and Orsin alone.

"You said you wanted to speak of something," Vasen said. "So speak."

Orsin walked in silence for a moment, perhaps deciding where to begin. "Your Oracle can see the future, yes?"

"'See' is a strong word, but yes. He has glimpses of future events."

"And yet he sent you—us, all of us—from the abbey at a time when he knew the boy would sicken, when he knew we would encounter the Shadovar riders."

Vasen shook his head. "'Knew' is too much."

"Either he's a seer or he isn't."

To that, Vasen said nothing. Shadows made slow turns around his flesh.

"Why would he take such a risk? An encounter with the Shadovar puts the entire abbey in peril. The worship of any god but Shar is outlawed in Sembia. And the Shadovar discourage travel unless it has official sanction. What if you had been taken?"

"I would never speak of the abbey to the Shadovar."

"Byrne? Eldris?"

"Neither would they."

"Well enough," Orsin said, accepting that. "But why take the risk? Did his vision fail him or . . . "

Vasen stopped and turned to look into Orsin's face. "Or what? Do you think he would risk the pilgrims' lives for nothing? Ours?"

"Not for nothing, no," Orsin said. "But I think something is happening. I think he sees it coming."

Vasen recalled the conversation he'd had with the Oracle outside his quarters. It must have shown on his face.

"You think it, too?" Orsin asked. "Don't you?"

They started walking again before the column caught up.

"I don't know," Vasen said, looking up at the sky. "Things have been strange of late."

"Yes," Orsin said, nodding. "My journey to the abbey. Our meeting."

"You think the Oracle arranged it?"

"Now you use words that mean too much. 'Arrange,' no. 'Foresee,' yes. But what does it mean? What did he intend?"

Vasen shrugged. "The spirits in the pass, too. That was odd."

"Yes," Orsin said. "They spoke to you of your father."

Vasen nodded. "And you know of my father. You follow the same god he did."

"And you and I met and here we are. There's more afoot here than we can see, Vasen. Maybe more than the Oracle could see."

"Possibly," Vasen said. "I'll ask him when I see him again. For now, the pilgrims are my concern."

Orsin seemed about to say something more, then said only, "Agreed."

Each walked alone with his thoughts for hours, pushing the pilgrims, monitoring the sky, the plains around them. Most of the day passed with nothing more eventful happening than Noll trying to walk on his own. Although weak, he managed, and his recovery brought smiles and brightened spirits. Elora rushed to Vasen and hugged him so tightly she momentarily took his breath.

"Thank you, goodsir," she whispered. "Thank you for saving my son."

Vasen felt his cheeks warm. The shadows around him swirled, caught up Elora, although she seemed not to care. Byrne and Nald grinned at his discomfiture, and discomfited he felt.

"You're welcome, milady."

"Thank you for your prayers, goodsir," Noll said to Vasen, all seriousness.

Vasen smiled, disentangled himself from Elora, and mussed the boy's hair. "I'm not sure it was the prayers. You're a tough one, Noll."

The boy smiled, his face still pale, and went to his mother's side.

The Dawnswords pushed the pilgrims as far and hard as they dared, then camped in a pine-shrouded declivity.

"No fire," Vasen ordered, and received groans in response. "Crowd together for warmth. I'll take first watch."

"And I'll take second," Orsin offered.

Byrne looked skeptical at that. "First Blade, I should take second watch. And Nald or Eldris third. Orsin is not one of us." He nodded sheepishly at the deva. "And I mean no disrespect."

"I take none," said Orsin, as implacable as a statue.

"He's one of us in the ways that matter," Vasen said. "And he can see in the dark as well as me."

"As you say, First Blade," Byrne acknowledged with a nod, and walked back to the pilgrims.

"Go eat, Orsin," said Vasen. "Then sleep. I'll wake you when it's time."

"As you say, First Blade," Orsin said with a nod and a mischievous wink, then walked off to join Byrne with the pilgrims.

That night, while the pilgrims lay on the wet ground and shivered in the wind, Vasen sat alone at the edge of the camp. He stared out at the inky plains. His father had known Sembia before the Shadovar had shrouded it in perpetual night. His father had fought to keep Sembia in light.

And, in the end, his father had failed.

You must not fail, Vasen.

The words that plagued his dreams.

Vasen pondered events until the end of his watch, then woke Orsin and fell asleep.

The next day they plodded on. A light rain fell, summoning exasperated sighs from the pilgrims. Notably, Noll kept his mouth clamped shut.

Three hours into the trek, Orsin put his arm before Vasen. "Stop."

Vasen's hand went to the hilt of his blade. He saw nothing, but held up his hand to stop the column. "What is it?"

Orsin cocked his head, as if listening. Vasen heard nothing but the soft patter of the rain.

"Why are we stopping?" Byrne called from behind, his tone overloud in the quiet.

Orsin stared into the distance. Vasen followed his gaze and saw it at last.

Black dots wheeled through the sky ahead, visible against the dark sky only because of their motion.

"It's the Shadovar again," one of the pilgrims, an elderly woman, said.

"No," Vasen called back. "Not the Shadovar."

"Crows," Orsin said.

"Yes," Vasen said. "Crows."

The wind picked up, carrying the caws of the birds, the distant sound as faint as a whisper. He and Orsin moved back to the column.

"What is it?" Byrne asked.

"Carrion birds," Orsin said.

"Something has died," Elora said, and put her hand to her mouth.

Vasen resurrected a smile and put a hand on Elora's shoulder, pleased to see no shadows dancing from his skin. "Take heart. It could be the carcass of a beast. Crows out here will swarm a dead deer."

Elora looked doubtful, her eyes worried in their nest of wrinkles. She put her hands protectively on Noll's shoulders. The other pilgrims, too, seemed uneasy, sharing concerned glances, whispering among themselves. A few looked up into the dark sky, perhaps fearing Sakkors itself would materialize out of the darkness, perhaps fearing another Shadovar patrol would happen upon them.

"Be at ease," Vasen said to them all. "There's nothing to fear."

He pulled Byrne aside. He felt Orsin's eyes on him all the while.

"There's a village on the other side of that rise."

Byrne chewed the corner of his moustache and nodded. "I know. Fairelm, it was called."

"It *is* called Fairelm. I'll go ahead and have a look. Keep the pilgrims here for now."

Byrne took Vasen by the arm and pulled him around. "Perhaps we should just avoid it. I don't want to compromise the safety of the pilgrims, and the doings of Sembia are not our concern."

"True," Vasen acknowledged with a tilt of his head. "But if something has happened to the village, someone there could need help. Our calling is more than just escorting pilgrims, Byrne."

"A light to chase darkness," Byrne said softly. His hand fell from Vasen's arm.　　Distant thunder rumbled, as if the sky disputed Byrne's sentiment.

"A light, indeed," Vasen said. He thumped Byrne on the shoulder.

"I still dislike putting the pilgrims at risk."

"As do I," Vasen said. "Take them over to that wood." He pointed at a nearby stand of broadleaf trees that swayed in the wind, leaves hissing. "Do what you can to put their minds at ease. I'll return quickly. The light keep you."

"And you, First Blade." Byrne turned and started gathering the pilgrims.

"Come, folks," he said, filling his voice with false cheer. "Rain is coming. Let's get under those trees and take a meal . . ."

As Byrne shepherded the pilgrims toward the wood, Vasen hefted his shield, turned, and found himself face to face with Orsin.

"Gods, man. You move like a ghost," Vasen said.

"I'll accompany you," Orsin replied.　　"Not hungry, I suppose?" Vasen asked with a smile.

"No," Orsin answered with a grin. "Not hungry."

"I'll be grateful to have you." Vasen signaled to Byrne that Orsin would accompany him. Together, the two of them hurried toward Fairelm. Orsin dragged his staff behind them, carving a temporary groove into the whipgrass and mud. The caw of crows pulled them onward.

Vasen smelled the faint, sickly odor of death before he and Orsin reached the edge of the rise.

They crouched low, and looked down at the village, maybe a long bowshot away. Small plots of farmland surrounded a core of single-story, sturdy wooden buildings, themselves built around a central commons and a large pond fed by a small stream. Several ancient elms stood here and there throughout the village, a dozen maybe. Vasen imagined the trees predated the Spellplague; they appeared to have come through unchanged. Two small rowboats bobbed on the wind-whipped water of the pond.

"There are many dead here," Orsin said, his voice a somber whisper.

A child's swing hung from one of the nearest elms, swaying eerily in the breeze, as if ridden by a ghost. The elms' canopies whispered in the wind.

"I see them."

Pieces of bodies lay scattered among the buildings. Vasen could make out heads, arms, torsos, the bloody flotsam of a slaughter. He noted the twisted forms of women and children, even livestock had been torn apart. Blood pooled in dark puddles on the road, stained the grass, spattered doors and the sides of buildings.

"What happened here?" Vasen whispered.

Orsin said nothing. He simply stared, as still as a statue, as still as a corpse.

Crows gorged on the feast, their cries a grotesque accompaniment to the quiet of *the dead*. Now and again a few would take to the air, cawing at one another, before they again alit and feasted.

"This isn't the work of an animal," Orsin said.

"No," Vasen said.

"The Shadovar, then?"

Vasen shook his head, shadows curling around him. "When the Shadovar wish to teach a lesson, they do so with magic and leave no doubt of their involvement."

"What, then?"

Vasen didn't know. There were many predators that prowled Sembia's dark plains, but this, this was something else . . .

Whatever had attacked the village had reveled in blood, in murder. He looked back to Byrne and the pilgrims. He could barely see them, huddled as they were under the broadleaf trees. A soft light flared—Byrne's holy symbol, light in the darkness. Perhaps he was leading them in prayer.

Vasen stood and drew his blade. Anything to be done in the village would require hard steel, not soft prayer. The weapon's edge glowed faintly in the shroud of Sembia's shadowed air.

"Come on," he said, and started down. Shadows gathered around him, a reflection of his anger. To keep himself centered, he concentrated for a moment and put his faith in his shield until it began to glow. The soft, rosy light warmed him but did nothing to dull his anger.

"If the attackers remain, they'll see your light," Orsin observed.

"Let them see," Vasen answered.

They walked through fallow barley fields, under several of the towering elms, and into the bloody streets. Somewhere a loose shutter or door slammed repeatedly against a window sash, like a pulse, like the dying heartbeat of a dead village.

The crows took wing, cawing in anger, as Vasen and Orsin neared the first of the bodies—an elderly man pressed face down in the mud. They kneeled beside him and flipped him over. His abdomen had been ripped open, his throat shredded. His wide, terrified eyes stared up at the dark sky.

"The claws and teeth of something large," Orsin said. "But he is not fed upon except by the crows."

"Just murder, then," Vasen said. He removed his gauntlet, placed a hand on the elderly man's brow, and with his other hand held his glowing shield over the man's face so that its light reflected in his eyes.

"Whomever your patron, let Amaunator's light help guide your way to your rest."

The other bodies and pieces of bodies they found on the outskirts of the village showed similar wounds. Vasen's heart ached over the dead children, who had spent their final moments in terror and pain. He prayed over everyone he found.

He and Orsin made slow progress, checking the bodies for signs of life, checking the interior of cottages for someone who might have hidden from the attackers. They found nothing but blood and the dead. Livestock had been slaughtered in their pens, cows flayed. Chicken feathers floated here and there in the wind like snowflakes.

Neither Vasen nor Orsin called out for survivors, although it would have made sense to do so. Breaking the quiet seemed blasphemous somehow.

He looked for tracks, some clue about the identity of the attackers, but the rain had washed them away. By the time they neared the center of the village, Vasen had resigned himself to finding neither survivors nor perpetrators.

"Ages turn, the world changes, but there is always horror," Orsin said.

"And sometimes beauty," Vasen said.

"But none here," answered Orsin, his eyes distant.

A shout shattered the quiet, a rage-filled roar that originated from somewhere ahead, the commons, perhaps. The sound summoned Vasen's anger. Shadows exploded from his flesh.

"Move!" he said to Orsin, and ran for the village center, blade ready. He channeled his god's power as he pelted through the mud, empowering his blade and shield. Both glowed white. But the shadows around his flesh remained. Light and shadow coexisted in the air around him.

"Wait," Orsin said, but Vasen did not wait.

When they reached the commons, shaded by the canopy of one of the large elms, they saw a woman slouched against the bole of the elm, her mouth slack, her eyes open. She looked alive. A man crouched beside her, head bowed, one hand on her shoulder, the other around a longbow. A sword hung from his belt. He had not noticed them.

"Step away from that woman!" Vasen said, slowing to a walk and advancing.

The man's head snapped around and his eyes fixed on Vasen and Orsin. His mouth twisted with rage in the nest of his beard. He stood.

"Shadovar! You brought this down on my home!"

Before Vasen could respond, the man had drawn and fired an arrow with startling speed. At almost the moment he released it, Orsin dived in front of Vasen and hit the ground in a roll. Vasen feared he had been struck, but the deva came up in a crouch, the arrow clutched in a fist.

"He's not Shadovar," Orsin said to the man, who had already nocked and drawn another arrow and sighted for Vasen's chest.

Vasen held his shield up, with its sun and rose, as evidence. He could see that the man was a victim of what had happened in the village, not a perpetrator.

The man walked toward Vasen, arrow still aimed at his chest. Circles darkened the skin under the man's eyes. A large, purple lump marred his brow near the hairline and blades of grass stuck out of his hair. His nose was crooked, and dried blood was caked in his beard and mustache. His lips were peeled back from his teeth in a snarl.

Orsin tensed, as if he might launch himself at the man, but Vasen signaled for him to be still.

Moving slowly, as he might to calm an excited animal, Vasen dropped his blade and lowered his shield. The glow went out of both of them. As his anger dissipated, the shadows curling around his flesh subsided. He stood before the man, exposed, vulnerable.

The man kept his eyes on Vasen's face and walked up to him until the point of the drawn arrow touched Vasen's breastplate. Tears had made tracks in the filth and blood covering the man's face.

"I'm not Shadovar," Vasen said. "We came to help."

The man studied Vasen's face and Vasen imagined how he must appear, with his dark skin and yellow eyes.

"You're not Shadovar," the man said, the words empty. The bow creaked against the tension of the drawn arrow.

"We're here to help," Vasen repeated.

"To help," the man repeated. He seemed dazed. Tears welled in his eyes and he audibly swallowed.

Holding the man's eyes, Vasen reached up, slowly, and closed his fingers around the arrow's tip. "To help."

The words finally seemed to penetrate the man's haze. He looked down at the sun and rose on Vasen's shield.

"You're a priest?"

"I serve Amaunator," Vasen answered.

The man's eyes overflowed but he seemed not to notice. Desperate, pained hope replaced the tears and sought validation in Vasen's eyes. He released the tension in the bowstring, dropped the bow, and took Vasen by the shoulders, shaking him in his distress.

"Help her, man. Please."

Before Vasen could respond, the man fairly collapsed into Vasen's arms and began to sob, as if whatever tension had been holding him upright had just been released.

"Please help my wife. Help her."

Vasen let the man's emotion run its course while Orsin looked on, sympathy in his eyes. After a time the man pulled back, stood on his own two feet, wiped his nose and face, obviously embarrassed.

"I'm sorry. I just. I need. Just help her."

He pulled Vasen toward the elm, toward the man's wife.

"What's her name?" Vasen asked, kneeling to examine the stricken woman.

"Elle."

"And your name?"

"Gerak."

"I'm Vasen, Gerak. This is Orsin."

The woman's long red hair hung over skin as pale as snow. Vasen leaned in to check her breathing and recoiled at the stench of her breath.

"What is it?" Gerak asked. "What?"

Vasen shook his head. He removed his gauntlets and took her face in his hands. She was warm, feverish. Her eyes were open but rolled back in her head. He opened her mouth, wincing at the stink, and saw the remnants of a black film sticking to her teeth and tongue. Worry rooted in his gut.

He took her hand in his, channeled some of Amaunator's power, and with it took the measure of her soul. He instantly cut the connection when he felt the growing corruption there. He tried to keep it from his face.

"What are you doing?" Gerak said.

"I'm trying to help her," Vasen said. Using his shield as a focus, he held a hand over Elle and prayed to Amaunator. When the shield glowed and his palm warmed, he took Elle's hand in his own and let the energy course into her, but he could see it changed nothing. When he was done, she remained feverish and unresponsive. He thought he knew why. Not even a more elaborate ritual could help her. She was beyond his arts. Maybe the Oracle could help her. Maybe.

"How long has she been this way?" he asked Gerak.

Gerak cleared his throat. "I don't know for certain. Hours. Did it work? What you did?" He kneeled and took his wife's hands in his own. "Elle? Sweets, come back."

"Let's get her inside," Vasen said, sharing a meaningful look with Orsin. The deva took his point and sighed.

"Yes, of course," Gerak said, and pointed. "There's our home that way. Come."

Gerak averted his eyes from the dead and led them into a one-room cottage that smelled faintly of vegetable stew. A large carpet covered the wood floor and modest, homemade furniture afforded seating.

While Orsin started a fire, Vasen and Gerak placed Elle in the bed and covered her to the chest in a quilt.

"You're home now, Elle," Gerak said, and smoothed her hair. He bent and kissed her brow.

Gerak pulled a chair over to the bedside and sat. Vasen remained standing, conscious of his shadow thrown on the wall by the fire.

"What happened here, Gerak?" he asked.

While holding Elle's hand, Gerak told them his story: how he had left Fairelm a few days earlier to hunt, how he had been attacked by a creature that had been Lahni Rabb.

"You mean she had been transformed into something?" Vasen asked, eyeing Elle and making connections.

Gerak swallowed, nodded. "A horrible, twisted form. The poor girl."

"Go on."

Gerak explained how he had hurried back to the village to find almost everyone slaughtered, save his wife. He told them of the two men, one deformed and scarred, the other huge and unkempt. He told them about Minser, about the cats.

"Cats?"

"Yes. Lots of cats lingered around him. They weren't from the village. They looked feral, larger than normal. I had an arrow on the skinny one but the bigger one took me unawares, gave me this." He indicated the purple bruise on his brow, the ruin of his nose.

Vasen took it in, turned the information over in his mind.

"Why?" Orsin asked. He sat in the chair with his hands crossed in his lap.

Gerak looked at him as if he had spoken another language. "Why what? Why did they do it? I don't know. How could I know?"

"Men always have reasons," Orsin said.

"Men could not have done this to the village," Vasen said.

"Not alone," Orsin agreed.

"Her fever is not breaking," Gerak said, indicating Elle. "How long before she improves?"

Vasen stared at him, saying nothing, saying everything.

"She . . . will improve?" Gerak said, haltingly.

Vasen spoke in a low tone. "I don't think her sickness is one of body. It's in her soul."

"Her soul? What are you talking about?"

"Gerak, I believe they put something inside her . . . "

Gerak might have surmised what Vasen had already guessed. He shook his head. "No, no, no."

"I felt it. And . . . it's growing . . . "

"No, no."

" . . . and I fear that what happened to Lahni . . . "

Gerak's voice grew louder and he slammed his palm into the arm of the chair. "No!"

" . . . will happen to Elle. I can't stop it."

There was silence but for the crackle of the fire and Gerak's heavy breathing. He stared at Vasen for a time, wide-eyed, as if stricken dumb by the words. He shed no tears. Perhaps he had already shed all he had. He pressed his hands together, as if in prayer, and placed them under his chin.

"Not my Elle," he said, as soft as satin.

Vasen said, "If the transformation runs its course—"

Gerak held up a hand. "Do not dare to speak what you're thinking in my house, in her house. Do not dare."

"That's not what I was thinking," Vasen said.

Gerak's eyes widened, as if he were surprised that it was what *he* was thinking. "Who can heal her? Another of your order?"

"There isn't time—"

"You don't know that!" Gerak said, half rising from his chair; then, more quietly. "You don't know that."

Vasen conceded the point with a tilt of his head. He did not know.

"She's pregnant with our child," Gerak said, his voice breaking. He looked at Vasen as if the words were an accusation.

Vasen did not wilt, and he knew he would not turn his back on Gerak, on Elle, on their child. Perhaps Elle and the child could fight on long enough for them to get her back to the abbey.

"The Oracle might be able to help her," Vasen said.

Gerak stared at him as if he did not understand. Finally, he said, "Oracle? *The* Oracle? The Seer of the Vale?"

Vasen nodded.

"Then . . . you two are from the Abbey of the Rose?"

Again, Vasen nodded. Orsin held his peace.

Gerak sat back in his chair, his exhalation audible through his teeth. "Minser."

The name sounded vaguely familiar to Vasen but he could not place it.

"Minser?" Orsin asked.

"A peddler. He—"

"Fat with a moustache and ready smile," Vasen said, placing the name. "He made the pilgrimage to the abbey once. His aunt was ill."

Gerak nodded. "The two men took him prisoner. They wanted him to lead them to the abbey."

Vasen half rose from his chair. "What? Why?"

"One of them was seeking the Oracle, Minser said."

Vasen stood fully, shadows swirling around him. "What would he want of the Oracle?"

"I . . . don't know."

"I need to get back to the abbey," Vasen said. "Quickly."

"I'm coming, too," Gerak said, standing. "And Elle."

"Gerak," Vasen said, trying to phrase the words gently. "I must move very fast."

"So we'll move fast. I know the terrain better than anyone."

"Gerak . . . "

Gerak's expression turned vacant, as if he were anticipating a blow. "Don't you dare say it. Don't. You are a servant of the light. Don't say it."

Vasen felt Orsin's eyes on him, felt the weight of his words to Byrne before he had come to Fairelm—his calling was more than escorting pilgrims.

"I'll help you bear her," Vasen said. "And we'll move as fast as we can."

"I'll help, too," said Orsin, standing.

Together, the three men hurriedly built a makeshift litter for Elle and pulled her along behind them.

"These were good people," Gerak said, as they picked their way through the streets, through the dead.

"We have no time to tend to their bodies," Vasen said. "I prayed over each, if that's any consolation to you."

To that, Gerak said nothing, and Vasen could not blame him. There was little consolation to be found in the destruction of Fairelm.

CHAPTER NINE

THEY DRAGGED ELLE'S LITTER BEHIND THEM, MOVING AS FAST as they could. Byrne saw them coming and raised his arm in a halting hail. Vasen waved in return and Byrne hurried out to meet them. His eyes went to Gerak, the sick woman, Elle, and questions raised his eyebrows.

Vasen did not waste words. "Everyone in the village is dead save these two."

Byrne's expression fell, although he did not look surprised. "Darkness falls. I am sorry," he said to Gerak. "The woman?"

"My wife," Gerak said. "She's . . . ill."

Vasen said, "The attackers are headed to the abbey."

That brought Byrne up short. "The abbey? Why?"

"They seek the Oracle. I don't know why."

"If they get to the pass, the spirits will stop them."

"Maybe," Vasen said, "But I'm taking no chances. You didn't see the village, Byrne. These are not ordinary men."

Byrne looked Vasen in the eye. "Well enough. Then we'll stop them together. Come on."

Byrne turned to go, but Vasen grabbed him by the shoulder and pulled him around.

"We'll stop them," Vasen said, nodding at Orsin. "You have to stay with the pilgrims, Byrne."

Byrne's eyes narrowed. He chewed his moustache, spit it out, and said, "I swore to protect the Oracle, the same as you, First Blade."

"And we also took a charge from the Oracle to protect Amaunator's pilgrims. Would you abandon them to Sembia's plains? Let them try to find their own way through the battle lines drawn across the Dales?"

Byrne colored, masticated his moustache anew, shifted on his feet.

"Say it," Vasen said, and Byrne did.

"You stay with the pilgrims, then," Byrne said. "You're a creature of darkness, First Blade. You can lead them better through this. Even now you sweat shadows. Even now you—"

Too late Byrne realized what he had said. His eyes widened.

Shadows coiled around Vasen but he kept his face expressionless. He'd heard the words, or read them on the faces of his fellow Dawnswords, many times. He was the first blade, but he was apart from his fellows and always would be. Like Orsin, he was a congregation of one.

"I stand in the light, Byrne Neev. The same as you."

"I'm sorry," Byrne said, flushing, but Vasen ignored him and continued:

"Faith defines me, not blood."

"I know, First—"

"And I've been in service to the abbey, and the Oracle, for much longer than you."

"Yes—"

Vasen's voice was rising as he spoke. "This decision is mine and you will abide by it."

"Of course."

"You *will* remain with the pilgrims."

"Yes, First Blade," said Byrne, chastened.

Vasen's breath came hard. The shadows around him swirled, nearly touching Byrne. He closed his eyes, inhaled, and calmed himself.

"I'm sorry," Byrne said, looking off to the side of Vasen's face. "I spoke inartfully, with heat, and I regret it."

"Words are not swords, Byrne," Vasen said. "I'm uncut, and it's forgotten."

Byrne sagged with relief.

"Keep moving, as fast as they can bear. By now, the Shadovar know we're out here. Watch for them. Watch for soldiers as you near the Dales."

Byrne nodded.

"After you've gotten the pilgrims to safety, return to Fairelm and see to the bodies as best you can. They deserve what rest we can give them."

"Well enough, First Blade."

"The light keep you," Vasen said to him.

"And you," Byrne said, coloring as he spoke the words.

Despite the harsh words, they embraced. Vasen started to walk toward the pilgrims, but Byrne put a hand on his breastplate to stop him.

"Has the Oracle ever seen for you, First Blade?"

"Of course."

"What did he say?"

The question took Vasen aback. "Each man's reading is his own, Byrne."

"He told me I would not die while the abbey stood. Those were his words."

Vasen swallowed, nodded.

"I don't know what to do with that," Byrne said.

"Nor I," Vasen said. "Let me tell the pilgrims I'm leaving."

"Of course."

After he'd explained things to the pilgrims, Vasen said to them, "Byrne and Eldris and Nald will see you safely north. There's nothing to fear. The light keep and warm you all."

They returned his greeting haltingly, and he turned to go before they began to ask questions. A soft touch on his forearm brought him around. Elora stood there, concern written on her features. Her hand slid down to take Vasen's.

"You shine, Dawnsword. Despite your shadows. Remember that. I wish you could have known my husband. He was a good man. Like you."

Her words touched him. He bent, took her face in his hands, and kissed her brow. "Thank you, Elora."

"I'm glad that we met," she said.

"As am I."

"I won't forget you," she said.

"Nor I, you," he said, then mussed Noll's hair. "Nor you. Take care of your mother."

"I will, goodsir."

With that, he walked back to Orsin and Gerak. "Let's go."

Before they started off, Orsin used his staff to draw an arcing line in the dirt before their feet.

"What's that?" Gerak said. "A horizon?"

"Of sorts," Orsin said, and they stepped over the line.

"Dawn or dusk?" Gerak asked.

"We'll soon see," Orsin answered, and they set off.

When they had gone about a spear's cast, Vasen turned to look back at the pilgrims. They were gearing up to go, but Byrne stood apart from them. He raised his hand in a farewell. Vasen answered in kind and turned away.

They moved as rapidly as they could, but Elle's litter necessarily slowed them.

"We're not moving fast enough," Gerak said, wiping sweat from his brow. "But we're not leaving her, Vasen."

Vasen said, "Of course we're not."

"How far is the abbey?" Gerak asked.

"Two days' hard walk," Vasen said. "Three at this pace."

Gerak looked down at his wife, pale on the litter. "She's with child. Did I already tell you that? We'd had trouble conceiving. She was so happy when she learned . . . "

"I'll take the litter for a while," Orsin said.

"By yourself?" Vasen asked.

"Aye," Orsin said. Gerak walked beside the litter, his fingertips brushing Elle's arm.

Vasen understood what had happened and knew that Orsin did, too.

Gerak was taking the first steps in saying goodbye to his wife and their child.

The Sembian plains looked the same in all directions—whipgrass with the occasional woods or forest—so Vasen dared not deviate from the course he knew. Using the landmarks he'd been following for years, he retraced the route he'd used to bring the pilgrims to Fairelm. The three men alternated carrying Elle hourly, although Orsin took extra shifts. The deva's endurance was otherworldly. Gerak and Vasen ended their turns sweating and gasping. Orsin ended his with a shrug and a smile.

While pulling Elle late in the day, Vasen noticed movement under the blanket that covered her.

"Watch out!" he said, and set her down, drew his blade, and threw back the blanket.

"Oh, gods," Gerak said.

Her legs had swollen to twice their normal size. A mesh of pulsing black veins lined them. Her abdomen swelled and roiled, as if something were moving within her. Gerak fell to his knees beside her and took her hand in his, held it to his brow. He did not sob and Vasen found this quite ominous.

"Is there anything you can do for her?" Gerak asked over his shoulder. There was no hope in his tone.

"I don't think so." Vasen kneeled beside Gerak and spoke in a low tone. "I'm sorry."

Sobs finally overcame Gerak's resistance. "Is she in pain, do you think?"

"I think not, no."

Gerak nodded, re-covered her with the blanket, and stood. "We keep going."

"Yes," Vasen said, his own eyes welling. "We keep going. We don't quit."

Over the next several hours, Elle's body continued to change. Her skin darkened, then coarsened. Scales and spines formed here and there on her flesh. Her body stretched, thickened. Her hair fell out in clumps. Vasen did not care to contemplate what might have been happening with the child she carried. He prayed it had died.

Throughout, the three men walked along in silence, none of them daring to say what needed said.

Night fell and the plains turned to pitch, but the three kept moving. The clouds masked the stars, and Vasen could determine the rough location of Selûne only because her light put a yellow smear in the sky. Gerak stumbled often in the dark, cursing, his breath a rasp.

After a time, fatigue made Vasen's mind fuzzy and he could barely stand. Gerak's breathing came in heaves. Even Orsin leaned on his staff, and his cheer was forced.

"We have to rest," Vasen said, and no one argued.

Orsin lowered Elle's litter to the ground and dragged his staff in a circle around the campsite. Gerak gathered kindling, dug a fire pit to hide the flames, struck flint to steel, and soon had a small blaze. It would not be visible in the gloom beyond a dagger toss. He pulled Elle's litter near to it. She looked monstrous in the firelight, the shadows playing over her deformities, her bloated body.

They ate the dried meat and bread from Vasen's pack. Gerak tried to feed Elle but she would eat nothing. He dribbled water into her deformed mouth, laid his bedroll on the ground beside her, and tried to sleep. His expression throughout seemed empty.

Vasen sat before the fire and stared across the flames at Gerak and Elle for a long while. Orsin sat across from him, so still Vasen thought he might have been asleep. But he was not, and after a while he removed a small flute from the satchel he carried and began to play, a quiet, uncomplicated melody that reminded Vasen of clouds.

"I didn't know you played music," Vasen said.

"I don't do it often," Orsin said. "Only when I'm sad."

Vasen's eyes grew heavy. He leaned back and floated on the notes of Orsin's tune.

"I'm glad you accompanied me back," he said to the deva.

"We've journeyed together often, Vasen Cale. In another age, we walked side by side into the volcanic den of Herastaphan the Dragon Sage, although we bore other names, then."

Vasen did not know if he believed Orsin, but he found the thought comforting.

"Spirits are not reborn, Orsin," Vasen said. "Spirits pass on to the immortal realms."

"What do you know of reincarnation, Vasen Cale?"

"Reincarnation?" Vasen chuckled. "I'll say I have little familiarity with it."

"Maybe not so little as you think. We have battled together before, you and I. Often."

Vasen slurred his words as sleep came. "I think we will again. Soon."

Screams jerked Vasen from sleep. He lurched to his feet, heart racing, blade in hand. Adrenaline cleared his mind. Orsin was already on his feet, staff in hand. Gerak, too, was standing, staring down at Elle, his face stricken.

She was screaming.

The sound reminded Vasen of a trapped animal, equal parts terror and pain. Strangely, her body did not move at all. She simply opened her mouth and wailed, the rest of her as still as stone. Her eyes were open, but vacant and bloodshot.

Gerak did not so much as glance at Orsin and Vasen. He kneeled beside his wife and placed two fingers over her lips.

"Hush, Sweets. Everything is fine. Hush, now. Hush."

Vasen did not know if Elle was responding to Gerak, but her screams lost volume, turned to a pathetic, hoarse wail, then stopped altogether. Her mouth and eyes remained open.

"Shh," Gerak said. "Shh."

During the night, Elle's teeth had lengthened and turned black. A dark ichor crusted at the corner of her eyes. Her chest rose and fell with the rapidity of a rabid animal.

Gerak put his head on Elle's breast and sobbed like a child. Vasen clenched his fists with frustration, helpless to do anything. Orsin looked on, his hands wrapped not on his staff but his flute.

The fire had burned down to embers. Vasen figured they had been asleep a few hours. He hoped Elle's screams did not attract any predators.

After a time, Gerak recovered himself enough to lean in close and whisper into Elle's ear. She gave no sign she had heard. Gerak stood, wiped the tears and snot from his face, and looked at Vasen.

"We're a day from the Oracle? Gerak asked.

Vasen nodded.

Gerak sagged for a moment, but picked himself up straight. "I need to cut my hair."

Vasen did not understand. His expression must have shown as much.

"It's too long," Gerak said.

Vasen still did not understand. "Gerak . . . "

Gerak withdrew a small skinning knife from a pouch at his belt and stood over his wife. He stared down at her, his eyes vacant. The knife hung loose in his hand.

"I'll cut it the way you like it, Sweets. Just the way you like it."

With that, he took his dark hair in his hand and began to slice it off in uneven clumps. His face was blotchy, his eyes wet, but he tried to smile for Elle as he worked.

Vasen watched the hair fall to earth and felt as if he were watching a murder. He glanced at Orsin, who looked as confused as Vasen.

By the time Gerak finished, his hands were shaking. He stood before his wife and posed as he might for a portrait.

"See, Sweets? Just as you like it."

Still shaking, his breath coming hard and fast, he kneeled beside her. He leaned in and kissed her on the cheek. Then he whispered in her ear while he placed the blade of the knife against her throat.

Realization dawned. Shadows swirled around Vasen. He started forward, stopped, dared not speak.

Tears finally broke through Gerak's resolve and began to fall. "I love you, Elle," he said, and slit her throat.

The blood poured out of her throat, not red, but black and stinking of decay. Elle did not move.

"I love you," Gerak said, as the blood flowed. "I love you."

In the last moments, fading pulses of blood oozed from the gash in her throat. Gerak stood and closed her eyes with his hand. His eyes were open but Vasen could see that he saw nothing. The light had gone out of him. He turned, dropped the knife, and walked away from the campsite.

"Gerak," Vasen called.

Gerak slowed but did not turn.

"Can you . . . see to her?" Gerak called back. "I can't. I can't, Vasen."

"I . . . of course," Vasen said.

Gerak nodded and walked off. Sembia's darkness swallowed him.

"He should not be out there alone," Orsin said to Vasen.

"He's alone wherever he is," Vasen said.

"He is now," Orsin said. He scribed a line in the ground, circling Elle's body.

"An end," Vasen asked.

"A sad one," Orsin acknowledged.

"Will you help me with her?"

"Of course."

Out in the darkness, they heard Gerak begin to wail, prolonged gasps of hopelessness and despair and anger that haunted Vasen while he and Orsin gathered wood for Elle's pyre. They stacked it away from the campsite, and when they had enough, they lifted Elle's body atop it and used embers from the fire to ignite it. The wood caught quickly. Thick black smoke curled into the sky and was lost among Sembia's dark shroud.

The two men stood in the light of the fire paying their respect to a woman they'd never known, to a child who would never be born. Vasen offered a prayer, although the words seemed too small for the occasion. Orsin played his flute.

In time Gerak emerged from the plains. He stood beside them in the fire's light. They all three watched Elle's body burn.

"Dawn and light follow the darkest night," Vasen said to Gerak.

"I'm not one of your faithful," Gerak said. "Spare me platitudes. Light and darkness have been gone from this realm for a long time, and now both are gone from my life."

"I'm sorry," Vasen said.

"I know," Gerak said, more softly, his head hanging. "You have my gratitude for trying to save her."

Vasen said nothing, simply stood beside Gerak.

"I brought food," Gerak said. He held up two coneys he must have taken while out on the plains.

"First we have to move," Vasen said. "The pyre will attract attention."

They broke camp and moved off into the night. After about two hours, Vasen called a halt. In silence, Gerak made another small fire in a pit, expertly gutted the coneys, stuck them with makeshift spits, and soon had them roasting. While they ate, Orsin spoke of his belief in past lives, that people close to one another meet again and again through time.

"Then . . . I could see Elle again?" Gerak asked. "In another life?"

"Yes," Orsin said. "Strong bonds stretch across many lives." His eyes went to Vasen.

"Would I know her?" Gerak asked. "Would she know me?"

Orsin smiled, walked around the fire, pulled Gerak close and kissed the top of his head. "I think you would, Gerak of Fairelm. Hold to that hope. But for now we walk this world, we three. Together. Yes?"

Gerak stared into the fire. "Yes."

After Orsin retook his seat, Gerak said, "I need to kill the men who did this."

"Yes," Vasen answered. "Yes, you do."

Riven sat cross-legged on the floor, his sabers unsheathed and resting across his legs. His girls sat beside him, the warmth of their bodies a comfort. Again and again he replayed in his mind all that he knew, all that he thought he knew, and still he felt as if he'd didn't know enough, that he was missing something.

But it was too late for second-guessing. Everything was in motion. Either he'd played matters correctly or he'd doomed them all.

He felt the shadows around him, the shadows in the plains outside that extended for miles. He felt the undead native to the Shadowfell, shadows and wraiths and specters and ghosts in the thousands, lurking in the darkness around the citadel. They, too, knew what was coming.

His girls sensed it at the same time he did. He felt the portals come into existence on the plains below the citadel, scores of them, each a flash of pressure in his mind. He felt his enemies step through and assemble in the plains in their multitudes.

Mephistopheles had finally lost the battle with his impatience. Or maybe Asmodeus had finally grown impatient with Mephistopheles, forcing the Lord of the Eighth's hand.

His girls stood up, hackles raised, and offered growls from deep in their chests. He patted them both as he stood.

"It'll be fine, girls," he said, and hoped he was right. "You're both staying inside, though."

They licked his hands, whined with concern.

"Get a move on, Vasen Cale," he muttered.

Outside, the blare of horns rang out over the plains, hundreds of them, followed by the combined shout of thousands of devils, the collective roar like a roll of thunder. His dogs howled in answer, crowded close to him. The horns blew a second blast, a third, as the armies of Mephistopheles arranged themselves to face him and his forces.

"To the hells with you and your horns," he said and walked to the nearest window to look out on what had come.

Telamont leaned on his magical staff and looked out the glassteel window of his tower library. The shadow-fogged air allowed only filtered starlight through its canopy, but Telamont could see well enough. The city of Shade extended before him, the dense jumble of its towers and domes and tiled roofs blanketed in night. It was his city, and he'd fought and schemed for centuries to preserve it and its people, along the way compromising . . . many things.

"Something's changed, Hadrhune," he said. "The world shifts under my feet."

Behind him, his most trusted counselor cleared his throat. "Most High?"

Telamont gestured with one hand, the shadows from his skin forming a wake behind the movement. "There's power in the air, odd stirrings in the currents of the world. It's troubled me for months. The gods are maneuvering, to what end I don't know."

"Most High, that's why—"

Telamont nodded impatiently. "Yes, yes, that's why I collect the Chosen. I search for them and when I find them I put them in cages, question them while I try to read the story of the changing world. And yet the question remains, and I still have no answers."

"Most High, Prince Brennus, with his unmatched skill in divination, could—"

Telamont's irritated gesture put a knife through the rest of Hadrhune's sentence, and it died in silence.

"Prince Brennus," Telamont said. "Is . . . unfocused of late."

He watched a patrol of veserab-mounted Shadovar knights cut through the shrouded air above the city, the undulating flight of the serpentine veserabs swirling the shadowed air with each beat of their membranous wings.

"Perhaps you should put this mystery from your mind, Most High? All of the Chosen we've captured can be killed within an hour. You need only give the word and I can inform the camp commanders—"

"To kill them now would be premature. Many of them don't even know what they are. Those who do don't understand what role they're to play. No, we keep them alive for the moment and learn what we can. Matters must clarify eventually."

"Most High, if I may be forward . . . "

Hadrhune paused, awaiting Telamont's permission for candor.

"Continue," Telamont said.

"Is it possible that the focus on the Chosen distracts from more worldly matters? The battle for the Dales goes well, but Cormyr and Myth Drannor must still be dealt with."

"Oh, war with Cormyr and the elves is coming," Telamont said. "Yder clamors for it. Our forces are prepared for them, but the Dales need to be pacified completely first. But this matter of the gods and the Chosen, this is something else, something . . . bigger. I need to understand it before events outrun me."

"Shall I state the obvious, Most High?"

Telamont said nothing, but he knew what was coming.

"There is one Chosen you have not imprisoned or questioned."

"Rivalen," Telamont said, and a cloud of shadows swirled around him.

"Yes," Hadrhune said, his velvety voice treading carefully. "You sent for him, but he did not respond. Yet."

"He will come," Telamont said, thinking of his son, the son he no longer trusted, the son he no longer understood.

"As you say, Most High. When he comes, perhaps with his newfound power . . . "

"His stolen divinity, you mean," Telamont interrupted.

Again, shadows churned.

"As you say, Most High," Hadrhune repeated, the doubt palpable in his voice. "In any event, if the prince *is* a godling, perhaps he has insight into what's happening."

"I think not, Hadrhune. The prince no longer thinks like a man."

Nor did he think like a Lord of Shade. He was lost in the nihilism of his faith. Telamont had scried him many times. Rivalen would stare into Shar's eye, unmoving for days at a time.

"Most High," Hadrhune said, "I concede that Prince Rivalen is unstable but . . . "

Telamont felt Rivalen's presence manifest in the room as a sudden weight on his consciousness, a density in the air, as if the room's dimensions changed shape to accommodate him. Hadrhune must have sensed it, too, for he gasped.

Rivalen said, "You speak of me as if I cannot hear every word you say, *child*."

"Child!" Hadrhune said, and sputtered in rage.

"You requested my presence," Rivalen said, ignoring Hadrhune, his statement directed at Telamont.

"No," Telamont said, still not turning, still staring out over Thultanthar. "I *sent* for you."

Rivalen became still more present in the room, weightier. The darkness deepened, thickened somehow. Telamont resisted the impulse to mentally run through the wards and spells that guarded his person.

"You don't send for me anymore, father," Rivalen said. "You request my presence. And I come if I will it."

Hadrhune recovered himself enough to say, "You will refer to him as the Most High, Prince Rivalen."

"And you will say nothing more or I will kill you where you stand."

Hadrhune gasped again to be so addressed, but he heeded Rivalen's admonition and said nothing more.

Telamont made his face a mask and turned to face his son.

By now, Rivalen loomed large in the room. Hadrhune, standing near him, indeed looked like a child. Rivalen's golden eyes glowed out of his sharp-featured face. He'd inherited the features from Telamont, but father and son shared very little else anymore.

"Divinity has made you ill-mannered," Telamont said.

"Prince Rivalen was never known for his grace," Hadrhune said.

Rivalen turned on Hadrhune, arm upraised as if to smack him. A sizzling mass of black energy gathered on his palm.

Hadrhune's eyes flared. He blanched, retreated a step, and held his staff defensively before him. Veins of blue light lit the crystal atop the staff.

"Rivalen!" Telamont shouted, and slammed the butt of his own staff on the tiled floor, causing a roll of thunder. "Violence is prohibited in these chambers!"

Rivalen froze, his narrow eyes fixed on Hadrhune, the annihilating ball of power crackling in his palm. "Your prohibitions no longer concern me, father. You couldn't stop me. Not anymore."

Telamont let his own power gather. Tendrils of shadows formed in the air, snaked around his hands, his staff.

"You're mistaken, child," he said, but wondered if Rivalen spoke the truth. He sensed the power in his son. Telamont had no doubt that he could hurt Rivalen, but he doubted he could kill him.

"He goes too far, Most High," Hadrhune said, his voice high-pitched, his breathing heavy and fast. He did not lower his staff, did not release the defensive spell burgeoning in its crystal cap.

"Run along, lapdog," Rivalen said. The ball of energy in his palm dissipated into nothingness.

"Most High—" Hadrhune began.

Rivalen clenched his fist and the crystal atop Hadrhune's staff shattered with a *pop*, raining pieces onto the floor. Shadows bled from the tip of the wounded staff. Hadrhune cursed, wide-eyed.

"I said leave," Rivalen said to him. "You aren't needed here."

Hadrhune's eyes burned, but he ignored Rivalen. "Most High?"

"You may go, Hadrhune," Telamont said, his eyes on his son.

The counselor bowed to Telamont, pointedly ignored Rivalen, and exited the chamber. Telamont knew Hadrhune would remain just outside the room with a group of elite Shadovar warriors, ready should they be needed.

"You were unnecessarily harsh with him," Telamont said.

"He is a fool." Rivalen walked past Telamont to the glassteel window that looked out on Thultanthar. "We fought so hard to preserve this after we fled Netheril's fall into the Shadowfell."

"We did," Telamont agreed. "And we fought hard to expand our reach when we returned to Faerûn. You were instrumental throughout."

Rivalen chuckled. "Flattery, father?"

"Truth, rather," Telamont said. "And now I could use your help once more."

Rivalen turned to face him. Shadows curled around him, as languid as a lover's caress. "With the Chosen and the gods and their plots?"

"You sense it, too?" Telamont said, momentarily surprised. "But of course you do."

"It's trivial," Rivalen said, and gestured contemptuously.

"Explain," Telamont said, irritated that anyone would call anything he mentioned "trivial."

"It's pointless. All of it. Everything." Rivalen gestured while he spoke, anger gathering in his voice, power gathering on his hands. "This game you play with gods and Chosen and empire. It's trivial. Do you not see that? We've wasted centuries on it, and to what purpose?"

"To what purpose?" Telamont said, taking a step toward Rivalen, his own anger rising. "For survival. And then for empire."

Rivalen's fists and jaw clenched. Shadows swirled around him. "Both are nothing. Both have always been nothing." He chuckled and there was a wildness in it. "It's all ending. This world. The gods. Their *Chosen*. They scramble to grab at phantasms. The Cycle of Night is already begun and it can only end one way. There's nothing left to do now but play our parts."

Puzzlement pushed aside Telamont's anger. "You think the world is going to end?"

"No," Rivalen said. He put his hands in his cloak pockets and his eyes flashed with the eagerness of a madman. "I know it's going to end. And I know how. So go on with your schemes and plots, your obsession with gods and their Chosen. Before the end, you'll see things as I do. This world is already a corpse. It needs only to rot away."

Telamont stared at his son a long moment. He realized he'd get nothing from Rivalen. His son was lost entirely to Shar, to nihilism, to nothingness.

"I think it's time for you to go, Rivalen."

Rivalen's lips curled in a sardonic smile. "You're right, father. And I don't think we'll meet again."

"You don't collect coins anymore, do you, Rivalen?"

Rivalen took his hands from his cloak and showed his father empty palms. "Why would I? What are coins to me? What is anything to me?"

"Indeed," Telamont said, and felt a deep sadness. He'd lost his son. His son had lost himself.

Rivalen bowed, the gesture half-hearted, almost mocking. "Goodbye, Most High."

The darkness shrouded Rivalen, and then he was gone, returned to Ordulin, to the thoughts and plans that plagued him, to the ideas that had, it seemed, driven him mad.

Telamont stood alone in the center of the room, his thoughts on the past, his wife, his sons as they'd been thousands of years before. He remembered his sons as children: Brennus's laugh, Rivalen's contagious chuckle. He remembered his wife's smile, what it felt like to hold her in his arms every night.

"My lord?" Hadrhune said.

Lost in his thoughts, Telamont had not heard Hadrhune re-enter the room.

"You never met Alashar, Hadrhune."

"Most High?"

"Never mind," Telamont said, and smiled softly.

"Most High, what of Prince Rivalen? Will he aid us in capturing the Chosen?"

"No," Telamont said, his thoughts hardening. "Rivalen is lost to us."

"I . . . don't understand. What will he do, then?"

Telamont faced his most trusted counselor. "What *won't* he do is the appropriate question."

Hadrhune licked his lips, dug his thumbnail into the damaged darkstaff he still held. "I'm not following, Most High."

Telamont walked to the glassteel window and stared out at Thultanthar.

"Rivalen wants to die, Hadrhune, but he wants to kill the world first."

Brennus stood at his ebonwood lectern in the three-story library of his manse in Sakkors. In the past he'd spent most of his time in Shade Enclave, but the capital city of New Netheril held small appeal for him anymore.

Books and scrolls from the various ages of Faerûnian history lined shelves that extended floor to ceiling on three of the library's walls—spellbooks, treatises on magical theory, histories from all over the continent, catalogs of arcane devices, lexicons of demonic and diabolical entities. The knowledge contained in the materials he'd gathered over the centuries could keep a sage occupied for a lifetime.

A highly detailed globe of Toril hung in the air in the center of the room, suspended only by magic. Its slow rotation mirrored that of Toril's. At Brennus's command, the globe could show Toril's terrain, its political borders and cities, or the lay of magic across the planet—where it was concentrated, where it was dead, the locations of various places of power.

Spicy, pungent smoke spiraled from a block of incense burning in a platinum censer atop a table near the globe. His homunculi perched on the table to either side of the censer like tiny gargoyles, clawing at the smoke and giggling as their hands split the streams of black smoke into finer ribbons. One jumped at the smoke as it rose, lost his footing, and tumbled off the table and onto the floor. The other laughed hysterically at his sibling's misfortune. Brennus watched them with a half-smile, wondering how constructs crafted of his own blood and essence could be so filled with humor and simple joy. Would he have been more prone to such things had his life taken a different turn? He remembered laughing often with his mother before she died.

Before she was murdered.

He'd changed after that. He'd obeyed the Most High's wishes and turned to divination rather than shaping. He would have been an entirely different man, with an entirely different life, had his mother lived. Strange how one vacancy could so change a life. Rivalen had not just murdered their mother. He'd murdered what Brennus could have been.

He eyed the books and scrolls piled high on the lectern before him, all of them connected in some way to the dead god Mask, his worshipers, Erevis Cale, the faith of Amaunator, Kesson Rel, and the Cycle of Night. He felt that he had all the pieces of the puzzle before him, but he could not quite form them into a coherent image.

He was missing something.

He was missing the son, Erevis Cale's son. The son had to be the key.

"Subject: Mephistopheles," he said, and charged the words with magic.

The shadows coalesced in several dozen places around the room and took the form of tenebrous hands. The homunculi looked up at the hands, eyes wide at the simple spell. Each of the magical hands lifted a book or scroll from a shelf and whisked it to Brennus's lectern. After setting down its burden, a hand would dissipate back into the air.

The homunculi watched the books float through the air and clapped with delight.

Brennus spent the next several hours learning all he could. He supplemented his mundane study with magical queries directed at entities in the Outer Planes. He used spells to pull knowledge from the informational currents that floated in the ether, learning what he could. More and more pieces formed.

Mask had been Shar's herald on Toril, and possibly her son. Shar existed on many worlds, in many planes, and always her goal was the same—the annihilation of worlds. The process, The Cycle of Night, had run its course on many worlds, leaving voids in its wake, and had begun on Toril. The hole in the center of Ordulin, the hole that Rivalen spent long hours pondering, was the cycle's seed.

But its growth appeared to have been slowed, or stopped.

In all his inquiries, Brennus could find not a single instance of the cycle ending on a world without that world's annihilation. Not one. The Lady of Loss had murdered billions with her nihilism. And his brother embraced it now.

We're all already dead, Rivalen had said.

His brother was murdering the world.

Brennus wanted Rivalen dead more than ever.

The guardian constructs flanking the door to the library—suits of archaic plate armor animated and given a rudimentary sentience by Brennus's spellcasting—lurched into motion and took offensive stances, halberds held before them.

At first Brennus thought his brother might have returned, but the alarm spell that pinged in his mind told him otherwise. In a few moments the library's door opened to reveal the thin, shadow-shrouded form of his longtime majordomo, Lhaaril.

The shield guardians moved before him, threatening him with their polearms.

Lhaaril's eyes flashed with surprise. The shadows drew closely about his finely tailored, elaborately embroidered robe.

"An experiment," Brennus explained. "I linked the shield guardians' perception to various alarm spells within the manse," Brennus explained. "They sensed you coming when your passage took you through the foyer. What is it, Lhaaril? I'm in the middle of things."

Brennus uttered a command word that returned the shield guardians to their neutral stance flanking the door.

"I have news, my lord," Lhaaril said. "One of the scouts has returned.

Brennus did not miss Lhaaril's emphasis on *one*. "One? Something happened to the other?"

Lhaaril shifted on his feet. The shadows around him swirled, betraying his discomfort. "It appears so. I think it best that the story come from the remaining scout."

The homunculi, no doubt sensing Brennus's piqued interest, sprinted across the library, clambered up his cloak, and took station on his shoulders.

Lhaaril dutifully ignored them, even when they stuck their tongues out at him.

"Shall I have him brought to you, Prince?"

"Yes, and right away."

Brennus deactivated the shield guardians before Lhaaril returned with the scout. Brennus searched his memory for the scout's name, found it—Ovith. The scout stood a head taller than Lhaaril, perhaps a hand shorter than Brennus. Plated armor, dented from many battles, encased his broad frame. His scabbard, however, hung empty from his belt. He put his arm across his chest and lowered himself to one knee.

"Prince Brennus."

On Brennus's shoulders, his homunculi mirrored Ovith's gesture.

"You may go, Lhaaril," Brennus said.

"My Lord," Lhaaril acknowledged, and exited the library, closing the door after him.

"Stand, Ovith," Brennus said to the scout, and he did. "Lhaaril says you have a tale to tell."

Ovith did not look Brennus in the eye when he spoke. "My Prince, Cronil and I patrolled the Sembian plains as you instructed, searching for any sign of the Abbey of the Rose."

Brennus had numerous pairs of Shadovar scouts scouring the Sembian countryside in search of the Abbey of the Rose and its Oracle. He suspected the life of Erevis Cale's son was tied up with the sun-worshipers, but he'd mostly given up hope. His men had found nothing but rumors for decades.

"We stopped to water our veserabs on the way back to Sakkors."

"Where? And be exact."

"At the River Draal, before it joins the River Arkhen, perhaps five leagues east of the Thunder Peaks."

Brennus held a hand up at his globe and put power in his words. "The River Draal, five leagues east of the Thunder Peaks."

Responding to Brennus's command, the globe in the center of the library turned to show the location he'd named. Brennus walked toward the globe, Ovith behind him.

"Twenty leagues in all directions from that point," Brennus said. "Expand."

The globe unwrapped itself from a sphere into a large, flat rectangle that showed the area Brennus had named. He noted the rivers, the mountains, his mind turning.

"Continue, Ovith."

"As we watered the mounts, Cronil heard something that alarmed him. He spotted a cave on the opposite riverbank and flew over to investigate. That's when we were attacked."

"The attackers emerged from the cave?"

Ovith nodded.

"Creatures or men?"

"Men, my Lord."

"Describe them, their clothing, their weapons, their tactics. Omit nothing."

Prompted by pointed questions from Brennus, Ovith explained how he and Cronil had been surprised, attacked by four men, all of them experienced combatants. Ovith could not be certain, but he thought two of them human, one a deva, and another . . .

"A shade?" Brennus asked, his mind and heart racing.

"Yes, Prince Brennus. I know how that sounds, but I saw him up close. He was a shade. And yet . . . "

"And yet?"

"And yet light was in his weapon. A rose and sun featured on his shield. And he wore this."

The homunculi leaned forward expectantly as Ovith removed something from his belt pouch and held it forth.

An exquisitely crafted rose cast in silver and attached to a few links of a necklace sat in Ovith's open palm.

"His holy symbol," Ovith said. "I snatched it from him during the combat. An accident, but I hope a fortuitous one."

"You've no idea." The shadows around Brennus stilled as he took the rose in his hand, felt its weight, the cool touch of its metal. The rose had a scratch on it, revealing shining silver under the dark tarnish.

Pieces started to fall into place, an image began to form. "A shade who is a worshiper of Amaunator."

"So it seems, my Prince. The abbey is real and we must have been near it. Why else would servants of Amaunator be at that place."

"Did they have mounts?"

"Not that I saw, Prince."

Brennus studied the map. His attention came back again and again to the Thunder Peaks.

"And this shade, he stepped through the shadows?" Brennus asked.

Ovith shook his head. "Not that I saw. No. He waded the river to reach me rather than stepping from one shadow to another."

"Did darkness regenerate his wounds?"

Again, Ovith shook his head, uncertainty clouding his expression. "Not that I saw, but he was a shade, Lord Brennus. I'd swear it. Perhaps not exactly like us, but a shade. I saw the way the darkness clung to him, his skin, his eyes."

"A half-shade, perhaps," Brennus said, closing his hand on the rose in his palm. A half-shade who was Erevis Cale's son. Brennus still could not see the whole picture, but he'd just found another piece.

"My Lord?"

"Nothing. How old did he appear to you, this shade?"

Ovith shrugged. "I can't say with any certainty. He looked like a human of thirty winters."

Too young, but he could have aged very slowly. Or he could be the grandson or great grandson of Cale, rather than the son.

"Did anyone say his name?"

"Not that I heard."

Brennus nodded, his mind racing, connections forming. "You've done well, Ovith. Return to the barracks and stay there. I may have more questions for you later."

Again Ovith put an arm on his chest and took a knee. "My Prince."

As Ovith walked out of the library, Brennus called to him, "Speak of this to no one. If you disobey me in this, I'll know."

"Of course, Prince Brennus."

After Ovith had gone, Brennus looked down at the rose. "I have you."

The Oracle, his perception focused by Amaunator's prophetic gift, walked the halls of the abbey, Browny padding along at his side. The Oracle's slippers whispered on the polished stone floors. Everywhere he saw the iconography of his patron—the blazing sun in murals, sunbeam images inset into the floor, blown glass globes lit with magical light. And here and there he saw the rose, the symbol of Lathander, the dawn guise of Amaunator. The Oracle's father had worshiped Lathander. They'd done the same work, father and son. Each had played his part. Perhaps they'd end the Cycle of Night, for Toril, at least.

After walking the halls, he returned to his sparsely furnished chambers on the abbey's second floor. The small room held his wardrobe, his bed, a pile of old wool blankets for Browny, and a prayer mat on the floor before the east-facing window. He kneeled on the mat and looked out the window. Browny sat on the floor beside him, chin on his paws.

The Oracle let his imagination pierce the shrouded sky, imagined golden sunlight, a blue sky.

"Night gives way to dawn, and dawn to noon. Residing in the light, I fear no darkness."

He took his holy symbol, a blazing sun cast in silver, and held it in his hand. "Thank you for letting me serve, Dawnfather."

He stood and went to his wardrobe. Within, buried under his winter bedding and the traveling cloak he never worn, lay a large, steel shield. The slab of enchanted metal and wood showed scars from many battles, but the rose enameled on its face looked freshly painted. The shield had been Dawnlord Abelar's. His father had cast it into a lake when his faith had temporarily failed him because the Oracle, then a boy, had been made to suffer. Years later, a vision had led the Oracle to the lake and he'd recovered the shield, knowing that he was to hold it in trust for another, to help during a dark time that would one day come.

A day that had arrived at last.

He could not see how it would end. The timeline of gods stretched too far into the past and future. He only saw how it would begin. He suspected the day's events would conclude in shadow, not light. His vision saw poorly into dark places.

He lifted the shield and tested it on his arm. It felt strong, sturdy, impassable, like the father who'd borne it. The shield's enchantment had kept the leather straps supple, even after one hundred years. He slipped it on, but the weight was far too much for him to bear with only one arm. Smiling softly, he slipped his arm free of the straps. He had not been born to be a warrior. He had been born to be a guide.

"Come, Browny."

Carrying the shield, he walked through the abbey, past the central worship hall, and into the attached living quarters. He went to Vasen's chambers, as sparsely furnished as the Oracle's own.

He saw much of himself in Vasen. Both of them had the need to serve others. Both of them had a father whose deeds had written many of the pages in the book of the son's life. Both of them were like two minds in one body. But they differed in at least one important way.

"You are a warrior," the Oracle said, and stood his father's shield against the chest at the foot of Vasen's bed. "Fight well."

Thinking of his father, he walked to the dawnlord's shrine in the eastern tower. He would await the servants of Mephistopheles there.

CHAPTER TEN

Sayeed and Zeeahd moved quickly over the plains, cutting through the shadowed air. Minser huffed and stumbled, sweating and wheezing, but the occasional cuff on the head from Sayeed kept him moving. The cats, too, herded him along.

"What will you do with me when we get there?" the peddler asked, gasping.

Zeeahd looked over his shoulder. "I'll decide when we arrive."

Minser's fearful gaze went to Sayeed, to the cats. He muttered prayers under his breath as he staggered along.

"No god is going to save you now, peddler," Sayeed said. "We're past that."

"*My* grace is all you can hope for," said Zeeahd, and a slight cough wracked his body.

The cats looked at Zeeahd curiously, hope in their evil expressions. Minser whined, perhaps fearing a similar fate to that of the woman in Fairelm. But Zeeahd's coughing ended without a purge.

Minser continued to pray under his breath as they walked.

Ahead, the dark, jagged spikes of the Thunder Peaks rose from the plains, the exposed spine of some enormous beast that seemed to reach all the way to the sky. Within an hour they walked the foothills. The terrain began to rise steeply. Valleys and gorges cut the face of the mountains. The pass they sought could have been anywhere. They'd have never found it but for Minser.

Minser led them on, his head bowed, his will broken. He stumbled and weaved as they walked, exhausted.

"You're certain of the way?" Sayeed asked him, and swatted the side of his head.

Minser blanched, mumbled something inaudible, and plodded on. He looked around from time to time, as if taking stock of their location.

"Speak, peddler," Zeeahd said, and another coughing fit afflicted him.

Sayeed was surprised to see his brother coughing again so soon after a purge. The disease within him must have been not only growing worse but doing so more quickly. Sayeed wondered if the changes wrought by the Spellplague in his own body were also worsening, but in a way he did not notice.

"You heard him," Sayeed said, pushing Minser to the ground. "You spoke of a pass. Where is it?"

Minser looked up to speak, but before he did he turned green and puked. He tried to cover his mouth as he vomited but that served only to spray it in all directions. The rapid travel had taxed him. Spitting and gagging, he pointed ahead at one of the narrow openings in the mountains. It did not look like a pass so much as a slit.

"If you're lying . . ." Sayeed said, and let Minser's imagination make the most of the threat.

The peddler shook his head, his chins jiggling.

"Give him a drink and keep him moving," Zeeahd said.

Sayeed tossed Minser a waterskin and the peddler gulped greedily.

"Get up," Sayeed said, and lifted the fat man as easily as another might lift a child.

When they reached the mouth of the pass, Zeeahd turned to Minser. The peddler quailed.

"You'll lead us through the pass."

Minser shook his head. "I don't know the way. There was a mist, and . . ."

"And what?" Zeeahd snapped.

"And nothing," Minser said, and Sayeed knew he was lying.

"Sayeed," Zeeahd said, and nodded at Minser.

Sayeed advanced on the peddler, who stumbled backward and fell, holding up his hands.

"Please, no."

"Then speak truth to me, peddler," Zeeahd said.

Minser's twisted expression evidenced the battle within him, but eventually fear won out.

"There were . . . spirits in the mist."

Zeeahd's voice was low and dangerous. "Guardian spirits?"

"I see no mist," Sayeed said.

"And you thought these spirits would save you, perhaps?" Zeeahd asked Minser.

To that, the peddler said nothing. His entire body shook with terror. The cats crowded close around him, mewling.

"There is no mist," Sayeed said again.

"How long ago did you travel the pass?" Zeeahd asked.

"Four years ago," Minser answered.

"The mist is gone," Zeeahd said, clearing his throat wetly. "There are no guardian spirits."

"Gone?" Minser said, his tone that of a little boy.

"Gone," Zeeahd said. "And with it, whatever hope you had of escape. Now move."

With Sayeed dragging Minser by the collar, they entered the pass. Its narrow, sheer walls closed in on either side. Tunnels, cracks, and other natural openings led off in other directions almost immediately.

"Which way?" Sayeed asked, shaking Minser.

"I don't know," the peddler said. "I told you, there was a mist. We were guided."

"By who?" Sayeed asked.

"By servants of Amaunator," Zeeahd said, as he kneeled before a boulder. He pointed near the base of the boulder and there, carved deeply into the stone, was the symbol of the Dawnfather—a blazing sun over a closed rose.

"They marked the path," Sayeed said.

Zeeahd stood, his hands on his hips. "So it seems. Do you remember other markers, Minser?"

"There was mist, but yes. They checked from time to time for markers."

"Good," Zeeahd said. "Very good. With them, we can find our way."

"So you can let me go now," Minser said. The quaver in his voice betrayed his fear.

"Yes," Zeeahd said. "We no longer need you. Have your release."

He waved at the cats and they swarmed the peddler, snarling. He screamed and tried to run as they bit and clawed. His exhausted legs would not bear him and he fell. The cats latched onto his body and tore at his flesh and skin. Blood and screams flew.

"Get them off! Get them off!"

Sayeed watched the murder, feeling nothing. Zeeahd laughed when Minser tried to pick up a nearby rock to strike one of the cats. The cat easily dodged the clumsy blow and sank its teeth into Minser's wrists.

"The light preserve me! The light preserve me!"

Death came slowly and painfully to the peddler. His screams bounced off the walls of the mountains. The cats, their fur soaked with Minser's blood, licked delicately at his savaged body. The peddler's lower lip dangled from the mouth of one of the creatures.

Zeeahd kneeled once more before the mark of Amaunator, stared at it as if committing its form to memory. After a moment, he stood, removed a pearl from his cloak, shattered it with a rock, and gathered the dust in his hand. He found a forked stick, sprinkled the pearl dust on it, and incanted the words to a divination spell Sayeed had heard him use hundreds of times over the years.

"Other than the symbol of Amaunator carved into the rock immediately before me," Zeeahd said. "Show me the nearest such symbol."

The forked stick glowed opalescent and seemed to tug Zeeahd around, the magic pulling him to the next marker.

"Come," Zeeahd said excitedly. "This way."

They left Minser's corpse behind them and, relying upon Zeeahd's spellcraft, moved from marker to marker, picking their way through the labyrinthine pass, their excitement growing with each marker they passed.

They heard a soft rush, growing as they moved forward— falling water. In time they exited the pass and below and before them stretched a valley ringed by sheer mountain walls, a long smear of green bisected by a slow-flowing river, itself fed by several cascades that poured from the cliff face. Dark tarns dotted the valley here and there.

Stone structures nestled among the pines near the river. Sayeed could see cleared land for cultivation, barns and other outbuildings, several livestock pens, an orchard of apple trees. A large central structure—the Abbey of the Rose, home of the Oracle—sat in the center of it all.

Built of granite taken from the mountains, the abbey was more cathedral than cloister. The diamond-shaped structure featured tall towers at the east and west ends. Glass was every-where. Large windows, not only in the walls but in the roof, would have bathed the interior rooms in light, were there any light in night-shrouded Sembia. A covered portico featuring slender columns ran around much of the structure. Several balconies jutted from the second floor and the towers. Flagstone courtyards on the north and south sides of the abbey provided gathering places.

Sayeed would have thought the building beautiful once, gentle in line despite the heavy stone of its construction. Either magic had aided the builders or they had spent greater than a decade erecting the building.

"There could be hundreds of priests and warriors in there."

"I see no one," Zeeahd said, concern raising the pitch of his voice.

The cats sat at Zeeahd's feet, disinterested in the spectacle, licking their paws. They left off only when Zeeahd hacked a cough and spat a black glob, which they pounced on and devoured.

Sayeed saw no one, either. The abbey appeared abandoned, the Oracle gone.

"What if he knew we were coming?" Sayeed said. "What if he knew?"

Despair rose in him, his affliction unable to spare him the black hole that followed failed hopes. "To have come so far . . ."

Zeeahd cleared his throat, spat, and stalked down the rise toward the abbey. "It isn't over yet."

Vasen watched the sky for Sakkors or any other sign of the Shadovar, but saw nothing. When they reached the site of the battle where they'd fought the Shadovar scouts, they found nothing. The veserab and the dead Shadovar soldier were gone.

"We should have hidden the bodies, or moved them, at least," Vasen said.

"There was no time," Orsin said.

"You fought Shadovar here?" Gerak asked, scanning the ground. "How many?"

"Two, with their mounts," Orsin said.

"And you killed them?"

"No," Vasen said. "One escaped."

Gerak seemed to consider that as they hurried on, moving at the double-quick. The effort left Gerak and Vasen sweating and gasping, but Orsin was untroubled. Vasen took the deva's endurance as inspiration and pressed on. Soon the plains gave way to the rocky foothills, and in a few hours, even the dim air could not mask the rising, jagged bulk of the pine-ruffed Thunder Peaks. Seeing them, Vasen felt both hope and foreboding.

"We're near the pass," he said.

Gerak studied the ground as they moved.

"Come on, man," said Vasen.

"Wait, look at these marks," Gerak said, his brow furrowed. "A lot of people passed this way. Yesterday."

"Us, with the pilgrims."

"We didn't walk this area," Orsin said. "We were over there."

Vasen realized Orsin was right. He went to Gerak's side. Whatever the man was looking at on the ground, Vasen could not see it. "How can you be sure it was yesterday?"

"The rain has been steady," Orsin said. "I would think—"

"Two things I do well, Orsin," Gerak said. "Archery and tracking. I'm sure."

Vasen and Orsin shared a look. Orsin spoke the conclusion both of them had drawn.

"The Oracle foresaw the attack. Everyone left the abbey."

Vasen was already shaking his head. He could not imagine the priests and the Oracle abandoning holy ground in the face of an attack.

"The Oracle is, infirm. He couldn't travel."

"He must have," Gerak said. "Unless . . . "

And all at once Vasen knew. He replayed in his mind the Oracle's words to him before he left the Abbey, the finality of the Oracle's farewell.

"By the light," he swore. "He ordered everyone away. He's there alone."

"Why would he do that?" Orsin asked.

Vasen snapped at him, harsher than he intended. "Who knows why seers do what they do?"

Orsin stared at him, blinking at Vasen's tone.

"I'm sorry," Vasen said, putting a hand on Orsin's shoulder. "He . . . said things to me before I left. They sound now like a farewell."

"Then we should move," Orsin said.

"Aye."

Valleys, gorges, and cutouts scarred the face of the mountains. But none of them misled Vasen. Following a path he could have walked blindly, he led his comrades over the rising terrain to the mouth of the winding pass that would take them to the abbey's valley.

"This way," he said.

The terrain rose steeply. Vasen guided them through a series of switchbacks and narrow, rock strewn passageways. Gerak seemed to be noting the terrain with care as they moved, nodding at noteworthy landmarks, presumably placing this or that marker in his mind.

"Small wonder none found the valley without aid," he said.

Vasen uttered a prayer to Amaunator and let the power flow into his blade, which glowed with rose-colored light. "We'll soon come to the mist. Guardian spirits live within it. Stay close to me and do not heed their whispers."

Speaking of the spirits reminded Vasen of his last trek through the pass. It felt as if it had been years ago, but it had been only a short time The spirits had spoken of his father and of Elgrin Fau. He wondered what he would hear now.

As the pass leveled off and widened, he saw the first marker—a boulder chiseled on its base with a tiny rose. At its base lay a crumpled form. His heart sank and he ran toward it, his armor clanking. Before he reached the body, he realized it was too large to be the Oracle.

He laid his shield on the ground and kneeled beside the corpse. The body was that of a human man—fat, balding, with a thick beard and moustache. His garish clothing was shredded, as was his flesh. He had died of blood loss after receiving hundreds of small bites all over his body. The rocks around him were stained brown. The torn remnants of his lips were peeled back from his teeth in a death grimace.

"Minser the peddler," Gerak said, coming up behind Vasen.

Vasen's eyes fell on the marker at the base of the boulder. Several drops of Minser's blood had spattered the engraved sun and rose.

"They must be using spells to move from marker to marker," he said. "We have to hurry."

Before standing, Vasen held his glowing blade above Minser's body and recited a prayer for his passage. He had time for nothing more.

"Go now into the light," he finished, raising his glowing blade skyward. "Be at peace."

"I think he would appreciate that," Gerak said, and with that, they left Minser behind.

Vasen expected the gray mist to form at his feet, crawl up ankles, expected his mind to fill with the confusing hisses and whispers of the spirits, but he saw nothing, heard nothing. He double checked the marker, stopped, looked around.

"I don't understand."

"What?" Gerak asked.

"The mist," Vasen said. "It should be here."

"You're certain we're in the right place?" Gerak asked.

"Yes," Vasen said. "I think. Come on."

He picked up his pace, counted his steps, and sought the second marker. Perhaps he'd made a mistake, taken a wrong turn. It happened from time to time with others.

And there was the second marker, a cliff face chiseled with the symbol of the sun. Normally he saw it only through swirls of mist, with the spirits' voices in his ears.

"By the light," he breathed. "They're gone. The spirits."

"How can they be gone? What does that mean?" Orsin asked.

Vasen did not know. The mist and spirits had been as much a mainstay of the pass as the valley's cascades, as the abbey itself, as his faith. Perhaps they, too, had been telling him goodbye when he had passed through them the last time.

"Move!" Vasen shouted.

Sayeed fell in behind his brother and the cats, his eyes on the abbey, looking for any sign of habitation. When they reached the cultivated earth and animal pens, they found that the livestock remained. Goats cowered in their open pens, bleating, fearful of the cats. The agitated flutter of wings sounded from the chicken coops, the doors thrown open.

"If they're gone, they didn't leave long ago," Sayeed said. "Else the animals would be starved. We can still catch them if they traveled on foot."

Zeeahd grunted as they stalked among the compound, his anger palpable.

The cats eyed the animals, mewled.

Zeeahd waved a hand dismissively. "What are the animals to me? Do what you wish. Kill what you wish. Only the Oracle matters to me."

As the devils wetly slipped their fleshy cells and set about slaughtering the panicked animals, Sayeed and Zeeahd explored the nearby buildings. They found root cellars, fermenting beer, wine, cheese, but no people.

"They're gone, Zeeahd," Sayeed said. "The Oracle is gone. He foresaw us coming and—"

Zeeahd whirled on him and slapped Sayeed's face, once, twice. "He's *not* gone! He must be here. He must. Otherwise . . . "

Sayeed grabbed his brother by the wrist and squeezed. Zeeahd did not so much as wince.

"Release me, Sayeed. Now."

Sayeed let his brother go.

Zeeahd's gaze drifted in the direction of the devils that had emerged from the cats. In their bloody glee, the fiends were leaping atop buildings, firing their quills at each other, at the animals, at nothing. Some of their spines trailed flames as they flew, and soon dozens of small fires started.

"Otherwise what?" Sayeed asked. "Finish your thought."

Zeeahd ignored him, turned, and eyed a low stairway that led to a columned portico and a pair of double doors that opened onto the abbey. Zeeahd inhaled in a hiss, put a hand across Sayeed's chest.

"What is it?" Sayeed asked, his hand going to his sword hilt.

"He's here," Zeeahd said.

"How do you know?"

"Because those doors are warded. Feel it?"

Sayeed didn't, but he trusted his brother's ability to sense powerful magic.

Zeeahd withdrew some items from his belt pouches as they walked toward the doors. He began to cast a counterward.

Standing in the shrine, looking upon the image of Jiriis and his father, the Oracle held his hand over the glow globe in the shrine.

When he lit it, he knew what it would bring.

"I will stand in the light and fear no darkness," he said, and waited for the ward on the doors to fall.

Vasen ran through the pass, his armor clanking, and even Orsin struggled to keep up. The moment Vasen heard the distant rush of the valley's cascades, he readied his shield and let the light die from his sword. Darkness cloaked them all.

"The light keep us," he said to his comrades.

He stopped at the mouth of the pass. The valley stretched out below him, a finger-shaped slash in the mountains covered in shrouded pine and scrub. The darkness and trees hid the river. The abbey and its outbuildings and walls nestled in a cleared swath farther in. The lands around the buildings looked like a black smear in the darkness. The glowglobes were unlit, their defiant glow extinguished. The windows, too, were dark, and the sight pulled Vasen up short. He'd never before seen the abbey sitting in darkness under the Shadovar's sky. It looked not like a place dedicated to the God of the Sun but a tomb, a surrender. The shadows around him swirled.

Orsin and Gerak tried to walk past him, but he stopped them with the flat of his blade.

"Wait."

"What is it?"

Screams pierced the valley's silence, carried up from the abbey on the wind. Not human, but animal, and . . . something else. The wind carried the stink of smoke.

"Something is burning," Orsin said.

"I smell it," Gerak said. He nocked an arrow but did not draw. "I can't see anything."

More screams sounded from below, the desperate, terrified bleats of the goats. All at once a dozen small fires lit up in the compound, the roofs of several storage sheds and several trees. Vasen heard cracking wood, the growls and snarls of some kind of beast. He could see movement in the shadows cast by the fire, but could make out no details.

"We get close," Vasen said. "Move quietly and quickly."

Orsin and Gerak nodded and they all started down. By the time they reached the bottom, two of the storage sheds were fully ablaze. The light from the fires raised shadows all over the compound. Vasen felt a twinge when he looked at the shadows, a feeling of connectedness. He crept onward.

They clambered over the low stone wall that kept wild animals from the fields, and when they did Vasen stepped on something slick and wet.

A pile of blood-soaked skins lay at his feet. Vasen lifted one of the skins on the end of his sword. They looked vaguely feline. Blood slicked the empty bag of fur.

"Those . . . look like the cats that accompanied the two men," Gerak whispered.

"They weren't cats," Vasen said, dropping the skin to the ground.

"Then what?" Gerak said, looking toward the abbey.

"We'll soon know," Vasen said.

They darted in a crouch across the fields toward the abbey.

The sudden flash of a light in one of the windows of the eastern-facing tower of the abbey caught Sayeed's eye.

"There is a light in the eastern tower," he said, pointing.

Zeeahd nodded, the flesh under his robe roiling and bulging, and continued his countercharm, using a silver wand to trace glowing symbols in the air.

Vasen, Orsin, and Gerak sheltered behind one of the outbuildings used to house visiting pilgrims and peeked around the corner. Smoke fogged the air, but the light of the flames allowed Vasen to see the marauders.

"Spined devils," he said.

The spined devils, which were about the size of a mastiff, prowled about on all fours. Hundreds of sharp quills, about the length of a man's hand, coated their hides. As Vasen watched, one of the creatures growled, tensed, and fired a half dozen spines from its back at a storage shed. The spines burst into flame as they flew and sunk deeply into the wood of the shed, the flames licking at the timbers.

Another spined devil burst through the fence of an animal pen, carrying the leg of a goat in its mouth. A second devil bounded into view from the right and tried to take the goat haunch from the first, the two fiends scrabbling over it like dogs.

"I can't see how many," Vasen said. "More than a handful, though."

"There were at least a dozen cat skins," Orsin said.

Vasen eyed Gerak, to see how well the man was holding up. Gerak met his gaze, nodded.

There were too many to try and cut their way through.

"We're looking for men, not devils," Vasen said. "We need to get to the abbey undetected."

"The smoke will help," Orsin said.

"Where is everyone?" Gerak asked.

Vasen could only shake his head and try not to lose hope. He looked out from around the building and saw no devils, although he could hear them above the crackle of burning wood. Just as he was about to give the order to run for the northern courtyard, a powerful impact shook the timbers of the shed. The three men flattened themselves against the wall, looking up, as they heard the chuff of a devil, the sound of claws on roof tiles.

Shadows poured from Vasen's skin.

Moving silently, Gerak drew an arrow, nocked, and took a knee a pace away from the wall, his bow trained on the roof.

The chuffing changed to a low growl.

Vasen met Orsin's gaze, gave him a nod. The deva nodded in return. They readied themselves and Vasen cleared his throat.

The devil lunged forward and the moment its head appeared past the edge of the roof, Gerak let an arrow fly and Orsin lunged upward. Orsin looped his hands around the fiend's neck and flipped it from the roof. It fell on its back, snarling, claws flailing wildly, an arrow sticking from its throat. Vasen hacked downward with his sword and split its throat. Stinking black ichor poured from the wound, stained the grass, and the creature went silent.

The three men sheltered behind the building again, listening. They heard nothing nearby. The devils appeared to be elsewhere on the grounds, burning and destroying.

"We move now," Vasen said. "Ready?"

"Ready," Orsin and Gerak said in unison.

They dashed out from behind the shed and made for the courtyard. Through the smoke and darkness, the large arch leading into the courtyard looked like a screaming mouth. The moment they broached it and set foot on the flagstones, Vasen saw the two men they sought.

They stood near the north-facing double doors. The smaller of the men held a thin rod in his hand with which he traced glowing runes in the air. He made a gesture of finality with the wand, and the jambs around the abbey's double doors flared white as the protective wards winked out.

Gerak drew an arrow and Vasen whirled his blade over his head. Anger and faith combined, flowed into his blade, and ribbons of rose-colored light trailed the weapon's arc.

"Get away from that door," Vasen called.

The men turned to face him. Behind and above them Vasen saw a light glowing in the upper window of the dawnlord's shrine, the only light in the entire abbey.

If the Oracle was still in the Abbey, that's where he would be.

The man who bore sword and shield was the largest human Vasen had ever seen. A battle-scarred breastplate covered his barrel chest. Shaggy hair and a thick beard obscured all of his features but his eyes, which looked as lifeless as coins.

The other man, also tall but thin as a willow reed, looked like a walking corpse. Parchment-colored skin was drawn tight over sunken cheeks and deep-set eyes. His thin lips parted in a snarl to reveal snaggle teeth.

"Kill them, Sayeed!" the thin man said to the large one. "I'll get what we need from the Oracle."

Before either man could move, Vasen swung his blade in a wide, final arc and flung the ribbons of light across the courtyard. The energy slammed into the thin man like a hammer blow, knocking him from his feet and leaving him stunned on the ground.

"You'll never set foot in the abbey," Vasen said.

The large man roared and rushed them. Gerak fired twice in rapid succession, but the large man blocked his shots contemptuously with his huge shield, never slowing his advance.

Two devils, perhaps hearing the shouts, bounded into the courtyard from the far side. When they saw Vasen, Gerak, and Orsin, they coiled, arched their backs, and a dozen flaming spines hissed across the courtyard.

Vasen jumped before Gerak—the man was unarmored—and protected both of them with his shield. Orsin leaped high into the air, and the remaining spines slammed into the stone wall behind them and fell to the ground, flaming.

Gerak drew, fired, and an arrow slammed into one of the devils. Meanwhile, Orsin leaped skyward on a column of shadow, the arc of his leap carrying him over the huge man, who halted in his charge to watch him sail overhead. Orsin landed in a crouch a few paces from the thin man, and a disc of shadow exploded a short distance outward in all directions from his feet. The wave of dark energy slammed into the thin man and sent him careening into the doors. Orsin clenched his fists, dark energy surrounding them, and advanced on him.

Vasen charged Sayeed, blade and shield readied and blazing with light. Sayeed whirled, his mouth a twisted snarl, sword and shield ready. They collided with a shout, a clamor of metal and flesh. The impact made Vasen's teeth ache, but he managed to slam his glowing shield into Sayeed's blade and loose an overhand strike at the man's skull. Sayeed parried with his shield, pushed Vasen back, and unleashed a vicious overhead strike that Vasen sidestepped.

When Sayeed's missed strike put the tip of his blade in the earth, Vasen stomped on it even as he slammed the edge of his shield into Sayeed's cheek. The combination should have snapped Sayeed's sword and skull, but the man barely flinched and the steel of his blade resisted Vasen's stomp.

Sayeed levered his blade up, knocking Vasen off balance, then swung his shield hard into Vasen's side. The blow sent Vasen stumbling sidelong.

Sayeed bounded after, stabbing for Vasen's ribs. Vasen managed an awkward parry with his shield, spun, and slashed downward with his blade, catching Sayeed's calf behind the protective plate of his armor. Blood spilled, and Sayeed grunted with pain but didn't fall. Instead, he stabbed at Vasen's chest, his blade slipping past Vasen's shield and scraping armor. Horrifyingly, the blade vibrated like a living thing, as if burrowing for Vasen's flesh. But the force of the blow knocked Vasen backward and the blade did not penetrate his armor. Sayeed advanced, blade held high for a killing stroke.

A hiss, thunk, and grunt of pain accompanied one of Gerak's arrows slamming into Sayeed's back. The big warrior roared, turned, and tore the arrow from his back. Vasen backed away and regathered his wits.

He glanced around, just in time to see a column of flame explode from the thin man's hands, slam into Orsin's chest, and send the deva careening backward across the length of the courtyard, where he crashed into a wall and sagged to the ground. His chest smoked as he struggled to rise. Another spined devil sprinted into the courtyard and charged him.

"Orsin!" Gerak and Vasen called as one.

Gerak's hands were a blur, firing again and again, as he backed toward the wall His bow and one of the devils charging him fell in a tumble, but the second shot went wide and he fumbled his sword free as the devil closed and slashed with tooth and claw.

Behind Vasen, the thin man opened the double doors of the abbey. Vasen cursed, torn between aiding his friend and pursuing. Before he could decide, the huge warrior loomed before him, roaring, and unleashed a flurry of blows that drove Vasen backward and prevented him from doing anything other than keeping sharp metal away from his flesh.

"Shoot him, Gerak!" Vasen called. "The other one! Shoot him!"

But Gerak was pressed against the wall, stabbing and slashing with his blade at two devils.

Anger flared in Vasen. Shadows whirled around his flesh. He channeled all the power he could into both blade and shield, causing both to glow, and lunged at Sayeed, loosing his own flurry of strikes, stabs, and slashes. The ferocity of the attack drove the larger man backward, toward the double doors, and the power infusing Vasen's weapons gave his strikes the force needed to knock Sayeed's shield and blade out wide, exposing his chest. Vasen put a straight kick into the larger man's torso, staggering him, then drove the glowing line of his blade to its hilt in Sayeed's chest.

He went nose to nose with Sayeed, whose mouth was filling with blood.

"We just want the Oracle," Sayeed gasped. "We need the son of Erevis Cale."

Shadows swirled around Vasen, around Sayeed.

"You've found him," Vasen said. "Know that as you die."

Sayeed's dead eyes widened with surprise and his mouth split in a bloody smile. He laughed, spraying Vasen with blood, and fell to his knees. He closed his hands around the hilt of Vasen's sword.

A pained shout pulled Vasen around. He tried to jerk his blade free as he turned, but Sayeed held it in a death grip.

A spined devil had Gerak pinned up against the wall. The devil lunged at him, but Gerak sidestepped the attack and slashed down with his blade. The weapon bit and sent several spines flying. The devil squealed, more with anger than pain, and not before catching Gerak's side with a claw that came away bloody. Gerak backed off, wide-eyed, his breath coming hard.

Orsin had regained his feet, and clouds of shadow clung to his fists and the ends of his staff as he battled with a spined devil. His weapon hummed, trailing a line of shadows.

Vasen turned, kicked Sayeed flat, put his foot on the man's abdomen, and tried once more to pull his blade free. Still it would not come loose. He cursed and left it.

Slipping out of the straps of his shield, he rushed toward Gerak, shouting the name of Amaunator as he ran, putting the power of his faith into his shield. The devil whirled as Vasen neared, and Gerak took the opportunity to stab it in the hindquarters. The creature snarled and loosed a handful of flaming spines that pierced Gerak's face and chest, sent him stumbling back against the wall, shouting with pain and frantically trying to pluck the flaming projectiles from his flesh.

Vasen held the shield with both hand, the metal and wood warm in his grasp. The devil leaped at him, jaws wide, and Vasen slammed the edge of the shield down on its neck before it reached him. The blow drove the devil flat into the earth, cracking bones, and the power infusing the shield poured out into the creature. It screamed, spasmed, and died. Vasen grabbed the now-dim shield and hurled it to Gerak.

"Take it!" he said. "You know how to use it?"

"I was a soldier," Gerak said, catching the shield. He was bleeding from his face. "What're you doing?"

"Going after the other one."

Gerak looked past Vasen, over his shoulder. "We haven't even gotten the first one."

Vasen turned to see Sayeed—inexplicably, impossibly—back on his feet. Vasen's blade stuck out his chest and back like a pennon. Sayeed stared at them, grinned, and slowly extracted Vasen's weapon in a gout of blood. The moment the weapon cleared his skin, the bleeding stopped.

"Gods," Gerak said.

"I have to go help the Oracle," Vasen called to his friends.

"Go," Gerak said.

"Go," Orsin said, pummeling a nearly dead spined devil with fists that dripped with dark energy. "We'll follow."

That was all Vasen needed. He sprinted for the double doors. As he did, he heard a hiss and thunk as Gerak put an arrow into Sayeed. The big man roared and fell to his knees.

Vasen leaped onto the portico and barreled into the side door. It burst open and he cut left, sliding to a stop and cursing.

A wall of fire blocked the hallway from floor to ceiling, the flames licking hungrily at everything within reach. Vasen felt the hair of his beard and eyebrows melt. He scrambled backward, blinking in the heat. The thin man must have conjured the wall of flames to prevent pursuit. Vasen did not hesitate. He covered his face with his hands and charged through the flames. Skin blistered and hair burned, but his armor protected him against the worst of it. Ignoring the pain of his charred skin, he stripped off his burning cloak and beat out the flames on his trousers and tunic.

The skin of his face felt raw, blistered. He would have channeled the light of his faith into healing energy, but he was without a focus—no holy symbol at this throat, no shield emblazoned with Amaunator's rose, no sword with his god's symbol cast into the hilt.

He drew a dagger and ran through the abbey's halls, speeding past the meditation cells, the storerooms, the library and study rooms, the stairway that led to the lower level.

He knew the thin man was heading toward the dawnlord's shrine in the eastern tower. Vasen could cut through the central worship hall and cut him off before he got to the eastern stairs.

He shouldered his way through the double doors that led into the main worship hall, running too fast to hear the noise until he'd entered.

CHAPTER ELEVEN

Drawn by the sound of the combat, devils swarmed into the courtyard, a roiling wave of spines, teeth, claws, and savagery.

"Shield me," Gerak said to Orsin, who'd moved to Gerak's side. The deva used Vasen's shield to protect them both as best he could.

Gerak fired rapidly, answering volleys of flaming spines with shot after shot from his bow. He shot Sayeed a few more times, too, keeping the big man on his knees, although he stubbornly refused to die.

Soon Vasen's shield was quivering with dozens of flaming spikes, while six spined devils and the seemingly unkillable giant had arrows sticking from their hides. The wounded fiends pelted wide around the courtyard, perhaps intending to come at them from both sides at once. Meanwhile, the huge man pulled Gerak's arrows from his chest, rose, and strode toward them.

"Gods," Gerak said. "Bastard won't stay down."

"We need to go!" Orsin said.

Sayeed shouted and charged.

Gerak double-nocked his bow draw and took aim at Sayeed. "Let's see how you like two."

He let fly and both arrows hit Sayeed squarely in the side. The impact knocked him down and he spun to the ground, shouting with rage. He sat up immediately, growling as he pulled the arrows clear of flesh and bone.

Two devils charged at Orsin and Gerak from either side. Orsin's staff hummed as he spun it overhead. Orsin ducked under a devil's leap and it slammed headlong into the stone wall. Bones crunched and the creature squealed. Orsin stomped on its head as he swung his staff at a second one leaping for Gerak. He hit it squarely in the side, and the impact sent it sprawling into the earth. Gerak put two arrows in its side and it rose on wobbly legs, snarled once, then collapsed.

Another hail of flaming spines hissed into the area, peppering their flesh. At least three caught Orsin and two hit Gerak in his chest. Gerak pulled them out before they burned his cloak, searing his fingers in the process.

"Aye," Gerak said. "We need to go."

"That way," Orsin said, nodding at the arch behind them, the one through which they'd entered the courtyard. Orsin reached into his belt pouch for something as they ran. A volley of flaming spikes whistled after them. At least one of them hit Gerak's side and stuck there, but Orsin pulled it out as they sprinted.

"Keep going," Orsin said. "Keep going."

The deva held a glass flask filled with a dark fluid. Flaming spikes flew all around them. The growls and tread of the devils sounded loud in their ears. Sayeed shouted challenges as he, too, gave chase.

Orsin threw the flask on the ground in front of them and smashed it with his staff as they ran by. A cloud of darkness exploded outward from it, so deep and inky that Gerak could not see his hand before his nose. A hand closed on his arm and pulled him along.

"It will only slow them!" the deva said. "Keep moving!"

Twenty paces later he and Orsin burst through the edge of the magical darkness.

"There," Orsin said, nodding at the abbey. They exited the courtyard and were coming around to the other side of the structure.

"Where? What?" Gerak said. He saw no door, and there were no windows at ground level large enough to accommodate anyone larger than a halfling.

"Get on my back," Orsin ordered, and took station before him.

"What?"

"Do it!"

Behind them, Sayeed burst from the darkness and ran toward them, his long, lumbering strides fearfully fast. The devils would be coming, too.

Gerak climbed onto Orsin's back, feeling slightly ridiculous. The deva adjusted his weight slightly and started to run. Gerak gawped at the man's strength. As they approached the side of the abbey, Gerak realized what Orsin intended.

"You can't mean to—"

A hail of flaming spines landed all around them.

The shadows around Orsin deepened and he picked up his pace. As they neared the portico, the deva's muscles tensed, the shadows around him flared, and he leaped into the air. He landed atop the portico with Gerak barely hanging on. Never breaking stride, the deva took two more running steps and leaped for a second-story window. He didn't make it, but he didn't have to. They crashed into the side of the abbey, both of them grunting at the impact, but Orsin gripped the sill and held on.

"Climb over me!" he shouted. "Quickly!"

More spines filled the air, thumped into the walls, a few struck Gerak and he cried out. Orsin did, too.

"Move!" Orsin said.

Using the deva like a ladder, Gerak scrambled over him and into the window. Orsin pulled himself in and fell to the floor under the window. Each pulled the flaming spikes out of the other. Orsin pulled another vial from his belt pouches.

"Healing," he said, and poured some of the cool, soothing liquid right onto Gerak's clothes and skin. Gerak felt immediately refreshed. He took the vial and poured the remainder onto the wounds on Orsin's legs.

Looking around, they saw they were in a library or study of some kind. The darkness made it hard for Gerak to see, but he made out desks and shelves full of scrolls and books. Several spikes whistled through the window and stuck in the shelves. Immediately the dry books and scrolls started to burn. Outside, they could hear the devils snarling as they scrabbled at the stone walls of the abbey. Orsin jumped to his feet and slammed the butt of his staff on the ground. A cloud of shadow formed around the top of it. He moved the staff before the open window, trailing a curtain of shadows that blocked the aperture.

"Those devils can fly," the deva said. "That won't hold them long. We need to move."

"We need to find Vasen," Gerak said. "Where do you think he is?"

One of the devils snarled right outside of the window, on the other side of Orsin's shadow curtain.

"The eastern tower," Orsin said. "Where I saw the light. Come on."

A devil perched on one of pews that lined the main worship hall, its claws splintering the wood. The devil held a brazier to its nose, sniffing at it. Vasen had no idea how it could have gotten inside the abbey.

Pews lay overturned. Tapestries had been torn down and shredded. Vasen smelled feces. The devil's castings lay about the room in stinking piles, including on the altar. Anger warmed Vasen's skin while the devil's head swiveled toward him, eyes narrowing, the slits of its nose dilating.

"You'll answer for this," Vasen said, his hand white around the dagger's hilt. The devil snarled and launched itself at him with preternatural speed, the force of its leap toppling the pew it perched on and carrying it across the length of the worship hall in a blink.

The creature's scaled, muscular body hit Vasen with enough force to drive him backward into the wall. His breath exploded out of him in a whoosh. A painting near him fell from the wall with a clatter. Claws, scales, and teeth seemed everywhere at once.

He squirmed, tried to bring his dagger to bear, but the creature used its weight and strength to pin him against the wall. Claws scrabbled over his armor, shrieking as they gouged metal. The foul breath of the creature, like decayed meat, made him gag. He pulled his head back as the creature's jaws snapped for his nose. Spit sprayed into his face. The devil's claws got under his armor and tore gouges in his side. Warm blood poured from the wound. The pain gave him strength. He freed the hand with the dagger and drove it into the devil's belly once, twice, but the creature's hide, infused with the dark magic of the Hells, turned its edge. He cursed, dropped the weapon, and tried to lever himself away from the wall.

The devil's mouth opened wide and bit at his face, missing his nose by a finger's width. The devil shook free one of its arms and slashed Vasen's cheek, just missing his eye. The blow staggered him and the devil bit for his throat. Instinct caused Vasen to slam his forearm, protected by a vambrace, into the creature's mouth.

The blow shattered teeth and the devil shrieked with pain, lurching backward.

He needed to arm himself. He feinted a lunge at the devil. When the devil retreated a step, he sprinted for the far door, bounding over pews. The devil growled behind him, its claws scrabbling on the stone floor as it pursued.

He wasn't going to make it to the door. He whirled just in time to intercept the devil's leap at his back. The weight of the creature drove him backward and down. He crashed into a pew as he fell, breaking the wood and cracking his ribs. But he used the creature's momentum against it, brought his legs in and up and pushed the creature off and over him. It fell with a crash among the pews two rows distant.

Vasen clambered to his feet, wincing at the pain in his ribs. Blood flowed, sticky and warm, from the wound in his side.

Without a holy symbol, he had no focus for his power and could not heal himself. He needed to get to his quarters, but now the devil stood between him and the far door.

He shouted and charged. Man and devil collided in a heap of scaled hide, armor, and flesh. For a moment each stood the other up, a counterpoise to the other, both striving to gain the advantage. The devil's broken teeth locked onto Vasen's shoulder, crushed his armor, and pain ran the length of his arm. He drew in close, hooked the devil's hind leg with his foot, and tripped it to the ground. They fell together, a tangle of fists and claws. Blood from Vasen's torn face dripped into his eyes, fell in droplets onto the writhing devil. The pain in his side felt like a hot brand had been driven through his ribs. He slammed a fist into the devil's face, bursting its eye in a spray of ichor. The creature roared, squirmed frenetically, its claws digging at his armor. He felt them tear through the links of his mail, start to maul flesh. He pounded his fists into the creature's head, over and over again. He felt his stomach get torn open, felt the blood pour sickeningly from the gash. All the while, he rained blows down on the creature. Vasen was weakening, failing, but he kept punching, metal smashing into flesh and bone, until he could barely lift his arms.

And then the devil lay still below him, its head a shapeless mass of scales, teeth, black ichor, and exposed bone. He stared at the gore for a moment, blinking.

Shaking his head to clear it, he rose, his breeches and tunic soaked with a mix of his own blood and the devil's foul ichor. He pushed his hair out of his eyes, looked around. Dizziness caused him to sway. Each beat of his heart spit blood from his body.

He had to find a holy symbol to focus the divine energy he needed to heal himself. He started toward the door that led to his quarters, but remembered the potions the priests stored near the altar.

He staggered across the hall, but his hopes fell when he saw the cabinet where the potions were stored had been torn open, the metal vials within scattered over the floor. Liquid healing elixirs stained the stone. He bent, groaning with pain, and examined each of the vials. No good. All of them were open and spilled. He touched some of the liquid on the floor, hoping its magic might have survived the devil's desecration, but found it inert. A few wooden roses—holy symbols—lay scattered on the floor, too, but all of them were fouled by the devil, unusable. He put a hand on his knee and pushed himself back to his feet.

The door on the far side of the worship hall looked a league away. Holding his wounded side, he staggered for it.

He pushed through the door without listening for anything beyond. If he encountered another devil, he would die. That much was certain. Fortunately, the corridor beyond was empty. He slumped toward his quarters. Doors hung askew from the rooms he passed, the contents within as fouled as the worship hall. Ahead, the door to his quarters lay flat in the hallway, torn from its hinges. He hurried forward as best he could, dripping blood.

His room was unmolested. His bed remained as he had left it. And the chest at the end of his bed . . .

His breath caught when he saw the shield there, leaning against the chest. He moved slowly into the room, favoring his side, as if the shield were a mirage that would disappear if he moved too fast. He eyed the rose enameled on the shield's face, scars from weapon strikes that were in no alphabet anyone could read but that scribed a history of the shield's battles. He'd heard descriptions of the shield in stories.

The shield had belonged to Dawnlord Abelar. Tales of the dawnlord had said the shield was lost. Yet here it was. The Oracle must have found it and kept it, a secret he shared with no one.

Growls sounded from somewhere down the corridor outside his room. Something heavy crashed. Ceramics shattered and something metal rang off the floor.

With shaking hands, Vasen took the shield. The metal felt warm in his hands, pure, and he knew it was as much a holy implement of his faith as any symbol he might ever wear around his neck. He held it before him so he could see the rose. Thin tendrils of shadow from his hands ran along the shield's edge. He frowned, tried to will them away, but they clutched at the shield as surely as his hands. He hoped the dawnlord would not object.

Channeling the power of his faith through the shield, he spoke a prayer of healing and the rose lit like a lantern, bathing him in its glow. The darkness leaking from his flesh resisted banishment from the light and lingered on the edge of the shield. But still the glow did its work. The gashes in his flesh closed, his ribs knit back together, and the pain and fatigue he felt vanished.

As the glow faded from the rose, he bowed his head, overcome.

The scrabble of claw on stone sounded from the corridor outside his chambers, closer now. He strapped the shield onto his forearm, found the weight of it ideal. He opened the chest at the base of his bed. His father's sword lay inside, wrapped in oilcloth. He reached for it, the shadows so thick and swirling about his hands that he could scarcely see his fingers. He took the wire-wrapped hilt in hand. The metal felt cool, the texture slick. Shadows slipped from the weapon to join those bleeding from his flesh. He lifted the weapon, slid off the oilcloth, and revealed a blade as black as a sliver of night, like deep water under a moonless sky.

The hilt seemed made for his hand, the weight made for his style. He took a few practice cuts, marveled at the way the weapon left a trail of dissipating shadows in its wake.

Chuffing sounded from outside the door, the sound of a fiendish hound on the scent. He heard claws clicking on the stone floor, the low, predatory growl of an animal on the hunt. He held a sliver of night in one hand and a circle of light in the other and he felt as if he could walk through the Hells themselves.

"Devil!" he shouted. "Account for your presence in my abbey!"

He started for the door, but before he reached it a crouched form filled the doorway, the raised spines on its back like a forest of blades. Its lips peeled back from its long fangs, and its sleek head moved back and forth as it eyed the room. Seeing no one else, its tongue fell from its mouth and it snarled at Vasen.

"Come," Vasen said, his anger rising, and beckoned it to close.

The devil hissed, tensed, whirled, and launched a dozen spikes at Vasen. They caught fire as they whizzed toward him. He sheltered behind his shield and most of the spines slammed into the metal and stuck there. A few thumped into the wall. Others hit the bed and caught it afire.

Vasen got out from behind his shield as the devil sprung at him, all claws, teeth, and rage. He braced himself and swung his shield left to right as the devil reached him. The slab of steel and wood flared with light as it slammed into the devil's head and neck, driving it sidelong into the wall near the hearth. The fiend squirmed, bit, and clawed, trying to get around the shield, but Vasen threw his legs back, leaned his weight into the shield, still blazing with light, and pinned the creature against the wall while driving Weaveshear into it again and again. The blade bit effortlessly through the devil's hide. The fiend writhed, shrieking as one blow after another sank deep into its vitals. Black ichor poured from its slashed guts. When at last it went silent and still, Vasen let it fall to the floor and jerked his blade free. Behind him, his bed was ablaze. Parts of the abbey were ablaze, too, and there was no way to stop it. Soon the entire structure would be gutted by fire.

He had to get to the Oracle.

He looked at his shield, still glowing faintly, and at his blade, leaking shadows. The shadows twisted themselves into a line that snaked out of the room and turned east.

A line to follow, he thought, smiling and thinking of Orsin.

Without looking back at his burning quarters, the room that had been his sanctuary for almost thirty winters, he followed the line of shadow emitted by Weaveshear and hurried to Dawnlord Abelar's shrine.

Zeeahd moved rapidly through the dark abbey. On the way, he encountered two of his devils, who must have gained entry through an upper window.

"Follow," he ordered them, and they fell in beside him.

Light trickled down the stairs that led up through the eastern tower, the light he'd seen from outside. The devils growled softly. Without a pause, Zeeahd and the devils climbed the stairs. A hallway opened into a circular shrine.

Two biers sat in the center of the room, but Zeeahd had eyes only for the frail old man who stood near them. He wore the elaborate red and yellow robes of a senior priest of Amaunator. His eyes glowed orange, and when they fixed on Zeeahd, Zeeahd halted in his steps.

"Oracle," Zeeahd said.

The old man's hand went to the holy symbol he wore around his throat, a sun and a rose.

"Do you know who I am?" Zeeahd asked, stalking into the room, the devils flanking him.

The Oracle stared at him, glowing eyes unblinking. "I know *what* you are."

"Then you know why I've come."

"You've come to further the purposes of forces beyond your understanding," the Oracle said.

The old man's confidence galled Zeeahd. The devils snarled, their claws scratching the floor. "I need an answer to a question, old man."

The Oracle smiled faintly, looked away from Zeeahd to stare thoughtfully at the image of the woman carved into the lid of the bier.

"She never married another. The woman whose image is carved into the wood here. Her name was Jiriis. I'm sure she never loved another, either. She committed her life to service, but lived it alone."

Zeeahd put a hand on the spines of the devils at his sides. Was the Oracle mad? Was he anticipating Zeeahd's question and answering him somehow.

"We all make sacrifices, it seems," the Oracle said.

"I don't care about that. Where is the son of Erevis Cale? Tell me. If he lives, tell me his location. If he's dead, tell me where I can find his corpse." When the Oracle said nothing, he added, "Tell me and no harm will come to you, but be certain that I'll have an answer, one way or another."

"I long ago accepted the harm that would come to me. I saw it in a dream. But it has been a good hundred years." The Oracle turned and looked down on the other bier. "Do you recognize the face here, Zeeahd of Thay?"

"You know my name?"

"Look on it and do what you came here to do," the Oracle said, his voice stern. "You recognize it, do you not?"

Zeeahd looked carefully at the image carved into the bier. His fury rose as he recognized the face, the face forever branded by pain into his memory. The stump of his thumb began to ache. The curse within him began to writhe.

"Abelar Corrinthal," he said, and the words came out a hiss, and the hiss turned to a cough.

"He was my father," the Oracle said, looking back at Zeeahd. "A good man. A holy man. Very unlike you, Zeeahd of Thay."

Zeeahd's coughing worsened as his rage intensified. He felt the growth in his belly, the sickening, squirming mass that resided within him, that wanted only to *become*. His damnation had started a hundred years ago, but he had held it at bay since then. He refused to let it finish. He would free himself before he let the Hells have him.

"Then I'll have something for you when we're done, son of Abelar," Zeeahd said between coughs and gasps. Black flecks peppered the floor. "The son, Erevis Cale's son, where will I find him? Tell me now or I'll make you suffer."

The devils growled at that, an eager sound.

The Oracle's glowing eyes fixed on Zeeahd. "You won't find him, Zeeahd."

"That is a lie," Zeeahd shouted. "You lie!"

He could take no more. He ran across the room, the devils loping after him.

The Oracle remained unmoved, and Zeeahd grabbed him by the robes and shook his tiny frame, spitting black spatters of phlegm with every word.

"Liar! Liar!"

The Oracle shook his head, his face placid. "I speak what I see. You will not find him."

A distant shout carried into the shrine from elsewhere in the abbey. Not far away.

"Oracle!" shouted a voice.

"You won't find him, Zeeahd," the Oracle said, and smiled into Zeeahd's face. "Because he has found you."

Zeeahd's ruined flesh goose pimpled. "What? What did you say?"

"He's found you."

Again the voice from below. "Oracle!"

"Then I will be free of this right now," Zeeahd said, and shoved the Oracle away from him.

"No," the Oracle said. "You will never be free. Your body will mirror your soul. That is your fate, Zeeahd."

Another shout, closer this time. "Oracle!"

The darkness squirming in Zeeahd's belly wriggled up his throat, caused him to cough, to heave. He clenched his stomach, heaved from the bottom of his belly, and gagged as he vomited a thick string of his pollution onto the floor, fouling Amaunator's sun. The glistening string lay there, a stinking mass of putrescence—hell reified in his innards and puked forth into the world. He stared at it, the Oracle's words replaying in his mind.

You will never be free. You will never be free.

The words snuffed whatever humanity remained in him. Zeeahd wanted the Oracle dead: He wanted the abbey burned.

"Kill him!" he said to the devils, waving at the Oracle. "Tear him apart!"

"That is denied you, too," the Oracle said, and, before the devils could pounce, a beam of bright light shone through the translucent dome in the ceiling, fell on the Oracle's face, and bathed him in clear light. His skin turned translucent in the glow, took on a rosy hue. He placed a thin, veined hand on Abelar's bier.

The devils growled but did not charge him.

"Kill him!" Zeeahd shrieked.

The beam of light faded, as did the light in the Oracle's eyes. His expression slackened, grew childlike. His mouth fell open partially and split in a dumb smile. He spoke a single word, his tone that of a lack wit, not the leader of a congregation, not the head of an abbey that had provided light in darkness for a century.

"Papa," the Oracle said.

The devils snarled and bounded forward. The Oracle closed his eyes and started to fall but before he hit the floor, the devils struck his body at a run and drove him to the stone floor. Claws and fangs tore into his body, ripping robes, ripping flesh. Blood spread in a pool across the floor.

The devils lapped at the gore eagerly, chuffing, snorting, but then they began to whine, then to shriek as their flesh began to smoke. The dead Oracle's flesh glowed on their muzzles and claws. They squirmed like mad things, snarling, growling, spitting, trying to get the Oracle's gore off of them. Their skin began to sizzle, bubble, and melt. They shrieked a final time as their hides sloughed from their bones, the spines falling like rain to the floor, their organs melting into putrescence.

Zeeahd could only watch it, mesmerized, horrified, as even in death the Oracle took his final revenge.

Rage rose in him, hatred, darker and fouler even than the sputum he'd left on the floor, hatred for Abelar, for the Oracle, for himself and what he had become, for daring to hope.

"Oracle!" came a third shout from down below, perhaps at the base of the stairs.

Zeeahd dared the devils' fate. He turned and kicked what was left of the Oracle's body, once, twice, again, again. Nothing happened to him, and he warmed to the task, venting his rage in violence. Bones broke, flesh split, and blood seeped from the rag doll corpse. But his outburst served only to amplify his rage, not abate it. He began to cough during his tirade, felt again the stirring in his innards, but did not care. He stared at the image of Abelar Corrinthal, carved in the wood surface of the bier. The peaceful expression. He spit on the image, slammed a fist on the wood. His skin split and blood marred Abelar's visage.

"You! You! You are why all of this has happened to me!"

He seized the lid of the bier and with a grunt threw it to the side, revealing the wrapped, mummified body within.

"You have rest!" he shouted to Abelar. "You have peace! And I have nothing but the promise of the Hells! Because of you!"

"The life he lived brought him peace," said a strong, firm voice behind him. "The life you've lived will bring you something far worse."

Zeeahd turned slowly, a snarl on his lips. The man who stood at the entrance to the shrine was only slightly shorter than Sayeed. Long, dark hair was pulled off his strong-jawed face in a horse's tail. The beard and moustache he wore did not disguise the violence promised by the hard line of his mouth. Dull, gray plate armor wrapped his broad body. He carried a shield emblazoned with a battle-scarred rose, a large, dark blade from which darkness poured. A thin stream of shadow led off from the blade back the way the man had come. Shadows emerged in flickers from his exposed flesh.

Zeeahd's fists clenched. "There is nothing worse!"

The man stepped into the room. Zeeahd backed off a step, his stomach writhing with hell.

Vasen took in the remains of the devils, the body of the Oracle, the defiled bier of Dawnlord Abelar. He fixed his gaze on the thin man.

"My name is Vasen Cale. My father was Erevis Cale. I'm the one you've been trying to find."

"And yet you found me," the man said, and a maniacal laugh slipped past his lips. The laugh turned to wet coughing.

Vasen took another step into the room, trailing shadows, bearing light. The man backed away from the bier, toward the double doors behind him. His eyes darted back and forth, as if he were awaiting something.

"Here he is, Lord of Cania," the man said, and pointed a bony finger at Vasen. "He's found. The son of Cale. Now free me of this!"

The man coughed, gagged. Vasen could make no sense of his babblings and didn't need to. He needed only to kill him.

He held up Abelar's shield and Weaveshear. "This is the dawnlord's shield and this is my father's sword. I'm going to kill you with them."

The man shrieked with despair, rage, and hate, spitting black phlegm as he did.

"Where is your promise now, Lord of Cania?" The man glared at the dark places in the room as if they held some secret. "I've done what you asked! I've done it! Here he is! Free me!"

"You're mad," Vasen said.

The man glared at Vasen, his breathing a forge bellows. "Maybe I am mad. And maybe I'll be freed only if you're *dead*!"

He raised his hands and a line of fire exploded outward from his palms. Vasen raised his shield and the fire slammed into the steel, drove him back a step. Shadows poured from Vasen's flesh, from Weaveshear, and those from the blade surrounded the fire in darkness and contained it.

Still the man continued to shout, an animal cry of mindless hate, the fire pouring from his hands, black spit pouring from his mouth.

Licks of flame ignited the biers and spread to one of the wall tapestries, which quickly turned into a curtain of fire. In moments the entire room was ablaze.

Vasen pushed against the fire, enduring the heat, one step, another.

"Vasen!" he heard from the stairway below. "Vasen!"

"Here!" he called, the flames licking around his shield.

Orsin and Gerak ran up to the doorway behind him and stopped, eyes wide at the conflagration. Gerak drew and aimed with his usual rapidity, but the thin man separated his hands and sent a second line of fire into the bowman. It hit Gerak squarely in the chest and knocked him against the wall. He quickly aimed another blast at Orsin, but the deva dived aside and dodged it.

The man laughed. "I'll kill you all! Then I'll be free. Watch, Lord of Cania! Watch!"

Gerak's bow sang and an arrow thunked into the man's shoulder. The man grimaced with pain, staggered back, hunched, snarling. His flames faltered. He raised his left hand to unleash another blast of fire, but again Gerak's bow spoke first and a second arrow sank into the man, this time his left shoulder. The impact spun the man around and he shouted with pain.

"Die," Gerak said.

A third arrow buried itself in his left thigh, and the man went down. He collapsed, coughing, spitting gouts of black phlegm.

Gerak stepped beside Vasen, nocked and drew again, sighting for the man's throat. Vasen lowered his shield and weapon and watched. The man deserved death, and Gerak had earned the right to give it to him.

Gerak's bowstring creaked as he drew back to his ear.

The man writhed frenetically on the floor, snapping the arrows stuck in his body, his arms wrapped around his stomach, screaming wildly, maniacally, between coughs. His body pulsed, roiled, as if something within him were trying to get out.

"It hurts!" he shouted. "Kill me! Kill me!"

"Give him no relief," Orsin said. "He deserves what pain comes his way."

Gerak sighted along his arrow, and after a long pause, lowered his bow.

The man rolled over onto his stomach, dark, bloodshot eyes staring out of the pale oval of his face. His teeth, crooked and stained black, bared in a snarl.

"I'll kill you! All of you!"

He lifted himself on his wounded arms, grunting against the pain, and staggered to his feet. He lifted a hand at them. Vasen readied his shield and Gerak readied a killing shot, but before the man could discharge any fire, his eyes filled with pain and fear. He went rigid, threw his head back, and uttered a piercing shriek of pain. His back arched and he cast his arms out wide, his hands bent like claws. Tapestries and the biers burned all around him.

"Suffer, bastard!" Gerak shouted. "Suffer like she did."

"We should go," Orsin said. "The other one's still alive, and many devils besides."

Vasen nodded. Shadows poured off of him, off of Weaveshear, and led off down the abbey's corridors.

Another scream from the man, a wet gurgle that ended in him vomiting a black rope of phlegm down the front of his robes. He put his hands on his face, screaming, as black fluid poured from his eyes, his nose, his ears, saturating his robes.

"This is not what you promised!" the man screamed. "This is not what you promised!"

Snarls and the heavy, scrabbling tread of clawed feet on the floor of the corridor behind the man grew loud enough to hear over his screams and the crackle of the flames.

"They're coming," Orsin said.

"You've seen what you need to see," Vasen said to Gerak. "Leave him to suffer or kill him. Your decision."

Gerak looked at the screaming man, seemingly insensate of all but his pain. Anger twisted Gerak's expression and he drew, nocked, and fired. An arrow sank to the fletching in the screaming man. He seemed barely to notice the wound as black fluid poured from the hole.

"Gerak," Orsin said.

But Gerak was past hearing him. He drew again, fired. Drew, nocked, and fired, the arrows coming so fast that Vasen was dumbstruck. In moments, six more arrows sprouted from the man's flesh . Black, putrescent fluid poured from the wounds, but still he stood, screaming, bleeding, dying, changing.

"We have to go!" Orsin said, as something large and strong slammed into the double doors behind the dying, bleeding man

The man uttered an inhuman shriek as the skin on his thin body cracked and split, blood and ichor spraying the room all around as something expanded within him, his flesh an egg birthing a horror.

"No!" he screamed. "No!"

Sharp claws burst in a black spray from the tips of his fingers. His spine lengthened with a wet, cracking sound, making him taller, thinner. He screamed in agony as the transformation twisted his body. His skull elongated, the jaw widened. His teeth rained out of his mouth as fangs burst from his gums to replace them. His voice deepened. An appendage burst from his back, a bony tail that ended in a spiked wedge of bone that looked like a halberd blade. The devil—a bone devil, Vasen realized—used its clawed fingers to help it slip the rest of the man's flesh and body, as if it were undressing.

"We *must* go," Orsin said.

Vasen took Gerak by the arm. "She's avenged, Gerak. Elle is avenged. Come on."

The bone devil stood like a man but twice as tall, its nude body the color of old ivory, the flesh pulled so tight over it that it seemed composed of nothing but skin, sinew, and bone. Hate burned in eyes the black of the phlegm that polluted the floor. Fingers on its overlarge hands ended in black claws the length of a knife blade. The devil clacked them together, as if trying out a new toy.

Finally the double door behind gave way and a half-dozen spined devils and Sayeed burst through. All of them pulled up at the sight of the towering bone devil.

Sayeed's emotionless, dead eyes went to the ripped pile of flesh gathered around the clawed feet of the devil, the face of the thin man still visible at the top of it, the eye sockets staring, the slack mouth open in a scream.

"Zeeahd?" Sayeed said, his blade limp at his side.

Orsin took hold of Vasen and Gerak, his grip like iron. "We have our path." He nodded at the line of shadows that led from Weaveshear down the hall, away from the devils. "We must go. Right now."

"This is freedom, Sayeed," the devil said, his voice deep and gravely. "Freedom at last."

Sayeed fell to his knees, staring at the devil. His expression went slack and Vasen saw something in him die. The spined devils abased themselves before their larger kin.

Vasen, Orsin, and Gerak turned and ran.

Before they'd taken five strides, he heard the bone devil say, "Kill them all."

Vasen turned to see the spined devils tumble into the hall behind them, all spines and scales and teeth. They launched dozens of spines from their twisted forms, the quills lighting up as they flew.

He channeled Amaunator's power through his shield and it blazed rose-colored light across the entire corridor. The quills hit the light and fell inert to the ground. Vasen turned back and ran on, following the twisting tendril of shadow put before him by Weaveshear.

The devils shrieked and gave chase, their claws clicking over the floors. Orsin plowed down the stair and through a set of doors, and Vasen slammed them shut behind them, hoping to delay the devils. He held Weaveshear before him, following the thread it offered. He had no idea where it would lead.

"It could be nothing!" he shouted to Orsin, indicating the thread of shadow that led them on.

"Follow it," Orsin said. "Trust me! It's happened before!"

Every corner they turned, every door they opened, Vasen feared encountering more devils, but the way remained clear. They burst through an outer door and into the northern court-yard, sprinting over the smooth flagstones and the shining sun symbol of Amaunator.

"The sword is leading us into the valley," Gerak said. "We'll be exposed in the woods. We should find a defensible spot and make a stand."

"Always you want to make a stand," Orsin said with a grin, pulling him along. "Keep moving!"

The devils burst through the doors behind them, caught sight of the three comrades, and loosed a hail of flaming spines. The missiles thudded into the walls, burning.

"Keep going!" Vasen said, and shoved Gerak forward. "Follow the line! Follow the line!"

They cleared the courtyard, the outbuildings and livestock pens, and sprinted into the pines. The devils pursued relent-lessly. Vasen could hear them roaring and growling not only behind but off to either side.

Brennus stood before the tarnished scrying cube, his mind racing.

"Look, now?" the homunculi asked. One of the constructs was perched on each of his shoulders.

Brennus nodded. He raised a hand and shot a charge of power into the scrying cube, activating it. The tarnish on its silver surface flowed together to make dark clouds, revealing the shining metal surface beneath.

Shadows spun around him wildly, aping the wild beating of his heart. He took the rose holy symbol in one hand, took his mother's necklace in the other, held them before him, the two pieces of jewelry crafted thousands of years apart, yet together forming another piece of the puzzle he'd long sought to solve.

He'd tried to scry the Abbey of the Rose hundreds of times and always failed. He had concluded that it was a myth. He knew better now. He'd tried to scry the son of Erevis Cale just as often, and also failed, and so concluded that Cale's son was dead or out of reach. But now he knew better about that, too. Before those examples, the only other person or thing he'd been unable to scry had been Erevis Cale himself, and that was because Mask had shielded Cale from Brennus's divinations. But Mask was dead, was he not? So who was shielding Cale's son?

Everything had come together at just the right time. He thought Mask must have somehow been at the root of it. Brennus was probably helping the Lord of Shadows somehow, and that was fine with him. By helping Mask, he was, presumably, hurting Shar. And hurting Shar meant hurting Rivalen. And hurting Rivalen was all he cared about.

"Now for the test," he murmured.

Possession of Cale's son's holy symbol would hopefully provide the focus he needed to pierce the wards, whatever their source.

His homunculi rubbed their hands together, reflecting his eagerness.

Holding the rose in his fingers, he held his hands above his head and incanted the words to one of his most powerful divinations. He focused the spell's seeing eye on Cale's son, on the Abbey of the Rose, and let power pour from him. Magic charged the shadows swirling around his body, veined them in red and orange, and they extended to the face of the scrying cube and joined with the churning black clouds of the tarnish.

The silver face of the cube took on depth, darkened, but showed him nothing. His spell reached across Sembia, feeling for the focus of the spell. Brennus continued to pour power into the spell until sweat soaked him, fell in rivulets down his face. He held the rose symbol so tightly in his palm that the edges bit into his flesh. The homunculi squeaked with fear and covered their eyes as ever more power gathered.

Dots of orange light formed on the surface of the cube, like stars in the deep. Controlling his exhilaration, he willed the scrying eye of the divination to move closer, realized that he was looking down from on high at a mountain valley. The orange lights were burning trees. Struggling to control a rush of emotion, he forced the eye of the spell downward so he could make out details. A river divided the valley. Tarns dotted it here and there. Ancient pines covered it in a blanket of green. Many of them burned, with fires blazing here and there throughout the woods. He saw movement among the trees all over the valley, but ignored it for now. Instead, he focused on the structures partially screened by the pines. Although dark, he recognized it as a temple or abbey.

"I have you," he said.

He moved the scrying eye to the frenetic motion he saw among the burning pines. Perspective blurred as the eye whirled across the valley, focusing on three men pelting through the woods. One of them, tall, dark-skinned, and with darkness clinging to his flesh, had to be the scion of Cale. The others, a deva and a bow-armed human, were his companions. Spined devils bounded through the woods in pursuit of the men. A single bone devil plodded through the woods, too.

The devils meant that Mephistopheles was somehow involved. Not surprising given the Lord of Cania's connection to Mask. Brennus could not let Cale's son be killed or taken by agents of the Archfiend. Brennus needed the son, needed to know what he knew, what he *was*, and how he could use him to harm Rivalen.

He studied the location with care, noted the details of the valley, the abbey, committed all of it to memory, and spoke aloud to his majordomo, Lhaaril. Latent spells in his abode projected his words to Lhaaril, wherever the majordomo might have been.

"Lhaaril, assemble a force of our trusted men and their mounts at the teleportation circle in the courtyard. This instant. No one else is to know."

The reply came immediately. "Yes, Prince Brennus."

Brennus considered returning to his chambers to arm himself with additional wands, but decided his spellcraft and the magic gear he carried would suffice. He pulled the darkness around him and stepped through it to an inner courtyard of his manse.

A single sheet of polished basalt paved the large, rectangular courtyard. The walls and spiked towers of the manse surrounded it on all sides. A large, thaumaturgic triangle was graven in the basalt, its grooves inlaid with tarnished silver. A servant stood near one end of the courtyard, holding the reins of Brennus's veserab mount, already saddled. As he approached, the servant bowed and withdrew, and the veserab hissed a greeting through the fanged sphincter of its mouth. It pulled its wings in close as Brennus walked to its side and slid into the saddle.

Meanwhile, his men began to appear. Pockets of darkness formed here and there in the courtyard, and fully armed and armored Shadovar warriors, their faces hidden by ornate helms, materialized from the darkness atop their veserab mounts. In moments, a dozen men and their mounts filled the courtyard. The veserabs jostled and shrieked at each other.

Brennus heeled his mount and the veserab lurched on its wormlike body into the center of the thaumaturgic triangle. His men did the same.

"We travel to a valley in the Thunder Peaks," Brennus announced. "The devils there are of no concern to you. There are three men, one who looks like a shade."

The men looked at one another at that, their body language suggesting a question.

"He is not Shadovar. He travels with a deva and a human. I want all three of them alive."

Forearms slammed into breastplates and with one voice, they said, "Your will, Prince Brennus."

With that, Brennus began the teleportation ritual.

CHAPTER TWELVE

Devils swarmed the woods. Vasen could hear them all around, lumbering through the brush, snarling.

"They're trying to cut us off!" Vasen said. "Faster!"

"I can hardly see anything!" Gerak said, nearly tripping over a log.

Vasen forgot that he and Orsin could see clearly in darkness and Gerak could not. He lit up his shield and the glow filled the forest. Shadows rose all around them. Vasen felt them knocking against his awareness, a sensation he'd never felt so strongly before. He stared at the sword in his fist, wondering.

Flaming spines flew, breaking his train of thought, and a devil bounded into their midst. It knocked Gerak to the ground and clamped its jaws down on his leg. He screamed, tried to roll out from under the creature while Vasen shouted and drove Weaveshear through the devil's side, impaling it on the black blade. The devil reared back, snarling with pain. Orsin appeared to the devil's right, his hands charged with dark energy. He slammed his fist into the creature's open mouth and drove it out the top of the devil's skull. The fiend collapsed in a heap, its shattered head leaking brains and ichor.

"All right?" Vasen asked Gerak, pulling him to his feet. More devils were closing.

"I'll manage," he said, wincing as he tested his leg. Before Vasen could say anything more, Gerak's eyes went wide and he pushed Vasen to the side while bringing his bow to bear. A snarl sounded from behind and above and Vasen whirled in time to see a spined devil leaping down from one of the pines at Orsin. Gerak's bow sang, and an arrow caught the fiend in mid-flight, sinking to the fletching in the devil's throat. The creature hit the ground writhing, its squeals of pain a rasping wheeze through the hole in its throat. Gerak fired again, hit the devil in the chest, and the creature went still.

All around them, pines and undergrowth were catching fire from the devil's spines. Growls and snarls sounded from all sides out in the woods. Once again Vasen felt the peculiar sensitivity to the shifting shadows around him. He felt their distance from him, their taste and texture. He felt them in much the same way he had come to feel his faith after he'd been called by Amaunator.

His god allowed him to draw on his faith, turn it into energy, and with it, serve the light. The shadows, too, were tools, and his blood allowed him to draw on them, use them, too, didn't it? Hadn't his father commanded the shadows?

He looked at his hands, saw the shadows leaking from his flesh, wrapping around Weaveshear. He felt the connection between the darkness in his flesh, the shadow he cast behind him from the light of his shield and the shadows all around them. Light and shadow were one, merged in him. He could move through them, if he wished. He knew he could.

"Vasen," Orsin said. "Vasen, we must go."

Vasen nodded.

"Too late," Gerak said, and started planting arrows in the ground near him, within easy reach. "They're all around. There's nowhere to go."

The woods blazed around them, the fires jumping from pine to pine. The air grew hotter with each moment. The scrub and beds of pine needles caught flame like tinder. Soon the entire wood would be ablaze. The devils slunk among the flames, a half-dozen maybe, the silhouettes of their fiendish forms moving among the trees and flames unharmed by the heat, their eyes glowing red in the flames. They moved with the slow certainty of predators, wolves who'd finally ringed their prey and brought it to heel.

"Then we fight here," Orsin said, and dragged his staff on the ground, tracing a circle around him, delineating his own personal arena. "You get your stand, after all, Gerak. There'll be other lives after this one, my friends. I hope we all meet again in one of them."

Vasen glanced back at the abbey but couldn't see it. It was lost to the smoke, fire, and the trees. With the Oracle dead and the abbey abandoned, the valley didn't belong to the light anymore. It belonged to the shadows.

To the shadows.

His perception narrowed down to a single thing—the vein of shadow spun out for him by Weaveshear, a dark line drawn across reality, reaching back to the abbey, stretching forward through the flames, past the devils, and out farther into the woods, a tether between past and present, with this moment standing at the intersection. The blade was the line that connected him to his father and his father's abilities.

He felt the tendril in his mind, felt its path as it wove through the woods, felt its end point.

He knew where it was leading them.

Gerak fired into the trees. Out in the dark, a devil screamed, but the rest continued to close. They were preparing for a rush. Orsin held his staff before him in both hands, his face serene, calm. The crash of a large form moving through the woods sounded from the direction of the abbey. The bone devil was coming. The gleeful shrieks and whines of the spined devils heralded the larger fiend's arrival.

The heat from the fire was increasing as the flames spread. The sky glowed orange. Clouds of smoke poured into the air.

"Look!" Gerak said.

Above the space where the abbey would be, a glowing green line formed in the sky and widened until it formed a large rectangle in the air. A portal. Dark forms moved on the other side of it, growing larger, larger, until they burst forth through a magical door.

"Shadovar," Gerak said. He took aim but it was too far for a shot.

A score of veserab-mounted Shadovar flew through the portal. The great, winged worms reared up when they materialized in the air, their wings beating rapidly. The riders tried to steady them. One of the Shadovar, backlit by the glowing portal, wore no armor and rode the largest of the veserabs. He looked down on the abbey, on the woods, his glowing eyes the color of polished steel.

Without warning a shower of flaming spines flew at the companions from all directions, dozens of them, a rain of fire. Most got caught up in the nearby trees and set them ablaze, but a score fell among the comrades. Vasen blocked most with his shield and the rest bounced off his armor, but Orsin and Gerak had no such protection, and both grunted with pain as spines pierced clothing and flesh.

"They're coming," Orsin said, plucking a flaming spine from his arms.

The devils came in a final rush. Their shrieks and growls reached a crescendo, and in the glow of the fire Vasen could see them bounding through the underbrush and trees toward them. From the direction of the abbey he saw the looming shadow of the bone devil, striding like a colossus through the pines.

"Stand next to me," Vasen said. "Now. No questions."

Above them, the veserabs keened as the huge beasts winged over the flames. Vasen heard the Shadovar shouting to one another, pointing down at the devils, at the comrades. The steel-eyed Shadovar in the long robes swooped toward them. He extended a hand, and energy gathered in his palm.

Vasen reached out for the shadows as Gerak and Orsin came to his side.

"What are you doing?" Gerak asked.

Orsin must have known. "What he was born to do."

When Vasen felt his mind take hold of the shadows, he drew them closer, deeper, darker. They swirled around him and his companions.

Vasen felt comfortable in the darkness, at home. The shadows dimmed the light of the world, but not the light of his faith. He could embrace both the heritage of his blood and the fact of his faith. He did not have to choose one or the other. He could have both.

The devils broke through the flaming trees. The Shadovar above discharged a black bolt of energy from his hand. Vasen touched each of his friends, stepped through the shadows, and took them from that place.

Frustration made Brennus white-knuckle the reins on his veserab. Ovith had led him to believe the son of Cale could not call upon any such powers. He cursed.

"Scour the woods!" he said to the riders who'd accompanied him. He spoke in a normal tone, but a spell put his voice in each of their ears. "Find them! Now!"

The heat and smoke rising from the burning forest made visibility poor. He wheeled his veserab over the woods, the river, the abbey. His riders did the same. Cale's son would not be able to walk the shadows far. Not even a true shade could take them far.

"You see them?" he called.

"No, my lord!"

"No, Lord Brennus!"

He felt an itch on his flesh, the touch of a powerful divination, and immediately knew from where it came: Rivalen. He cursed again. His brother would be coming.

Below, a handful of spined devils prowled the blazing woods, bounding through the inferno. A bone devil strode among them. He looked back to the abbey, which sat dark and apparently abandoned, more like a mausoleum than a sanctuary of Amaunator that had evaded Shadovar detection for a century.

"What changed?" Brennus asked himself.

"No one home," said one of the homunculi perched on his shoulder.

"But why? Why now?"

Holding the rose of Amaunator by the few remaining links of its lanyard, Brennus intoned the words to another divination, focusing the magic around the son of Erevis Cale. When he finished the spell, he felt it latch onto its target. The rose symbol lifted from his palm and flew toward the east, pulling against the lanyard.

He did not bother to alert his men. Eager, he spurred his veserab to the east. The huge creature veered, beat its wings, and flew like a shot quarrel through the air.

"Have him now?" one of the homunculi asked.

"Yes," Brennus said. "We have him. But the nightseer is coming."

The homunculi cowered in Brennus's cloak, shivering.

The three comrades materialized in the woods on the eastern side of the valley. Mountains loomed before them, forming a dark wall. The rush of the cascades sounded loud in Vasen's ears. Wind whispered through the pines. The relative quiet felt expectant.

"The tarn," Orsin said, nodding.

"You said it was holy," Vasen said.

The line of shadow extending from Weaveshear led off into the woods, toward the tarn.

"What tarn?" asked Gerak. "What just happened?"

In the distance they could see the orange glow of the burning woods. The dark, winged forms of the veserabs flitted over the inferno. One of the Shadovar had peeled away from the burning woods and flew in their direction, each beat of his mount's huge wings devouring the distance.

"The Shadovar are coming," Orsin said.

Vasen started toward the tarn at a jog. "Come on."

They followed the line of darkness that connected Weaveshear to the water. Standing at the tarn's edge, they looked down into water so dark and still it looked like a hole. The shadows from the sword plunged into the depths.

"So?" asked Gerak, looking over his shoulder.

Orsin looked to Vasen.

Vasen stared at the water, licked his lips. "We follow it."

Gerak looked at him as if he were mad. "Into the water?"

A series of shrieks from behind turned them around—a veserab. The canopy blocked their view of the approaching Shadovar, but Vasen knew he was close.

"Yes, into the water."

"There are better places to hide," Gerak said. "I could lead us—"

"It's not to hide. It's to go."

"Go? Go where?" Gerak asked.

Vasen shrugged. "Go where . . . I'm supposed to go. I know how this sounds. But I also know I'm right."

Gerak shook his head, cursed softly. He looked at Orsin. "This makes sense to you?"

Orsin nodded slowly. "It does."

"Well, past lives make sense to you, too, so I don't credit your opinion much."

Orsin chuckled at that.

Gerak eyed the water warily. "I don't swim," he admitted at last.

Vasen smiled, then lied. "Me, neither. But I don't think we'll need to."

Closer shrieks from the veserabs, the susurrus of beating wings.

"I'm asking you to trust me," Vasen said.

Gerak looked from Vasen, to Orsin, back to Vasen. "If you're wrong, I'll find you in our next life."

Again Orsin chuckled. Vasen joined him. "Well enough."

The shadows ten paces from them swirled, deepened, and two pinpoints of steel gray light formed in their midst. The darkness coagulated into the form of the Shadovar leader. His lower body vanished into the darkness, so that he appeared to disincorporate below the knees. His thin, angular face showed no expression. His hands glittered with rings. Two tiny creatures, their skin like clay, perched on his shoulders—homunculi.

"Wait," the Shadovar said, and extended his hand. Energy gathered on his fingertips, writhing tentacles of shadows.

Vasen didn't wait. He raised his shield, brandishing Dawnlord Abelar's rose, and channeled his faith into it. Rose-colored light exploded out from it in a blaze of beams, casting the entire meadow in bright light. The Shadovar and his homunculi cried out, shielding their eyes from the sudden glare.

"Go!" Vasen said, and tried to push Orsin and Gerak into the water.

But before any of them could jump in, the sky above them ripped open with a thunderclap, the sound so loud that it made Vasen's bones ache and flattened him to the ground. Ears ringing, he raised himself to all fours.

"I've sought you for decades, son of Cale," said a deep, resonant voice from above, a voice so full of power that it seemed to use up all the air. Vasen could hardly breathe. "And here you've been all the while, hiding under my nose."

Vasen staggered to his feet, his shield still blazing, and looked up.

Another Shadovar descended from a glowing green rift in the dark clouds. He had no mount. He rode only the column of his power. Darkness spun around him, mingled with the swirl of his dark robes. Power went before him, palpable in its strength. He seemed more . . . present than anything else in the world, more solid, more *there*. Golden eyes blazed in the dark hole of his face.

"Rivalen," said the steel-eyed Shadovar, his tone dark with hate.

Vasen knew the name. Prince Rivalen Tanthul, the Nightseer of Shar, rumored to be divine.

"Rivalen," Orsin whispered. "One of the three."

"We must go," Vasen said softly, helping Gerak and Orsin to their feet. He edged them toward the water.

Rivalen reached the ground, a cloud of darkness swirling at this feet. His entire lower body was lost to the shadows. He looked as if he were riding a thunderhead as he walked toward them.

"You aren't leaving," Rivalen said. "None of you are."

"Rivalen," the other Shadovar said.

"Be silent, Brennus," Rivalen said, and made a cutting gesture with his hand that lifted Brennus from his feet and drove him backward into one of the pine trees. Either wood or bone or both cracked from the impact.

"You think your infantile plotting is unknown to me?" Rivalen said to Brennus. "You think your intent is unknown to me?"

To Vasen's shock, Brennus climbed to his feet. "No," he said, his steel eyes flashing. He held something up in his hand, a jeweled necklace. "I've made my intent plain. And nothing has changed."

Rivalen's eyes never left Vasen. "You're mistaken, Brennus. We've found the son of Cale. Everything has changed." He waved his hand and the light went out of Vasen's shield. "Enough with that shield."

Brennus's gaze went from Rivalen to Vasen and back to Rivalen.

Vasen backed toward the shadowed tarn, Gerak and Orsin beside him. He held his shield and Weaveshear at the ready, although he expected neither to be of any use.

"I don't fear you, Shadovar," Vasen said, and meant it. "And my name is Vasen."

Rivalen smiled, revealing small fangs. "You should fear me. You have your father's spirit, Vasen. But it won't save you. Or the world."

Rivalen glided toward them, the ground seeming to vibrate under the weight of his power.

"Run, you fools!" Brennus shouted to Vasen, and started to incant the words to a spell.

Rivalen's expression hardened, his eyes flashed.

Vasen whirled, grabbed Orsin and Gerak by their arms, and shoved them into the tarn before they could protest. They sank out of sight instantly. He looked over his shoulder, and he jumped in himself.

A column of flame extended from Brennus's hand and engulfed Rivalen. Rivalen stood unharmed in the midst of the fire, the dark eye of a blazing storm, and loosed a jagged bolt of green energy not at Brennus but at Vasen.

Vasen interposed sword and shield as his feet hit the water. He expected death or worse, but the energy of the spell was drawn to Weaveshear like metal shavings to a lodestone. The weapon seemed to absorb much of the power of the magic, although the force of the spell still sent Vasen skittering over the surface of the tarn like a skipped stone.

He sank into the water with the energy of the spell still sizzling around his blade, the green glow lighting the otherwise inky confines of the tarn. The water seemed to seize him in its grasp, pull him downward, as green lines of energy from Rivalen's magic snaked around the blade, around the hilt. Vasen thought to release the blade too late and the energy touched his flesh.

He screamed, expelling a stream of bubbles, as a jolt of agony coursed through his body and his heart seized. He felt as if his ribs had been shattered. His vision blurred and he struggled to remain conscious. His body spasmed, and even with his darkness-enhanced vision he could see nothing. He expected a splash to sound from above—Rivalen pursuing to retrieve his corpse—but he heard nothing, just the quiet of his own agony.

He knew he was dying because the water felt not cold but warm, pulling him rapidly down, drinking him in, swallowing him whole. In his rush to escape he'd killed not only himself but Gerak and Orsin. They'd all drown, lost in the shadowed tarn forever.

Darkness swirled around him, a manifestation of his regrets, his pain, his failure. He was falling, falling forever into the deep.

"See you soon," Rivalen said to Vasen, and flew to the edge of the tarn. He saw only the ghost of his reflection on the deep water, his golden eyes staring back at him like stars.

The tarn must have been a latent portal, activated by Weaveshear. He knew in that moment Drasek Riven must have put it there. It amused Rivalen to think of Riven, a small minded fool with his plots and counterplots, trying to foil Rivalen's own. Riven was just another pawn in Rivalen's game.

Brennus's chuckle pulled him around. "Not even a godling gets what he wants all the time. You failed, Rivalen. You wanted Vasen Cale and you failed to get him."

Rivalen laughed, loud and long. "I wasn't here to capture him, Brennus. He has a role yet to play. I was here to make sure that *you* didn't capture him. It's you who've failed. You've who've done nothing but further my ends. You see nothing, little brother, and at every turn do as I wish."

Shadows swirled around Brennus "You lie!"

Rivalen laughed more. "Your bitterness is sweet to the lady."

Brennus's steel eyes blazed with anger.

"I don't have to kill you to hurt you, Brennus. Remember that. Now run back to Sakkors, obsess about mother and revenge, and watch, helpless, as my plans end this world."

Brennus visibly bit back whatever words he might have said. His shoulders sagged as shadows gathered around him, deepened, and transported him back to whatever hidey-hole he had prepared for himself.

Rivalen smiled after his brother left. Brennus had once more had his hopes crushed. He was almost ripe for the picking, ready to serve as Rivalen's tool in translating *The Leaves of One Night*. Brennus's despair and bitterness ran deep.

Rivalen rose into the air on a column of darkness and power, surveying the valley. He had one more matter to which he must attend.

The Shadovar who served his brother had vanished, presumably following Brennus in flight. A handful of spined devils ran amok in the wood, burning everything flammable, torturing what animals they could find and catch. The valley was ablaze in fire and torment, a miniature version of the Hells. A bone devil prowled the pines among its smaller kin, aimless in its strides.

Rivalen saw Mephistopheles's hand in it. As always, the Lord of Cania sought the divine power that Drasek Riven and Rivalen had taken from Kesson Rel. The archfiend, too, must have guessed that Vasen Cale was the key to unlocking the divinity from its three holders.

Of course, Mephistopheles wanted the power only to give him the upper hand in his war against Asmodeus. Rivalen didn't want it at all. He wanted to use it, feed his goddess with it, and in so doing, restart the Cycle of Night and end everything.

Rivalen rode the shadows to the abbey. Much of it was ablaze, but fire and smoke could not harm Rivalen. He walked among the flames, amused that the home of the sun god finally radiated light, but only in its immolation. Tapestries curled as they burned. Roof timbers gave way in a shower of sparks. Stone cracked, fell in a hail of rubble.

Amid the ruins Rivalen found the corpses of two spined devils and the body of an old man, beaten beyond recognition. No other bodies.

That gave Rivalen pause.

The Oracle must have known an attack was coming. So he'd sent everyone away.

What else had he known?

His feet carried him through the fires to what appeared to be a shrine. The room included two burned biers, one knocked from its pedestal, the lid defaced and burned, the body that had been within burned to an unrecognizable cinder. He wondered who had been interred there, then reminded himself that it didn't matter. The world and everyone in it, including him, would soon end in nothingness

He pointed a finger at the ceiling and discharged a ray of energy that disintegrated a perfect circle through it, revealing the dark sky above. Through that he flew up and out into the night.

He rose high into the sky, one with the darkness, and looked down on the narrow gash of the flaming valley, the burned-out abbey.

Below, the devils continued to burn the woods and kill whatever creatures they could find.

"Mephistopheles's creatures," he said, irritated at their presence.

He moved from the darkness in the sky to the darkness under the canopy of the woods, a few paces from two of the spined devils. His sudden appearance halted their loping strides through the undergrowth. They crouched low, spines raised, teeth bare. He gestured, let power flow from his hand, and ripped every spine from their hides in a shower of flames and ichor. They yelped with agony and fell rolling to the ground, their raw, exposed flesh accreting pine needles and dirt. The cloud spines hung over them. He reversed all of them, pointed the barbed tips downward, and drove all of them back into the devils' flesh. They shrieked and died.

He felt the darkness around him, the velvet of its touch across the entire valley. He sensed the location of another devil, stepped through the shadows to it, and, with a flick of his finger and a minor exercise of power, turned it inside out.

He moved to another, another, methodically destroying each of the creatures in ever more grotesque fashion.

"Stay in your hole in Cania, Archfiend," he said, as a blast of life-draining energy left another spined devil a lifeless bag of hide and bones. "When the time is right, we'll meet in Ordulin. All of us will."

He saved the bone devil for last. The thin, lumbering creature stalked through the pines, its mouth open in a pained scream. It thrashed about wildly with its overlong arms and clawed hands, the long, curling tail that ended in a sharp spade of bone.

"Freedom!" it shouted, the word nonsensical, the tone tinged with madness.

Rivalen stepped from the shadows before it, let it see him. It halted, crouched, and flexed its claws. Its lower jaw dropped open, the fangs dripping with foul saliva. Stupidly, it pelted toward Rivalen, shrieking for blood.

Rivalen raised a hand, palm outward, and immobilized the creature in mid-stride. Dark energy whirled around it, holding it fast, keeping it silent. Rivalen stalked forward, contemplating suitable ends.

He felt a presence in the trees behind the devil, and an armored man burst out of the tree line. He was as tall as Rivalen but built as thickly as a barrel. He bore a large single-edge sword and a square shield in his hands. Dark, dead eyes stared out of a face barely visible for the thick beard he wore. Rivalen sensed the minor enchantments on the man's shield, sword, and armor, but it was the twisting, odd signature of the magic affecting the man himself that kept Rivalen from annihilating him where he stood.

"Get away, Shadovar!" the man said, pointing his sword at Rivalen. "Back, I said."

He advanced on Rivalen with blade and shield at the ready.

Curious, Rivalen retreated a step, hands held up in a gesture of harmlessness.

Rivalen tried to mask his power but the man seemed to pick up on it as he neared. He stopped his advance, a stride or two before the immobilized devil.

"Just leave us," the man said.

"Us?"

The man's eyes moved to the bound bone devil, back to Rivalen. "Leave, Shadovar."

Rivalen took a step forward, let more of his power manifest. Perhaps sensing what Rivalen was, the man fell back a step, eyes wide.

"You've a fondness for devils? Who's this creature to you?"

The man found his nerve and looked up sharply, as if Rivalen had slapped him. "He's no creature, shade. He was—*is*—my brother."

Rivalen understood the implication immediately. "And now he serves Mephistopheles?"

"He was betrayed by Mephistopheles! We both were!"

Rivalen saw an opportunity, used his power to put guile into his voice. "And the archfiend's betrayal turned him into . . . that?"

The man nodded hard, once.

"What's your name?" Rivalen glided forward, closing the distance between them.

"What difference does it make? It's all lost now. Everything. It was all for nothing."

The words pleased Rivalen. He pulled the man's name from his mind. "Sayeed. Your name is Sayeed."

Sayeed's brow furrowed. He took another step back, sword and shield ready.

"There's nothing to fear," Rivalen said, waving a shadow-strewn hand dismissively. "A minor cantrip. Your name hovered at the forefront of your thinking because I asked the question. You serve the archfiend as well, Sayeed?"

The man's jaw tightened as he chewed on rising anger. "I serve myself. And my brother."

"Your brother is gone. Whatever he was, that isn't him."

Sayeed's expression fell but only for a moment before he recovered his stoicism. "We were—"

He cut himself short, shaking his head.

Again, Rivalen knew his words before he spoke them. "You were cursed. But not by the archdevil?"

"No, not by him. The Spellplague changed us."

"Ah," Rivalen said with a nod. "But Mephistopheles promised you release." Rivalen gestured at the bound devil, Sayeed's transformed brother. "And that is how an archfiend honors his word."

The man glared at Rivalen, his hands opening and closing on the hilt of his sword. "A Shadovar is no better."

Rivalen smiled. "Oh, you are world-weary, Sayeed. I see it clearly. I've known others like you, many others." His memory flashed on Tamlin Uskevren, whose pain Rivalen had used to twist the young nobleman to his ends. "The world has treated you harshly. Hope wanes. Despair rises, replaced by bitterness. It's warranted. You're afflicted by hardship. I was, too, once. The Lady offers a place to lay such weight."

Sayeed shook his head, looked away, but Rivalen saw something awaken behind the indifference. "The Lady? Shar?"

He said the word as many did, in hushed, fearful tones.

Rivalen stepped close to Sayeed, the two of them eye to eye, Sayeed caught up in Rivalen's shadows.

"Shar, yes. The Lady of Loss knows your pain. What burden do you bear, Sayeed brother of Zeeahd? I'm her servant. Confess it to me."

Sayeed swallowed. "No. It's mine to bear."

Rivalen admired the man's stubbornness. "Share it. Perhaps I can help ease the weight."

Sayeed stuck out his chin. "I require no help."

Rivalen recognized the ground Sayeed stood on, offering the last bit of defiance. He saw potential in the man, a

PAUL S. KEMP

possible use. His despair and bitterness ran deeper, perhaps, than even Brennus's. Shar had put Sayeed in Rivalen's path, and Sayeed was but a small step away from where Rivalen needed him to be.

"Well enough, then," Rivalen said. "Luck to you."

He turned and glided away, allowing Sayeed a few moments to think.

"You'll leave us?" Sayeed said to his back.

"What are you and your cursed brother to me, Sayeed?"

Rivalen started to gather the shadows around him.

"Wait!" Sayeed called, and Rivalen knew from the man's tone that he had him. He let his hand brush the holy symbol of the Lady he kept on an electrum chain about his neck.

"You said you could help," Sayeed said.

"I said 'perhaps I could help.' You're yet to give name to your affliction."

"My affliction," Sayeed said, and started to pace in agitation. "My affliction."

Rivalen waited, letting matters take their course.

Sayeed walked a circle, an animal filled with pent-up anger. His voice gained volume as he spoke. "My affliction is that I'm no longer a man. I don't taste food or drink. I don't take pleasure in a woman's touch! I feel nothing! Nothing! Not even pain!"

Before Rivalen could act, Sayeed slid his hand along the length of his sword. He didn't wince. Blood poured from the wound, but only for a moment before his skin closed. He held up his hand for Rivalen to see. It was unmarred.

"I'm not alive, but death is kept from me. Can you help me with that, Shadovar? Can you? Kill me if you can!"

Rivalen thought of Shar's eye, of *The Leaves of One Night*. He stepped close and put his hand on Sayeed's shoulder.

"I can help you. Indeed, I can."

Sayeed looked up, his eyes clear, as dead as those of a corpse. "I want . . . help."

Rivalen steered Sayeed around until he faced his transformed brother. "You'll have it. And you will help me in the process. Will you do that, Sayeed? Help me? Help the Lady?"

Rivalen felt Sayeed's body sag at the request, but he nodded vacantly. "What things?"

"A small thing, but important. I need you to read something, is all."

"Read something?"

The man was lost, broken, as soulless as a living human could be. He was exactly what Rivalen needed. He would serve even better than Brennus.

"I'll explain in time. But now you must do something else." He nodded at the bone devil. "Kill it. Kill what's left of your brother. Kill what's left of your life before today, before this moment."

Shaking his head, Sayeed tried to step back but Rivalen held him fast, shadows swirling around him. "That's my brother. I can't. I won't."

Rivalen tightened his grip on Sayeed's shoulder. A man who felt pain would have cried out. Sayeed gave no response.

"That is, indeed, your brother, but you must do as I say. He's a tool of Mephistopheles, Sayeed, and Mephistopheles betrayed your brother and you. But you will have your revenge. I vow it. You will see Mephistopheles suffer. But first, you must do as I've asked."

Sayeed stared at the bone devil, the towering fiend held helpless by Rivalen's spell.

He needed reassurance, so Rivalen gave it to him.

"This is how it must be. Free him, Sayeed. Give him death. End his suffering."

Sayeed's jaw tightened. He nodded, his mouth set, his brow furrowed. He took his blade in both hands. "Release him."

"There's no—"

"I won't execute him while he is helpless!"

"Very well."

A minor exercise of will freed the bone devil from the spell. Instantly, the creature rushed forward, bony claws raised high, the spike of its tail curled up over its head.

Rivalen backed away as Sayeed ducked under the devil's claw slash and sidestepped the spike of its tail, which drove deeply into the soil. Sayeed rode his momentum into a spinning slash that severed the devil's leg and sent it toppling to the earth.

Sayeed was atop it before it could rise to even a sitting position.

"I hate you!" he screamed, and drove his blade into the devil's chest again and again. "I hate you for this!"

Rivalen didn't know if Sayeed was speaking to him or his transformed brother or to Mephistopheles, and he didn't care.

"Your bitterness is sweet to the Lady," he muttered.

Sayeed would be perfect. Perfect.

Presently it was over. The devil's body was chopped apart, ichor staining the grass. Sayeed wiped his blade clean on the turf and sheathed his weapon over his back.

"You did him a service," Rivalen said. "And now you'll do so for me. The Lady's eye is on you, Sayeed. She sees you clearly."

He gathered the shadows about them both and rode the darkness from that place to Ordulin.

Brennus materialized in his safe room in Sakkors, a vaulted, lead-lined chamber stocked with multifarious magic wands, staffs, scrolls, and potions, and warded with the most powerful abjurations he knew. Two iron golems greeted his arrival with creaky nods; the towering metal constructs were obliged to attack anything and anyone that appeared in the safe room unescorted by Brennus.

He doubted his defenses would be enough to keep Rivalen out, should his brother choose to attack, but it would at least allow Brennus advance warning.

He collapsed into a chair, the shadows about him whirling madly. His homunculi emerged from his cloak and, instead of taking their usual perch on his shoulders, curled up in his lap, shivering. He rubbed their heads and in time their shivering stopped. Brennus's rage, however, did not abate.

He reached into his cloak and removed his mother's platinum necklace—the jacinths looked dull in the darkness, like extinguished stars—and the rose holy symbol once borne by Vasen Cale. He resolved to die before leaving his mother's murder unavenged. He simply needed to find a weakness in Rivalen, a crack in his defenses.

Rivalen's words haunted him.

Rivalen knew it all. Rivalen had foreseen it all. Brennus could not stop him, could not avenge his mother's murder.

"Rivalen is going to destroy the world," he said.

He would have done anything to stop Rivalen, to kill him, but Brennus could see no way to do so.

He had to try to get to Cale's son. He was missing something. He had to be missing something.

Because if he wasn't, Rivalen would soon kill everything.

Vasen seemed to fall forever. He had no idea which way was up. He was turned around, air-starved, dying. He prepared to inhale a lungful of water, to end it all, when strong hands grabbed him by the cloak, felt for his arms, and pulled him upward with a lurch.

He emerged into darkness, gasping, shadows churning around him. A drumming sounded in his ears, a rhythmic beat that seemed to shake his entire body. He heard a roar, like the cascades of the valley but more ominous. As his vision cleared and the shadows around him diminished, he expected to be staring into the golden eyes of Rivalen Tanthul. Instead, he found himself staring into the tattooed face of Orsin, the deva's white eyes filled with concern.

"He lives," Orsin said.

Vasen sat up with a lurch, coughing, spitting dark water. The drumming he'd heard was not coming from his ears, nor the rush from the cascades. He sat on a polished obsidian floor in a small, rectangular chamber . . . somewhere.

The air, viscous with shadows, felt thick in his lungs. As he had back in the woods of the valley, he felt the shadows all around him, felt them everywhere, to the limit of his perception. And he was connected to them, tethered. A swirling mass of darkness obscured the floor in one side of the room.

"That's where we came out," Orsin said.

"Came out?" Vasen said. His mind was fuzzy.

Gerak stood at a narrow window nearby, looking out. His body looked bunched with stress. The drumming and roar came from outside the window.

"Can you stand?" Orsin asked him.

When Vasen nodded, Orsin pulled him to his feet. His entire body ached and his chest still burned. The energy from Rivalen's spell had left a painful scorched patch on the skin of his hand. He sheathed Weaveshear. The weapon felt at home on his belt.

"Where are we?" Vasen asked.

"You tell us," Gerak said over his shoulder. "Come here. Look."

Vasen and Orsin joined Gerak at the window and both of them gasped.

The narrow window focused the volume of the drumming and roaring and the sound hit them like a gale. The three comrades stood in a high tower of obsidian, part of a larger keep or castle that featured delicate spires and high, smooth walls, the whole of it awash in shadows.

Outside the walls, surrounding it on all sides, was a horde of nightmarish size. Devils stood in ranks, thousands of them, some horned, armored, and as tall as giants. Others short and fanged, like the spined devils. Some flew in the air on membranous wings. Some oozed or crawled. Large horned devils, their red skin emitting flames the same way Vasen's skin emitted shadows, moved among the multitude. Weapons bristled everywhere: pikes, axes, swords. The size of the force took Vasen's breath away. Shadows poured from his flesh. And throughout the horde the same heraldry was featured, huge oriflammes that showed a black hand and a sword, both sheathed in flames.

"Gods," Vasen breathed.

"We're in the Hells," Gerak said, a hint of panic in his tone. "We must be."

Vasen felt the shadows behind him deepen, fill with power. He turned to see a short, lithe man step from the darkness, although the shadows clung to his form in a mist. A goatee hid a mouth that looked like it never smiled. His angular face, the dark skin pockmarked with scars, looked sharp enough to cut wood. Twin rapiers hung from his belt and he held a pipe in his hand. Black smoke curled up from the pipe to mix with the shadows.

"You're not in the Hells," said the man, his accented voice rich with power. "You're in the Shadowfell. And it's about time. Things are moving quickly now, and so must we."

Orsin assumed a fighting stance while Gerak fumbled for an arrow.

The man's mouth formed a sneer, showing stained teeth. The shadows about him whirled. He drew on the pipe, inhaled deeply, blew it out in a dark cloud.

"Wait," said Vasen to his comrades, and held up his hand.

"Thinking before you act," the man said with an approving nod. "Your father was the same way. Most of the time."

"You're Drasek Riven," Vasen said. He had to be.

Riven nodded, took another draw on the pipe.

"The Left Hand of Shadow," Orsin breathed.

Riven looked sidelong at Orsin. "If you fall to your knees, shadowalker, I promise you I'll stab you in the face."

Outside, the roar of the fiendish army and the beat of the drums rose higher, seemed to make the entire citadel shake.

Riven seemed barely to notice. He had eyes only for Vasen. "We don't have a lot of time for explanations. You're going to have to do as I tell you."

As if to make his point, a blare of horns from outside sounded.

"I don't even know what's happening," Vasen said. "I just watched my abbey burn, saw the Oracle die. We fought devils, Shadovar—"

"Shadovar? Which Shadovar?"

"What?" Vasen said. He was still processing events.

"Rivalen," Orsin offered.

Riven's face darkened. Shadows swirled around him. "Rivalen left Ordulin? What did he say?"

"He didn't say much of anything," Vasen said, and shadows boiled from his skin.

Riven paced the room. "He saw you and let you go?"

"We escaped," Vasen said. "He didn't *let* us do anything."

"What are you saying?" Orsin asked.

"I'm saying you're here because he let you go. If he wanted you dead, you'd be dead. I didn't . . . see that." He looked sharply at Vasen. "Do you feel anything unusual when you look at me?"

Vasen shook his head. "I don't understand. Should I?"

Riven stared into his face. "He changed you, Vasen. Or rather I changed you . . . Shit, shit, shit. Did I miss something? What am I overlooking? I thought you'd know, that you'd come here and know."

Shadow churned around Vasen, too. "You thought I'd know what?"

Riven whirled on him. "Know how to get this out of me! And out of Rivalen and Mephistopheles! You're the key, Vasen! You're supposed to be able to get the godhood out of all of us."

A long silence followed.

"I don't know how to do that," Vasen said at last.

Riven stared at him a long moment, their shadows, their lives, intersecting, crossing.

"I see that," he said at last, and took a step back. He exhaled, shadows churning around him. "Fine. Things are where they are. We have to keep going."

"Going where?" Gerak asked.

"To the Hells," Riven said. "Vasen is going to Cania to rescue his father. Erevis Cale is our best hope now."

"You're mad," Vasen said. "My father's dead."

"No, Riven said. "He's alive. Trapped in magical stasis. And you're going to get him out."

CHAPTER THIRTEEN

THE SHADOWS BLANKETED SAYEED and he heard, or maybe felt, a rushing sound. When the darkness lifted, it revealed a ruined city shrouded in night.

"Ordulin," Rivalen said.

"The maelstrom," Sayeed said. "I was here when it was still a city."

"It's something else now," Rivalen said.

Shattered, half-collapsed buildings dotted the area, jagged and crooked, like rotten teeth poking from the earth. Swirling shadows darkened the air. The wind blew in fierce gusts. Green lightning split the sky again and again. The ruins smelled like a graveyard, an entire city murdered and left on the face of the world to rot. Chunks of stone and statuary littered broken roads once filled with carriages and wagons and commerce. A hundred years ago, Sayeed had walked Ordulin's streets under the sun. Now he walked its ruins in darkness, himself ruined.

As they went Sayeed wiped his hands on his trousers, again and again, but whatever stained them would not come off to his satisfaction. He'd killed his own brother. He had no one, nothing for which to live. He had only a single desire, powerful and true, and that was to die. He was a hole. There'd be no filling him ever again.

"It's dark here," he observed.

Rivalen, half-merged with the shadows, his golden eyes like stars, said, "Always."

Thunder rumbled.

"I want to die," Sayeed blurted. The words sounded limp, dead as they exited his mouth. "You promised me that. I need to die."

"I know," Rivalen said, and lightning lit the sky in veins of green. "I can oblige. Come."

Undead prowled the ruined city: wraiths, specters, living shadows. There were hundreds, thousands perhaps. They broke on Rivalen's presence like water on stone, flowing around and over him, never approaching too closely.

Rivalen said, "Many thousands of years ago I murdered my mother to show the Lady the truth of my faith."

Sayeed said nothing.

"As she died, she asked for my hand."

They came to a wide flagged plaza. Building-sized chunks of dark stone littered it here and there, as if they'd rained from the sky. Hovering over the center of the plaza was a void, an emptiness. The sight of it made him dizzy and mildly nauseated. Paper flitted around it, into it, out of it, as if it were chewing on them and spitting them out.

Sayeed could not keep his eyes on the void, not entirely. It seemed to slip away and he never quite saw it squarely. But he saw enough, he felt its emptiness, felt the bitterness that poured from it, the spite. It was a mirror. In it he saw himself.

"Give me *your* hand," Rivalen said.

Sayeed turned, looked into Rivalen's golden eyes, at his extended hand, the flesh swathed in shifting lines of shadow.

"Give me your hand, Sayeed. You'll have what you wish. I'd thought to have my brother's . . . aid in this, but you will do better."

Sayeed extended his hand.

Rivalen took it, his flesh cold and dry, his grip like a vise.

"Come. You must stand before Shar's eye. She must see you."

Rivalen pulled him along toward the void, the eye, the mouth, the hole.

As he drew closer, he realized that the emptiness he'd felt, the pit in the center of his being, the hopeless feeling of loss, of solitude, was a trivial reflection of what he felt emanating from Shar's eye.

"Wait," he said, and tried to stop, to pull away from Rivalen. Rivalen's grip tightened, a vise. "It's too late for that."

"No!" Sayeed said and tried frantically to pull away. "No, wait!"

Rivalen pulled him along as if Sayeed were a child, the Shadovar's strength preternatural. Another step, another.

"Stop! Stop!"

Shadows boiled around Rivalen. His golden eyes flashed. "You wanted death, Sayeed! You'll have it! But first I need you to translate!"

"No! No!"

For the first time in a hundred years Sayeed felt something. Shar's eye put a seed of fear in him, and it soon blossomed into terror. He felt her regard emanating from the hole—the hate, the spite, the hopelessness, the unadulterated contempt for everything and anything. He screamed, his sanity slipping from him.

Rivalen drove him to his knees before the eye. The wind rushed around him. The papers orbiting the eye, moving in and out of it, gathering in a cloud before him. Her eye bore down on him like all the weight in the world. It pinioned him to the earth, tiny before it. He felt himself wither under her regard. He was an insignificant, trivial thing. He'd been such a fool, such a ridiculous fool. The Spellplague had changed him into something other than a man . . .

"Feast on her words," Rivalen said, putting his hands on either side of Sayeed's head.

But Sayeed had changed himself into something other than human, killed his own brother. Tears fell.

"Your bitterness is sweet to the Lady," Rivalen said, and his fingers burrowed into Sayeed's head, squeezing.

Pain lanced through Sayeed's skull. He felt as if his eyes would pop from his head. His mouth opened wide in a scream that went unuttered, for the pages of the book floating in the air before him flew into his open mouth, one after another, rushing down his throat, filling his mouth, stuffing him. He gagged, grunted, he couldn't breathe, he couldn't breathe, and through it all he felt Shar watching him, her eyes freighted with contempt.

Rivalen was holding little more than a rag doll in his hands, a hollow man useful now only as a vessel by which to translate the divine language of *The Leaves of One Night*. Not quite a corpse, not quite alive.

"Light is blinding," Rivalen said, stating one of Shar's Thirteen Truths as he forced dark, unholy energy into Sayeed's limp form. "Only in darkness do we see clearly."

Sayeed's body spasmed, charged with baleful energy. Rivalen released him and Sayeed slumped to the ground, an empty penitent with his back to the sky and his eyes to the ground, suspended forever between life and death, able to participate in neither.

Sayeed's bitterness and hopelessness, the essential core of his being, were the reagents that would transform Shar's words into something her nightseer could understand.

Impatient for revelation, Rivalen tore Sayeed's cloak and tunic from his back, ripped his armor from his torso and cast it aside, exposing the bare skin of Sayeed's back. Small black lines squirmed under his skin, causing it to bubble and warp, the ink of Shar's malice. The lines twisted and curled, formed themselves into tiny characters, and then into words, and words into promises.

Riven read them eagerly, the holy word of his goddess written in darkness on the skin of a man trapped in perpetual despair. He vacillated between elation and apprehension. The transfigured words of *The Leaves of One Night* were said to state the moment of Shar's greatest triumph and the moment of her greatest weakness.

He leaned forward, traced a trembling finger along Sayeed's back as he read. Shadows poured from Rivalen's flesh, knowledge from Sayeed's.

As Rivalen read, he began to understand. And as he began to understand, he began to laugh.

Rain fell. Thunder rumbled. Shadows swirled.

He looked up into Shar's eye and wept.

"All is meaningless," he said, intoning Shar's fourteenth, secret Truth. "And nothing endures."

He stood, the wind whipping his cloak and hair, and looked over his shoulder to the west.

They'd be coming, and their bitterness would be sweet to the Lady.

"Run to your father, little Cale," Rivalen said. "Then bring everyone to me."

Surprised silence greeted Riven's words. Gerak broke it.

"This is madness. You can't, Vasen. This is a fight for gods, not men."

"He must," Riven said, and his one eye bored into Vasen. "You must."

"I'll do it," Vasen said without any hesitation. "When?"

"Now," Riven said.

"I'll come, too, of course," said Orsin.

"Of course you will," Riven said. "After a hundred years, you shadowwalkers are still the same. All balls and no sense."

Orsin grinned. "A compliment from a god?"

"Take it as you wish," Riven said, but his tone indicated that he had, indeed, meant it as a compliment.

"Gerak, you can stay here," Vasen said, then looked to Riven. "He can stay here, yes?"

Riven shrugged. "He can, but I won't be able to look out for him. We have to move. Come on."

He headed off through a door and down a hall, and the three men fell in behind him.

"I don't need looking out for," Gerak snapped.

"If you stay here you might," Riven said.

Ten steps later, Gerak said, "I'll come."

"Gerak . . ." Vasen began.

Gerak cut him off. "Where else would I go?"

"So we're all madmen," Vasen said. "Well enough."

As they hurried through the shadowed, stone corridors and staircases of the Citadel of Shadow, two fat dogs fell in beside Riven, trotting and puffing along. Like Riven, they seemed clothed in shadows.

"My girls," Riven explained with a father's pride. The dogs took a liking to Gerak, and despite the woodsman's dark mood, he made a point to pet them as he walked.

"Good dogs," Gerak said.

Riven descended a stairway, picking up his pace. Outside, the drums and horns of the host of the Hells continued to thump and bray.

"They'll be attacking soon," Riven said. "You need to be gone before that."

"You going to hold them off alone?" Gerak asked. "Where are your forces?"

"They're around," Riven said.

"You'll send us to the Hells?" Vasen asked Riven.

Riven nodded. "I'd free Cale myself but the moment I showed, Mephistopheles would sense me there. Everything would fall apart."

"What's everything?" Orsin asked.

"Wish I knew," Riven said.

"How will we get back?" Orsin asked.

"Cale," Riven said.

"Cale?" Vasen asked. "What if he can't?"

"He can. He must. Vasen, you can free the divinity in me, in Rivalen, and in Mephistopheles. When you do that, Mask will return. And when he returns, the Cycle of Night will be stopped.

"What's the Cycle of Night?" Gerak asked.

"I don't have time for all of this!" Riven snapped. He inhaled to calm himself and looked at Vasen. "You say you don't know how to do it. I believe you. So Cale must. He must, Vasen. Mask kept him alive and in stasis for a reason. He'll be able to get you out of there."

"And if he can't?" Vasen asked.

"Then we all die. And eventually Shar gets her way, restarts the Cycle of Night, and all of Toril dies, too. That's the shape of it. Well enough?

Vasen nodded, trying not to show how overwhelmed he felt. "Well enough."

Riven held out a hand. On his palm sat an opalescent black sphere, about the size of a sparrow's egg. "This is a sending. Use it when you have your father out. Break it and speak and I'll hear. Clear?"

Vasen secreted the small gemstone in one of his belt pouches. "Clear."

They stood before a pair of large doors that Vasen assumed must open out onto the plain. The sound of the army outside caused the doors to vibrate. Dust floated in the air.

"Question," Orsin said to Riven.

Riven raised his eyebrows, waiting.

"It's personal."

Riven tapped a foot impatiently. "You want a kiss?"

Orsin laughed.

"Come on, man," Riven said. "Ask it."

Orsin said, "You want the divinity out? That's what you said. But why would you go back to being a man after being a god? *How* can you go back?"

Riven stared at Orsin a long time. "I never did like you shadowwalkers much."

Orsin stared at him, but said nothing.

Riven eyed each of them in turn. "When I open those doors, you just wait here, no matter what happens out there. When the time is right, I'll send you to Cania. Move fast, free your father, and get out. He's trapped under a cairn of ice and shadow."

The three men nodded. Shadows swirled rapidly around Vasen. His heart hammered his ribs.

"After you free him," Riven said. "Tell him to take you to the plaza in Ordulin where he and I faced Kesson Rel. He'll know where I mean."

Gerak said, "Ordulin's in ruins, haunted."

"What's that to you now?" Riven said. "You're standing in the Shadowfell. Soon you'll stand in the Eighth Hell. How's that for a daytrip, woodsman?"

He thumped Gerak on the shoulder and the bowman, despite himself, grinned.

Riven said, "Ordulin is where this ends. One way or another."

Shadows leaked from Vasen's flesh. He thought of the Oracle, his father, Derreg, his mother. "What'll happen in Ordulin?"

"The end happens in Ordulin," Riven said. Then, to Vasen, "Use Weaveshear to cut through Mephistopheles's wards around your father's cairn. You tell Cale . . . it all comes down to him."

"I will," Vasen said.

"I'll send you to Cania when the time is right. Be ready. Do not try to help me. Do not move from here until I move you."

"When will the time be right?" Orsin asked.

"When I get Mephistopheles to show," Riven said. He winked. "Shouldn't take long."

He touched the double doors and they swung open and the blast of sound from the army almost knocked them over. The stink of brimstone flowed in, filled the air.

Riven had his sabers in hand. "Good luck," he said to the three companions, then darted out the doors in the cloud of shadow. He shouted as he went, his voice a match for the drums of Cania's legions.

"To me, dead of Elgrin Fau! Once more to me!"

A great moan went up. It seemed to come from everywhere, from below Vasen's feet, from the walls of the Citadel of Shadow, from the air itself. The three men stared, awestruck, and thousands upon thousands of living shadows, human-shaped but dark and cold, emerged from the earth, from the walls of the Citadel, from the shadowed air. Their red eyes glowed in the darkness, a constellation of coals and hate, as they swarmed forth behind Riven.

"Those are the guardians of the pass," Vasen breathed, his flesh growing goose pimples. "The Oracle knew all along. He must have sent them."

A keening and more moans sounded from the left and right, from above. Out of the mountains from which the Citadel was carved swooped a black tide of more undead—towering nightwalkers, clouds of shadows, keening banshees, wraiths, specters, and ghosts. It was as though the entire Shadowfell had vomited forth its denizens, tens of thousands of them to face the legions of Mephistopheles. The air was black with undead, and leading them all, swathed in shadows, bounding across the plains, was Drasek Riven, the God of Shadows.

"Gods," Gerak said, wide-eyed, his bow slack in his hands.

Orsin had his holy symbol in hand and he prayed softly over it, watching his god in the flesh.

Vasen looked away from the battle, took his tarnished silver holy symbol in hand, the rose given him by the Oracle, and intoned his own prayer.

"Light, wisdom, and strength, Dawnfather," he said. "Light, wisdom, and much strength."

Riven sprinted out to face thousands of devils, the dead of Elgrin Fau flew behind him like a black fog, rose out of the earth in the thousands. Riven picked up the mind link left in his consciousness by Magadon.

Meet me in Ordulin, Mags, he projected. *The plaza in the center of the maelstrom. I don't know how this is going to end. Cale will be there. Just be ready.*

Riven's mental voice reverberated through Magadon's consciousness like a gong. His adrenaline spiked. He stood.

"Cale," Magadon said, and grinned.

I need you now, Magadon projected to the Source. *Will you help me?*

From the cold embers where the last flickers of the Source's consciousness still glowed, he received an affirmative answer.

I'm coming to you, Magadon said.

He pictured the huge chamber in the center of the inverted mountain in which the Source floated. He'd been there before, when he'd lost himself. Now he'd go there again, now that he'd found himself. He pictured it in his mind, as clearly as if he were looking right at it. He drew on his mental energy, orange light haloed his head, and he moved himself there.

The Source, a huge, perfectly symmetrical red crystal, hung unsupported in the air, perpendicular to the smooth stone floor. Its facets hummed with power, power that kept an entire city afloat.

The hemispherical chamber in which the Source had lived and dreamed and felt and hoped for thousands of years had no doors. The Source's home was a cyst in the core of the mountain on which Sakkors floated, an abscess, with no means of nonmagical ingress or egress. The Source glowed red, bathing the large chamber in light the color of blood. The fading but still regular waves of its mental emanations struck Magadon with the regularity of a heartbeat.

The semicircular ceiling of Source's chamber was crafted into polished rectangular plates that reflected the image of the Source over and over again, reflected Magadon's image over and over again, a reminder of the thousand lives they'd lived together in the Source's dreams.

Magadon did not draw on the Source's power, not yet, but the air was so rich with it that some diffused into him without his intent. His mind expanded. His thoughts sharpened. His power doubled, tripled. He smiled at the rush, but held onto himself, held onto his purpose.

Please take Sakkors toward Ordulin. As fast as you can.

The Source did not respond. Its consciousness was floating deep in its dying dreams.

Magadon drew on some of the power suffusing the air around him, used it to burrow his thoughts deep into the Source's mindscape.

Can you hear me, my lovely? There's nothing to fear. Can you take Sakkors toward Ordulin? As fast as you can? Can you do that?

He smiled with relief when the Source answered him.

The entire city lurched as it suddenly slowed, stopped, changed direction, and flew toward the Ordulin maelstrom at speed.

He hoped Sakkors's citizens would realize that something had gone wrong and start leaving the city. If he had to, he could use the Source's power to augment his own and send everyone on Sakkors a powerful mental compulsion to leave. Whether they would be able to get off a floating city zooming through the sky was, of course, another matter.

Brennus cursed in frustration. Even with the rose holy symbol in his hand, his scrying spells could not pick up Vasen Cale.

He was about to start another divination when Sakkors lurched to a stop, causing him to stagger. His scrying cube shifted position, its weight causing it to score the stone floor as it slid, the sound of its movement like a scream. Through his windows, he heard stone crack outside, the rumble of a collapsing building, the shouts of citizens. His homunculi, sent skittering across the polished stone floor, loosed a string of expletives.

"What just happened?" he asked, but there was no one in the room to answer him.

Without warning, the city started moving again, to the southeast, and fast, faster than it had ever moved before.

More cracking and rumbling from outside, more shouts. The city's structures were not built to withstand such movement.

Brennus ran to a window, trailed by his homunculi. He saw nothing to indicate an attack, nothing to . . .

And then he realized what must have happened. Something was wrong with the mythallar that powered the city. He knew it was sentient, unlike the mythallar that powered Thultanthar. Had it gone mad? Was it being controlled?

And then he realized something else.

Sakkors was moving directly toward Ordulin, toward Rivalen.

He cursed, hurriedly composed a sending to his father.

Something is wrong with Sakkors's mythallar. The city is speeding toward Ordulin. Rivalen may have control. Come if you can.

"Stay here," Brennus said to his homunculi. He renewed the various magical wards that protected him, drew the shadows about him, pictured in his mind's eye the chamber in which the Source floated, and moved himself there.

The moment he arrived in the chamber, a knife stab of pain in his skull sent him to his knees. He groaned and the shadows around him whirled.

"Rivalen!" he said through gritted teeth. Somehow his brother must have . . .

He felt a consciousness sifting through his brains, sorting through his thoughts. Not Rivalen, then.

"Prince Brennus," said a voice. "I wonder if you remember me."

The voice sounded familiar to Brennus, but he could not quite place it.

"You and your brother took me prisoner and tortured me. Long ago. Forced me to awaken the Source."

"The Source?" At first Brennus did not understand the reference. "You mean the mythallar?" Realization dawned. "You're the mindmage. Magadon Kest."

A spike of pain in his temples made him wince. His head felt as if a hot poker had been driven through his skull. He could not organize his thoughts enough to raise a defense. His wards were useless against mind magic.

"The mindmage," Magadon said. "Yes."

Shadows roiled angrily around Brennus. He tried to section off a part of his mind to give him a moment to raise a mental screen or shadow step from the room, then . . .

"I can't allow that," Magadon said.

"Get . . . out . . . .of . . . my . . . head," Brennus said.

"I can't do that, either," Magadon said.

"Why are you . . . here?" Brennus said. Blood dripped from his nose, spattered the floor. He lifted his head. "What are you doing?"

The mindmage sat cross-legged in the center of the chamber, directly under the mythallar. Long horns jutted from his head. He regarded Brennus with his unusual eyes, the dots of his black pupils floating on otherwise colorless orbs. His face looked entirely at peace. Above him, the huge, glowing crystal pulsed with power, tremulous lines of energy moving along its length at regular intervals.

"I'm here to stop you and your brother."

The words sounded sincere but made little sense. Brennus endured the pain in his head and slowly climbed to his feet. "My . . . brother? Rivalen?"

"Of course, Rivalen," Magadon answered, and another stab of pain drove Brennus back to his knees. He felt warmth in his ears. Blood.

"Stop . . . us . . . from . . . what? I want . . . Rivalen . . . dead!" Brennus said.

"Liar."

"Look for yourself! See if I'm lying! Look!"

Magadon's brow creased in a question.

Brennus felt mental hands moving through his mind, examining, probing. He did not resist. He let Magadon see everything, feel the depths of Brennus's hate.

"He murdered your mother," Magadon said softly.

"I saw him do it," Brennus said.

"I know," said Magadon, his voice surprisingly sympathetic. The polished reflective planes in the chamber showed the meadow where Rivalen had murdered Alashar. She lay among the flowers, a hand outstretched.

"Hold my hand," she gasped.

Brennus averted his gaze. "Please, I don't want to see it!"

The images vanished.

"He showed that to you, your brother. And you showed it to me."

The pain in Brennus's head subsided. He could only nod.

"I'm sorry," Magadon said. "You have to leave now, Prince Brennus . . ."

Hope lodged in Brennus's chest. "No, let me help—"

The shadows deepened to Brennus's right and the Most High stepped through them, his platinum eyes ablaze, darkness swirling around him. Magical wards sheathed him, so powerful they distorted the air around him. He took in the scene at a glance, leveled his staff at Magadon, and loosed a bolt of black energy that would have withered an archangel.

The energy slammed into Magadon's chest and drove him across the chamber. He hit the far wall with enough force to audibly drive the breath from his lungs. But it didn't kill him. His eyes focused on the Most High and a violet light glowed around his head.

The Most High groaned, staggered, put a finger to his temple. The shadows around him spun rapidly. Lines of blood trickled from his nose. He leveled his staff once more at the mindmage.

"Stop!" Brennus said, stepping between them and holding up his arms. He stood directly under the Source. The polished panels showed their reflections over and over again, the three of them repeated to infinity.

Magadon stood, wobbly. The Most High held his ground, keeping his staff at the ready.

"What is this, Brennus?" the Most High asked.

"Show him," Brennus said to Magadon. "Show him what you saw in my head. Show him."

And the mindmage did. The walls of the mythallar's chamber showed Brennus's memory of the image Rivalen had shown him: Rivalen's murder of his mother amid a field of flowers, her extended hand, his refusal to take it even as she died, her final wish, that she be the instrument of his downfall.

Telamont watched it unfold in silence, the shadows roiling around him the only indicator of his inner turmoil. When it was done, Telamont looked to Brennus, and the light in his platinum eyes had dimmed.

"That is what you accepted all theseyears," said Brennus. "That is what you were willing to compromise over. Your wife, Most High. My mother. Rivalen did that. Rivalen. He must pay for it, whatever the cost to us, to the empire."

"How?" Telamont said.

He sounded so strange to Brennus, his voice less commanding, more like the father Brennus remembered before Alashar had died.

"The how is already in progress," Magadon said.

Brennus had almost forgotten he was in the room. "Rivalen is mad, Most High. You know this. He wants only to die and take the world with him. He must be stopped and he must pay."

"I can't kill my own son," Telamont said. "I won't."

"Father—"

"Just leave," Magadon said. "Take your people from Sakkors and go. You don't have to kill anyone. We'll stop him."

Telamont stood to his full height and his voice recaptured its typical imperiousness.

"You ask me to abandon a city of the empire."

"Sakkors is already dead," Magadon said. "The Source—the mythallar—is dying. When it does, its power will go out. The city will fall from the sky. It has hours."

For a moment, Telamont said nothing, then, "You lie."

"No," Magadon said, simply, and sadness filled his voice. "I wish I did. But it's dying. Check if you wish."

Telamont's eyes narrowed. His fingers traced arcane symbols in the air as he cast a divination. When he sensed the spell's result, he gasped.

"You see?" Brennus said.

"You can't save it," Magadon said. "There's nothing to be done. Sakkors will fall."

Still Telamont said nothing, and Brennus imagined the thoughts roiling in his father's mind.

"Father?" Brennus said.

Staring at Magadon, the Most High said, "We'll get everyone off of Sakkors. But I won't help you kill my son."

"Even after what you saw?" Brennus asked, incredulous.

The Most High hung his head. "Even after that."

Shadows swirled around Brennus, mirroring his anger.

Magadon said, "Go. You have little time."

After they'd gone, Magadon returned to his place under the Source and kept deathwatch. He reached out first to Riven, through the mind link between them.

If you can perceive this, I'm on my way, and I'm bringing Sakkors with me.

With the power of the Source at his command, he'd be near a godling himself.

Assuming, of course, that the Source stayed alive long enough for him to make use of it.

He reached out with his mind from time to time to check on the progress of Brennus and Telamont. Augmented by the power of the Source, he was able to feel it as Sakkors emptied. Shadovar soldiers fled on veserabs. Those who had them fled on magical transport or via spell. Those who had no other way were transported to earth by Brennus and Telamont, by way of spell, by way of the shadows. They moved rapidly, efficiently, and within an hour the entire populace of Sakkors was gone. All but one.

Brennus Tanthul remained, a solitary figure standing at the edge of the plateau on which the abandoned city stood, the figurehead affixed to the prow of the ship-city. Magadon imagined Brennus looking east toward Ordulin, toward the maelstrom of shadows that darkened the sky, all the while sharpening his anger on the whetstone of his hate.

Magadon reached out for Brennus's mind. *You'll remain, then?*

I can't leave, Brennus said. *I must see him pay.*

Magadon had felt the depths of Brennus's hate for his brother. He did not feel like he could deny the Shadovar what he asked.

Don't interfere with anything, Magadon said.

To that, Brennus said nothing.

The wraiths and specters of lost Elgrin Fau blanketed the battlefield in a cloud of darkness. The undead native to the Shadowfell joined them, flowing forward like a dark tide around the towers and walls of the Citadel of Shadow.

Cania's armies stood arranged in precise formations, units of scaled and hulking horned devils, lithe, crouching bearded devils clutching glaives, buzzing wasp devils, a horde of spined devils, their bodies covered in a thick coat of long quills, and all the larger, more powerful armed and armored devils who commanded them. Pennons and oriflammes announced the units and their pedigree, and tens of thousands of weapons

THE GODBORN

and horns and scales and fangs made a forest of sharp edges
and points against which the cloud of incorporeal undead and
Riven threw themselves.

As the forces collided, the moans of the undead vied with
the roar of the devils, the beat of their drums, and the blare of
hundreds of horns. Columns of hellfire flew in all directions,
beams of baleful energy, clouds of poison. Missiles of bone
and steel and magic from fiendish archers rose in shimmering
clouds and fell in a dark rain on the undead army.

With each step Riven moved through the shadows, covering a spear cast of distance with each stride, appearing and
disappearing with the rapidity and rhythm of a heartbeat. He
appeared amid a squad of horned devils, a whirlwind of steel
and darkness, beheaded six of them, and stepped through the
dark. He materialized behind a towering, insectoid gelugon, and
drove his sabers into the crease in its white carapace between
its neck and the base of its skull. Dark ichor flowed as the devil
spasmed, fell, and died. He stepped through the shadows and
into the center of a horned devil regiment. With a thought he
covered all of them in a cloud of swirling, deep darkness in
which not even their fiendish blood allowed them to see. But
he could. And he dashed up and down their ranks slashing,
cutting, stabbing, leaving scores of dead devils in his wake.

He rode a column of shadow into the sky and from there
took a moment to assess the battlefield.

Undead vied with devils for as far as he could see, their lifeless touch pulling the otherwise immortal life from the fiends.
But the devils, powerful, organized, and well-led, held ranks
and responded with barrages of hellfire, beams of magical
energy, and organized charges of their ranks. The undead
fell by the score, dissipating with a moan into dark, stinking
mist. A nightwalker, a faceless undead, humanoid in shape, as
black as a moonless night and taller than a castle tower, strode
among a regiment of horned devils, crushing the devils in pairs
and trios with the weight of its tread. Wasp devils swarmed it

349

from above while a unit of flaming, armored devils on burning horses charged it from below. It fell, moaning, and the fiends cut it to pieces before it dissipated to nothingness. But still the undead came on, fearless, heedless, their numbers beyond count, and fiends fell to the dark earth, their bodies withering as the undead pulled out their life force. Thousands of fiendish corpses dotted the field.

A flight of shock troop devils—huge, blocky winged devils covered in red scales and dull iron armor, wheeled toward him. Each bore a huge sword and shield in its muscular arms. Riven hung there on his column of shadows and let them close in.

When they drew near he extended a hand and a wide net of sticky shadows shot from his fingers. The devils, too big to maneuver deftly, could not avoid the dark strands. It caught up all of them, wrapping their bodies and wings in sticky fibers of reified shadow.

Wings fouled, the devils roared and fell out of the sky. As they plummeted, Riven stepped through the darkness and onto one of the devil's backs. He drove his sabers into the base of the devil's skull, silencing its roars, then stepped to another, did the same, stepped to another, killed again. He killed six and stepped away before they hit the ground, their huge forms crushing lesser devils and throwing up clods of soil and grass.

Around him the battle raged. Devils and the dark hordes of the Shadowfell moaned, shouted, and died. Shadows spun around Riven. A green beam of energy and a column of hellfire shot out at him from his left, struck the shadows that shrouded him, and died in their darkness. He pointed a hand, loosed a line of life-draining energy from his palm, and withered an entire line of flaming devils and their mounts. They squirmed and shrieked and slowly imploded as his power stripped them of animus.

He'd killed dozens of devils and done nothing to cloak his power, but still Mephistopheles had not shown.

"Let's try this, then," Riven said.

Spinning and whirling his way through a score of gelugons, his sabers leaving a flotsam of insectoid limbs and heads behind him, he scanned the field for his target. He spotted him in moments, a pit fiend named Belagon, one of Mephistopheles's most powerful generals. Flames and smoke sheathed the heavily armored pit fiend the same way shadows shrouded Riven. The devil stood several times the height of a man, and his blazing sword and flaming whip slew undead by twos and threes with each blow.

Riven stepped through the shadows to stand before him.

"Godling," said the fiend. He beat his huge wings and they shed enough smoke and flame to engulf a village. Riven stood in their midst, unharmed.

"Dead thing," Riven answered, and launched himself at the fiend.

His sabers moved so fast they hummed, as he ducked, stabbed, slashed, and spun. Despite its size, the fiend answered in kind, its huge blade spitting flames as it parried, stabbed, and slashed. The two of them fought in a cloud of shadows and smoke and flame and power, and any devils or undead caught up in the cloud died screaming.

Belagon's whip cracked as the fiend tried to wrap Riven's legs in its flaming lines, but Riven leaped the attempt and slashed down with both sabers, severing the whip. He sidestepped a stab from Belagon's sword, pointed both sabers at the fiend's chest, and loosed a spiraling column of divine power. It slammed into the fiend, driving him backward several strides, tore through his breastplate, and tore a gory divot in the exposed flesh of his chest.

The fiend shouted with rage, the flames that surrounded him igniting into a conflagration. He charged Riven, blazing sword held high. Riven sidestepped the downward slash—the blade put a furrow in the earth—slid to the fiend's side and drove both blades through his armor and into his abdomen.

The devil squealed and collapsed, writhing in pain, ichor spurting from his gut. Riven rode the shadows to his side and drove both his blades into his throat. The pit fiend gurgled and his flames died, as did the fiend. Riven crouched atop the dead pit fiend's chest, an ichor-stained saber gripped in each fist, a cloud of shadows and smoke roiling around him.

"Come out, come out, whither you hide," he said to Mephistopheles.

Vasen, Gerak, and Orsin watched the battle in awed silence. Magical energy and fire lit the otherwise dark air of the Shadowfell, criss-crossed the field in blazing lines and pillars and columns and streaks of killing force. The undead blanketed the diabolical forces, so many and so thick that it looked as if a black fog had settled on the fiendish legions. The sound of shouts and screams and drums and moans was surreal. Vasen tried to keep his eyes on Riven, but Riven moved from shadow to shadow so quickly, covering as much as a bowshot in a single stride, that it was impossible to keep up. But wherever he appeared, the one-eyed man-god left dead devils in his wake.

They watched Riven fight a pit fiend in a fog of shadows and smoke and fire, watched him fell the devil with as much effort as it would have taken a skilled warrior to disarm a child.

Orsin held his holy symbol in hand and muttered prayers under his breath.

Gerak and Vasen stood with their mouths hanging open, waiting for words to fly in and give them something to say.

A boom sounded, so loud it shook the doors of the Citadel of Shadow, and for a moment stilled the battle. A line of fire formed in the sky above the battlefield, a slit in the fabric of the planes. Smoke and heat and power poured from it, the screams of the damned. The line extended laterally, then vertically, until it looked as if a flaming door hung suspended in the air over the slaughter.

A shadow filled the door, a towering dark figure of muscle and wings and horns and power.

"Mephistopheles," Vasen breathed.

Across the battlefield, Vasen saw Riven's face turned not toward the archdevil but toward the Citadel, toward them. Riven gestured and the darkness around the three companions intensified, fat ropes of shadow swirling around them. Vasen, sweating shadows of his own, closed his eyes, offered a hasty prayer to Amaunator, then snapped them open.

"Ready yourselves," he said. "We go."

The shadows engulfed them entirely. Not even Vasen's shade-born vision could pierce them. He felt a tingle in his stomach and a lurch as of rapid motion.

CHAPTER FOURTEEN

R IVEN WATCHED MEPHISTOPHELES HURTLE OUT OF THE portal, a dark bird of prey, the archdevil's body surrounded by dark energy that crackled with each beat of his wings. The bare-chested, muscular archfiend eschewed any visible weapon or armor.

The devils on the ground roared excitedly at his appearance. A dozen shock troop devils, larger than those Riven had felled earlier, swooped toward their master. Mephistopheles hung in the air and surveyed the battle. His eyes fell on Riven.

"Let's dance," Riven said, bouncing on the balls of his feet.

The archfiend and the shock troop devils beat their wings and flew toward Riven like shot arrows. Riven surrounded himself in a protective cloud of shadows, rode the darkness into the air, and materialized to the side of the archfiend, slashing and stabbing the moment he appeared.

Mephistopheles anticipated his sudden appearance and pulled up, parrying Riven's blades with his bare hands and arms, which might as well have been adamantine. Riven's blades bounced off the archfiend's skin, barely scoring the flesh. The devil's fists and claws glittered with green energy as he punched, clawed, and grabbed at Riven. Green beams of power shot from the archdevil's eyes, vied with Riven's protective shadows.

Riven channeled more power into his blades, moved from shadow to shadow around the archfiend, appearing to Mephistopheles's right, slashing, disappearing and reappearing to his left, stabbing, throughout dodging the blows of the archfiend and the shock troop devils who flew around the combat and tried to get in slashes when they could.

Riven opened a dozen tiny gashes in the archfiend. Finally Mephistopheles reached through his protective sheath of shadows and grabbed Riven by an arm. Riven did not relent in his attack, hacking with his saber, gouging the archfiend's iron skin. Beams of viridian energy shot from Mephistopheles's eyes but shattered into a rain of harmless motes when they struck the shadowy shroud that protected Riven.

Roaring in frustrated rage, Mephistopheles beat his wings, spun a tight circle in the air, and flung Riven earthward. But the moment the archfiend released Riven, he flipped in mid-air, extended a hand, and a long rope of shadow formed from the air of the Shadowfell, one end in Riven's hand, the other looped around Mephistopheles's throat. Riven's precipitous fall pulled it taut, choked Mephistopheles, and swung Riven around and back up toward the archfiend. As the archdevil grabbed at the makeshift garrote wrapped around his throat, Riven slammed into him from behind, at the same time loosing two downward slashes that opened Mephistopheles's flesh. Black ichor oozed from the gashes, and the archdevil raged.

He beat his wings, whirled, and slammed a fist aglow with magical energy into Riven's face. The force of the blow, combined with whatever magic augmented it, penetrated Riven's protective shroud, shattered his nose, and sent him careening earthward, tumbling head over feet. A shock troop devil zoomed at him, hacked at him with its sword, and struck him in the side. The shadows protected him, but the impact made him spin faster.

No matter. Every shadow in the Shadowfell belonged to him; every shadow was part of him.

He rode the darkness out of his fall and into the shadows above Mephistopheles. He reversed his grip on his sabers, pointing them down, and as he fell drove them into Mephistopheles's back, just above the wings. The blades sank in half their length and ichor spurted from the holes.

The archdevil roared, arched, his wings beating furiously, their impact knocking Riven away and once more sending him earthward. Three shock troop devils tucked their wings and fell with him, swinging their blades as they plummeted. Riven, his back to the ground, parried with his sabers as he fell. He felt the ground rushing up and knew that a hundred more powerful fiends were waiting to pounce on him the moment he hit.

He channeled divine power into the cloud of shadows around him, turned it acidic to non-divine beings. Caustic shadows left him unharmed but melted flesh from the shrieking shock troop devils. They beat their wings frantically, but the cloud had already reduced their wings to shreds. In mere heartbeats, they'd been reduced to bones, and a shower of gore fell on the waiting devils below.

Riven rode the darkness back to the Citadel of Shadow, just inside the open double doors. The shadowstuff in his flesh reknit his nose, healed the other minor wounds he'd received during the battle.

Mephistopheles wheeled over the battlefield, his own wounds already healed, black energy firing from his fists, annihilating undead by the score. He was searching for Riven.

"Show yourself, man-god!" the archfiend shouted. "I'll rip your godhood from a hole in your throat!"

Riven thought himself a match for Mephistopheles, at least in the Shadowfell, but the archdevil's legions were slaughtering Riven's undead forces. None of the lesser devils presented a threat to Riven individually, but thousands of them, in combination with Mephistopheles, posed a threat. And Mephistopheles was immortal, and had lived for ages. He knew how to draw on his sliver of divine power in ways Riven did not.

Of course, Riven didn't need to defeat Mephistopheles. He just needed to hold him and his army off long enough for Vasen to rescue his father.

"Hurry up, Cale the Younger," Riven said, and darted back out into battle.

Cania hit them before the shadows lifted. A wind so cold it felt like knives sent Vasen's teeth to chattering. Screams filled the air, the stink of burning flesh, the smell of brimstone. Distant cracks boomed, the sound so loud it seemed as though the bones of titans might be breaking. Bestial grunts and growls carried on the biting gusts.

When the shadows that transported them dissipated, they all three stared in horror at the terrain. They stood on an icy promontory, exposed to the wind. A sky the color of blood glowed above them, the sun that lit it little more than a distant torch. Ice extended in all directions, huge jagged shards jutting from the cracked, windswept landscape.

Thick rivers of magma cut through the ice, glowing veins of flame in which tortured souls writhed. Devils stalked the river banks, stabbing at the damned with their polearms, pulling impaled souls from the magma. Huge, malformed devils blotted the sky in distant flocks. Vasen could not make out their forms at such a distance, but their squirming, awkward flight made him vaguely nauseated.

Vasen had seen it before in dreams, but still it sickened him.

"Don't look," he said, but Gerak and Orsin seemed transfixed, overwhelmed by what they saw. Vasen grabbed each of them by the arm and shook them harshly. "Look at me. Look at me."

They did, and he saw from the look in their eyes that what they'd seen had marked their souls. They'd never unsee it. If they lived, it would haunt their dreams for the rest of their lives.

It would fall to him to keep his companions grounded. His dreams and his faith had armored him against Cania's horror. The fire in his spirit could not be quenched, not even by the Eighth Hell. He held his shield forth and uttered a prayer to the Dawnfather.

"Strength to our spirit, Dawnfather. And resolve to our purpose."

He channeled his faith through his shield, and it glowed with a rosy light that touched each of them, warmed them, comforted them. Immediately Vasen felt his spirit lighten, felt the darkness and cold retreat. Gerak and Orsin, too, seemed less haunted.

"Stay strong," he said to them, as he drew Weaveshear. Both nodded. "It's an awful place, but it's just a place."

"Just a place," Gerak said, clutching his bow, his voice higher than usual.

A line of shadows poured out of Weaveshear and flowed down the side of the promontory, toward the plains below. Vasen followed its path with his eyes and saw where it was headed.

A mound of snow and ice rose out of the frigid plain. Dark lines swirled around the mound, ropes of shadow that were unmoved by Cania's wind.

"There," he said, and pointed with Weaveshear.

He tried to feel the correspondence between the shadows where they stood and the shadows near the mound, but he couldn't quite feel it. Perhaps he needed to practice the skill more, or perhaps the wards around the mound prevented the connection. Either way, they'd have to move on foot.

"Let's go," he said.

A bellow sounded from above and behind them, so loud it nearly knocked them from their feet. Ice cracked in answer to the sound. A huge shadow darkened the earth.

Vasen turned, looked up, and gasped.

A huge form blotted out the sky behind them, a flat, undulating carpet of doughy, black-veined gray flesh a bowshot across. Tiny eyes stared dumbly out of a ridge of flesh in its front. A mouth like a cave hung slackly open, showing a diseased, malformed tongue and rotting, pointed teeth each as tall as a grown man. Vasen had no idea what kept the creature afloat, but each tremulous beat of the fleshy folds that served as its wings sent a wind groundward that smelled of corpses.

The three men gagged, pulled cloaks over their mouths.

Forms moved atop the creature, red-scaled devils, a score or more. If they saw the three companions . . .

"Down!" Vasen said. "Down!"

But it was too late. The huge beast bellowed again, the sound dislodging a shower of ice and snow from the earth, and angled downward. Dozens of the muscular, red-skinned devils leaped off the creature's back, falling through the sky like a red rain. Each of them bore a vicious looking glaive. A squirming nest of short tentacles grew from their faces and jaws like a grotesque beard. They whooped as they hit the ice and pelted toward the companions.

"They saw us!" Vasen said. "Run! Now!"

While his two companions leaped over the edge of the promontory and slid down the side, Vasen aimed his shield at the oncoming wave of devils and intoned a prayer to the Dawnfather. His shield flared white and a wave of holy energy shot forth from it in a wide line. It struck the leading devils and knocked them off their feet. Of those coming behind, some leaped over their fallen brethren, while others tripped on them and fell in a tangle of limbs and claws.

Vasen turned and jumped down the edge after his comrades. He'd misjudged its steepness and hung for a terrifying second in open air before he slammed back down on the edge and skidded down the slope on his backside. He tried to slow himself with his shield and blade but could not get purchase in the ice. Hitting the plain below sent a painful shock through his legs. Orsin pulled him to his feet. Gerak had two arrows nocked and sighted back up the ledge.

"Move!" Vasen said. "Move, Gerak!"

From above came the whoops and hollers of the pursuing devils. One of them leaped high over the lip of the promontory, glaive glittering in the red light of the plane. Gerak loosed both arrows at once and the devil's whoop turned to a pained squeal.

Vasen grabbed Gerak and Orsin and ran for the cairn of his father as the body of the devil Gerak had shot crashed to the ice beside them.

Hollers, growls, and snarls sounded from behind them. Vasen spared a look back to see a score of devils pouring over the ledge, scrabbling down its side, reaching the plain and pelting after the companions.

"Don't look back!" he said. "Just run! Run!"

They careened over the ice, slipping as they ran, their breath pouring out of them in frozen clouds. Gerak fell once, as did Vasen, and both times Orsin, surefooted even on the ice, helped them rise and keep running.

The growls grew louder behind them, the sound of their fiendish claws digging into the ice. They closed on the mound, the shadows from Weaveshear mixing with those emanating from the mound.

A shadow fell over the plain—the huge, flying devil looming over them. It bellowed as it flew over and past them, the sound like a thousand war drums. The three companions gagged on the stink of the creature. It swooped low and they all three dived onto their bellies to avoid getting hit, sliding along the ice.

The enormous creature could've flattened them by simply landing atop them, but it did not touch down for some reason. Perhaps its physiology prevented it from touching the ground. Vasen hoped so.

They rode their momentum back to their feet and sprinted onward.

The devils were closer. Vasen could almost feel their breath on his back.

"Keep going!" he said. "Keep going!"

As they closed on the cairn, Vasen could see a dome-shaped distortion in the air around it.

The wards.

Weaveshear would have to cut through them or the three of them would die on Cania's plains, torn apart by devils.

He did not slow as he approached the wall of the wards. Instead he raised Weaveshear high, shouted at the sky, and slashed at the translucent wall with the blade of his father.

The wards of an archdevil audibly and visibly split. Glowing veins of power flared all over the dome. Weaveshear opened a gash in the dome about the size of a door, leaving the rest of the ward structure intact. The three piled through.

Immediately Orsin turned and dragged his staff across the ice, scribing a line across the opening.

"Gerak and I will hold them here!" he said to Vasen. "Go get your father!"

Vasen nodded, sprinted for the mound, the shadows from his sword and flesh mingling with those of the mound.

Behind him, Gerak's bow sang. Devils roared and cursed. He looked back to see Orsin standing in the open gash in the wards, his staff humming and leaking shadows as it spun. The devils could try the opening only one at a time, and Orsin's staff, elbows, fists, and knees cracked against devilish hide and armor. Behind him, Gerak fired an arrow every time Orsin afforded him an opening.

Vasen turned to the mound. Shadows swirled around him, a tangible thing, kith to him. The mound was cracked in many places. He slammed his shield into the ice but it did not even mar its surface.

He cursed, glanced back at his comrades to see a claw tear into Orsin and drive him back a step, bleeding. Before the devil could follow up, Gerak loosed an arrow that struck the devil in the throat and sent it staggering back into its fellow fiends. Orsin lunged forward and slammed the butt of his staff into the devil's face, shattering fangs and sending the fiend careening backward.

"Hurry, Vasen!" Gerak called, without looking back. "There's too many!"

The huge flying creature hovered over them, and another of the big creatures, perhaps having heard the bellow of the first, was coming toward them from their left, its bulk filling the sky. Two score more of the bearded devils rode its back.

Shadows poured from Vasen's flesh. He stared down at the cairn, under which his father lay. He'd free him with his father's weapon.

He raised Weaveshear, the blade shedding shadows the way a pitch torch shed smoke. He hoped its power could cut through the ice that entombed his father as well as it had cut through the wards of an archdevil. He whispered a prayer to Amaunator and stabbed downward, driving the blade into the ice all the way to the hilt.

A crack spread from where he'd struck. Beneath him the mound rumbled. The crack expanded into another, and then another, each crack spawning yet another until an entire network of lines crisscrossed the cairn. Shadows poured from them, like black steam escaping a heated kettle. The mound continued to vibrate, the shaking becoming more violent. Shadows churned around the mound, spinning and whirling. A hum filled the air as power gathered.

"Watch out!" Vasen shouted.

He grabbed Weaveshear and slid off the side just as the mound exploded in a cloud of shadows and ice and snow. The force of it knocked him backward, and for a moment, the shadows and snow and ice swirled so thickly that he couldn't see.

He glanced back to see that the explosion had knocked Orsin and Gerak and all of the devils to the ice. Already they were climbing back to their feet, their expressions dazed.

"Hold them off!" he shouted, his voice dull and distant to his still ringing ears.

The mound was gone. A crater marred the plain where it had stood. Shadows poured out of it. Vasen staggered up to the side of the crater and at the bottom of it, saw his father.

Erevis Cale lay stretched out in the ice, eyes closed, hands crossed over his chest, as if he were a corpse someone had arranged for burial. He was bald, clean-shaven, taller than Vasen, with a prominent nose and strong jaw. He wore fitted leathers and a dark cloak. Shadows spun around his dusky flesh. He looked much as Vasen might have guessed.

"Erevis! Father!"

His father didn't move.

Vasen cursed, slid over the edge of the crater, heaved his father's body over his shoulder, and clambered out.

"I have him!" he called to Gerak and Orsin.

Orsin unleashed a furious onslaught of blows with his staff, driving back a pair of devils who tried to get through the hole in the wards. He bounded back, dragged his shadow-tipped staff across the ground, and snapped it over his knee. Instantly a curtain of darkness rose up from the line Orsin had scribed, crackling with energy, filling the gap.

Orsin ran toward Vasen. Gerak backed toward him, firing arrow after arrow as he moved.

Vasen laid Erevis on the ground, the shadows around father and son intermingling in a blended darkness.

Vasen slapped him on the cheeks. "Erevis! Father!"

No response.

Gerak and Orsin reached him. Gerak continued to fire. Orsin was dripping blood from deep scratches in his face and arms.

"Hurry, Vasen," the deva said, his eyes on the curtain of force he'd raised.

Vasen nodded, put a hand on his father's brow, whispered a prayer, and channeled healing energy into Erevis. Vasen's hand glowed with a warm, rosy light, the energy of the god of the sun healing the First of Mask's Chosen in Faerûn.

They all exhaled with relief when Cale's eyes opened, glowing yellow in the shadowed gloom. His gaze narrowed and he grabbed Vasen by the wrist, his strength shocking.

"I dreamed of you," Cale said. "You're my . . . son."

Shadows swirled around father and son. Vasen swallowed.

"I am, and I dreamed of you," Vasen managed, for a moment nearly overcome. For years he'd heard his father's voice only in dreams.

Behind them, the devils cursed and growled, poked at the curtain of power Orsin had raised.

"That wall won't last," Orsin said.

"We have to go," Cale said, sitting up.

"Riven said we need to go to Ordulin," Orsin said.

Cale's gaze grew distant for a moment, perhaps as he consulted the content of the dreams he'd had while entombed. When his focus returned, he nodded. "*The Leaves of One Night* are in Ordulin. That's where the Shadowstorm started, so that's where Shar's little book is. Good. We go, then."

"And when we get there?" Orsin asked.

Cale took in the holy symbol Orsin bore, his absence of weapons. "You're a shadowalker? One of Nayan's?"

"Nayan . . . has been dead a long time. But I am one of his, yes. I can't walk the shadows as they did, but they answer me in other ways. My name is Orsin."

"Gerak," said Gerak to Cale. The woodsman drew and fired, and a devil squealed.

"When we get there," Cale said. "We read the *Leaves*. They're said to contain Shar's moment of greatest triumph but also her moment of greatest weakness. Her moment of weakness has to be the return of Mask, her herald. Has to be. If that happens, the Cycle of Night gets frozen forever."

Vasen shook his head. "But Riven said I have to unlock the divinity in him, Rivalen, and Mephistopheles. I don't know how to do that."

"Yes, you do," Cale said. "Mask had this planned long ago, and you dreamed it, the same as me."

Cale and Vasen stared at one another a long moment, then both spoke at once.

"Write the story."

With that, Vasen took the small gem from his pocket, shattered it. A clot of shadows formed before his face. He spoke into them.

"We have him, Riven. We're with Erevis and he's alive."

The shadows he'd spoke into dissipated, presumably carrying their message to Riven in the Shadowfell.

Cale stood and drew the shadows around them.

"We go," he said.

Vasen's voice sounded from the shadows shrouding Riven.

We have him.

That was all Riven needed to hear. He charged across the battlefield, stepping through the shadows as he went, cutting down lesser devils each time he appeared. Mephistopheles pursued him from above, shouting. Bolts of energy shot from the archfiend's palms, narrowly missing Riven and putting huge smoking divots in the earth. Riven dived, rolled, spun, and sprinted, dodging the archfiend's attacks, playing for time. He ran through everything he knew. He hadn't missed anything but he didn't know enough. He'd schemed for decades to arrange for everyone needed to arrive in Ordulin. But after that . . .

He wasn't sure what would come next. Just as Mask had split his divinity up among a few Chosen, so had he split his plan up among many of his servants. Riven might have been the most powerful of them, but he could see only pieces. He'd gambled everything in the hope of some sudden revelation.

His wandering thoughts distracted him. Mephistopheles materialized before him, haloed in dark power, having teleported into Riven's path. The archfiend stuck Riven with a fist, discharged the power in his hand, and sent Riven tumbling head over heels, momentarily stunned. Dozens of devils swarmed him, glaives and swords and claws and teeth trying to cut through his protective shadows and tear at his flesh.

I'm not leaving, Magadon projected to the Source. *I just need to see.*

The Source's response was muddled, but grateful. It was fading.

Rich with power drawn from his bond with the Source, Magadon reached out for Brennus, who maintained his station at the westernmost point of Sakkors.

I need to see through your eyes for a moment, he projected.

When Brennus did not object, Magadon created a sensory link between them, allowing him to see through the Shadovar's eyes.

Sakkors flew through Sembia's shadowed sky at tremendous speed. Far ahead loomed the black wall of the Ordulin Maelstrom. Lines of lightning lit the thick clouds, endless flashes. The dark clouds roiled and churned, as if agitated, as if something within them were angry and waiting.

Rivalen stood over Sayeed, the man's despair palpable, his skin covered in Shar's holy words, his mouth stuffed with the pages of *The Leaves of One Night*. Riven was coming with the son of Erevis Cale to read those words, but the words did not say what they hoped. He placed a hand on Sayeed's back and the man trembled under his touch.

"The death I promised you will come. First the world, then you, then me."

And then release.

More trembling from Sayeed.

Rivalen took his holy symbol in hand, stared into Shar's eye, felt the wash of her power over him. She'd taught him what he needed to know. His life had been an incremental crawl toward revelation and truth.

"Nothing endures," he said, intoning Shar's Secret Truth. "Nothing."

Long, many-forked lines of green lightning lit the black clouds. Thunder growled. Shar's eye pulsed with power, with anticipation. She wished to incarnate, to feed. She would have her wish soon.

He stepped through the darkness to stand atop a large chunk of the ruined tower once occupied by Kesson Rel. There, he waited. His enemies were coming. When they arrived, he would destroy them, free his goddess, and then watch the Lady of Loss devour the world.

Cale, Vasen, Orsin, and Gerak materialized at the edge of the plaza in Ordulin. It looked much as it had when Cale had set foot there long ago to face Kesson Rel. Cracked stone and crumbled buildings littered the area like the tombstones of titans. Green lightning lit the shadowed haze in a ghostly light. The wind gusted. A fog of shadows swirled in the air.

In the center of the plaza hung a slowly turning void, a cold emptiness that stretched back through time and space forever. Shar resided in the eye; Cale could feel her in it, the weight of her malice, the pressure of her regard. Her existence did not fill the emptiness; it defined it. He felt nauseous.

"Dark and empty," he said.

Prone before the eye, hunched and shirtless, was a man. Words covered the skin of his back, the sight of them unnerving, somehow. His eyes were open but appeared to see nothing. His mouth, too, hung open, but parchment had been stuffed into it. His cheeks bulged with so much of it they looked distended.

"Gods," Orsin whispered. "That's Sayeed."

"It's grown," Cale said, nodding at the eye. He'd seen the void long ago, when Kesson Rel had first created it.

A presence manifested, weighty, power radiating from it in waves.

"It's soon to grow more," said a deep voice, Rivalen Tanthul's voice, from right behind them.

They whirled as one to see the nightseer standing right behind them, his golden eyes glowing out of the darkness of his hood. They shouted, brandished their weapons, but too late. Rivalen spoke a single word, and the power contained in it knocked them all to their knees, all but Cale.

Weaveshear absorbed and deflected the power in Rivalen's spell, but the force of it turned the blade warm and drove Cale backward. He kept his feet and skidded backward across the plaza, toward Shar's eye. He could feel the Lady of Loss glaring into his back.

Vasen, Gerak, and Orsin lay on the ground, groaning.

Rivalen stared at Cale, his golden eyes narrowed, head cocked in a question.

"Cale?" Rivalen asked.

Cale had faced Rivalen before, when Cale's god had been alive and Rivalen had been only a man. Now Cale, a man without a god, faced a onetime man who was now a god.

He charged, and Rivalen did not even move. Cale crosscut with Weaveshear, but the blade rang against the shadows swirling around Rivalen as if they were made of steel. Rivalen grabbed Cale by the face with one hand, spoke a word of power, and discharged unholy energy from his palm. Ordinarily the shadowstuff in Cale allowed him to resist the effects of magic, but not when the magic came from the hand of a god.

Pain pulled a muffled scream from Cale. His skin blistered and popped. Bones cracked. Casually Rivalen cast him aside. Cale hit the stone of plaza in a heap, rolling over, groaning while the shadowstuff in his body undid the damage Rivalen's spell had caused.

"I wasn't sure I'd see you again, Cale," Rivalen said. "I didn't know if your son would succeed. It's good that he did, though. You've arrived here alive only to die."

Rivalen grabbed Orsin and Gerak by their cloaks and lifted them in one hand, then grabbed Vasen in the other. He carried them all toward Shar's eye, and Cale feared he would throw them into the eye.

Cale rolled over, gritting his teeth at the pain, and rose to all fours. The shadowstuff in him reknit his bones, closed the blisters on his skin. He watched Rivalen toss the three men on the cobblestones, near the prone man.

Cale rose, stepped through the shadows, and materialized behind Rivalen with Weaveshear raised for a decapitating strike. Rivalen turned, a contemptuous expression on his face, and intercepted the strike with his bare hand. It didn't even cut his flesh. He tore the weapon from Cale's grasp and tossed it aside.

Cale growled, lunged forward, drove the top of his head into the bridge of Rivalen's nose.

He might as well have struck a stone wall. Rivalen sneered, grabbed Cale by the throat, and lifted him from his feet.

"You're just a man, Cale. These events are beyond you."

Cale gagged, choked, kicked Rivalen in the chest, but the blows did nothing. Rivalen, too, was beyond him.

"Listen to the words of your son," Rivalen said.

Rivalen kneeled, still holding a struggling Cale at arm's length, and touched Vasen.

Vasen's eyes snapped open, widened when he saw Rivalen and Cale. He reached for a blade, but his scabbard was empty. Rivalen grabbed him by the arm, pulled him upright, and slammed him down by the figure hunched before Shar's eye.

"Read it," Rivalen commanded. "You came here to read it, didn't you?"

Vasen looked back at him, at Cale, his eyes glowing yellow in the shadows.

"You thought I didn't know why you came? You think I didn't know Mask's plan? I knew all along. I knew it all. You gambled everything to come here and read the Leaves. So let's hear it read."

Rivalen shook Cale as he spoke. Cale, unable to breathe, started to see sparks. His vision narrowed to a tunnel, and at the end of it was his son.

"Read it!" Rivalen said. "Read it aloud."

Magic infused the phrases, turning the command into a compulsion.

Vasen turned and in a slow monotone began to read the words written on the back of the hunched figure, the words of *The Leaves of One Night*.

Rivalen shook Cale again. "Listen. Hear what your son says, Cale."

Compelled by Rivalen's spell, Vasen uttered blasphemous words dictated by Shar herself. The sound made Cale wince, hurt his ears. As Vasen intoned the black syllables, Shar's eye began to spin faster. It emitted an unsettling, discordant hum.

Desperately, Cale kicked and punched at Rivalen, blows that would have left a human insensate or dead but that had no effect on Rivalen. Cale could scarcely breathe. He was fading.

He had to get away. Before he lost consciousness, he let himself feel the shadows around him, in the plaza. He grasped at them, pulled them around him, and rode them across the plaza, to the darkness behind a fallen sculpture. He collapsed there, gasping, blinking. Darkness leaked from his skin. The shadowstuff in him began to heal the damage Rivalen had done to his windpipe.

He peeked around the statue to see Rivalen with his arms held out, shouting into the dark sky. "Watch then, Cale! Watch as your son ushers in the end! There's no moment of weakness written in the Leaves! I've read it! Do you hear me? There's only her moment of triumph! Do you hear, Cale! Do you!"

Shar's eye expanded, spun faster, and the hum turned to a roar like rough surf. The ground of the plaza began to vibrate. For all Cale knew, all of Toril might have been vibrating. The power emanating from the eye charged the air. Little balls of lightning exploded all over the place. Acrid smoke mixed with the shadows, all of it an echo of a world Cale had once visited, a world destroyed by Shar.

He'd survived his own death only to watch the world die.

Riven regained his bearings in moments. He let divine power explode outward from him in all directions. The force of it blew the devils a spear cast away from him, like dry leaves in an angry wind. He stood, shadows coiled around him, and faced Mephistopheles.

The archfiend alit on the battlefield twenty paces from Riven, his eyes glowing red with hate, his hands aglow with power, his wings beating a slow promise of Riven's death.

"Couldn't wait any longer, eh?" Riven said, his tone mocking. He sheathed his sabers. "Overreached, did you? Asmodeus has grown unhappy with his lapdog, eh?"

Mephistopheles's brow furrowed in anger. "You know nothing, mortal, and you don't deserve the power you stole. You don't even know how to use it. It's right that I tear it from your flesh while you scream."

Riven sneered, shadows boiling around him in an angry cloud. "That's a high-pitched bark you have, lap dog. Yap, yap."

Mephistopheles roared, beat his wings, and bounded toward Riven. Power crackled around the archfiend, buckling the earth as the archfiend closed in.

Riven waited, waited, braced himself, and at the last moment threw himself at Mephistopheles. Instead of dodging the archfiend's grasp, he clutched Mephistopheles's hands in his own. The two of them spun, each gripping the other, vying for advantage. Dark power surged into Riven, blistered his skin. He grimaced against the pain, the shadows whirling around man and devil darkening, deepening.

"Hey," Riven said through the pain.

Mephistopheles looked into his face, a question in his red eyes.

Riven sneered. "Let's go for a ride."

The shadows turned black as ink and pulled both of them across the plains and to Ordulin.

CHAPTER FIFTEEN

Abruptly the sound emitted from Shar's eye changed pitch to a hungry whine. Vasen continued to recite the words of *The Leaves of One Night*. He spoke the words only slowly—he was resisting Rivalen's compulsion—but the spell forced him to speak the unspeakable, them clearly, loudly.

Rivalen cocked his head, as if listening for something far off.

"Here they come at last," he said, and faded into the shadows.

A churning cloud of deep shadow formed in the plaza, sparking with energy, and out of it tumbled Riven and Mephistopheles. Shadows and baleful energy swirled around devil and man. They gripped each other by the hands, shadows and unholy power sizzling between their palms as they struggled.

Mephistopheles roared, beat his wings, and shoved Riven back, the effort raising veins and sinew in the black skin of his chest and arms. Riven stumbled backward. Mephistopheles extended his arms and shot a column of swirling hellfire from his palms. It burned through the shadows that protected Riven, slammed into his chest, and drove him backward, his cloak and flesh charring. Riven rolled out of the path of flames, grimacing against the pain, and put a hand to his temple.

"Riven!" Cale shouted, and started to draw the shadows around him.

Riven looked at him sharply and Cale felt the weight of his gaze, the power in his regard.

"Stay where you are!" Riven barked.

Mephistopheles saw Cale, too, and turned to face him. "Cale! How did you escape my realm?"

Rivalen emerged from the darkness near Vasen, near Shar's eye, his hands at his sides, leaking power. "And now we're all here and the end is come."

"So you say," Riven said. "But—"

Appendages shot like striking asps from Shar's eye, long ropes of darkness that squirmed forth and grabbed Riven and Mephistopheles, coiling around them, cutting off Riven's words.

"No!" Mephistopheles roared, before one of the appendages shot into his open mouth and down his throat, gagging him.

More and more appendages squirmed forth from the now-shrieking eye, wrapping around the two gods, cocooning them in Shar's darkness. Mephistopheles writhed and fought, dark energy flaring from his exposed flesh. Riven did not struggle, and soon both were entirely covered.

Immediately the thick twist of appendages that led back to Shar's eye began to pulse, like a gulping throat. And with each gulp Shar's eye grew incrementally larger. With each gulp, the power of the empty being that lived behind the eye grew.

"And so dies the herald," said Rivalen.

Cale understood immediately what was happening. Shar was coming. She was consuming their divinity, and when she ate it all, she would emerge and devour the world. And it had started with Vasen reading *The Leaves of One Night*. He had to stop it and he saw only one way. He had to kill the man on whom the Leaves were written. He prepared to step through the shadows, but before he did, he felt a familiar itch behind his eyes. Magadon's mental voice, strained, sounded in his head.

Erevis?

Cale could hardly believe what he was hearing. He put his back against the statue's pedestal, sank down and into the shadows. *Mags? Mags?*

Erevis, it's so good to hear—

Later, Mags. Where are you?

Almost to Ordulin. I'm with the Source on Sakkors.

The Source!

Erevis, I have to mind link Riven to you, to us. I want you to prepare yourself.

For what?

This.

Cale felt the connection open between him and a god. Agonizing pain coursed through Cale. His body felt as though it were on fire. He was feeling what Riven was feeling, tiny bits of himself getting chewed off by Shar's maw.

Cale might have screamed. Or he might have just been experiencing Riven's screams.

Behind the pain, he sensed the sweep of Riven's mind stretching across time and worlds, the understanding so vast and deep that Cale recoiled. And behind that, he felt the hopeful voices of the faithful pleading with Riven for a sign, the burden all gods carried.

The . . . book, Riven projected. *Her weakness . . . in . . . the book.*

There is no weakness in the damned book!

Has . . . to . . . be. Find it . . . or we all . . . die.

The mind link with Riven closed.

"Shit, shit, shit," Cale said.

Rivalen's deep voice rang out. "This is over now, Cale. Are you bitter? Do you see now the fool Shar has made of you and your ridiculous god?"

"Shut up," Cale whispered. To Magadon, he projected, *Mags, I need you to link me with my son.*

Let me see through your eyes.

Cale looked at Vasen and felt Magadon's consciousness settle into his vision. A deeper itch behind the eye, a short, sharp pain in his left temple. The connection between them opened.

Vasen? Cale said.

No response. Cale felt waves of resistance, self-loathing, rage, but still Vasen read the words and still Shar fed.

Listen to me, Vasen. You have to find the moment of weakness in the book. It's there.

Still no response.

Think of everything you've seen, everything you've heard and done. It's there, Vasen. Mask had a plan. He set all this up. He's a better schemer than Shar could ever hope to be. It's there somewhere. You just have to see it.

Still nothing.

It's there, Vasen. You'll find it. I have faith in you.

Rivalen emerged from the shadows before Cale, powerful, dark.

Cale lurched to his feet, stabbed with Weaveshear, but Riven sidestepped the blow, grabbed Cale by the cloak, and slammed him against the pedestal. Ribs snapped and Cale gasped with pain.

"You can't hide from me, Cale. The darkness here belongs to me."

He slammed Cale again into the pedestal, causing ribs to grind against ribs, opening his skull. Cale saw sparks; his vision blurred. The shadowstuff in his veins worked to heal the damage, but he was still barely holding onto consciousness.

Cale? Magadon projected. *Cale, I'm almost there. But the Source is dying . . .*

Cale did not respond to Magadon. Instead, he spoke to his son.

Faith, Vasen. I have faith. Write the story. Write it.

Rivalen slammed him once more into the stone pedestal.

Agony, and all went dark.

Write the story. Faith.

Vasen's mouth formed the words he read on the poor, trapped man who hunched before him. Hateful words. Dire words. Words of death. Words that should never be uttered. Words that promised an end to everything. And yet he could not stop his lips from forming them, his voice from speaking them.

Faith.

There was no moment of weakness written in the book. There were only words that described Shar's imminent victory, her incarnation, her feast on the world and everyone in it.

He looked between the words, sought to discern a code, a hidden text. He saw nothing and despaired. And he knew his despair was a betrayal, that Shar fed on his despair as she fed on everything.

He grabbed onto his father's words, pulled them close.

Think of everything you've seen, everything you've heard and done. It's there, Vasen. Mask had a plan. He set all this up. It's there somewhere. You just have to see it.

His voice, compelled by the nightseer's spell, continued to utter blasphemies of its own accord, but his mind was his own. He pored over his past, things Derreg had said, things the dead of the pass had said, things the Oracle had said.

The Oracle. Faith. Write the story.

For men like us, Vasen, faith is a quill. With it, we write the story of our lives.

The story of our lives.

He thought of Orsin, prone beside him, maybe dead, thought of the spirals and whorls and lines that decorated the deva's skin.

The story of Orsin's life, scribed on his flesh.

A man writes his story in the book of the world.

And in that moment Vasen understood. Shar's moment of weakness wasn't written in *The Leaves of One Night*, because Vasen wasn't supposed to read it. He was supposed to write it, and his faith, a faith of light and hope and courage, was the quill.

The light is in you, Vasen. Brighter than in the rest of us because it fights the darkness in you.

He smiled and stumbled over one of the words written on the flesh of the man before him. Rivalen's spell dragged another word out of him, another, and then no more.

With painful slowness, Vasen dragged a finger across the ground before him, scoring the dirt and dust with a line. A new beginning.

He reached down within himself, the core of his being, the light of his soul, to the faith that had sustained him for his entire life, the faith that allowed him to live under a sky that never saw the sun.

"A . . . light . . . in . . . darkness," he said.

Cale! Cale!

Magadon's mental voice returned him to consciousness.

I'm almost there. The Source is dying, Cale. When it does, Sakkors will fall.

Rivalen held Cale aloft by his cloak, near Shar's eye, near the pulsing black tentacles vomited forth by Shar's eye.

But something had changed.

Vasen was no longer speaking the words of *The Leaves of One Night*. And the eager, satisfied roar that had come from Shar's eye had changed to a plaintive whine.

"What is this?" Rivalen said, the shadows swirling around him. He shouted at Vasen, his voice full of power. "Read! Read it!"

"A . . . light . . . in . . . darkness," Vasen said.

Rivalen stalked toward Vasen, dragging Cale, Shar's whines filling the air.

"What did you say?"

"From ends, beginnings, from darkness, light, from tragedy, triumph," Vasen said. "Night gives way to . . . dawn. Stand in the purifying light of Amaunator who was Lathander."

As he spoke, his skin grew luminous, grew brighter, brighter.

"Stand . . . in . . . it."

The sound from Shar's eye rose to a shriek. Vasen's light burned the shadows from around Rivalen and Cale. Rivalen dropped Cale and staggered back, shielding his eyes. Cale blinked, his eyes watering.

Vasen burned brighter, brighter, a sun in the night of the Ordulin Maelstrom. Rivalen gave a pained shout. Shar's appendages writhed in the light, began to smoke and disintegrate, releasing Riven and Mephistopheles.

Vasen's light burned brighter, blinding.

Squinting, Cale saw that the flesh of the man hunched before the eye was clear of Shar's words. His son had erased *The Leaves of One Night*.

The hunched figure suddenly lurched up, opened his mouth, and vomited forth the pages of the Leaves that had been forced down his throat. Each page burned to ash when it touched the light emanating from Vasen. After he'd expelled the book from his mouth, the man sighed and fell face forward onto the plaza, dead.

Beside Vasen, Gerak groaned and stirred.

Cale moved to assist him, shielding his eyes from the light. "All right?" Cale asked him.

Gerak nodded, his expression dazed, blinking in the glare.

Behind Cale, Rivalen, Riven, and Mephistopheles all screamed as one. Cale turned and watched Vasen's light push the divinity from them and cast it as long shadows on the ground behind them. All three stood on their tiptoes, backs arched, mouths open in silent screams.

Magadon's voice sounded in Cale's head. *What's happening? What's that light,   Cale? It's beautiful.*

Cale stared at Vasen. *It's my son, Mags. It's my son.*

"Cut them apart," Vasen said. "With Weaveshear. Cut them, Erevis."

Cale sprinted across the plaza and picked up his weapon. It bled shadows, but Vasen's light consumed them as rapidly as the blade could birth them. He went first to Riven.

The shadow of divine power extended behind the assassin, attached to him at the heels. Cale raised Weaveshear high and chopped down, severing the connection between the man and the god. The blade smoked and pitted but did its work. Riven sighed and sagged to his knees.

Free of its connection to Riven, the divine power, the shadow, slid across the plaza, formed an arc, a dark line scribed on ground lit in the blazing light of Cale's son.

"Are you all right?" Cale asked him.

Riven, pale, breathing hard, could only nod.

"Hurry!" Vasen said.

Cale went next to Mephistopheles, then to Rivalen, severing both from their godhood. Weaveshear was brittle by the time Cale cut Rivalen's divinity from him.

"No!" Rivalen said.

"Yes," Cale said, and kicked him hard to the ground. The Shadovar hit the plaza face first and Cale heard teeth scrape stone.

The shadows of divine power Cale had cut from Rivalen and the archfiend slid across the plaza as had Riven's, elongated into arcs, joined themselves to one another, forming a black circle on the stone—Mask's symbol.

Shar's eyes spun and whirled, whined for the power it craved, the power that would allow her to incarnate and feed. All that stood between the eye and the power was the light of Vasen Cale.

"What now?" Cale shouted to his son.

"Someone has to take it!" Vasen shouted. "The Herald has to incarnate! I can't keep this up, and if the light goes, she'll devour it all and then . . ."

He didn't need to say anything more. Cale understood. *That* was why he'd been brought back, why Mask had seen to it that he lived when he should have died.

Mephistopheles must have understood, too, for he rose to all fours and crawled for the divinity.

Cale bounded toward the archfiend, but before he reached him the wounded, weakened archfiend suddenly sprouted an arrow from his side. The shaft sunk to the fletching and he groaned.

"That's for Fairelm," Gerak shouted.

The bowman stood beside Vasen, another arrow already nocked and drawn.

Before Mephistopheles could take another crawling step, Gerak shot him again. Again the devil wailed.

"For Elle," Gerak said.

Still Mephistopheles did not fall. Spitting blood from between his gritted fangs, he crawled for the divine essence.

"And this one for me," Gerak said, shooting a third arrow that took the fiend in the throat.

Mephistopheles gagged, got up on his knees, back arched, spattering the plaza with his black ichor.

Cale seized the opportunity. He shadowstepped into the darkness behind the fiend.

"I owe you something, too," he said, and drove Weaveshear through Mephistopheles's back and out his chest. Gore poured forth.

"That's a century overdue," Cale said and twisted the blade. The weapon snapped in his grasp, leaving a long shard in the archdevil.

Mephistopheles, trying to push his innards back into the holes in his flesh, gagging on his own fluids, tried to speak, managed only to gurgle, then dematerialized, a piece of Weaveshear still stuck in him.

Cale cursed at the archfiend's escape. He looked across the plaza and shared a nod with Gerak.

Standing in the light of his son's faith, his own faith gone, Cale stared at the three shadows painting a circle on the stone of the plaza. His own, normal shadow stretched out before him, almost touching them.

"I'm failing, father," Vasen said, and his light began to dim.

Shar's eye continued its hungry hum, its rapid rotations, its eager seething.

Cale needed only to take a step forward, let his shadow touch the divine shadows, and . . .

A hand on his shoulder pulled him around: Riven.

He stared into the pockmarked face of his friend, now just a man, the scarred, empty eye-socket, the scraggly beard.

"I'll do it," Riven said.

"Riven . . ."

"Stay a man, Cale." Riven looked down, shook his head. "You were in my head. You . . . saw. Godhood makes you into a bastard, and I ought to know. It's too late for me on that score."

Cale shook his head. "No, I should—"

"Cale, you've got your son, your life, go live it."

Cale stared into Riven's eye a long while, finally nodded. They embraced like the long-lost brothers they were.

"Been a long road," Cale said.

"Truth," Riven said. "Odd one, yeah?"

"Odd one," Cale agreed.

Riven thumped Cale on the shoulder and stepped past him. For a moment his shadow stretched out next to Cale's. Then he stepped forward into the circle scribed in darkness on the stone. Riven's shadow bisected the arc.

The circle began to spin, to shrink, closing in on Riven. He gasped, threw his head back, and shouted, his voice like thunder. Despite Vasen's light, shadows leaked from Riven's skin, swirled around him, embraced him. The spinning circle of power tightened and Riven seemed to grow larger, more present, the shadows swirling around him denser.

And as divinity flooded Riven, enlarged him, Shar's eye shrank correspondingly. The rotations of the eye slowed as it shrank; the screams more plaintive until fading entirely.

And then it was over.

Vasen's light faded and Riven, fully divine, stood in the plaza shrouded in a cloud of shadow. He looked out at Cale, the hole of his eye seeming to stretch back through time and place.

"You're still terrible at making plans," Cale said, a half smile on his lips. "And I'll be thrice-damned before I pray to you."

Riven, or Mask, turned and looked at him. "I'd be disappointed if it were otherwise."

The darkness drew tight around Riven. He merged with it and was gone, gone to where gods go.

Cale blew out a heavy sigh, turned, and hurried to Vasen's side. He and Gerak helped Vasen to stand.

"You did it," Cale said, pulling him close.

Vasen nodded, his face drawn. He leaned on Cale. "We all did it."

"What exactly did we do?" Gerak asked, looking around.

Vasen shook his head, kneeled beside Orsin, placed his hands on him, and uttered a prayer to Amaunator.

Cale expected to see Vasen's hands glow with healing energy, but nothing happened. Vasen hung his head.

"What's wrong?" Cale said, shadows spinning around him.

"That was the price," Vasen said, his voice cracking. "It burned it out of me."

"Burned what?"

"The calling, the connection." Vasen made a helpless gesture with his hands. "I don't know, but it's gone."

"It doesn't work that way," Cale said. "It's still there."

"I don't feel it," Vasen said.

"You will," Cale answered.

Vasen shook his head, looked down at Orsin. He tapped the shadowalker's cheeks, shook him gently. "Orsin. Orsin."

The shadowalker opened his eyes.

"You all right?" Vasen asked.

"I . . . think so," Orsin said. "Is it over?"

"It's over," Cale said, and he and Vasen pulled Orsin to his feet.

"Where's Riven?" Orsin asked.

Cale half smiled, the shadows swirling around him. "Riven is . . . gone. He's Mask. Or Mask is Riven. I don't know."

Orsin clutched his holy symbol, murmured a prayer to the Shadowlord.

Cale, Magadon said. *I'm not going to make it there. The Source is almost gone. Sakkors is coming down.*

It's all right, Mags. You did enough. Get out of there. It's over.

But it wasn't over.

A moan from behind turned them all around. Rivalen stood on wobbly legs, the nightseer no longer a god, but just a man. His golden eyes looked at the tiny, withered, shrunken distortion that was all that remained of Shar's eye.

"It can't be," he said.

It struck Cale then. No shadows spun around Rivalen. Vasen's light had stripped him of them, at least for a time.

Gerak nocked and drew. Orsin assumed a fighting stance and shadows formed around his fist. Vasen and Cale stalked toward Rivalen, Cale holding the jagged remainder of Weaveshear.

Brennus is coming for Rivalen, Erevis, Magadon projected. *Don't interfere.*

What?

Magadon didn't respond but Cale took him at his word. He held up a hand to stop Gerak from firing.

"I'm still the nightseer," Rivalen said, glaring at them with his golden eyes.

The shadows darkened around Rivalen and a second Shadovar stepped from the shadows and took Rivalen. He was shorter, slighter of build, with steel-colored eyes.

"No. You're a murderer. And you belong to me."

"Brennus!" Rivalen said.

The shadows swirled and both of them were gone.

The Source was barely cognizant of Magadon. Its light was almost out. They were somewhere within the Maelstrom, over Ordulin. When the Source was gone entirely, the city would plummet from the sky.

I have to go now, Magadon said. *Thank you for everything. Rest well, my lovely.*

The Source did not perceive him.

Magadon sent the Source feelings of comfort, of affection, drew on its power for the last time, and transported himself to the plaza he'd seen through Cale's eyes.

"Mags!"

The half-fiend had let his hair and horns grow long. His asp eyes, white but for the pupils, crinkled in a grin.

"Erevis!"

They embraced.

"You let your hair grow," Cale said to him.

Mags eyed Cale's bald pate. "You did not. And we need to go. Right now."

"Aye," Cale said.

Past Mags, through the shadowed sky, Cale saw the mountain of Sakkors plummeting earthward. Ordulin would be pulverized.

Orsin dragged his staff on the ground, scribing a line on the plaza's stone.

"A new beginning," he said.

Cale nodded. "Let's go see what it brings."

He drew the shadows of maelstrom around all of them, and took them from there.

Brennus stood behind Rivalen, holding his brother's arms against his sides. He had his mother's necklace in his hand, too, pressing it hard into Rivalen's flesh. Both of them looked up at Sakkors as it fell toward them. Rivalen struggled, but he'd been weakened too much. He could not shake Brennus's grip.

Brennus put his lips to Rivalen's ear. "We raised Sakkors from the sea, you and I. And now we'll stand under it as it falls. Think of mother as you die, Rivalen. She was the instrument of your downfall."

"Don't, Brennus. Don't."

Brennus smiled as Sakkors fell. Shadows swirled around him.

"It's done," Brennus said. "Your bitterness is sweet . . . to me."

Rivalen shouted defiance as the mountain crashed down on them. Brennus only grinned.

EPILOGUE

Gᴇʀᴀᴋ ᴡᴀʟᴋᴇᴅ ᴛʜᴇ ᴄᴏʙʙʟᴇsᴛᴏɴᴇ sᴛʀᴇᴇᴛs ᴏғ Dᴀᴇʀʟᴜɴ, head down against the rain. Soldiers were everywhere, tramping through the streets, filling the inns. Sakkors may have fallen, but Shadovar and Sembian forces were still on the march, and Daerlun was readying for an attack.

He hadn't been in a city for long time, and the close confines made him uncomfortable. He'd promised to meet Vasen and Orsin there, but it had been the better part of a tenday and still no word. It might have been better that way. He didn't know how much more appetite he had for any of it. The things he'd seen . . .

Rumors ran like the trots through Daerlun's populace, fed by charlatans and diviners and those who sold information for coin.

"Something terrible had happened in Ordulin," some said. "A second Shadowstorm was coming, this time for Cormyr."

"Sakkors had fallen."

"Shar is walking Toril," others said.

"No," said others. "Mask has been reborn."

"No, you're wrong," said still others. "Mask was never dead."

Gerak never bothered to correct anyone. Hells, he'd been there and he still wasn't entirely sure what he'd seen. He just knew he'd seen too much. He'd spent his days since in various common rooms around Daerlun, drinking and trying not to think about what he'd seen, where he'd been. He had a feeling that what he'd seen in Ordulin was merely the beginning, that Toril had hard, painful days ahead.

He had painful days ahead himself. Fairelm was gone, Elle was gone, their child was gone. And he . . . didn't know what to do. He had no family, no home, no anything save the next ale cup and the next drunken, dreamless sleep. He considered Vasen and Orsin comrades, friends even, but the two of them shared a unique bond, and he knew he'd always be on the outside of it.

The rain slacked to a light drizzle. He plodded through the mud, picking his way through the wagons and hooded pedestrians of the city. Ahead he saw a painted wooden sign swinging in the wind: *The Bottom of the Cup*, it read. His kind of alehouse. He needed a shave and a bath, but first he needed another drink.

He reached into his trouser pocket, took inventory of the silver and copper coins there. Enough metal jangled to get him through another few days. He picked up his pace, heading for the tavern.

A voice from the alley to his right stopped him short. "Gerak."

Gerak turned, blinked, his flesh growing goose pimples. Riven stood in the mouth of the alley. He wore his cloak, his sabers, his sneer and goatee, and his presence crowded out everything else on the street. Behind him, the alley was cast in deep shadows, so dark that Gerak could not see into it.

Riven regarded him with one knowing eye and one empty socket. "Where you headed?"

Gerak looked around. No one else seemed alarmed at the presence of a god on the street. He walked up to Riven, cautiously, the way he might a dangerous animal.

"What do you want?" he asked.

"You don't look good."

"I'm fine. Just about to grab a drink, is all."

Riven sneered. "You look like you've already had a few."

"Maybe I have," Gerak said. "What's that to you? A god has come to lecture me about my habits?"

It occurred to him in passing that he was snarling at a reincarnated god; Mask stood before him.

"That's because I know those habits," Riven said. "You just did a big thing, saw wonders, right? But now it's over. And you got no family or home to come back to. You're feeling alone, kind of empty. Not even anyone you'd call friends to visit with, or at least not good friends."

Gerak started to protest, but Riven silenced him with a raised hand and a nod.

"Oh, I know. You want to say Vasen and Orsin are your friends, and you'd be right. But you know how things are. Those two, they're like brothers. You, you're just a sometime cousin. They welcome you, but you're not necessary. Is that about it?"

"I guess that's about the shape of it, yeah. You're familiar?"

Riven nodded. "I know how that is, yeah. And when it's like that, when you have nobody, the bottom of an empty ale cup seems like a good friend. That's the road you're on. You see that, right?"

Gerak didn't answer, but he saw it. He saw it well.

"You know what kept me from that?"

Gerak heard movement in the shadows behind Riven, a soft chuffing. He recognized it right away. Riven's girls stepped out of the shadows, each to one side of their master. They blinked in the natural light of the Prime, noses raised at scents they probably hadn't smelled in decades.

Seeing them instantly lightened Gerak's spirits. He kneeled and held out a hand. They looked up at Riven, as if for permission.

"Go on," Riven said, and they did, waddling up to Gerak, licking his hands. He rubbed their flanks, their muzzles.

"Good girls," Gerak said. "Good girls."

"They can't come with me," Riven said, and Gerak pretended not to hear the break in his voice. "And even if they could . . . "

Gerak looked up at Riven. "You want me to . . . ?"

Riven had eyes only for his girls. Shadows swirled around him. He nodded, once. "I don't know how long they have now, but I want them to spend whatever time they have left in the sun, in *their* home, not mine."

Gerak's gaze fell at that. His eyes welled. "Their home is with you."

"Not anymore," Riven said. "It's with you now. You take care of them, give them a home, and they'll give you one. No more ale cups. Don't disappoint me, Gerak. I'll be watching."

"I won't," he said, smiling and rubbing the dogs.

"Goodbye, girls. You saved me, and I love you."

Gerak was silent a long moment. Finally he looked up and asked, "What are their names?"

Riven was already gone.

Orsin had left Vasen and Erevis to commune in solitude with his god. He'd picked his way through the Valley of the Rose, following the same path Vasen had once led him down, until he stood beside the dark waters of the shadowed tarn. The shroud the Shadovar had put over Sembia remained, but cracks appeared in it, lines of red cast by the setting sun. Shadows darkened the vale, the water. The towering pines behind him whispered in a soft breeze. Insects chirped.

Orsin felt the many lives he'd lived converging around the one he lived now, as if all of them had been a prelude to this, his finale. His people believed that the soul reincarnated again and again across time and worlds in an attempt to perfect itself or achieve its purpose. Perhaps Orsin's spirit had finally achieved its goal in standing beside Vasen. He had trouble imagining future lives before him, certainly he could imagine none richer.

Days before he had worshiped a dead god. But his god had been reborn before his eyes. He'd been a congregation of one, but that would not be so for much longer.

He pulled his holy symbol out from under his tunic and held it in one hand. The disc felt warm to his touch, alive. He stepped into the shadow of a pine, at the edge of the shadowed tarn, and with his staff scribed a prayer circle around himself. He kneeled and prayed.

"Lord of Shadows," he intoned. "Hear my words."

Shock gave way to a smile when he heard Riven's voice in his head.

Fine, but first get off your damned knees, Shadowwalker.

Hands clasped behind his back, Telamont looked through the glassteel window out on Thultanthar. It floated alone in the empire's sky. Rivalen's hopes had raised Sakkors from the depths of the Inner Sea, and his ambition and nihilism had brought it down in ruins.

The empire had lost a city, but Telamont had lost two sons. He'd wept only twice in the last two thousand years. Once when he'd first learned of Alashar's death and once when he'd learned for himself that his own son had been her murderer.

Outside, Thultanthar's towers and domes and soaring roofs rose out of the gloom.

"I don't know what's coming, Hadrhune," he said over his shoulder.

His most trusted counselor cleared his throat. "Most High?"

"The world has changed, and is changing yet. Our reach is shorter. And I've lost two of my sons."

"Yes, Most High. Shall we . . . continue the program with the Chosen?"

Telamont sighed, nodded. "Yes. Capture and hold what Chosen we can. Interrogate them all. Someone must know something. In any event I imagine their power will be of use to us when we see events more clearly."

"The gods themselves seem to be involved in affairs."

"Indeed, Hadrhune."

The Shadovar had not yet returned to Toril when the so-called Time of Troubles took place, when the gods themselves walked the earth and the entire divine order had been upset and reordered. Telamont feared similar changes afoot currently. He'd struggle to maintain the empire during such upheaval.

"Most High," Hadrhune said, his tone stilted and uncomfortable. "There is one other thing. It's a bit . . . strange."

Telamont turned to face his counselor.

Hadrhune stood near the door, deep in shadows, his glowing eyes like steel stars in the black constellation of his face.

"What is it, Hadrhune?"

Two small, bald gray heads poked out of Hadrhune's cloak, tiny ears raised and alert. They looked on Telamont with terror, but behind the fear their opalescent eyes looked profoundly sad.

Telamont froze. Shadows roiled around him. "Are those . . . ?"

Hadrhune nodded. "They are, Most High. Prince Brennus's constructs. They should have died when . . . he died. I can't explain it."

"We lost," the homunculi said in their high-pitched voices.

"Me, too," Telamont said.

"Forgive me, Most High," Hadrhune said, pushing the homunculi back into his cloak. They squeaked in protest. "I should not have troubled you with this."

"No, you did the right thing," Telamont said. "Leave them."

"Most High?"

"Leave them with me, Hadrhune. Is that unclear?"

"No, Most High. Of course. Shoo," he said to the homunculi, and shook them from his cloak.

They hit the ground and cowered, keeping one hand each on Hadrhune's cloak, eyeing Telamont fearfully.

"That will be all, Hadrhune."

"Of course, Most High."

After Hadrhune left, the homunculi crowded close together, hugging one another, trembling.

"Most High hurt us?"

"No," Telamont said softly. He kneeled and held out a hand, the same way Alashar had held out a hand to Rivalen. "Come here. Take my hand. It's all right."

They crossed the smooth floor in hesitant fits and starts, nostrils flaring, eyes diffident. When they reached him, Telamont ran a finger gently over each of their heads. They relaxed and cooed.

"My son was your master," Telamont murmured. "He made you. Loved you, maybe."

"Master loved us," they echoed, nodding. "Him come home soon?"

Telamont's eyes welled for only the third time that he could remember. "No. He's not coming home anymore."

Cale kneeled in the grass before Varra's simple headstone. Her name had been etched into the limestone slab, underneath an etching of the sunrise. A partially decayed orchid lay in the grass before the stone.

Shadows poured from Cale's flesh as he replayed the last moments they'd shared together. He remembered the smell of her hair, the feel of her smooth skin under his hands, the weight of her atop him. They'd made Vasen that night.

He dragged his fingertips over the cold limestone slab.

"I'm sorry," he whispered.

He felt Vasen's eyes on him. His son. Their son.

"I shouldn't have left her," Cale said over his shoulder. "I went back later but it was too late. She was gone."

"You did what you had to, what you thought was right. There's no room for regret in that."

"There's room for regret in everything," Cale said. "How did she die?"

Vasen cleared his throat. "She sacrificed herself for me. She died loved, though. And not alone."

"I'm glad."

"I didn't know her," Vasen said. "No one knew anything about her, and she died before she could tell anyone much. She spoke of you, though."

"How do you know that?"

"My fath—Derreg told me."

Cale nodded. Tears pooled in his eyes, fell down his face. He thought of the first time he'd met Varra, in a dark tavern in Skullport.

"I'll tell you about her sometime," Cale said. "Just . . . not right now."

"Of course," Vasen said, shifting on his feet.

Cale looked at the headstone beside Varra's, also adorned with a decayed orchid. The name etched in the stone read "Derreg, son of Regg."

"Derreg raised you?" Cale asked.

"He did," Vasen said, and Cale heard the pride in his voice.

"I knew Regg," Cale said.

"I know."

"If I could thank Derreg, I would."

Cale heard a smile in Vasen's tone. "He was not the kind of man who needed thanks for doing the right thing."

Cale smiled in turn. "He was indeed Regg's son, then."

Cale ran his fingers over Varra's headstone a final time and stood. "We should go."

"Go where? What's next?"

Cale looked his son in the eye and smiled.

ABOUT THE AUTHOR

While his mind is often in the Forgotten Realms®, Paul Kemp's body lives in Grosse Pointe, Michigan, with his wife Jennifer, their twin sons, and their two daughters. He is a graduate of the University of Michigan–Dearborn and the University of Michigan law school. He enjoys single-malt scotch, good books, and blood-soaked rituals designed to return the world to the Old Ones.

ACKNOWLEDGEMENTS

As always, my thanks to Ed, Bob, Fleetwood, and James.

ALSO BY PAUL S. KEMP